Double Exposure

Two Crime Novels by
R. Allan McCall

Book One – *The Floater*

Book Two – *Cat and Pearly*

ISBN 0-7414-2180-1

Published by:
INFIN∞ITY
PUBLISHING.COM
1094 New DeHaven Street, Suite 100
West Conshohocken, PA 19428-2713
Info@buybooksontheweb.com
www.buybooksontheweb.com
Toll-free (877) BUY BOOK
Local Phone (610) 941-9999
Fax (610) 941-9959

Printed in the United States of America

Printed on Recycled Paper

Published July 2005

Also by this author:

The War Affair

Perilous Odyssey

This one is for my children, and theirs as well

BOOK ONE

The Floater

1

"**W**hy did you slap him, Maury?" Lieutenant Weatherby asked.

"Because he deserved the same treatment he gave me, a kick in the groin. But I was soft-hearted and opted for a lesser punishment for him trying to ruin my sex life."

"Take it from the top, please. You spotted the stolen car, with the kid sitting in it. What did you do?"

"I told him to get out of the car and put his hands on the roof. He called me a fucking pig, and sat there defiantly sipping beer out of a can."

"Anyone else in the stolen car?

"Yeah. A young chick, who ran away while I was trying to deal with the young Cairncross boy. When I hauled him out by the scruff of his neck, he kicked me in the balls. That's when I decided nobody kicks me in the family jewels and gets away with it, least of all, an insolent little juvenile delinquent with a record as long as your arm."

"Come on Maury. You are about six-three and, what, about two-fifty? Anyway, it was an unequal contest. You are supposed to be able to subdue little kids without losing your temper and beating them up."

"I didn't beat him up. I simply massaged his face a little bit to shut him up. Loot, in addition to grand theft auto, that little jerk should be charged with resisting arrest, assaulting a police officer and D.U.I. When I searched the stolen car, I found a six-pack of Coors under the front seat, with five empty cans, in addition to the one in his hand."

I could tell by the supercilious expression on his face that the lieutenant was not buying. He had his arms folded across his chest, like a braless bimbo trying to support her oversize boobs.

"How was he supposed to know you were a police officer, Maury? After all, you were in plain clothes, and supposedly off duty when you spotted the stolen car and let your temper get the better of your judgment. You did not read him his Miranda rights when you arrested him, did you?"

"What the hell. How was I supposed to read him his rights when he was trying to make me a soprano? I don't imagine, having called me a fornicating pig, that he thought I was his fairy godmother."

"Skip the sarcasm Sergeant. You know the proper procedure, and you failed to follow it. You fucked up again, Maury. Big time."

"What do you mean *'again'* for crissake?" I could feel the blood rising under my collar, knowing this was going to be a no-win situation. For months now, Weatherby was out to get me, and seized on every nit-picking opportunity to shove the knife a little deeper up my backside. "Tell me one other time I failed to read a perp his Miranda rights. Name one other time. You can't. You fucking well can't and you know it."

"That's beside the point. Once is more than enough. His lawyer will jump on it and have the case thrown out of court."

"As you said yourself, Loot, I was supposed to be off duty. I was trying to do the city a favor by apprehending a felon. I could have just as easily ignored the little son-of-a-bitch and continued on my way. Instead, I made an arrest with the smartass kid struggling, kicking, spitting at me and screaming bloody murder. People were gathering around in the parking lot, probably thinking I was a child molester, or some other kind of a wierdo. It was not the time or place to worry about the niceties of arrest procedure. I read him his rights later at the station."

"Not good enough, Sergeant. Not nearly good enough."

Weatherby. My nemesis. Thin, hawk-like features. Sallow complexion. Insignificant moustache. Insignificant man. Slicked back, black hair glistening with some kind of pomade. Trying to look judgmental and superior.

"Well," I asked, "are you going to allow the charges to remain against the kid or not?"

"Grand theft auto, yes," he replied. "But it won't stick. His father's lawyer has already picked upon the fact that you did not give him his rights at the scene, when you arrested him. And no judge will buy the fact that a big cop like you was grievously attacked by a thin little sixteen-year-old."

"I'd like to see the sneaky little brat kick you in the gonads, Loot. You'd forget to read his rights in the heat of the struggle, just like I did."

Come to think of it, I would really like to do it to Lieutenant Weatherby myself.

"Never mind what I would do, Sergeant. It's what *you* didn't do that matters." I noticed that the lieutenant had started using my rank, instead of my usual moniker, getting all formal and official. To put it mildly, the Harvard-grad lieutenant was *not* one of my favorite people. Last year, he was brought in over my head, because of his brilliant academic background. At twenty-nine, he thought he knew all about the detective business and dealing with his subordinates. Naturally, there was some initial resentment on my part. I am forty-one and have been with the Naples Police force for twenty-one years. So, based on experience, I thought I should have received the promotion. I could have handled the disappointment, if he had not been so damned officious.

"OK, so I shouldn't have lost my temper, I suppose," I admitted ruefully. "But I'm pissed off with these juvenile delinquents getting off without any punishment. It makes a mockery of the law."

"The problem is," said Lieutenant Weatherby, "there are charges of police brutality and unnecessary use of force outstanding against you, putting the Naples Police in a very bad light with the public and the media. This is particularly the case in this instance, because the kid's father is a prominent citizen."

"That is exactly what burns my ass, Lieutenant. It's not what the kid did that matters; it's the fact that his father is well-connected and no judge is going to put the kid behind bars where he should be. A few years from now, if he keeps defying the law, he will be a hardened criminal."

"Well, don't worry about *his* future, Sergeant. You would do well to think about your own."

"Are you saying, Lieutenant, that because I sort of applied some practical justice, that my future is in jeopardy?" It would not surprise me if there was smoke coming out my ears. "Is that what this conversation is all about? Are you going to make me the fall guy, while that young jerk gets a suspended sentence again?"

The lieutenant looked uncomfortable. "Something like that, Smith. It's the culmination of a lot of things with you lately. You seem to be completely cynical about the job. Your attitude concerns me. Maybe you have been on the force too long."

He looked down at his desk and opened what appeared to be my personnel file. "Says here you joined the Naples Police when you were twenty. And now you're forty-one. With this screw-up on your record, you might as well forget any hope you might have had of promotion. I would suggest you would be wise to consider your options. Early retirement, with a reduced pension, would seem to be your best choice."

I looked at him incredulously. "Well, you arrogant asshole." I could feel myself getting hotter and hotter. "Twenty-one goddam years, five commendations, a great relationship with your predecessor, and now, just because you consider me some kind of a threat to your job, you are trying to get rid of me. Let's admit it, you hate my guts, and the feeling is mutual. Sure, I'll take early retirement." I took out my badge and slammed it on his desk. "You can take the stupid badge and shove it where the sun never shines."

Without another word, I walked out of the office and slammed the door. Heads came up all over the squad room. Then I remembered the police-issue .38 Smith & Wesson in my shoulder holster. I withdrew it and re-opened the door with the gun in my hand, held by the barrel.

Thinking I was going to shoot him, the lieutenant dived under his desk.

Despite my anger, I could not help laughing out loud at his panic reaction. Quietly, I walked over to his desk and gently placed the revolver on his desk. He peered out from under his desk, his brown eyes wide with terror.

I was still laughing at the scene in the Lieutenant's office, as I walked past all the other plain-clothes detectives and uniformed cops and out into the brilliant sunshine.

4

A sergeant actually laughing at his own firing? That's me. Of such weird events are legends made. I was now an unemployed legend.

The next day, as I was cleaning out my desk, my phone rang. At first, I did not pay it any attention. But it kept ringing. Finally, I picked it up, to silence the damned thing.

"Yes?"

"Sergeant Smith?"

"No longer," I corrected. "*Mister* Smith. Who is speaking?"

"This is Captain George Allen, I would like a word with you, before you leave. Would you drop by my office when it's convenient?"

I hesitated, before answering. Captain George Allen was one of the good guys in this operation. But, he was also the one whom approved Lieutenant Weatherby's appointment last year.

"Um, I'm sorry Captain. In my present state of mind, I'm not very good at 'words'. I would just as soon take my things and leave quietly."

"Stay there. I'll come down, Maury."

The Captain's office was on the next floor up. He appeared just as I had finished packing a few personal things in a cardboard box.

I kept thinking about Weatherby diving under his desk yesterday. There may have been a slight smile flirting on my lips.

"Lieutenant Weatherby told me about your abrupt resignation yesterday, Maury. And about your reopening his door, with your gun drawn."

"Sorry about that, Captain. Returning the department's revolver was an afterthought, but he over-reacted. I did not point the gun at him. I was holding it by the barrel. That way, I could only shoot myself if there were a bullet in the breech. But I always kept the safety on. Can I help it if the lieutenant is gun-shy and has an over-active imagination?"

He laughed. "Anyway, Maury I was sorry to hear about the bad feelings evident in your confrontation. But you didn't have to scare him half out of his wits. I was hoping you would

apologize to him and then we could patch up any misunder-
standings between the two of you."

"Sorry. I have no apologies to offer. He has been on
my case ever since his appointment last year. As far as I'm
concerned, he is a vindictive son-of-a-bitch, a lousy administrator and an arrogant asshole. That about sums it up from my
perspective."

The captain's steely, gray eyes bored into my baby
blues. I did not blink.

"Hmm," he murmured. "You don't mince words, do
you, Maury? Well, that's too bad. If you can't get along with
your superior officer, it is probably just as well you turned in
your badge. I very much regret to see the detective division
lose a good man. But, you must understand that we have to
maintain discipline and morale in the shop." He held out his
hand in a farewell gesture. "Goodbye and good luck."

As he was leaving my oversized cubicle, with its Sally
Ann furniture, Captain Allen paused and turned. "Incidentally,
several of your friends on the force spoke to me about arrang-
ing a farewell bash in your honor. Can you make it to Mitch's
Bar and Grill tomorrow night?"

I smiled. "Sure. And, Captain, no hard feelings, right?
Will you be there?"

"I wouldn't miss it. But it will have to be in an *unofficial* capacity.".

I remember very little about the beery bash at Mitch's,
except that the banquet hall was packed with off-duty cops and
some patrolmen who snuck in for a quick one anyway. True to
his word, Captain Allen attended in civvies. and turned a blind
eye to a few minor transgressions on the part of his staff.

It was a memorable send-off into the world of unemployment. I was toasted and roasted. I became gloriously
drunk and had to be delivered home at three A.M. by a couple
of my pals.

The next morning I paid the price, with a hammering
hangover – a memorable lesson in the wages of sin. It was a
good thing my daughter Melanie was visiting a girlfriend for a
sleep-over, sparing me an unsympathetic teasing.

2

Naples, Florida July, 1995

It is a wonder any marriages in the detective division last longer than the first year. In their personal lives, detectives are at the mercy of robbers, rapists, scam artists and murderers who have no respect the family lives or priorities of police personnel. From the standpoint of law enforcement, offenders tend to break laws at the most inconvenient times. And there is a certain urgency in solving such crimes, because the older the cases become, the harder they are to solve.

In the Smith household, our marriage lasted twelve long years, with Loretta complaining incessantly, admittedly with some justification, about the long and unpredictable hours mandated by the nature of the job. "Your dinner is in the oven *and spoiled.*" became her favorite accusative greeting when I returned home at the end of a long day's – and sometimes night's - work. She also contended frequently that I thought more of the police force than I did of our marriage. Increasingly, as the whining continued, that became true.

Finally, in July, 1995 we agreed that we would both be happier if we went our separate ways. In discussing the divorce settlement, Loretta made it clear she did not want the responsibility of raising a child as a single person. So, despite ending up a great deal poorer, all was not lost. I got custody of my daughter Melanie, a great little kid whom I loved dearly. And I figured, on balance, I got the best of the settlement.

Through all the trials and tribulations, Melanie showed a maturity beyond her ten years – probably greater than either of her parents.

Because I ended up bereft of house and wheels. I decided to rent a car temporarily, while we searched the environs of Greater Naples to put a roof over our heads. I could hardly use a police cruiser for accommodation hunting.

The sales person who greeted Melanie and me at Mercury Realty was Joanne Carter, a honey-blonde with a gorgeous figure and upbeat personality to match. Joanne pointed out that I could save myself the expense, as she would be escorting me and my daughter in her Lincoln Town Car, to view the various apartments that might be of interest. For shopping and other personal chores I could use taxis at lower cost than a full-time car rental. I appreciated her compassionate response to the sorry state of my finances.

After many frustrating walk-throughs, our search for new digs ended at a condo development in East Naples, with the unoriginal but glamorous name *The Pallisades.*

With a low down-payment, I was fortunate to take immediate possession of a recently constructed two-bedroom, two-bath, 1300 square foot condominium on the second floor of a low-rise building, overlooking a small man-made lake and lovely green golf fairways. Fortunately, five new appliances were included in the purchase price.

As every developer knows, with god-like ease, lakes can be created, on demand, in the former swampland of Southern Florida, most of which is barely above sea-level. It is only necessary to dig a large hole in the Spring and a lake will appear by the end of the Summer rainy season.

According to scientific prognostications, when global warming eventually melts all the Arctic glaciers, most of South Florida will again be covered by the ocean, from which it emerged eons ago.

After the purchase agreement for the condo was signed, Joanne's work was essentially completed, but I kept making excuses to see her again and again. I was trying to get up enough nerve to ask her for a date. But, on a detective's salary, diminished by the deduction for alimony payments to Loretta, I felt I had little to offer one of Naples' most successful real estate gals. I was afraid she would tell me to wait until I was Police Commissioner or at least Chief.

Fortunately, I was to learn later that she was interested in me as a person, and not in my social status or rank in law enforcement.

3

Gulf of Mexico, September, 2005

My boat, *Melanie* is an ancient Sea Ray, a 24 ft. fiberglass-hulled fishing craft with an open cockpit and central control station with a folding canvas Bimini top for protection from the sun. She is powered by twin 150 h.p. Mercury outboards.

Prior to my divorce, my personal watercraft was named *Loretta*. After my former spouse cleaned me out financially, I had a sign-painter change the name on the stern to *Melanie*. My initial attraction to Loretta gradually diminished as her recriminations became louder and unreasonably hysterical. From my standpoint, the end of our union was a welcome relief. That was back in 1995 when my daughter was ten. Now she is a beautiful young lady of twenty, attending university in Fort Myers.

Early on a bright sunlit morning in September, 2005, I decided to take Pooch, our wire-haired terrier, for an offshore fishing expedition in the Gulf. We set off, wending our way, at no-wake speed, through the tall, red and green navigational buoys marking the safe channel through Naples Bay.

The wide bay gradually narrows to Gordon Pass about one hundred feet wide, as the bay funnels into the Gulf of Mexico. A few more sets of channel markers guide boat traffic out of, and into, the mouth of the pass.

Like a forward lookout, Pooch was perched on a seat in the bow, enjoying the modest sea breeze. The little terrier looked over his shoulder at the helmsman. I knew, from experience the little speed demon wanted me to turn up the revs on the twin outboards that were easily capable of pushing the Sea Ray at sixty knots with the throttles advanced to the top end of the scale. I obliged his need for exhilarating forward progress, but at only half that speed.

The view to the North was of a five mile long, slightly curved, white sandy beach, punctuated every few hundred feet by wooden groins installed by waterfront residents, to keep their valuable sand beaches from drifting away. A few beach-walkers could be seen strolling along in the modest surf, enjoying the refreshing, cool air of early morning. A handful of colorful umbrellas had already sprouted on the five mile strip of sand. Visible in the distance, the wooden pier projected into the Gulf like a long finger pointing toward Cancun, many miles across the Gulf of Mexico. Luxurious homes line the waterfront, framed by palm trees and protected from occasional storms by seawalls of stone and concrete.

The famous Naples pier, rebuilt after a hurricane wiped out the original structure in the sixties, reminded me that Naples began its existence as a small and charming fishing village many years earlier.. At that time, the settlement was accessible only by water, because no roads had yet been built. Eventually, the two-lane coastal highway, US 41, reached Naples from the North, and the quaint village began to develop into a popular winter resort for snowbirds – escapees from the ice and snow of Northern states and Canada. Then when Interstate 75 touched the Eastern outskirts of Naples, growth became explosive. Collier County became the fastest growing county in the country. In the winter months, the population soared to four or five times its summer figure, into the hundreds of thousands.

Some local residents deplored the trend to big city status, with all the concomitant problems. But only landlubbers had to be concerned about the excesses of humanity. Out here on the Gulf there was still plenty of room to move around and lots of fish to take one's mind off shore-based concerns, including my recently achieved unemployment. I set the course on a magnetic compass heading of 290 degrees and relaxed in my swivel chair to enjoy the feeling of freedom and the bracing, salty air.

The light onshore breeze of ten knots caused only modest swells in the water, barely enough to cause the bow of the V-shaped hull to make the customary slapping vibration, as it cut through the waves. When I figured in my head, by dead reckoning, that my favorite fishing grounds had been reached, I cut the motors and allowed the Sea Ray to drift. Pooch bounded off his bow seat and stared at me, until he was handed a dog treat, part of a well-established ritual. When the boat's forward motion stopped, he took his Milk-Bone dog biscuit to the vacated helm seat, seeking the protection of the Bimini top from the blazing September sun.

My protection from the solar rays, UvA and UvB, came from a liberal application of Coppertone Sport sun-block No. 30 to my bare shoulders and legs. By this stage, of course, I had removed my tee-shirt and wore only a pair of light cotton shorts. My skin was well tanned, but my forefathers must have lived in Northern climes as I am blue-eyed and fair-haired, and I tend towards freckles when over-exposed to the great orange globe in the sky.

With cut-up portions of snook, I baited two lines and set the long fiberglass poles in outrigger holders mounted on either side of the transom. Then I opened a can of cold Coors from the on-board fridge, which I had filled earlier from a cooler. In my view, fishing without a beer is like bread without butter. Or a sundae without a cherry on top. Besides, one has to avoid dehydration!

I had barely become comfortable in a stern seat, when one of the poles bent in a C shape, quivering to indicate a catch. Pooch barked twice, his signal that I should get off my backside and tend to the business at hand. I responded by stowing my beer can in a receptacle mounted on the gunwale. He stood beside me, excitedly wagging his curly tail, while I played the critter, sight unseen below the surface.

When caught, *clever* fish try to find some underwater object to which they can swim, so that they can snag the line and cut themselves free. (Good line-snaggers are outboard motor propellers and anchor rodes). I like to think, modestly, that I have more brain power than any form of marine life. I think that any fish fool enough to swallow a piece of dead meat on a hook can't be a candidate for a Pulitzer Prize in rocket science. Nor can I for that matter! But in case I am underestimating the piscine population, whenever I stop the boat to start fishing, I invariably make a practice of raising the twin motors out of the water, in trail position, and eschew the practice of dropping an anchor.

It took several minutes of playing the catch underwater until its struggling slowed down. At that point, I took the landing net in my left hand, the line in my right and scooped the flopping fish on board. It was the first close look I had at the catch, and I was disappointed.

"Dammit, Pooch," I said. "It's a friggin' trigger fish. They always put up a good fight, but they don't make good eating. Anyway, back she goes."

I removed the still-struggling five pound fish from the net, being careful to avoid 'the trigger', a sharp spear-like dorsal fin that gives the species its name. Then I heaved it back in the Gulf, much to Pooch's dismay."

Fishing and catching improved as Saturday morning wore on. I brought aboard two black grouper of about ten pounds each and a twelve pound red snapper, both great eating species. In between these catches, I had to battle two more unwanted trigger fish, which I hastily and carefully released. I suppose, by selectively keeping only the 'good' fish, I could be considered guilty of downgrading the overall fish population in the Gulf. But I have been accused of worse misdemeanors.

Looking at my watch, I observed that time had flown while I was having fun. It was suddenly 10:15, so I decided to wrap it up. Indicating to Pooch that he should resume his lookout position in the bow, I took over the helm position once more, pushed a couple of buttons to lower the twin Mercs back into the salty brine and restarted the motors at idle speed.

We had barely moved a hundred feet before Pooch started barking excitedly. I looked around in a 360 degree circle, but could not see any other boats in the vicinity, only a large sailing craft on the horizon a couple of miles distant.

The dog did not stop barking, so I left the motors idling, grabbed my binoculars and walked forward to the bow where the little tail-wager was perched. When I arrived beside him, Pooch started acting like a Mexican jumping bean on a hot griddle. I could now see a white object off the port forward quarter, just a few inches above the surface of the water.

A couple of curious ring-billed gulls were circling above the floating object, probably hoping for an easy meal. I returned to the helm and steered in that direction. As we drew near, Pooch started to growl at the white patch.

13

Now I could see clearly that the object was a human body. *A dead human body*, grossly distorted by gases released in the body, due to internal decomposition of its organs. The body was floating head down, the gray hair on its head waving with the currents of the light wave action. It was wearing a pair of sloggy slacks and a white long-sleeve shirt, discolored with algae. The feet were bare and had been nibbled on by wee fishies. Surprisingly, the body had not been mutilated by sharks. But some toes were missing and it looked like the face may have been chewed on by birds or perhaps other predatory fish.

Ugh! A floater. A rotten smelling body that had been in the water for several days.

I tried to decide what to do about Pooch's discovery. I could not just leave it there. But I did not want to bring the bloated body aboard either. So, I returned to the helm station where I kept a hinged-top catch-all box of ropes, bobbins, anchors and various other marine miscellany. Tying a lasso knot on one end of a ten foot length of nylon line, I reached over the side and managed to encircle one of the legs of the corpse. I tied the other end to a cleat on the boat.

By the time the fastening process was achieved, Pooch had stopped growling and was now looking at his master questioningly.

"I don't know, Pooch. Let me think for a minute," I said.

What I was thinking about was *which* marine patrol of law enforcement I should call. I knew, from my years with Naples Police, that their Marine Service usually confined their patrols to within one thousand yards of the five-mile long sandy beach. Beyond that, Collier County Sheriff's Marine Patrol had jurisdiction up to twelve miles offshore.

The State of Florida had a marine patrol, as well, over-lapping the local patrols if they considered it necessary. But, I did not want to get involved with the State guys. They could be a pain in the ass, if one let them. The higher up the food chain you went in law enforcement, the more they could com-plicate one's life. I decided my life was complicated enough already. Why complicate the complications?

For emergency calls, I keep a list of radio frequencies for the Coast Guard and the various law enforcement agencies on a plastic laminated card attached to my helm console. So, I lit up my single sideband marine radio and called the Collier County Sheriff's Marine Patrol. The response was almost instantaneous.

"Collier County Sheriff's Marine Patrol. Deputy Fred Baker here."

"Hi Deputy. This is Maury Smith recently of Naples Police."

"How ya doin' Sergeant. Or, rather ex-Sergeant....sorry!"

"I'm doing okay. But there's a guy tied to my boat, out here in the Gulf, whom isn't doing so well."

"You mean a swimmer, or a corpse?"

"A floater. Very dead. Male, I believe. Caucasian judging by the few square inches of skin remaining.. May have been a swimmer, but not a very good one. Looks like he has been out here for several days. And, I'm damned if I want to bring the corpse on board. So, I've got him tied to the side of the boat, and I figure on staying put until you guys come and pick him up."

"How do we find you Smitty? Do you have a G.P.S. system on board."

"Nope. Can't afford those expensive gadgets. I rely on dead reckoning to find my way around the Gulf. I can give you a compass heading. To find me, set a course of 290 degrees, from the mouth of Gordon Pass, without allowing for compass deviation. I am about seven miles offshore. My boat is a white twenty-four foot Sea Ray, named *Melanie.* She's powered with twin Mercury outboards.

"How many aboard your boat?"

"Just me and my dog. You'd better bring a partner and a body bag. Oh, yes, and a couple of face masks to breathe through. The body smells to high heavens. Looks to me like retrieving the corpse is a two man job. *Your two men,* if you don't mind."

"Okay, Smitty, Stay right there. Drop an anchor. We'll be there within thirty minutes, give or take."

"Gotcha," I replied. "But don't take too long. The smell is getting to me. And my dog looks like he might throw up. He's lying on the bow seat with his paws over his nose."

4

Naples, Florida September, 2005

When I walked in the front door of our apartment with Pooch on my heels, my daughter Melanie was stretched out on the love seat in the lanai, her legs tucked under her. She looked up from reading a book.

She was dressed in a beige tee shirt and matching shorts. Her brown beach sandals lay discarded on the floor. In appearance, she was remarkably similar to her mother, Loretta, who could also be classified as a looker. But there the similarity ends. In temperament they are as different as day and night.

Loretta is a whiner, always unhappy with her lot in life. Not that she had an easy time as the wife of a cop. But the more she complained, the more she believed her complaints. Even the good times we had together were minimized, in her mind, when stacked up against the occasional inconvenience of having to cancel attendance at a neighborhood party, or of not having her husband available on time for an evening meal.

Melanie, on the other hand, has an easygoing, extroverted personality and tends to roll with the punches that life always dishes up, such as being left with her father as a single parent, and, to some extent, estranged from her mother. My grown up daughter still loves to tease, joke around and has a great sense of humor.

As I dropped the white plastic cooler in the vestibule, Melanie got up to greet me and my four-footed fishing partner. Pooch made a big deal out of running over to her, his tail wagging and front paws raised to confirm his unconditional love.

"Hi Dad," Melanie said. "What's in the cooler, as if I didn't know."

"Dinner for a week, my dear. Main course, anyway. Or, as your mother used to exclaim, 'Not fish again!' Sorry, Mel; they don't raise beef out in the Gulf."

"I don't mind fish, Dad, as long as we can space it out."

"Not a problem, Mel. We can go to Morrison's Cafeteria or Perkins Family Restaurant, for in-between meals."

She smiled. "Funny thing, Pops. I thought you said The Everglades Room at The Naples Beach Club. I must be getting hard of hearing."

We both laughed. I said: "You do love to tease your old man, don't you my dear. Actually, I'll see if the tooth fairy can arrange a blow-out next week, when I get my pension check. You can get all dressed up, looking like a million bucks and make all the other Neapolitans jealous."

"Just kidding, Pops. Don't waste your money." She gave me a light peck on the morning stubble I had not yet shaved off. "Oh, I almost forgot, you just missed a phone call from the Collier County Sheriff's office. Something about wanting a statement from you."

"Uh, huh. I'll get back to them after I shower."

"What's up, Dad? Or is it a big secret?"

"Pooch made a surprise discovery out on the Gulf this morning."

"He did? What kind of a discovery?" She put her arm around the little dog and hugged him, as though he could talk.

"He spotted a corpse. A floater. Out near my favorite fishing spot."

Her jaw dropped. "You mean a *dead* body?"

"Yep. Most corpses are dead, you know."

"Cripes, Dad, I wish I had come along. You guys have all the luck."

"That'll teach you to get up early. It's us early birds that get the dead bodies. Right Pooch?"

Before heading for the shower, I went to the fridge and pulled out a can of Miller's High Life. I mumbled something about it being Miller Time.

"Any identification?" Melanie asked, not wanting to let the subject drop. "Do they have any idea who it is, or was?"

"I don't know. I didn't stick around while they examined the body. It was an older person, probably male, judging by the clothing. He was slightly the worse for wear. The little fishies and birds had been nibbling."

"Any indication why he drowned?"

"I haven't a clue. There will have to be an autopsy."

"Gee, Pops, you'd better finish your beer, have your shower and get down to the Sheriff's office."

I picked up the morning paper, sat down and skimmed the headlines while I sipped my beer. "Yeah, okay. No panic."

"You seem to be taking this whole thing pretty casually, Dad. I bet it'll make the front page of the Sunday papers."

"Sweetie, it's hard to get excited about an unidentified body. The mystery doesn't bother me, because I'm not a cop any more."

"Aren't you even curious?" she asked, with a hint of frustration. "It might be someone important."

"Melanie, ease off. If I find out anything, you will be the first..."

I was interrupted by the phone ringing.

"Hello. Yeah. This is Maury Smith. Yes, Deputy. I know you have to have a written statement, and complete a report. I can't tell you anything you don't already know. But I'll be there as soon as I have a shower to get rid of the awful smell. Meanwhile, you might wish to do the same, so we won't offend each other."

I had just stepped out of the shower when Melanie called me to the phone again. Carl Forbes identified himself as a police reporter for the Naples Daily News. Obviously news of the floater had traveled at the speed of light. I figured the guy must have an inside source at the Sheriff's office. Of course any number of people might have seen the body bag being unloaded. In which case, someone might have phoned the news room to report their sighting, in the hope of receiving an honorarium – or bribe – for reporting breaking news.

"No thanks Mister Forbes," I said. "I don't see any point in posing for a picture of myself in front of my boat. And, no, I don't think it is a big coincidence that I found the body, considering my former police employment. My dog spotted the body first. He's a very shy animal and does not like to have his photo taken."

"What breed is the dog?" Forbes asked, still hoping for a photo op.

"Just a mongrel. Has a lot of pit bull in him. So he can be very vicious, if harassed."

"Any idea whom the drowned person might be, Mister Smith?"

"I haven't a clue. You'll have to ask the Sheriff's office, if you want more information."

When I hung up, Melanie was standing in the doorway with her hands on her hips, looking indignant. "Da-ad, you know perfectly well that Pooch is a wire-haired terrier. Pit bull indeed. You are a fibber."

I laughed. "That's me, Mel. Fibber Smith – prevarications with a purpose. I wanted to spare Pooch photo trauma. Besides, if he finds out he is a hero for spotting that floater, he'll demand more treats. Then he'll get fat, and I'll have to answer to the vet for allowing him to put on weight."

I had just finished donning a fresh pair of Dockers, golf shirt and a pair of Nikes when the phone rang again. Melanie picked it up.

"For you, Dad." Melanie had the foresight to put her hand over the mouthpiece. "WINK-TV reporter by the name of Sadie, Some-thing-or-other."

"I just left for the Sheriff's office," I whispered conspiratorially. "Tell her to get the story from Pooch."

5

Naples, Florida October, 1995

Back to the past. To 1995, the year of my divorce. A psychiatrist might call it rebound syndrome, but I had trouble getting Joanne Carter out of my mind. Actually it was impossible. We had not seen each other for several weeks, because I had run out of plausible excuses to visit her office. I was afraid I might be forgotten in her busy life. While still concerned about the possibility of a negative response, I felt it was time to gamble and ask for a date – for better or for worse.

Like most real estate agents, her business card, which I held in my hand like a precious jewel, showed the numbers of her office, pager, and home phone. People of Joanne's ilk, who were trying to move a lot of properties wanted their clients to be able to communicate readily with them.

I did not want to make a personal call to her office, or over the airwaves to her pager, so I waited until nine o'clock one evening and phoned her at home. My research revealed that she lived in a modern villa, in a development named Fox Run, an exclusive gated community off Davis Blvd. One day I had surreptitiously checked her address, by following close to the rear bumper of another car that had a remote control to open the black, caste iron, double gates. Her one-storey villa, with a two-car garage, backed onto the private Fox Run golf course. Obviously, she was doing well as a realtor.

Her phone rang five times before her answering machine picked up the call. The recorded message, in Joanne's business mode was very impersonal. "You have reached 751-0423. Please leave your name, number and a brief message, and I'll get back to you."

On the fateful Friday evening of our date, I dressed in my best blue slacks, white short-sleeve shirt and a colorful madras jacket. As I was leaving, I admonished Melanie to be in bed by 10 P.M., saying I would be home by that time to check on her. I left Joanne's number, and the name of the restaurant, in case of emergency. She already had her mother's number, although I knew she would only call Loretta as a last resort. I warned Melanie not to answer the door while I was out.

Joanne met me at the door of her villa, dressed in a shimmering silk, almond-colored cocktail dress with a low neckline. The only concession she had made to adornment, were a pink coral necklace and matching earrings. Her blond hair was gathered in an upswept mode, revealing the delicious curve of her throat. A pair of Gucci sandals matched the color co-ordination of her outfit.

I stood speechless, overwhelmed by her beauty, and like a befuddled Elmer Fudd, I forgot to hand her the small corsage of flowers I was holding in my hand.

She giggled. "Good evening Maury. Something for me?"

"Oh, sorry Joanne. Just a little corsage. My god you are beautiful tonight."

"Flattery will avail you everything, sir. Or at least a peck on the cheek and a tour of my digs. Do come in, Maury. You are looking sharp yourself, in that pretty jacket." She reached up and gave me the promised little smacker.

We were in the tiled vestibule. To the right was a clothes closet and two-piece powder room. Beyond that the long living room and dining room, separated only by an archway. Everything was beautifully decorated. She led me to the spacious kitchen and then to the corridor serving three bedrooms and a full four-piece bathroom serving the guest room. Off the master bedroom was another full bathroom. Such luxury!

I asked her why, living alone, she needed three bedrooms. She showed me that one was made up as a den-cum-library equipped with stereo equipment and television. And pointed out that the sofa could be converted into a bed for additional guest overflow.

"As for the dedicated guest bedroom, I do have the occasional family member from home and I can't let them sleep in the garage," she quipped. "Come out to the lanai, Maury, let's have that glass of wine I promised. Red or white?"

"Whatever you are having," I replied. "It is not necessary to open both."

"How gallant of you. Then it will be a Sauvignon Blanc. And I'll let you remove the cork."

Naples has pretty good mosquito control, but I was pleased to see that her lanai was screened in, as was the *pool* at the back. Now I really was impressed!

We sat together on a chaise lounge swing, ready to sip the cool wine from long-stemmed glasses. Surrounding the pool was a hibiscus hedge in full bloom. Nearby, a jasmine bush gave off the sensuous aroma of the white flowers. A full moon cast rays of light, filtering through variegated foliage of the trees separating the pool from the verdant fairway of the golf course. A very romantic setting! I put my arm around her shoulders, and she didn't object. In fact, she kind of snuggled into the crook of my arm and let out a sigh.

Joanne held up her glass of wine. "Cheers, Maury. I'm looking forward to a pleasant evening together. I am so glad you called."

"Cheers! I'll be honest, Joanne. It took a lot of courage to phone you. I was afraid of rejection. As long as I didn't ask you for a date, I could not be told to get lost, in a nice way of course. So I kept putting it off."

She looked perplexed. "Why would I do that, Maury? You are a nice man, and very handsome. If you have had bad luck with your marriage, you must not let that make you antisocial. Naples needs more eligible, single men. Not fewer. There are a lot of lonely widows and divorcees in this town. And, now that you are free, you are fair game."

"But I'm just a lowly cop," I protested. "And you are a classy, beautiful woman. Look how you live – in the lap of luxury, while I am simply trying to make ends meet on a cop's salary, with alimony payments to meet and a daughter to raise. That's why it took a lot of nerve to ask you for a date."

"Well, I'm delighted you did. And I don't consider *any* cop as being lowly. Law enforcement is an honorable vocation, and very necessary to protect us all from the bad guys of this world. Besides, you won't always be a corporal. I predict you'll be a lieutenant or captain before you know it."

I laughed. "Thanks for the promotion. At least I've made it to the detective division, which is more interesting than being a traffic cop, or on patrol in a cruiser. Once in a while I get to use my brain to solve a case. And I don't have to wear a uniform, except on formal occasions."

"To change the subject, where are you taking me on our first date? I love surprises."

"I thought we might try the King Arthur's Court," I said. "If that appeals to your sense of chivalry and ancient historical legend."

"It does, indeed appeal, Maury. Although, out of context with their theme, that restaurant is reputed to offer the best stone crab claws in the area."

As I held the passenger door open for Joanne to enter the rented Le Baron, she exclaimed. "I love your wheels. Convertibles are so glamorous and romantic. May we have the roof down, please. It's such a lovely evening."

"Certainly," I replied. "I left it in the up position, as protection against the wind, in order to avoid messing your lovely hairdo."

She smiled and pulled a silk scarf over her head, knotting it under her chin. "There. That's all the protection I need. So, lower away."

"Here goes, then. Watch out for flying birds, particularly wood storks!" I released a couple of clamps above the windshield and pressed a button marked 'Roof'. Obediently the roof began its downward journey to fold itself into a compartment behind the back seat.

"If this is a new car, Maury, I like your taste," Joanne said.

"I cannot tell a lie, Joanne. This is a rental for the evening. As you may recall, I lost my old clunker in the divorce settlement. No doubt Loretta has since turned it in for an upgrade, now that she has a good job as a legal secretary."

Joanne turned to me and smiled. "I thought it might be a rental, Maury. But, I am flattered that you would go to so much trouble for our date."

When we turned into the parking lot in front of the restaurant, I hit the roof button again to raise it, this time to protect the seats from evening dew. By the time the roof was again in the up position, a young parking attendant had opened the passenger door for Joanne. He asked me if I would like valet parking.

"Yes, please," I replied. "But I should mention that I am a cop. And, if you so much as put the merest scratch on this vehicle, I'll charge you with reckless driving."

The kid laughed, as he jumped in behind the wheel. He was still laughing as he burned rubber, while careening the convertible around to the rear parking lot. Some joker! I did not share his sense of humor.

"So much for idle threats," I said to Joanne, as I escorted her into King Arthur's Court.

The hostess, dressed in period costume, as a maiden of yore, found my name on her reservation list. I noticed her name tag spelled 'Marian' and I wondered if she were a reincarnation of the famous Maid Marian. Then I remembered that I was getting King Arthur and Robin Hood mixed up. Oh well!

"Ah. Mister Smith and guest. Welcome to Camelot. I have a nice table for you, if you'll just follow me. I followed Joanne, who in turn followed Maid Marian to the 'nice' table near the back of the busy restaurant. Neapolitans love to eat out, particularly on Friday nights. (T.G.I.F.) So I was pleased that we did not have to wait for a half hour or so in the bar, for a table to clear.

When we were seated, the maiden lady handed each of us a large menu. It was printed in Old English type font, on heavy vellum parchment. Images of knights in shining armor, carrying lances and heraldic shields, mounted on prancing horses, decorated the borders. I looked for, but could not find King Arthur, or the legendary Round Table, presumably due to lack of space on the menu. I did notice, however, that our dining table was circular and covered with a tablecloth bearing more images of chivalrous knights, heraldic shields, lances, swords, and other weapons of mass destruction.

"The house special entrée is stone crab claws," volunteered the fair Maid Marian. "And they are delicious. The wine waiter will be with you shortly."

The 'shortly' wine waiter was also in costume. He wore a chemise of plush velvet with sleeves flounced at the shoulder, blousy, striped pantaloons and long, white stockings. On his feet were shoes, with bows on the instep, like the Quakers wore, and probably still do.

In the spirit of the restaurant's name and promotional theme, I asked Joanne: "Wouldst thou like a Sauvignon Blanc Bordeaux, Geneviere?"

"Sounds perfect, Lancelot, old boy," she replied.

After we sipped our goblets of wine for a few minutes, a young waiter showed up. He was dressed in costume similar to the wine waiter. We both ordered the house special – stone crab claws. We could do no less, considering all the promotional hype, including well-planted word-of-mouth rumors about the delicacy.

"Maury, I feel a trifle guilty about depriving innocent stone crabs of their claws," Joanne said, while we waited for dinner to be served.

"Oh, don't give it a thought,." I replied. "Did you not know that the harvesting of stone crab claws is tightly controlled, to protect the little beasties from extinction?"

"How, may I ask?"

"When one claw is removed, the wily crab can grow another to replace it."

"You don't say."

"But I do. Furthermore, this protection continues into old age, until the crab raises a stumpy claw and begs for mercy.".

"How goulish!"

I continued undeterred. "Crabmen, unlike fishermen, do not take the lives of their prey. They do not remove a claw until his or her other claw is sufficiently developed to permit the crab to defend itself from attack by natural predators."

"Well, you have certainly made me feel much better about our upcoming feast, Lance. I did not know you were so well informed about the creatures of the sea."

I grinned. "Hey, I'm a fisherman of some renown. Anytime you would like your freezer filled with the bounty of the deep, I am at your service."

The entrées finally arrived, just in time to interrupt my immodest boasting.

Each of our two pewter platters bore eight – count 'em – claws, hiding within their shells precious morsels of crab meat. The casings of the claws resembled sand-colored porcelain and were equally as hard as fire-hardened ceramic tile. To crack them, we were supplied with metal pincer-like implements, similar to nut-crackers.

I watched as Joanne made a feeble attempt at cracking a casing. She appealed to my male hubris for assistance. "Would you please show me how to do this, Maury?"

"Certainly, m'dear," I said, eagerly. "Sir Lancelot will come to the aid of the fair Lady Geneviere. Watch me carefully."

I grasped the cracking device and inserted a claw taken from her plate. "It just takes brute strength and ignorance, and I have plenty of both."

As the hard claw casing cracked, my right thumb slipped off the handle of the metal pincers, and the skin was pierced by a sharp fragment of claw casing.

"Ouch," I yelled involuntarily. "It got me!"

Nearby patrons turned to see me stuff my bleeding thumb in my mouth, like a two-year-old child. They smiled with sympathy. Or perhaps empathy.

Our waiter heard my exclamation and raced to my first aid with a large, white napkin. Obviously, such wounding incidents were not uncommon in Camelot. As soon as I had staunched the bleeding, he returned with a plastic Band Aid. The short-lived crisis was over. And my cheeks were red with embarrassment.

"She sells *sharp* seashells by the seashore," I murmured, as formerly curious eyes turned elsewhere.

"Good thing I'm not a hemophiliac, or my blood would not clot. Nor would my crud blot."

Joanne giggled at my discomfiture. "So much for brute strength and ignorance. They are not equal to the sharp shells she sells."

"Cunning crustaceans," I further observed, "creating havoc on their careless claw captors."

"Crafty creatures being quite cruelly creative! I wonder where stone crabs got their name?" Joanne mused, as she took a forkful of tasty crabmeat.

"Glad you asked, m'dear," I said, making the story up as I regained my aplomb. "You see, eons ago, there was a fernlike plan with lacey leaves growing on the bottom of the sea. Crabs loved to chew on it, because it gave them a high. In other words, they got *stoned* on the leaves. Hence the name stoned crab, abbreviated to stone crab."

Joanne laughed. "You have a vivid imagination, Maury. But that's okay – I enjoy fairy tales."

"That being the case, I'll finish my story."

"Please do. I don't like being left at the bottom of the sea."

She took a sip of wine and, with her napkin wiped a tear of laughter off her cheek.

"One day, the crab police happened along while the stone crabs were high and acting silly. The offenders were arrested and brought before Judge Davey Jones. After hearing the testimony, he sentenced the felonious crabs to surrender one claw each, so that they would have difficulty chewing on the pot plants. You owe the claws you are eating to undersea marijuana. And I owe my cut thumb to one of those silly crabs."

"Enough already," Joanne said. "I'm beginning to assign personalities to the claws on my platter. Any more stories and I'll be unable to enjoy the tender meat inside."

After we finished the delicious entrée, Joanne said: "You don't seem much like a policeman, Maury, although I am not much of an authority on cops. As a little girl, I was always a little bit frightened of the police, wearing their guns and billy clubs."

"Where were you raised, as a little girl, Joanne?"

"I grew up in Elkhart, Indiana," she replied. "I was very young when I married Tim there. Our marriage lasted less than a year."

"Oh. That explains it. You are a hoosier. And they are notoriously afraid of the police. That's why I frighten you."

She smiled. "You don't frighten me, Maury. At least, not here without your gun and billy."

I kept a straight face. "Please leave my billy out of this discussion."

"Okay. But you remind me of a big, friendly St. Bernard."

"Ye gods, madame. First you insult my billy, and then you say I look like a dog."

"No," she declared. "You are not a dog. You are a nut, a macadamia nut. A complete fruitcake when you make up stories. But, that's why I like you. You have a sense of the ridiculous – a good sense of humor."

I reached across the table and patted her hand. "I'm glad you like me, Joanne. Because I *really* like you. Anyway, tell me about your former husband – why you split up so soon."

She sighed audibly. "I'll make it brief, Maury. Tim was always a heavy drinker. I didn't hold that against him, because I enjoy a drink myself. But it was not long before I realized that he was an alcoholic – a binge drinker. He lost his job and made only a token effort to get another one, preferring to live off the income I was earning as a real estate gal. When I criticized his drinking and lack of gumption, he abused me physically. But, he only beat me up once. I pulled up stakes and headed for Florida. It did not take long to get my realtor's license here and I have never looked back. It was the best decision I ever made."

"Where is your former husband now?"

"I have no idea. I keep in touch with my parents. But certainly not with him."

"What a sad story," I said sympathetically. "I gather you did not have any children?"

"Fortunately, no," she replied wistfully. "Having a child would have complicated matters. As it was, I did not have to endure a bad marriage, just so that a child would have a daddy. I love children, but I don't want to be a single parent."

"Yeah. Loretta didn't want to be one either. That's how I ended up with Melanie."

"You got lucky there. She seems such a bright and loving child. Now that I've told you my reason for divorce, what about yours?"

"Not much to tell. Loretta could never adjust to being a policeman's wife. It's certainly no bed of rose petals. But I finally got tired of her incessant complaining and suggested she adjust to reality or take a hike. She took the hike. Presently she is working in a legal office. But rumor has it she has her eye on an up-and-coming young lawyer. It would not surprise me if she remarried soon."

"Isn't it surprising that she gave up Melanie in the divorce settlement? Most mothers fight to keep their children."

"That's true, Joanne. But I think Loretta considered herself more attractive to a future husband, as a single person, than with the baggage of a child by a previous marriage. She always put her own welfare ahead of anyone else's. I am sure my ex-wife had a future partner in mind, hoping she would do better than she had done with me. Meanwhile, Loretta is entitled to have Melanie with her on a visitation basis. But she has not taken advantage of that provision in the settlement as yet."

The young waiter who rendered first aid to my sore thumb showed up. We both ordered sinful desserts and coffee.

"And Melanie – how has she reacted to losing her mother?" Joanne asked after he departed.

"She has rolled with the punches, so to speak. I think she had become as tired as me of her mother's constant complaining. If she felt rejected, she has not shown it. I believe she is better adjusted than either of us. And she is at an age when she appreciates a little more independence, and a little less mothering. Besides, she knows I think the world revolves around her, and she responds accordingly with affection and natural good humor."

"What a kid!"

"Yep. One in a million, I think."

"I am just sorry she does not have *two* loving parents," Joanne said.

"Well, I am sorry for your unfortunate experience, too, Joanne. I hope you will not hold a grudge against the male gender as a result."

Joanne laughed: "Oh no. I don't think badly of men in general. I just got a bad apple, and I hear there is supposed to be one in every barrel. But one bad apple does not make me want to give up apples forever."

"Good," I said, "speaking on behalf of apples in general and me in particular."

"But that does not mean I want to rush into marriage again," she said. "Not for some time, anyway. Once burned...well you know the saying, and the feeling."

"I sure do," I agreed.

"Well then, that's settled." Smiling, she reached across the table, repeating my earlier gesture, covering my hand with hers. "Let's make a pact here and now. No permanent commitment for either of us, until one or the other decides to end the pact. Meanwhile, let's be good friends and enjoy each other's company."

"Remaining free to enjoy the company of others, of either gender, even lovers," I suggested. "Hey, I'll take your friendship any way I can get it, Joanne."

"Right. I think we both need time to recover from post-breakup trauma," she added.

"So when can I see you again?" I was beginning to wonder if all this pact stuff was her way of saying goodbye.

She laughed at my question. "Down boy. This date is not even over yet. "I'm sure we'll be seeing lots of each other. As friends. *Very good friends!*"

The little red LeBaron convertible returned us to her villa, with fenders unscratched and the parking lot attendant uncharged with careless driving.

I was invited in for a nightcap.

My first date with Joanne ended with a long and blissful kiss, as I was leaving.

While driving home, I thought of our agreement. It seemed harmless enough. But I hoped this mutual freedom situation would not last forever. Little did I know that it was like a serpent lying in the grass, waiting to strike when least expected.

I pulled the key to our apartment from my pocket, feeling a trifle guilty about having left Melanie alone.

When I opened the door, Melanie was sprawled on the floor in front of the television. I looked at my watch, which read 10:45.

Melanie scrambled to her feet, looking guilty herself. "What time is it, Dad?"

I gave her a parental look. "Forty-five minutes past your bedtime, young lady. How come you are still up?"

She decided the best defense was to adopt an offensive strategy. "You are late, too, Dad. You said you would be home by ten o'clock. Besides, I couldn't get to sleep until I found out if you kissed her goodnight."

"It's none of your business. But yes, I did. Is that alright with you?"

"Sure, Dad. She is a very nice lady. And beautiful, too. I would have been worried if you hadn't."

"Well, your worries are over. Now off to bed with you."

"Will you tuck me in."

"Of course, Melanie. But no more conversation at this late hour."

7

Naples, Florida September, 2005

Following my resignation from the Naples police, I started thinking about future employment, to supplement my reduced pension income. I was hoping to find some way to make use of my training as a detective. Of course, the closest alternative to working for a public service such as the Naples Police would be to join or start a private detective service. But, becoming a 'private eye' would require a drastic change of mind-set. I had spent most of my life working for a public institution funded by the city.

I decided to approach the question by attempting to weigh the pros and cons of such a move.

I had the impression that private investigators usually have to work alone, with minimal resources at their beck and call. The police, on the other hand, have unlimited resources, both locally, and outside their own jurisdictions, they can call on as needed. They work as partners, or at least, as part of a team. P.I.s need to rely more on individual effort, as well as on such unofficial contacts as they might have with police, to obtain favors which might help in bringing cases to a favorable conclusion.

Television has dramatized private investigators (P.I.s), by usually putting them in a favorable light. The medium has seldom featured the seamy side of the job. Catching wayward husbands or wives in compromising situations is not nearly as glamorous, or attractive to TV viewers, as seeing P.I.s solve crimes the police have had to shelve due to excessively heavy work loads or because of lack of evidence.

If I should decide to become a private investigator, I would want to be able to concentrate on those assignments that would be more in keeping with my experience in police detective work and less in boring surveillance activities or family disputes.

But, would picking and choosing my case work be economically viable? Or would I have to remain a slave to the almighty dollar?

Finally, in view of my recent dispute with my boss resulting in my resignation, should I even consider trying to work for someone else? Would I not be better off to start out as an entrepreneur – as my own boss?

I knew I was not going to find answers to my questions without talking to someone in the business of private investigation. That is when I remembered an old friend and school mate, Dan Short.

Despite his name, Dan is anything but short. He is slightly taller than me, which puts him about six-four in his stocking feet, or even barefoot for that matter. Dan Short owns and operates his own one-man detective agency, with an office in a strip plaza on Airport-Pulling Road in East Naples. I spoke with him briefly on the phone, and he invited me to visit his emporium.

"Maury, old cock!" Dan greeted me at the door of his office, bypassing a dowdy-looking receptionist, when I walked in. "Good to see you. Grab a chair and take a load off. Your timing is good. The coffee is fresh. How do you take it? I can't offer real cream or sugar. So, your choice is Creamer and ersatz sweetener."

I laughed. "Fortunately I take it black, as it comes from the pot, thanks Dan."

He poured a couple of cups as I dragged a chair in front of his desk. When he settled in a well-worn oak swivel-chair, he started the conversation.

"Want to tell me about it, Maury?"

"About what, Dan?"

"About kissing off the lieutenant, of course. And making him duck under his desk."

I should not have been surprised that word of my unique resignation had become street talk – the circumstances of my resignation made me a legend in my own time.

"As you have probably heard," I said. "The loot and I did not hit it off. So I am temporarily between jobs – a euphemism for the ugly word 'unemployment'. I am thinking about getting into the private eye business, but I haven't gotten beyond the thinking stage. I have a lot of questions, but few answers. I know you have been a P.I. for a number of years. So, I was hoping you could clue me in."

"Sure, Maury. Do you smoke these things?" He pulled out a package of cigars from his jacket and offered one to me. I held up my hand. "Thanks, but no thanks, Dan. I gave up smoking a few years ago. But you go ahead and I'll enjoy it vicariously. Tell me all about the PI business. I admit to being a neophyte when it comes to the private sector."

After he lit up, he settled back in his chair, pulled out a lower drawer in his desk, turned sideways and put his feet up on the open drawer.

"First of all," Dan said, "in the State of Florida private investigators are called Detective Agencies. And the business is highly regulated by the state. To get a license, applicants must serve a two year apprenticeship. Were you thinking of starting out on your own, Maury?"

"Yes, I was. But I can't wait two years. Damn! I had to take a reduced pension when I resigned from the police. And I am trying to put my daughter through university. I can barely meet expenses"

"Well, you might get special consideration in view of your long experience with the police. But starting your own shop will require some up front investment. Cash flow will not be instantaneous."

"Yeah. I guess I am wasting your time, Dan."

"No you are not, my friend. There is a job right here, Maury, if you would be interested."

"That is very good of you, Dan. But I learned something about myself on the police force. Obviously I don't take orders very well from anyone, even a nice guy like you. But don't get me wrong, I am flattered with the offer."

Dan raised his big meat hook of a hand. "Stop already. You didn't let me finish. Since your phone call I have been thinking the whole idea through. I don't want an employee; what I want is a partner. And I think, with your background, you would fill the bill admirably. As a full partner, you would not have to take orders from me. We would be on equal terms."

"Why would you want to give up full control of your own firm, Dan?"

"For a very good reason, Maury. Since I started the business twenty years ago it has grown to the point where I have to work fourteen hours a day just to keep up. I am unable to handle all the case work alone. Now, a partnership would require some investment from you, to balance out and even up the share each of us will hold in the firm's assets. But that could be done gradually."

"I don't have any ready cash, Dan."

"That's okay. We could have a legal contract drawn up, to make the partnership an accomplished fact, to take effect as soon as you get your license from the State. I think they might partially waive the apprenticeship rule in your situation, in view of the years you have spent with the Naples Police. Particularly considering the many years you have spent as a detective."

"Well, you have certainly given me a lot to think about, Dan. As the new bride said – this is all so sudden."

"Just take your time to think it over, Maury. The offer stands until you get back to me, one way or the other. If you say you are interested, I'll be completely open with you. I'll show you the books and the kind of cases I've been working on – the whole nine yards." Dan smiled the big old smile of a crack salesman. I think he knew he had me hooked, line and sinker!

8

To spare Melanie the grizzly details, I had pretended to be disinterested in the body that Pooch had discovered in the Gulf. But my detective instincts would not allow me to just forget it. Of course, the County Police would be doing a lot of investigative work to establish the identity of the corpse. But if they knew who it was, they were not releasing any information to the news media. Curiosity got the better of me and I decided to phone the Sheriff's Office.

I asked for Deputy Fred Baker of the Marine Patrol. Luckily, he was available – just going off duty.

"Hi Maury," he said, when I told him who was calling. "What can I do for you?"

"Just curious, Fred." We were on a first name basis by this time. "Did you have any success in identifying the corpse?" I asked. "You know, the floater."

"Hey, man, giving out information on a case under investigation...."

"Is a violation of public trust," I finished the mantra for him. "But as a responsible member of the public, I trust you, and you know you can trust me. Besides, my dog discovered the body, and I believe his master should have special consideration."

He laughed. "Well, you can pass the message on to your dog, Maury. Tell him we still don't have a clue. Mister John Doe, as we call him, apparently had no criminal record, and no service record. So he could not be traced through his prints. As your dog knows, everybody in the world has not been fingerprinted."

"Right. My dog wondered if the man could be traced through his clothes."

"Nope. We drew a blank there. He was wearing the sort of clothes that are sold all over America."

"And his teeth?" I asked.

"Tell your dog the teeth were dentures, and must be at the bottom of the Gulf. Not enough stickum, I guess."

"In other words, a complete mystery. Right?"

"I'm afraid so," he replied. "If you or your dog can give us any clues, the Sheriff would like to close the case."

"On behalf of Pooch, thanks for the update, Fred. If we hear of anything, we'll get back to you."

"Have a nice day."

9

I phoned Dan Short the next day and told him the new bride says yes. He sounded very pleased. I was looking forward to getting back in harness.

My completed application for a private investigator's license was mailed to the State of Florida in Tallahassee by priority post. Dan followed up with a phone call to a friend in the state capital who was in the office responsible for issuing licenses. He used his considerable powers of persuasion to get my apprenticeship period shortened to three months.

Meanwhile, we changed the signage at Dan's office to Short & Smith Detective Agency. An attorney drew up partnership papers allowing me to buy into the firm on the basis of a personal promissory note, payable over a period of five years. But in the interim, as soon as my license was issued, I would be a full partner.

A storage room at the back of the building was converted into a private office for me. Some new furniture was installed, as well as a networking computer system, so that Dan, the receptionist and the new partner would have ready access to the Internet, the world's greatest database.

A seriously underperforming reception gal was given her walking papers and was replaced with a clever, bright and cheerful Latino, Josie Gonzales.

Now we could post a sign *Habla Espanol.* (We figured it was not necessary to have a sign saying we speaka da English).

Using the well-documented theory that it pays to advertise, we started running a catchy small-space ad regularly in the Naples Daily News.

Time passed, as Shakespeare pointed out, at diverse paces. I showed up at the office of Short & Smith from time to time, between fishing trips and spending a lot of time at the beach. Three months passed eventually and my self-inflicted holiday was over. In mid-December Dan phoned to say that my license to practice as a bona fide private detective had come in the mail.

My first case turned out to be an interesting experience, but not without some anxious moments.

The day before I started back to work full time, Josie had taken a message from Mrs. Gary Golding, who said she had seen our little ad in the paper. She explained to Josie that she knew me from a successful investigation I carried out for her last year while I was with Naples Police Department. It was a jewel robbery. The perp had jigged the security system and liberated some very expensive jewelry from the lady's bedroom safe, while Mrs. G and her husband were attending the Naples Philharmonic one evening. Through an underworld contact – a reliable informant – I was able to identify the thief, who had a record of break and enter. Her jewelry was recovered. Both she and her insurance company were very pleased. The only individual not pleased with the outcome of the case was the jewel thief, who was sentenced to five years as a habitual criminal.

The Golding residence was in a very upscale section of Old Naples with an appropriate name – Port Royal. Although the residents of that exclusive enclave were not necessarily of royal blood, they were, of necessity, very well-endowed with monetary wealth. To own property in Port Royal they had to be millionaires, or even billionaires. They had to be able to afford their palatial homes, most of which backed on to canals where they could park their equally expensive yachts.

Whoever named the streets and canals of Port Royal must have had the heart of a buccaneer and the soul of a devout alcoholic – Galleon Drive, Spyglass Lane, Treasure Trove, Morgan's Cove, Smuggler's Bay, Gin Lane, Rum Row.

Then there was the Port Royal *Club,* play place of the rich and … But then, outsiders could not be sure there was any *play*ing, except maybe card games. Who knows? Only the members and their guests!.

Anyway, the Club is located opposite the gates to the Port Royal community itself, on the beach side of Gordon Blvd. It is sufficiently far back from the high water mark that plebians and other beach-walkers do not bother the members, except maybe by gawking from a respectable distance. Whatever is inside the Club is housed in a handsome red brick building, which is surrounded by nicely landscaped grounds. The Port Royal Club surely offers a lifestyle to which every upward mobile young Neopolitan should aspire, but few will achieve.

Did I remember Mrs. Golding? Of course I did. And she remembered me, at least enough to leave a message, asking me to call her. Her husband, I recall, owned an investment bank. He had retired with enough loot to buy a sinfully gorgeous house on one of the preferred lots in Port Royal, backing onto a canal, where he could dock his fifty foot Hatteras yacht.

I returned Mrs. Golding's call of the previous day and apologized for the delay in getting back to her. After the usual pleasantries, she said she would like to talk with me about taking on a project of an investigative nature concerning her daughter. I made an appointment to visit her at 2 P.M. Then I went in to explain the situation to my partner, Dan. I asked him if he had any advice for me in handling my first case for the firm of Short & Smith. He was at his ebullient best when I told him the background.

"Wonderful, Maury!" he said enthusiastically. "Glad you are going to get your feet wet, right off the bat. An old time dick like you does not need any help or advice from me in how to handle an investigation. But you will be new to our billing procedures. So, open a paper docket for your expenses receipts to charge the client, plus an administration fee of 17.65%, which is equivalent to 15% coming off the top. And you will want to start a computer file on the case. The usual deposit, if you take the case, is one thousand dollars. But that is not a hard and fast amount. Just use your own judgment. If I had a client living in Port Royal, I would not worry too much about getting paid. But sincerity money up front is always welcome."

When I drove through the winding, tree-lined boulevards of Port Royal I was impressed once again by the beautiful architecture of the homes and exquisitely landscaped grounds. The Golding residence was no exception. Like all the other Port Royal properties, the wide, circular driveway was of interlocking brick, leading to a three-car garage which was built into a modern, two-storey building of understated elegance. A gleaming black Mercedes convertible coupe was parked in the driveway. If cars could think, my little Ford Focus sedan would have felt intimidated.

Answering the chimes, a Jamaican maid, dressed in a black and white frilly outfit, led me through a maze of rooms to the back patio, where Mrs. Golding was ensconced on a chaise lounge. She was dressed very briefly in halter top and very short shorts, showing a shapely pair of legs.

"Sergeant Smith! How good of you to come," she greeted, as she got up of the lounge and offered a small, soft hand. I noticed, as we shook hands, her ring finger displayed a diamond of semi-walnut size, encircled with a subservient border of small emeralds. I recalled that this was one of the items in last year's stolen jewelery case. Since she was wearing it, even in an informal setting, it occurred to me that there was less chance of it being stolen again, unless a thief also took the body.

"Sorry, Mrs. Golding," I said. "I am no longer a sergeant. Just a plain mister now."

A plucked, thin eyebrow was raised a little. "Such rubbish! The Naples Police have lost a fine detective. But I am so glad you are available through your private agency."

Mrs. G. was of indeterminate age. Her glowing tan and bleach-white hair made her seem to be in her early to mid thirties. But closer inspection revealed marks behind the jawline indicating a face-lift had eliminated wrinkles that usually occur after age forty. Her voice was husky, the mark of a devotee to cigarette smoking. Her green eyes had an appraising look. She exuded an aura of sexuality.

"Please do sit down and make yourself comfortable," she said, indicating a padded poolside armchair beside a round glass-topped table.. "Would you like something to drink? Coffee? Tea? Scotch? Champagne?"

I laughed. "Thanks, but coffee would be just fine. I take it black."

She got up and pressed a button on the wall, and then took a chair beside mine. I could smell her perfume. Chanel 5 can be very distracting!

We were seated under a large, striped awning, providing shade from the hot sun. A kidney-shaped pool of Olympic dimensions stretched out beyond the faux fieldstone patio. A ten foot privacy wall encircled the pool and its surround right up to the walls of the house. Peeping Toms would be frustrated unless they were good climbers or could rent a helicopter.

The maid appeared in response to Mrs. G's button pushing.

"Two mochas, please Marjie. Skip the sugar and cream."

Mrs. G. donned a pair of sunglasses and encouraged me to do the same. "The sun reflecting off the water can burn holes in your eyebrows, Mister Smith." she said. "And what would a Private Eye be with holes in his eyes?"

I pondered that one, as I obeyed her instruction. "A holey PI Mrs. Golding?" I ventured.

She smiled, showing even white teeth. "A blinded private dick, Smitty. I trust you don't mind my calling you Smitty? My name is Cynthia. Let's drop the formality."

"As you wish, er…Cynthia. Do you want to tell me about the investigation concerning your daughter?"

"What I am about to tell you is in strictest confidence, Smitty. I do not even want my husband, Gary, to know I called you."

"Certainly. I may be new to the PI business, but I do know there must be confidentiality between client and investigator. I take it your husband is not home this afternoon?"

"Correct. Gary is away, so we should not be interrupted."

Marjie the maid arrived through the sliding glass doors and carefully placed a brown mocha coffee on a woven straw coaster in front of each of us.

"Thank you Marjie," Cynthia Golding said. "You may have the rest of the afternoon off. But, I'd like you back by five o'clock as I've invited a few friends in for cocktails this evening."

The tawny maid did a little bow. "Certainly Ma'am. I'll enjoy some time at the beach."

Cynthia waved her away imperiously, with a flick of her wrist. She picked up a long holder and withdrew a cigarette from a pack handily available on a nearby side-table. I pulled a Bic lighter from my pocket, flicked it on and held the flame for her to light up. She stuck the cigarette in the holder slowly, in a suggestive way, leaned over, steadied my hand with her long, soft fingers while she drew in the first drag. I tried not to stare at the sight of her cleavage. She was well-endowed in the breast department. I wondered if they were real. Real enough to cause a stirring in my groin, anyway.

"Cigarette, Smitty?" she asked archly, as she caught me giving an appreciative glance at her long, tanned legs."

"Um. Thanks, but I only carry the lighter out of long habit. I am a reformed smoker.".

"Righto Smitty. Let me explain my concerns about my daughter. First, I might be embarrassed if your investigation turns out to be unnecessary. I may be away off base, but if so, I can only apologize in advance."

She took another long drag from her cigarette, while she gathered her thoughts. I remained silent. I learned as a police detective interrogating suspects that silence is often the best way to draw out information. The subject person feels uncomfortable and tries to fill the vacuum.

"A little background might help," she began, "my twenty-year-old daughter is from my first marriage. Her name is Sarah. My first husband died in an auto accident, leaving a large sum of money in a trust for our only child. The trust provides Sarah with a monthly income until her twenty-first birthday, at which time she becomes entitled to the principal. She will be twenty-one on February 8, 2006 – about three months from now."

I continued to remain silent, simply nodding so that she would continue uninterrupted.

"When I married Gary, two years ago, Sarah did not like the idea of living in the same house as her step-father. Like a lot of self-made business people, Gary tends to be a trifle over-bearing and strong-willed. Sarah is also strong-willed, and has an independent streak in her personality, aided and abetted by her private income. Shortly after my marriage to Gary, Sarah left home and rented a modest apartment in Fort Myers where she was attending Edison Community College.

She shared the accommodation with another girl. After graduation, she and Sarah parted company. So she is living alone now."

Finally, I decided to break in to give her larynx a brief rest. "I suppose you must miss her, Cynthia. Does she keep in touch?"

"Oh yes. She phones me about once a week, when she knows Gary is not going to be home. Other than that, I don't see her unless I am specifically invited to her apartment."

"You mean, without your husband?"

"That's right, Smitty. She considers herself a grown woman, who does not need the aggravation of talking to someone whom she does not like. I am quite certain the feeling of dislike is mutual. I have the feeling Gary prefers she live elsewhere."

I pulled out my ubiquitous little black book, a habit learned in the Naples Police. I jotted down the name Sarah. Then I had to ask her last name – the family moniker with which she was born.

"Briscoe," Cynthia replied to my question. "Sarah Bernhardt Briscoe. Her father thought she might become an actress."

I smiled at the thought that a proud parent might wish a famous actress' name on a child with the hope that it might provide thespian talent on the recipient.

"I'll give you my daughter's address and phone number before you leave," Cynthia said. "But I would suggest you do not contact her directly. As I said, she is very independent-minded and would resent any interference from me in her personal affairs. So, you can understand why I did not want to go to the police about my concerns."

"I understand," I said. "Please go on."

We both paused to take sips of the exotic coffee, which was served in small, fragile cups. I resisted the temptation to turn my cup over to see if the cups were as valuable as they appeared.

"The last time I was in Fort Myers," Cynthia said, "visiting Sarah in her apartment, was on November 25th. We discussed plans for Christmas. She said she was going to have some friends in on several occasions, and assured me that she would not be lonely. She absolutely refused to consider coming over here. I asked her if she needed any extra money for Christmas shopping. She just smiled mysteriously and said that money was the last thing she needed. I thought that was a strange answer, as her monthly income from the trust fund is only $1900 a month – not a lot, considering her rent and other living expenses."

"Seems odd, all right."

"She said she had been making some investments that have really paid off. Really paid off were her exact words. I did not want to pry into her personal affairs, but I was worried that she might be doing something foolish. I suggested she might want to get some investment advice from Gary, but of course, that went over like a lead balloon. That was when she said her extra income was from some sort of religious investment, for a worthy cause."

"Worthy causes, don't usually provide income," I suggested. "On the contrary, religious donations or investments do not often pay any dividends – just income tax deductions."

"Sarah handed me this folder," Cynthia said, pulling a four color brochure from her beach bag. "She said she could hardly wait to invest the principal from her father's trust, as soon as it became available in February. That's when I became alarmed and decided to call you, Smitty."

She handed me the folder. It was obviously professionally designed, and colorfully printed on glossy stock. On the front cover was an ethereal picture of Christ, arms extended to welcome the reader. The image was back lit, with a halo over his head. A caption at the bottom read: *The Heavenly Ministries invite you to share in our Holy Abundance.*

Inside, the text was minimal. But there were some very heart rendering photos: A collage, consisting of an Oriental baby, clad only in diapers sitting on a war-torn railroad track, with tears streaming down its cheeks… a small black African boy, with distended belly, obviously suffering from malnutrition…a Red Cross nurse administering an inoculation to a black teenage girl…a European woman pushing a two-wheeled cart, transporting her three children and all her worldly possessions into a refugee camp. The only caption said *Give generously and the Lord will provide.*

The back cover read: *Your generous gifts will be rewarded.* Under the caption was a Donor Card with provision for name, address and telephone number of the donor. And, of course, suggested amounts starting at $100, which could be ticked off, along with method of payment.

At the bottom of the Donor Card, the text read,.

Please mail to:

The Everglades Church of Redemption,

Box 517, Fort Myers, Florida 33010

"May I keep this folder?" I asked.

"Certainly, Smitty. That's why I kept it."

"Did your daughter explain how her 'investment' in the church paid rewards?" I could not keep the skepticism out of my voice.

"She gave a complicated story about how the donations or gifts to the church were being used to help poor children and destitute families in Third World countries. In return, out of gratitude, the countries involved provided goods and materials to the so-called Heavenly Ministries Trading Company at below market prices. This was supposed to allow the Everglades Church to dispose of the goods in the marketplace through a subsidiary marketing company –HMTC Marketing."

"Uh huh. And no doubt that was how the holy profits were obtained?"

"Sarah said they did not use the word profits. They were called Heavenly Abundance Rewards."

"Okay. Go on," I said.

"She said she invested One Hundred Dollars at the outset. That was all she could spare at the time. A month later she received a check in the mail for Fifty Dollars, along with a Thank You card. The face of the check had a miniature reproduction of the pictures in the folder, along with a caption 'Heavenly Ministries – Abundance Reward'.

"So, she received a fifty percent dividend, or profit in only a month, and ostensibly received her money back?"

"Right. The check, she said, was drawn on a bank in Fort Myers. Thinking there must have been some mistake, she phoned the church and spoke with the Minister. He told her there was no mistake, that her One Hundred Dollars had been pooled with other donations and had produced a Heavenly Abundance of Fifty Dollars. He added that her initial One Hundred Dollar investment was still working to help the poor people in Third World Countries. He encouraged her to add to her investment whenever she could. She did not need the Fifty Dollars, so she said she endorsed the check back to the church, thus increasing her investment to One Hundred and Fifty Dollars. At the end of the next month she received a check for Seventy Five Dollars, which she turned back to the church to increase her investment to Two Hundred and Twenty-Five Dollars.   And that's the story, Smitty.   What do you think? Too good to be true?"

"Oh yes!" I added only one word. "Ponzi."

10

Obviously, Cynthia's daughter lived in a sheltered world, a place where money grew on trees, where investment paid fifty percent or more a month.

"I beg your pardon. What was that word?"

"Ponzi, a well-known scam. A Ponzi scheme is one of the oldest scams on earth. Before a swindler by the name of Charles Ponzi came over from Italy, such a scam was called 'a bubble' Have you ever heard of the famous South Sea Bubble?"

"A bubble? You mean it might burst?" she asked.

"Yes, because a fraud artist can only rob Peter to pay Paul so long before the whole thing collapses."

"Please tell me more about this Charles Ponzi. How did his scheme work, Smitty?"

"Ponzi started selling Promissory Notes paying fifty percent over forty-five days. He ultimately collected millions of dollars from gullible and greedy investors. He claimed he could share with others the profits he made from arbitraging Postal Reply Coupons of various countries, due to different rates of exchange."

"Arbitraging, Smitty?"

"Yes. It means buying something in one country and selling it simultaneously in another, and making a profit on the differing exchange rates. All hogwash, of course. But people will believe what they want to believe. He was simply paying the Promissory Notes off with new money coming in from investors. When the incoming money stream finally dried up, Ponzi was unable to pay off his Notes."

"And, the same thing will happen with Sarah's so-called investments?"

"Yes. And there's likely more to the church's Ponzi scam. Such a fraudulent scam works best when combined with a Pyramid program."

"That sounds Egyptian."

"Such a program is named Pyramid because it's peaked at the top and broad at the base, like an isosceles triangle. Let's say the church wants to ensure a continuing source of income by appointing salespersons on a commission basis. The original salespersons can then appoint additional salespeople and receive an overriding commission on the money collected by their appointees. The sales base keeps broadening. And the funds collected flow up to the top, minus commissions, of course."

"Is that kind of a thing illegal, Smitty?"

"Depends on what is being sold. If it's a legitimate product, for example brushes, or cosmetics – two examples that come to mind – the purchasers are receiving value for their money. So that is considered legal. But if the product being sold is a phony investment scheme, even one operated by a church, I believe it would be considered fraudulent and illegal."

"You seem to be well-informed about scams and fraud." She said.

"More than the average detective. You see, I worked on the Fraud Squad for a couple of years. You'd be surprised at the number of people who get bilked out of their life's savings in various scams. Senior citizens are particularly vulnerable. So they are picked on by fraud artists more than the general population."

She put the butt of her cigarette in an ashtray and inserted another from the pack into the holder. Small wonder she had a husky voice. I could hardly fail to supply fire from the Bic again, having established a precedent.

After taking another drag, and blowing out a plume of smoke, she said: "As I mentioned earlier, my main concern is that my daughter may go ahead and invest the principal of the trust in this church investment. It is very important that we do not let that happen."

"From what you have told me, I think there should be *another* aspect of this situation you should be worried about."

"What is that, Smitty?"

51

"The question of whether Sarah has been recruited as a salesperson. If she has become part of the scheme, she will have committed a felony. She could be charged as part of the conspiracy to commit fraud."

Cynthia Golding suddenly looked panic stricken. "Oh no! I had never thought of that possibility. Good Lord, Smitty, I don't want my daughter to go to jail. And I don't want her to lose her inheritance. What can you do to put a stop to this foolishness?"

"One of the problems with trying to shut down a Ponzi operation is to get proof. Because a church is involved, it has the appearance of legitimacy."

"Sure." Cynthia agreed. "Churches are always involved in fund-raising."

"It's almost a perfect cover." I said. "They can claim that the funds are required for missionary projects, to pay for operating expenses or to pay off a mortgage. The question is *how* they are raising the money, not *whether* they are entitled to do so. If they are promising, through their actions, to pay ridiculous interest rates, on so-called investments, repayment of investors' capital is obviously unsustainable. It is only a question of time before the whole scheme collapses. By then, whoever is behind the phony fund-raising will no doubt have taken off to greener pastures."

"Oh, dear," Cynthia worried, "what can be done to protect my daughter from herself?"

"I may find myself in a bit of a bind," I pointed out, "if I can get proof that the Everglades Church of Redemption is being used as a front for a confidence racquet, I may be obliged to call in the local police. If it turns out to be a widespread operation, the State police or even the FBI might become involved."

"I guess you will have to do whatever is necessary, Smitty. But I hope you will try to protect Sarah."

"I will certainly do my best," I assured her. "One thing I can do is contact the minister of the church. How I can best approach him will take some thought. He might be willing to co-operate if he thinks his neck is going to be on the line. In any event, I think I should have a word with Sarah before I alert him and his cohorts."

I could see that Cynthia was very distraught. "Now that you have explained her possible deeper involvement as a salesperson," she said, "I now think you should talk to her like a Dutch uncle. Headstrong as she is, she probably would not listen to me."

As I was leaving, Cynthia wrote out her daughter's address and phone number in Fort Myers on a small recipe card. "Good luck, Smitty. I am so glad I called you. I want to be kept informed, of course. But I don't want my husband, Gary, to be in the loop at this stage. So don't phone me, I'll phone you."

I was half way out the front door, when she called me back. "Wait a minute, Smitty. We haven't discussed your fee."

I paused for a few seconds. This was new territory for me.

Noting my hesitancy, Cynthia Golding pre-empted my response.

She said: "Oh, what the hell, Smitty. Take this for starters. I trust you."

She reached into her purse and handed me a roll of ten one hundred dollar greenbacks. Then she gave me a peck on the cheek. "Go break a leg, Mister Detective. Put the bastards in jail."

11

Dan Short was at his big, well-worn desk when I arrived back at the office after my afternoon session with Cynthia Golding. His balding head was bent over a document of some kind, Winston Churchill reading glasses perched on his rather bulbous nose.

He had a dubious habit of sporting a toothpick or a wooden match in his mouth, and today was no exception. I think it was an adult substitute for a child's pacifier. Perhaps his mother had denied him the pleasure of her nipple when he was a baby. Another possibility, I mentally speculated, was that he needed something in his largest facial orfice to replace the feeling of a nice Cuban cigar, without the attendant risk of being charged as an accomplice of Fidel. The final, and absolutely last likelihood was that he had been influenced by a television series in which the great detective, Sherlock Holmes, invariably clenched a long-stemmed pipe in his teeth when he solved crimes before the very eyes of the amazed Doctor Watson. In that far-fetched scenario, I expected him to address me condescendingly, with the remark "Elementary my dear Smith."

Whatever the reason, I was not about to quarrel with my new partner about his harmless habit. He might, with good reason, retaliate with a sermon about my alleged hair-trigger temper. Just a myth, actually, created by a certain police lieutenant for his own depraved purposes. Or, so I believed.

Without comment, I handed, Dan the roll of one hundred dollar bills which Cynthia Golding had given me as a down payment towards my fee and future expenses. He stretched his generous mouth into a broad smile. I hoped he would not accidentally swallow his toothpick.

"What ho," Dan said, as he counted the bills. "That's the idea, partner. Get the filthy lucre up front, in case the client changes his or her mind."

"It is a her, Dan. And you may credit one grand to the account of Cynthia Golding."

I went on to sketch out, in broad terms, what Cynthia had told me about her daughter's intention to invest the proceeds of her father's trust funds in the apparently fraudulent Ponzi scheme of the Everglades Church of Redemption.

"So you think the daughter might have become a salesperson for this scam, Maury?" Dan asked.

"It is a possibility, Dan. She sounds pretty naïve about how and why the so-called Heavenly Abundance funds are paid out. Gullible as she is, Sarah could easily be talked into becoming a part of the scheme, in which case she could be charged as a co-conspirator."

"How are you going to get proof that the operation is illegal and still protect her?"

"First I have to convince her that she is being duped by some unscrupulous con men. Do you mind if I get some help from Josie? I need a female accomplice to get past the young lady's defenses."

"Not at all," Dan said. "If Josie is willing, you have my blessing. I don't want to know what dirty tricks you have in mind. Anyway, good luck. I'll keep this money handy in case I have to bail you both out of the county jail."

Sarah's mother had given me her daughter's unlisted telephone number. Presumably it was unlisted to guard against con artists, boiler room operators and other predators of that ilk. I decided to take a page out of their book.

"Josie," I said in my most persuasive manner, "how would you like to help me keep a young girl out of jail?"

She smiled. "It sounds more interesting than answering the phone all day. What do I need to do?'

I explained that a young girl by the name of Sarah Briscoe was being both naïve and pig-headed, and was possibly in danger of ending up in jail with some scam artists.

"We need to outsmart the con men, Josie, by adopting fake personas."

"You mean aliases?"

"Yes. We have to get past Sarah's defenses, and the sure fire way seems to be to pretend a connection with the Everglades Church of Redemption in Fort Myers, a church she worships, if you will excuse the pun, because they have been paying her big bucks."

She looked a little puzzled. "I see. Well, I don't really see. But I am sure it will all be clear in due course. It sounds like a lark. Count me in."

"Good girl. You may call it a lark, or a mocking bird. Or possibly an albatross that will drop nasty doo-doo on the necks of the crooks planning to separate a lot of innocent people from their life's savings. Our little game is going to start with a phone call, from you to the divine Sarah."

When Josie phoned Sarah Briscoe's unlisted number, a girl's voice answered, presumably Sarah being cautious. I was listening on the extension phone.

"You have reached 941-540-3669, please identify yourself, or stay on the line and leave a message, with your name and number, at the tone."

Josie raised her eyebrows at me, but carried on.

"Ms. Briscoe this is Josie Gonzales. I am in the Accounting department at the Everglades Church. We have discovered a discrepancy in the account of one of the investors you brought in. And we need your help to clear it up."

"This is Sarah Briscoe. I picked up your call, Josie. Which investor are your referring to?"

"Sorry Sarah. I don't want to discuss this on the phone," Josie said. "May I come out and see you personally, at a time convenient to you?"

There was a pause. "Could we make it this evening, Miss Gonzales?" Sarah asked.

"Sure we can," Josie replied. "You just name the time."

"How about seven-thirty?" Sarah suggested. "Give me a chance to have my dinner and clean up a bit?"

"That will be fine. Oh, by the way, I will have Reverend Smith with me. He is from the Diocese accounting office. He would like to meet you."

Sarah sounded worried: "Can't you tell me what this is all about, Josie?"

"Not a major problem, Sarah. We'll look forward to seeing you at seven-thirty."

Josie said goodbye to terminate the conversation, leaving Sarah with a big question mark hanging in a balloon over her head.

I told Josie she was an angel. Admittedly, a very deceptive one, who might have trouble at the Pearly Gates. She had already agreed to come with me to Fort Myers to be assistant gumshoe for the evening.

For my disguise, I rented and donned a white clerical collar from a local costume outfit that caters to actors, costume party-goers and Halloween weenies. Deceptive detectives were not their usual customers, but I tried to look like a thespian – John Geilgud playing Father O'Hara.

Fort Myers is about thirty miles from Naples via Interstate 75. My Ford Focus transported us in economical style, without ostentation, to the downtown intersection of US 41 and Daniels Road in about forty minutes. The landmark Bell Shopping Center loomed on my right. I turned onto US 41 North and drove one long block into a maze of side streets off the busy highway.

Ford Foci do not usually come equipped with GPS, but an erstwhile police detective should not need high tech help in finding his way in a maze. It is simply a case of trying all possibilities until one finally pays off. At last, I brought the wheels to rest outside a low rise apartment building, nestled behind a hedge of pink oleander. The number on the building indicated that Sarah Briscoe lived inside. A small sign associated her name with Apartment 2C on the second floor.

Although the yellow-brick building appeared to have only four apartments, there was a security system of sorts. The only visible way to gain access to any of the four suites was through a small vestibule through a locked door.

Pressing a little button beside an intercom, I stood back and gave Josie room to speak into the mike.

"Who is it?" asked the disembodied voice of Sarah.

"It's Josie Gonzales and Reverend Smith," Josie replied.

"Okay. Come on up." A buzzer sounded, to tell us the door was unlocked. We advanced through the dimly lit lobby to a staircase and up a flight of stairs to the second floor.

After I used a knocker to announce our arrival, the door opened, with the safety chain still attached to the door. A young girl's oval face peered through the crack at the slight Latino and the large Diocesan. After some indecision, to my relief she undid the chain, allowing us to enter. I think the sight of my turned-around collar did the trick.

Sarah obviously had her mother's attractive genes, if not her disposition. Cynthia had warned me about her prickly nature. Fair hair, bright greenish eyes, upturned button nose and an unwelcoming frown on her brow.

"What's this all about?" she asked while we were still looking around for a place to park our perfidious carcasses.

I tried to look like a devout clergyman, a man of God, while thoughts of a Trojan Horse, and Greeks with evil intentions bearing gifts galloped through my mind.

"May we sit down?" I asked innocently. "I am Smith. This is Gonzales." I said, pointing first to myself, then to Josie, trying to inject a bit of humor into the tense atmosphere. "We are here about the Everglades Church of Redemption." Up to this point I had told the truth.

"So she said," Sarah said, pointing at Josie. "Yes, you may sit down. But you did not answer my question."

Before answering, I looked around for a suitable place to light, finally settling on a straight-backed chair at the small dining room table. Josie followed my lead and sat on a similar chair beside me. Sarah sat across from us, on the other side of the table. Her frown was still etched on her high forehead.

It was difficult to differentiate between the dining room and the living room. It was really one room, each area identified by its furniture – Sally Ann Classic. The low ceiling made the room seem cramped. But then it would have seemed so, even with a vaulted ceiling. I tried to visualize how the place would look after she came into her inheritance in February, that if Ms. Briscoe and her Heavenly brethren were not in jail by that time, awaiting trial.

Deciding to cut to the chase without further ado, out of my inner pocket I drew a business card and flashed my State of Florida Private Detective's license.

"These should answer your question, Ms. Briscoe. Or, Sarah, if I may be permitted to use your first name."

Naturally, she looked shocked. "Private Detective! What the hell?" She glanced at my circular collar and added: "Oh excuse me."

I smiled to myself at the power of the clergy.

"No dammit," she said. "Don't excuse me. "What do you mean by coming into my apartment, wearing a disguise? You have no right to be here. So, get the hell out. Both of you! I'm going to call the *real* police." She pulled a small cell phone out of her jeans and apparently started to dial 911.

"Cool it Sarah," I said. "You are in serious trouble. If you call the *real* police, I won't be able to help you stay out of jail."

She hesitated, having dialed 91, without the final '1'. "What do you mean? Let's cut the crap, Mister Smith. Explain yourself or get out," she demanded, pointing at the door.

"You are a participant in a fraudulent scheme, Sarah," I pointed out quietly. "I have been hired to keep you out of prison. I am sorry that I had to use a disguise to get in to talk to you. But it will be in your best interests to listen carefully and answer a few questions honestly."

"What fraudulent scheme? I have done nothing wrong."

"Sorry, but I have reason to believe that you have committed a felony by participating in a scam being operated by the Everglades Church. I need to know the extent of your personal involvement in the so-called Heavenly Abundance scheme, if I am to save you from being arrested, along with the actual conspirators who dreamed up the scam. Josie is my assistant at S&S."

She looked at my business card again. "Short & Smith. You are from Naples," she said accusingly. "That means my mother must have sent you."

"Bingo," I said. "She didn't think you would listen to her advice. So she hired my firm to help shut down the phony get-rich scheme and save your butt from landing in the state prison. Yes, it was your mother's idea, although I personally think a few months in Florida's correction system might improve your attitude."

She put her cell phone down on the table. "There is nothing wrong with the church's Reward program, Mister Smith." she said defensively. "It is just a method of raising money to help poor and destitute people in Third World countries. Out of gratitude, those countries reciprocate by making goods available at very low prices to the trading company with which the church is associated. The profits from the sale of those imported goods are returned, in part, to investors. It's very simple. The church helps the people in the foreign countries and the governments of those poor nations in turn help the church."

She reeled off the spiel like a robot, as though she had recited it many times before.

I was smiling indulgently, while shaking my head. "Uh huh, Sarah, it won't wash. If you believe that plausible story, I'd like to sell you the long bridge over the Caloosahatchee River. It's all a con job, my dear girl. You have been duped. They are operating a Ponzi scheme, paying dividends out of money that keeps rolling in from greedy new investors, or 'donors'. In the classical sense, they are robbing Peter to pay Paul. But eventually Peter will stop producing enough money and the whole deck of cards will collapse. Many so-called investors will lose everything they have contributed – many their life savings."

"Not so," she countered. "I have received more money in Abundance payments than I have ever donated. And the church has taken me into the inner circle. I am now a Disciple, and am paid a healthy commission on every new contribution I or my Flock bring in."

I winced when she confirmed my earlier misgivings. "Your 'Flock' being other salespeople whom you have brought in to the operation. And you get part of their commissions, like an overriding commission, right?"

She nodded, but did not answer.

"That really complicates matters. As a salesperson, or Disciple, if that is the phony name they like to use for hucksters in their pyramid selling scheme, you and the members of your Flock are as guilty of fraud as the bad guys who thought up the scam. To put it bluntly, Sarah, you are up to your pretty little ears in trouble – unwittingly perhaps, but nevertheless you could very well be caught up in the police dragnet when this illegal operation is closed down."

"But, I haven't done anything wrong," she protested, as she got red in the face..

"Did you sign anything, when you were invited into the inner circle?"

"No. Not that I remember. But, what if I did? I was glad to help the church improve the lives of poor people abroad."

I was still shaking my head, amazed at her apparent naiveté. "Well, Sarah, at least your motives *sound* good. Or, perhaps they were at the outset. Donating money to a church, or any worthwhile charity for that matter, is commendable. But when you talk about how the Everglades Church has doubled your money that is as unreal as Santa Claus or perpetual motion. Surely, you, a college graduate, should be able to see that this Heavenly Abundance scheme is simply appealing to people's greed, and in some cases their ignorance, to raise funds in an illegal manner. You are certainly not ignorant, so your motivation comes right back to greed."

Like a small child, caught with her hand in the cookie jar, she stuck out her lower lip and looked as though she were going to start crying. "I am *not* greedy," she declared. "I just wanted to help the church and less fortunate people abroad."

"Then why don't you prove your good intentions by returning all the money you say you have collected from your donations to the church?"

She sniveled and wiped away a tear from her cheek. "Why should I do that? I have worked really hard for that money."

"It would demonstrate your altruism – your selfless desire to help others, that you say motivated you to become involved in this scheme in the first place. Perhaps, that way, you could protect yourself from charges of fraudulent activity, as an insider in this operation when the law moves in to shut it down."

She knew she was backed into a corner. In frustration, she lashed out at me: "Why don't you mind your own fucking business, Mister Smith? You've done nothing but issue threats and warnings since you came in here under false pretenses.

You should be ashamed to wear that collar and use an imper-sonation to make wild accusations against the house of God."

I got up from my seat at the table. "Come on Josie," I said, ignoring Sarah. "I'll report to her mother that she refuses to admit her guilt and deserves to go to jail."

Taking my cue, Josie got up and followed me towards the front door.

"Hold it, please," Sarah said, more contritely. "Are you going to the police?"

"Yes," I replied. "But not right away. I need some proof first. But when I do, without any remedial action on your part, it is very likely you will be arrested for conspiracy to commit fraud. So be it. You need an attitude adjustment, and some time in prison should straighten you out."

I waited, with my hand on the doorknob for her inevi-table reaction. I thought I could imagine alarms going off in her stubborn head – or police sirens.

"Wait a minute, Mister Smith," she said urgently. "Are you saying that, if I pay back the Heavenly Abundance money I have been paid, I cannot be charged?"

"It is not quite that simple, Sarah. You and your fellow salespeople have caused other investors to lose their money. But you would certainly be in a far better position to fight any charges, having shown your remorse. Also, in the final out-come, you would be able to prove that you have not benefited financially. I doubt if any judge or jury would find you guilty in those circumstances."

She took a deep breath. "Oh, all right. If that is the only way I can stay out of jail, I will do as you suggest. Come back, please."

Taking a checkbook out of her purse, she sat down at the table and wrote out a check for Eleven Hundred Dollars payable to the Everglades Church of Redemption. Handing it to me, she said, "There. That is how much I was ahead, includ-ing commissions. Will you deliver it for me and tell them I am no longer a Disciple?"

"Certainly, Sarah. Congratulations! You have made the right decision. Your canceled check will be your receipt. So get it from the bank and keep it in a safe place. Here, write on the back of the check: *'In full payment of any and all profits*

I have received from participation in church financial activities.'

She did as I asked.

"I will present your check to Reverend Marvin Clarke tomorrow, after morning service. He will no doubt be surprised and pissed off at the same time.

In a subdued voice she asked, "When will I know whether I will be charged, Mister Smith?"

"When the police investigation is complete, Sarah. Meanwhile, keep your fingers crossed.

When we were driving back to Naples, Josie asked, "Would you have walked out, like you started to do, if she had not called you back?"

I smiled. "That was obviously a bluff, of course, Josie. She may have sensed it, but was afraid to call me on it. You did well, by the way."

"I didn't say a word, Mister Smith," she reminded me.

"See. You knew when to *not* say a word. Smart girl."

"She laughed. "You clergymen are all the same. Trying to win people over."

12

Fort Myers Sunday, December 18, 2005

Of all the days in the calendar of Pope Gregory, including Blue Monday and TGIF Friday, I have least liked to work on a Sunday. Although some parts of the Christian religion are controversial, I believe the scriptures got it right when the seventh day was declared a day of rest.

But if I was to save prickly Sarah from herself, and at the same time get a first hand look at how the Everglades Church was bilking the public, I had to give up half of my day of rest and point my little Focus in the direction of Fort Myers.

At least I was going to a church service on the Sunday before Christmas, the day of Christ's birth. I figured that should earn me some browniepoints with the big guy upstairs.

For the occasion, I was suitably dressed in a short-sleeved white shirt, serious dark blue suit, matching socks – probably a first for me – and soft black shoes with Velcro closures. Melanie's earlier attempts to persuade me to wear a tie were in vain, the weather forecast being in the humid high eighties.

Finding a vacant spot in the parking lot beside The Everglades Church of Redemption turned out to be a challenge. The lot was jammed. I was glad, for once to be driving a compact vehicle, which I sandwiched in between two GM behemoths. The time on the dashboard clock read 10:45.

The church building turned out to be a stereotype – white stucco walls, steeply sloped roof, topped by the inevitable high steeple pointing at heaven. The front entrance featured a large gothic arch, through which parishioners and investors were streaming, including women with purses to carry away monetary loot, if their husbands' pockets would not suffice. Of course, some were thinking only of worshiping

64

Almighty God. But others, of a more avaricious nature, were attending to worship the almighty dollar.

I found an empty aisle seat in the back row, beside a young family, consisting of two nicely dressed parents and two energetic pre-teen children. My seat was beside the daddy.

"Going to be a warm day," I said, to break the ice.

"Yeah," he responded. "I'd rather be on the golf course, but the wife insists. You know how it is."

"Sure do," I agreed. "With me it's fishing. But I hear they make it worthwhile to come to a church service. Thought I'd check it out."

The mommy must have heard our conversation, over the scuffling sound of her restless children. She leaned forward to add her two cents worth. "It's unbelievable. Last Sunday, instead of a having a collection, they gave out a five dollar bill to each member of the congregation. They called it a Heavenly Abundance from God, made possible by profits earned by the Heavenly Ministries Trading Company, which is associated with the church."

"Wow. That's a lot of seed money," I said, under my breath.

"Beg pardon?" asked the daddy, who probably missed the handout last Sunday, while he was collecting bogies on the golf course. Obviously, he was not going to make the same mistake twice in a row, thanks to pressure from the missus.

"It just occurred to me that you and yours will be twenty bucks ahead, if they repeat the give-away today."

The mommy piped up again, before her husband could reply. "Oh, no. We are not supposed to keep all the Abundance money. There will be a Donations receptacle at the door. See these white envelopes. Well, you write your name and address on the outside of one, and enclose whatever you wish to donate, starting with five dollars. The ministry will open an investment account for you, and it will earn dividends, payable monthly. Very few people keep the five dollars, preferring to invest it to earn more at the end of the month."

"I see," I said. "But from the church's standpoint, what's the point, if they don't get to keep donations from the congregation?"

The daddy shrugged. "Power of suggestion, I guess. Beats me. Seems to work, anyways, considering the payback they offer."

"And what is that?" I asked innocently.

"We have a friend who earned fifty percent more than he donated, after only thirty days," he said.

"Could he withdraw his original donation, plus the dividend?"

"I suppose he *could,* but he would be foolish to do that, wouldn't he?"

"No, he leaves it in his account so it will earn more at that extraordinary rate."

"Extraordinary, all right," I agreed.

Further conversation was interrupted by the church organ bursting forth with loud music. The dramatic sound rose in a crescendo, and then gradually diminished as a figure dressed in a white robe mounted stairs up to a high pulpit. Topping the robe, the figure wore a high, white hat, reminiscent of the headpiece usually worn by the Pope when in full regalia.

The slanting rays of the morning sun streamed through the multi-color stained-glass windows, dappling a colorful pattern on the long, white robe.

"Is that Reverend Marvin Clarke?" I whispered. "Or is it the Pope?"

"I believe it's the Reverend," the daddy whispered back.

"Quite an outfit," I observed.

Raising his arms, like an NFL referee signaling a touchdown, the minister intoned in a deep voice, "Let us pray."

Most of the congregation got on their knees to pray, using the knee-rail, and putting their hands together in traditional prayer mode. I could only watch, mesmerized by the whole professional production and the gullibility of the people who expected to get something for nothing.

"Heavenly father," intoned the sonorous voice of Reverend Clarke, "we humbly thank thee for the abundance you have given to us, enabling us to share more than ever our good fortune with the poor and destitute populations of far-away countries. We ask you to bless this congregation with the riches and worldly wealth of the United States of America, so that this unselfish sharing may continue to help others. Amen."

Many voices responded with "Amen."

The organ began again. A choir of thirty or so singers dressed in white robes, like the minister, took the cue to raise their voices in singing a stirring rendition of 'Onward Christian Soldiers'.

By raising his hands, with palms facing up, the minister indicated that the whole congregation should stand and join in. The sound became overwhelming, a few enthusiastic people even stamping their feet in imitation of marching. At the line *'with the cross of Jesus'* a large rear-screen projection unit lit up behind the choir loft. A series of haunting images, of underfed, weeping children and teary mothers appeared, and segued into a scene of a truck bearing the name 'Heavenly Ministries Trading Company' speeding to their rescue.

The organ music died down, but remained in the background as Reverend Clarke's voice boomed from the microphone on the podium.

"Christmas season is a time for rejoicing in the birth of Jesus, and what better way to celebrate His birth than in singing the traditional songs of the Yuletide season. Therefore, the sermon today will be very brief. We are all familiar with the saying 'It is better to give than to receive'. And yet the Heavenly Ministries, with whom the church is associated, makes it possible to improve on that saying, by changing it to 'It is better to give *and receive.*"

The sound of the organ, which had been lowered while the minister spoke, was raised again in a dramatic crescendo for emphasis, and then down again.

Resuming his theme, the minister said, "Giving *and receiving.* That is what Christmas is all about. Let us remember the story of the Three Wise Men, who traveled from afar to bring to the new-born infant Jesus rare gifts of gold, frankincense and myrrh. And, of course Joseph and the Virgin Mary *received* those gifts, with their son lying in a manger, in the little town of Bethlehem."

Led by the organ, the choir began to sing 'Oh, little town of Bethlehem', accompanied by the congregation. The carols 'Silent Night' and 'Good King Wenceslas' were next. Even a lost soul like me, enjoyed the familiar songs and carols.

When the song-fest ended, the spotlight again high-lighted Reverend Clarke, standing on the raised dais, in his impressive white outfit.

"We are particularly blessed today," he said, "to have with us the man who made it possible for us to help thousands of children and their families in many parts of the world. He is a philanthropist, a man of unselfish and outstanding character, having donated huge sums of his own money to the cause which he founded, and to which the Everglades Church of Redemption has recently subscribed. Please welcome Mister Elliot Jones, Chairman and Founder of the Heavenly Ministries." Reverend Clarke again gave the palms up signal so that the congregation would rise. He started the applause and many others joined in.

Another organ upsurge greeted the humble philanthro-pist, Elliot Jones. He strode across the raised platform and shook hands with the minister, who had stepped down from the pulpit.

In stature, Jones reminded me of stocky Nikita Kruschev, the former Russian intimidator of shoe-pounding fame. He wore a sedate gray suit made of shimmering Italian cloth with a matching gray shirt and brick-colored tie. A white carnation decorated his button-hole. His arrival was marked by a smattering of applause, which swelled louder with encour-agement from ReverendClarke and the accompanying organist.

Proceeding to the pulpit, Jones waved in acknowl-edgement to the crowd. "I too will be brief," Jones promised. "I just wanted you to know what two of our client countries have said about the work of Heavenly Ministries in helping their poor people." He produced a couple of telegrams from the inner pocket of his jacket.

"From a government in Africa, that prefers to remain unidentified. 'The transfer of funds arrived yesterday. Food and clothing, purchased from your generous monetary assis-tance, are already on the way to our needy people. God bless you and your wonderful supporters. Please keep up the good work.'"

He paused for effect, and to wait for the applause to die down. "This message is from a war-torn country in Central Europe. 'A shipment of fine glassware is on its way via the Heavenly Trading Company. It is priced well below market value, in appreciation of your financial aid to our poor and displaced people. These are trying times, and our government appreciates the help extended by you and your donors. A million thanks for your benevolent help.'"

"So you see, my friends," Jones went on, "your donations to the church are relieving poverty and helping homeless and displaced people attempting to rebuild their lives in many Third World countries. I am pleased to donate personally to this worthwhile cause. I wanted to thank each and every one of you for your participation in this heavenly blessed undertaking."

Again, Jones and Clarke shook hands, while the congregation applauded, and the organist played 'Amazing Grace'. The philanthropist departed off stage right.

Resuming his position on the pulpit, Reverend Clarke said, "We will now ask our apostles to share Heavenly Abundance with the congregation, by distributing to each an every person here a token gift of Five Dollars. This gesture of sharing is the direct result of a very successful sale of the shipment of fine glassware by Heavenly Ministries Trading Company, to which Mister Jones referred in his report. You are all welcome to spend, as you see fit, this small example of the church's appreciation for your continued support of our Offshore Heavenly Outreach Program. Many of you have donated additional funds to help in this worthy cause, and have realized substantial dividends on the funds you have invested through your donations. Anyone who wishes to participate, may use the white envelopes in the pew racks in front of you to enclose cash, checks or monthly pledges – you may even return the Five Dollar bill as part of your investment, if you wish. All donations will be acknowledged by a receipt mailed to your home address. The money will be invested in your name and used to help those poor and needy folks abroad who cannot help themselves. God bless you all and best wishes for a very Happy Christmas."

After receiving the Five Bucks and placing it in one of the white envelopes, I tucked the envelope in my jacket inner pocket for evidence. Reverend Clarke and his partner-in-crime Elliot Jones proceeded up the aisle to the front door where there was a large donation box for the white envelopes.

I waited at the back of the line, as members of the congregation filed slowly past the pair and out of the church.

As I approached the two glad-handers, Clarke and Jones, I noticed that they appeared to be no less the caricatures that I had noted from a distance. Reverend Clarke was tall, thin and angular – a replica of Ichabod Crane. Elliot Jones closely resembled the infamous Nikita Kruschev –built like a bull with closely-cropped grizzly gray hair.

I kept a straight face as I was greeted by the two con artists.

"I have a rather large donation I would like to give the church for its Offshore Outreach Program," I said, addressing Ichabod. "But I would prefer to discuss it in the privacy of your office, if you don't mind."

He appeared to be taken aback by my request. But he soon recovered, with dollar signs flashing in his greedy brown eyes.

"Ah, certainly," he replied, glancing at Jones, who nodded his approval. "Your name, sir?"

"Smith," I replied with a smile, and added, "a very common name, much like Jones."

The cynical bit of humor passed without comment, apparently unnoticed.

"Well then, Mister Smith, Clarke said affably, "why don't we go to my office."

He turned to Elliot Jones. "You will excuse us, Elliot? Meanwhile, do have some coffee, which the ladies are serving in the basement lounge."

"Of course, Marvin. You go ahead," Jones replied.

"Then, just follow me, gentlemen," Clarke said, as he ghosted away in his white robe and Pope-like chapeau.

When we arrived at the basement lounge, Elliot Jones dropped off and headed for the coffee being served by elderly ladies, obviously volunteers.

Reverend Clarke's office was at the far end of the larger business office, separated by a sturdy wall from the lounge and loitering members of the congregation who preferred coffee or tea to the urgent need to spend or donate their Five Bucks.

Clarke took out a clutch of keys on a brass ring and selected one to open the locked door to his private office.

Meanwhile, my searching gaze picked out semi-hidden cameras, following our every move, presumably feeding pictures to security personnel elsewhere in the church premises.

I noticed that the large business office of this thriving enterprise was not lacking for high tech equipment. At each of ten low-partitioned work areas was a computer monitor and keyboard, presumably connected by cable to a main-frame server in a glass-partitioned area in one corner of the large room. This would provide a networking facility for recording the incoming and outgoing Heavenly Abundance. Today, however, all work stations were free of workies, perhaps temporarily, while the loot from the white envelopes was being collected.

I followed the Rev into his private office, a far different environment from the utilitarian outer workplace. Thick Persian carpet. Expensive-looking oil-paintings. Padded leather armchairs. I set myself down in one of the latter, while the white-robed minister perched himself on a swivel chair behind a large cherry-wood desk.

"Well, Mister Smith, what do you have in mind?" he asked, in a business-like tone.

I did not reply verbally, but simply slid an envelope containing Sarah Briscoe's check across his desk, so that he could open it.

With obvious eagerness, he pulled out a letter-opener with an ornately carved handle from his drawer and proceeded to open the sealed envelope. He removed the check and looked at the amount of Eleven Hundred Dollars, which did not exactly stagger him, although he grunted with a modicum of satisfaction. Then he looked at the signature and the name and address of Sarah Briscoe.

With raised eyebrows, he asked, "What's this? Sarah Briscoe is donating Eleven Hundred Dollars? I thought you said....?"

"The explanation you want is on the back," I pointed out.

He turned the check over and read the disclaimer I had suggested she write, followed by her signature.

"What's this all about, Mister Smith? Sarah is one of our Disciples, and a very good one."

"Not any more," I said in reply, without elaborating.

"What do you mean by that?" he demanded.

"She has resigned, and wants nothing more to do with your church and its fraudulent financial activities."

He ignored my accusation and said. "Obviously, we can't cash a check with such an endorsement on it."

"That's your choice, Mister Clarke," I replied. "If you do not want the funds, just give me the check and I will see that it is placed in safekeeping."

"Safekeeping for what?"

"To be used in evidence in your forthcoming trial. I am going to see that you and everyone connected with your Ponzi/Pyramid operation are charged with fraud."

His elongated face started to turn red. Without speaking, he got up and went past me to the door.

"Stay right where you are, Mister Smith," he hissed, as he left the room.

Within one minute he was back, followed by Elliot Jones. It was the latter who took over the conversation. He now had the check in his hand.

"What the hell is this? And who are you?" he demanded to know.

Without replying, I handed him my business card and held up my Florida Private Investigator's license, without handing it over.

He glanced at the business card, and handed it to Clarke.

"I understand," Elliot Jones said, "that you have made a threat to Reverend Clarke concerning our money-raising activities for the church. As a private detective, I assume you are familiar with the laws of libel and slander. If you persist in your unfounded allegations, you will charged."

I smiled, not surprised by his temerity in trying to take the offensive.

"Nice try, Mister Jones," I said. "That would be welcome. By all means, call in the Law, to save me the trouble."

He frowned menacingly, and screwed up his face in anger. Not a pretty sight.

"Who are you working for anyway?" he asked.

"That," I said, "is not your concern. But obviously, considering the check in your hand, I am representing Sarah Briscoe in this matter. On my advice, she wants immunity from prosecution, and protection from any further association with your con game."

He paced the room in obvious frustration. I wondered if he would use a Nikita Kruschev ploy and start beating the Rev's desk with his shoe.

Finally, he stopped pacing and held up the check. "If we keep the check and cash it, does that put an end to this matter?"

"For now, Mister Jones," I replied. "But I can make no promises for the future."

In a fit of rage, he tore up the check and threw the pieces in my face. "In that case, Smith, get the hell out of here. This meeting is over. And, if I were you, I'd keep looking over my shoulder."

With his veiled threat ringing in my ears, I took the white church donation envelope from my pocket and tore it up in small pieces, which I tossed in the smoldering face of Elliot Jones. Too bad to waste the five bucks!

I walked out of the room, without looking over my shoulder.

But, in the light of subsequent events, no doubt I would have been well advised to take his advice.

13

Naples, Florida Monday, December 19, 2005

It was quite a shock to wake up in a strange room. But I figured it was far better than not waking up at all. The acrid smell of antiseptic intruded on my benumbed senses. I suspected I must be in a hospital. While my nose was working fine, this was one of those times when it was better not to open my eyes too quickly. First one eye, not all the way. Then the other one, squinting through compressed eyelashes. Now, both together. One, two, three...blinding sunlight! Close them again, and start over.

When I had finally managed to open both eyes fully, without too much pain, I realized there was a matronly nurse beside my bed. She had just opened the blind on the window, allowing sunlight to pour in, partially blinding me. Keep this up and I'll need a seeing-eye dog.

Raising my right arm to ward off the unwanted dazzling rays, I moaned in protest. Without apologizing, the nurse lowered the blind slightly, figuring I suppose, we had reached a compromise. Then I realized that the reason I had raised my right arm was because my left arm was bandaged and about twice its normal size.

That made me wonder, in a moment of panic, about my other appendages. I tried to move my legs. They responded, slowly and painfully. I had trouble moving my toes, but that was not unusual. Motel beds, and even crank-up style hospital beds are seldom long enough to accommodate my tall frame. So, toes take a beating from compressing bed-sheets.

Forget the toes; I began to realize that my whole left side was one big ache. Bruise marks and contusions were evident when I lifted the sheet to look at my nether region. Even my face was bandaged. *What the devil happened to me?*

Eventually, I assumed, I would be sporting all the colors of a rainbow.

Last, but by no means least, I had the mother of all headaches.

The white-gowned, black nurse, wearing a starched black and whitecloth appurtenance on her head, approached my bedside. I pointed to my bandaged arm, questioningly, as I didn't feel much like talking.

She simply nodded. "Sprained muscles and tendons. Not broken." Then I pointed to where my wristwatch was supposed to be. "Time?" I asked.

She consulted her own watch. "Eleven-thirty."

"What day?"

"Monday." She was a virtual encyclopedia of information.

"Naples Community Hospital?" I asked.

"Yep."

There was a knock on the door. A uniformed State Trooper stuck his head in the doorway. "Okay to come in?" he asked.

The nurse answered, "Might as well. He's awake now. Sort of."

The trooper walked over to me and offered his hand. I took it listlessly, and without enthusiasm.

"I'm Joe Pilaski, Highway Patrol," he said. Tall guy, about thirty. Small moustache. Reflective sun glasses hanging from his shirt pocket. Ballpoint pen clenched in his teeth, like a matador with a rose. Broad-brimmed hat in one hand, small black book in the other. He dropped his hat on the side-table and withdrew the pen from his teeth.

"Coupla questions," he announced, looking at the nurse for permission.

She nodded and departed the scene.

"I have some questions, too," I groaned.

"Me first," he replied. "I arrived on the scene of your accident about twenty minutes after it happened. A passing motorist called it in on a cell phone. How much do you remember, Mister Smith?"

"It's starting to come back," I said. "The sons-of-bitches!"

He paused over his black book. "What is that supposed to mean?"

I answered his question with one of my own. "Was a black Lincoln Navigator there when you arrived?"

He looked puzzled. "Not that I remember. A few cars had pulled up to the side of the road. Wondering if anyone had survived the crash, I suppose. But I don't remember a big sports-ute."

"Probably gone by then," I said. "And, it was *not* an accident."

"How do you mean?" Looking puzzled.

"The fucking Lincoln ran me off the road," I said. The driver wanted to kill me. I was investigating a suspicious bunko scheme in which he was involved."

"You are a private investigator, right?"

"That's right, officer, and an ex-cop with Naples police," I said.

"Well, Mister Smith, that's quite an accusation. Do you know who this person is, and do you plan to lay charges?"

"Not without evidence," I replied. "You could help by checking on the body and paint shops in the Fort Myers area, to look for a black Lincoln Navigator with a scratched right front fender. There may be paint off my car, where we made contact."

He looked skeptical, wondering perhaps, if I was dreaming all this up, to excuse the fact that my Ford Focus ended up in a farmer's field on a bright sunny Sunday afternoon.

"I'll turn that part of the investigation over to the Fort Myers Police and the Lee County guys. They know the local repair shops better than the State Highway Patrol."

"And, that's it?" I asked.

"Not quite, sir. I'd like the name or names of the suspects – the bad guy or guys whom you said caused the accident."

"Never mind," I said wearily. "I'll see that the bastards are brought to justice."

"Well, if it was a hit-and-run, charges should be laid against the perps," he pointed out.

"Yeah, I know. I'll think on it and get back to you. My mind is fuzzy right now." I responded, trying to end the interview.

"Uh huh. Be sure to call Highway Patrol if you remember the name or names of the suspects." He snapped his black book shut and picked up his boy scout hat. "You know, concealing a criminal act is a felony itself."

"Yeah, yeah," I said impatiently. "I know, I know. Leave it with me." I waved him away like I was brushing off a fly, and tried to turn over, to block him and the sunlight out of my vision.

He took the hint and left. The nurse returned. Spotting the name tag on her white gown, I asked, "Enid, where are my belongings?"

She pointed to the drawer in the night table beside my bed. "In that drawer. And, there is an itemized list that the E.R. people made up when you came in on a stretcher. There were some strange wires on your body that they wondered about."

I read the list: "Was there not a small tape recorder anywhere around the scene on or off the highway?"

She shrugged. "Not to my knowledge. No mention of such a thing." She looked at me rather strangely.

"The list of things in my wallett, does not include my driver's license. That appears to be missing," I pointed out.

"If it's not there, it's missing," she answered logically.

Damn! The license had my home address on it.

"Enid, I need a phone real bad. My daughter is home alone. I expected to be back in Naples Sunday afternoon."

Just then there was a light knock on the door. Joanne peeked in timidly. Not waiting Enid's permission, I waved her in with my good right arm. She carried an armful of cut flowers wrapped in plastic. Joanne had a look of great concern screwing up her lovely face.

"May I come in for a couple of minutes nurse?" she asked politely.

Enid nodded, and stage-whispered softly, in my presence, "He may have had a concussion. He's not making much sense." Then she bustled out of the room.

Joanne smiled and kissed me on the forehead. "I see you've already made a big impression on the nurse, Maury."

"We have had a wonderful conversation, Hon. And I am so making sense. Has Dan Short been around?"

"He was here earlier," she said, "but you were asleep. Said he would be back later."

"Joanne, I am worried about Melanie. She was home alone when I left for Fort Myers yesterday. Would you mind phoning my number, to see if she is all right?"

"Certainly, Maury. I tried earlier, but there was no answer. I thought she might be on her way here, or out walking the dog."

She pulled a little cell phone out of her pocket and punched in my home number.

With a frown, she said, "No answer, Hon. I'll go right over and check it out. Don't worry. She is a competent young gal and can look after herself."

At that point, Enid opened the door for Dan Short. She warned both visitors about the fragile state of my health, and backed out, closing the door.

"How are you doing old buddy?" Dan asked. "Sorry to hear about your accident."

"It was no accident, Dan. But we can talk about that later. I am really worried about my daughter, Melanie. Would you go right over to the apartment and see if she is all right?"

"Sure, Maury. What makes you think she may not be okay?"

"The Ponzi boys are starting to play rough," I said. "Forced me off the road.

"How would they know where you live?"

"They took my driver's license out of my wallet, while I was unconscious. I guess they went to see what kind of leverage they could get on me so I would not try to put a stop to their con game. Melanie may have answered the door, without knowing what was going on."

"Jesus, Maury, you don't think she has been kidnapped, do you?"

"I don't know what to think. But why not? They tried to murder me on the Interstate. I threatened to blow the whistle on their phony operation."

"Shit! Oh, excuse me, Joanne." Dan said. "I'm out of here. Stay cool, partner. I'll phone you from the condo."

"Here's the key, Dan," I said, reaching into the night table. "Please hurry."

When Dan left, Joanne sat down beside my bed. "What's going on Maury? I used to worry when you were on the police force. Now, it sounds like you are in over your head as a private detective. You seem to attract trouble."

"Sorry you had to overhear that conversation, Joanne. But the truth is I called out a couple of bad guys, underestimating their reaction so soon. It seems they will stop at nothing to prevent their cozy little con game from being drawn to the attention of the police. Their collection scheme all seems so plausible because they are using the church as a legitimate cover. And that makes it difficult to obtain proof that the operation is fraudulent. I had some damning evidence on a hidden tape. But they removed the recording while I was counting sheep in a field off I-75."

Joanne put her hand on my forehead. "Have you had anything to eat or drink, Maury?" Just her touch had therapeutic properties to sooth the savage beast – my raging headache..

"Actually, I just woke up a few minutes ago. Would you please ring the nurse. I need a couple of aspirin to go with that glass of water on the sidetable."

The wait for Dan to call seemed interminable. In fact, it was only about twenty minutes, before Enid brought a phone and plugged it in.

"Maury, I am calling from the apartment. You had reason to worry. The dog is here, all alone. Your daughter is missing."

I looked at Joanne. She could tell it was bad news.

Dan continued, "I talked to the folks in the apartment below yours. They said the dog has been barking most of the night, driving the neighbors crazy. They heard noises upstairs in the wee hours, and got to the door, just as a vehicle was driving away. That's when the barking started. They agreed that they should have called the police. But they thought it was your car that they heard, and they didn't want to stick their noses into your business."

I tried to stay calm, but it was not easy. "Dan, look around. See if you can find a note, or any message. I will be there in a few minutes. Don't go away."

"You're in no condition to leave the hospital," Dan protested.

"Forget it. I'm on my way." I hung up before he could say anything further.

Joanne overheard, and said, "Are you nuts, Maury? You can't leave here in your condition."

"The hell I can't, Joanne," I said, getting out of bed.

I staggered and swayed a bit when my legs hit the floor. But I managed to get to the clothes closet unaided and started to dress in my street clothes, which were soiled but wearable.

"Well, if you are going to be pig-headed, I might as well help," Joanne said, helping me on with my shoes.

In about three minutes, with reluctant assistance from Joanne, I was dressed and gaining strength from surging adrenaline.

"Will you drive me over to my condo?" I asked.

She gave me a look of exasperation. "Sure. If you are intent on acting crazy, I can't stop you, Maury."

We headed out the door, with me limping along on Joanne's supporting arm. As we passed the nursing station, Enid jumped up and held her hand up like a traffic cop. "Mister Smith, what are you doing? You can't leave the hospital."

"Yes I can, Enid. Thanks for your concern, but I have an emergency at home – a matter of life and death."

"Well, it might be your death, if you are not careful." she said.

"Tell Accounting to send the bill to Naples Police Department. I still have medical coverage for six months.

"But…"

Limping towards the elevators, I said over my shoulder, "Sorry, no time to argue."

We got on the elevator, with Enid standing, hands on hips, shaking her head.

As I eased myself into the passenger seat of Joanne's Lincoln, she smiled indulgently at me like I was a disobedient child. "You are impossible, Maury. But I'm as concerned as you about Melanie. I hope you can find her."

With my urging, we ran a red light or two in getting to *The Pallisades* development in record time. Dan met us at the front steps and helped me up the short flight of stairs leading to the apartment. Pooch greeted us, with his tail wagging, when we opened the front door. Then he started whining softly. Who says dogs can't communicate?

I collapsed on the sofa. "Find anything, Dan?" I asked.

"This was in the mail box, Maury." He handed me a piece of torn kraft paper, holding it by the edge. I did the same, thinking of latent prints. The message, in heavy black marker, read:

KEEP YOUR MOUTH SHUT! IF YOU BRING IN THE POLICE, YOUR DAUGHTER WILL DIE.

On the flip side was part of a Publix Supermarket logo. To add insult to injury, they had used a kraft bag from my own kitchen. The remaining piece of the bag was sitting on the counter in the kitchen, where Joanne was busily trying to calm her nerves by brewing some tea.

The black marker, I discovered was from the kitchen drawer.

She read the note over my shoulder. "My God, Maury! Poor Melanie! What are you going to do?"

I have always prided myself on being able to keep cool under stress. But in this case, with my innocent daughter being used as a pawn in the game being played by these predatory bastards, my coolness was tinged with a strong dose of anger and resolve.

"First, I am going to feed Pooch, so he will stop whining, although his distress may be partly due to the way his mistress was roughly handled. Then I am going to confront the Ponzi boys and make them wish they had never been borne. Kidnapping is a federal offense, if the victim is of 'tender years'. That is open to interpretation. So, we don't *have to* call in the FBI. It is not that difficult to know who is behind this. What do you think, Dan?".

Dan said, "I'm with you all the way, Partner. I think the Feebies should be notified, because we might need their help. But that does not mean we should just sit on our hands and hope for the best. We are experienced detectives and quite capable of taking some action ourselves in the meantime. But first, bring me up to speed on who we should go after."

"Let me update you quickly, Dan," I said, while I fed Pooch and filled his water dish. He ate and gulped water like there was no tomorrow. "First, I went to the Sunday service of the Everglades Church in Fort Myers, with the express purpose of getting Sarah Briscoe out of the mess she had gotten herself in. Secondly, I wanted to get some evidence to prove that the so-called Heavenly Abundance scheme was nothing but a fraudulent operation to bilk a lot of innocent but greedy people out of their money, in some cases their life savings."

"You wired yourself and recorded some conversation with the con artists?"

"Right. Reverend Marvin Clarke and his henchman, Elliot Jones. But the small tape recorder was removed while I was unconscious, after being run off the road on I-75. If you are coming with me, Dan, I'll fill you in, while we are driving to Fort Myers."

Joanne intervened. "Surely you don't intend to go to Fort Myers in your condition, Maury. Let Dan go to see Reverend Clarke and this man Jones. You look like the last rose of summer…"

"With a bug on it," I said, completing the saying. "But save your breath, Hon, because I am determined to find my daughter, with Dan's help. The two of us will go and Dan can do the driving. There's no way I could stay here twiddling my thumbs, with Melanie's life in danger."

"Oh, all right, Maury," she said, realizing that further argument was not going to get my daughter back. "But please take it easy. I will look after the dog until you return."

"Thanks, Joanne. You are a doll," I said, giving her a quick hug. "Why don't you stay here and we'll keep you posted by cell phone. Come on then, Dan. Let's go to the office first, and send faxes to the Bureau and local police, so that we can't be accused of keeping a kidnapping under wraps. By the time they get their wheels in motion, we will be well on our way to Fort Myers."

14

Dan and I reached our office during the noon hour. Josie was seated at her desk, having a sandwich for lunch. She had proven to be very conscientious about staying in the office during the day, if both of the principals of Short & Smith were out.

We decided to draft the fax message and have Josie hold it for about thirty minutes, before dispatching it to the Naples Police, the Fort Myers Police, the State Police and the FBI. We both thought the local and State Police would defer to the Feds, but would offer their help if requested.

Josie looked alarmed when I walked in, bandages and all on full display. I told her not to worry, that I looked worse than I felt. She nodded, but obviously was not convinced. Anyway, she said Mrs. Golding had phoned twice. I explained that I did not have time to call her back, and that I would call as soon as I returned.

Dan and I sat down and worked on the wording of the fax message. The final version, printed on Short & Smith letterhead, was as follows:

FAX MESSAGE

Date: Monday, December 19, 2005

TO: Federal Bureau of Investigation, Washington, D.C.

COPIES TO: Naples Police Department

      Fort Myers Police department

      Florida State Police

SUBJECT: Missing Person

MISSING, BELIEVED ABDUCTED

MELANIE SMITH

SEX: FEMALE

AGE: 20

RACE: White, Caucasian (U.S. Born)

HEIGHT: 5 ft. 7 inches

EYES: Blue

PROBABLE DRESS: Tan Tee-shirt, blue jeans, white sneakers

HOME ADDRESS: 2101 Pallisades Blvd. Apt. 202, Naples, FL

NOTE: Subject is daughter of Maury Smith of this office.

TIME OF ABDUCTION: Between the hours of 12.01 A.M.
and 6. A.M. today, from her home
address.

NOTE FROM KIDNAPPERS READS:.

*KEEP YOUR MOUTH SHUT! IF YOU BRING IN POLICE,
YOUR DAUGHTER WILL DIE*

Pending instructions from FBI, or local police, principals of
Short & Smith are pursuing leads.

Signed, Short & Smith,

Private Detective Agency

Following my suggestion, Dan Short opened the office
safe and took out two 9 m.m. Barretta revolvers, two sets of
handcuffs, cash to cover expenses. Then we took off speedily,
in Dan's Pontiac Bonneville, up Davis Blvd to Hwy. 951 and
from there to Interstate 75.

The usual thirty-minute drive to Fort Myers was covered in twenty minutes, with Dan's lead foot allowing the
powerful motor no mercy. He pulled the big vehicle into the
parking lot of The Everglades Church of Redemption, off
College Parkway at 1:45.

Consciously trying to avoid limping, I led the way through the main floor of the church to the basement. Seated in front of the closed door to the general office, was a heavy-set man, with Neanderthal features, including pug-nose, sloping forehead and brush cut hair, obviously a security guard.

He rose to meet us.

"We are here to see Reverend Clarke," I said matter-of-factly.

"Do you have an appointment with Reverend Clarke," he asked.

"Yes and no," I replied. "Yes, we will see him, And no, we don't need an appointment."

Placing his right hand on the handle of the sidearm in a holster on his hip, he said, "If you have no appointment, you cannot enter the office, so I suggest you both get lost."

Pug-nose turned out to be a slow draw.

Dan stepped around me and pointed his Beretta at the man's head.

"Open the door, or lose your head," Dan said quietly.

The man's eyes widened and almost crossed as he looked down the barrel of Dan's little revolver. He decided he wanted to keep his head, even with the sloping forehead. Slowly and carefully, he reached for the ring of keys attached to his belt and turned to open the door.

After warning the guard that he would be shot if he made any false move, Dan put the weapon back in his pocket and followed the man into the general office, with me limping along behind.

All work cubicles in the general office were fully occupied by women at computer terminals or counting donations. Cash was visible everywhere and discarded white envelopes filled waste baskets. As we passed down the side aisle, we were hardly noticed, as everyone was preoccupied with their assigned duties.

When we reached the door to the minister's office, Dan spoke to the guard. "Open the door, and no fancy stuff, or say your prayers – your last prayers."

Pug-nose obeyed, and we all entered. Reverend Clarke looked up from behind his huge, cherry-wood desk. He was wearing a white shirt, with sleeves rolled up. His black slacks were supported by wide, blue-striped braces – a far different dress mode than his white robe and Pope-like hat of yesterday.

I figured he must be short-sighted, because he squinted at us and said to the guard. "I asked not to be disturbed, Bernie. What is the meaning of this intrusion?" Then his gaze wandered over to Dan and finally to me. "Oh, Mister Smith, what are you doing back here?"

"Surprised to see me alive?" I asked him.

"What is that supposed to mean?" he responded.

"Someone driving a black Lincoln Navigator tried to commit vehicular homicide yesterday on I-75. I was the intended victim." I said accusingly. "You and your partner-in-crime, Elliot Jones, are prime suspects. This is my business partner, Dan Short. You might wish to talk to us privately."

He caught the hint and said to the guard, "Er, Bernie you may leave us."

"Will you be all right, sir?" Bernie asked.

"I doubt if these gentlemen intend to harm me. Just a friendly discussion, I believe," he said, looking at Dan and me hopefully.

"That's right, Bernie," I said. "We have no intention of harming Reverend Clarke, unless you call in reinforcements. In which case, all bets are off, and we will have to review our options. So, run along like a good guard and keep the riff-raff out."

"Do as Mister Smith says, Bernie," Clarke said. "Just don't call for help."

Bernie looked uncertain, but opened the door and stepped outside.

Dan followed him to the door and pushed a button on the latch, locking it.

Although uninvited, I sat in an armchair opposite Reverend Clarke. Dan stood beside me. It felt good to rest my battered bones.

"Mister Clarke," I began, "I will come right to the point. Last night, my daughter was abducted from our apartment, while I was in the hospital in Naples. A note was left, warning me that my daughter would die if I contacted the police. I do not intend to be intimidated by a couple of crooks trying to murder me and then snatching my daughter. *I want her returned unharmed and without delay.* We have already notified law enforcement authorities, including the FBI, of the abduction. So, it is not just a question of whether you and Elliot Jones will be prosecuted for fraud, but also with the additional charges of attempted vehicular homicide and kidnapping. As you know, kidnapping is a federal offense, punishable by execution. At the very least, you will get life in prison."

"My God," said the minister, "I did not have any part in any of this. I do not know what Elliot Jones has been up to, but I certainly don't condone the illegal actions of which you are accusing us. If Mister Jones did what you are saying, he did it without consulting me. I am a man of God, and would not, under any circumstances, aid and abet such criminal behavior."

"That may be true, Mister Clarke," I said. "You may plead your innocence to the FBI and later to a judge and jury. But, if you wish to receive any special consideration, you had better co-operate with us in getting my daughter returned unharmed."

He shrugged and threw up his hands. "What can I do? Our church has just recently subscribed to the Heavenly Ministries program, because we were desperate for funds. Our mortgage was overdue, and our congregation was dwindling until we joined up with Elliot Jones to raise money and pay off our debts. It seemed to be the only way to keep the church solvent financially."

"Be that as it may," I said impatiently, "Right now I want your help in getting my daughter back. You can start out to make amends by telling us where we may find Elliot Jones."

"I believe his home is somewhere in South Georgia," Clarke said evasively. "The Heavenly Ministries Trading Company operates out of Augusta, Georgia. I will give you his address."

"Are you saying he is no longer in Florida?"

"Frankly, I don't know. He did not tell me where he was going when he left here in a hurry, after the service yesterday.

"You mean after the confrontation in your office. Right?"

"Er, right. He left shortly after you did.".

"To follow me along I-75 and try to kill me by running me off the road."

"As I said, I know nothing of that. I am sorry to hear of it, if true."

I was getting exasperated, fencing with the evasive minister. "What do you mean, 'if true'? Are you doubting my word? Do you want me to call in the State Highway Patrol officer and have him read his report? Let's cut the bullshit, Clarke. Where does Elliot Jones hang out when he visits Fort Myers?"

Reverend Clarke paused. "Oh, he has a yacht which he lives on," he finally mumbled the words under his breath, as though it was completely irrelevant.

"A yacht? Why the hell didn't you say so in the first place, dammit. Where does he park the freaking yacht?"

"Well, officially, he keeps it in Tampa, or Tampa Bay, I guess."

"Look Rev, I don't give a flying fuck about 'officially. Where does he dock it in the Fort Myers area?"

He winced when I started using barrack language, but I couldn't care less. Getting information out of him was like pulling molars.

"Um, I think at a marina on the river."

"The Caloosahatchee River?"

"Yes. He docks it on the river," he finally admitted.

"Now you are going to tell me you don't know what marina, or exactly where on the river. Right?" I wondered how many years in prison I would get for throttling a clergyman.

"Sorry, but I don't know," Clarke said. "He just phones me and we discuss things over the phone. Or, he comes here unannounced. According to Elliot, our church is just one of several participating in the Heavenly Ministries program. So he has to move around a lot. As you know, most important Florida cities are situated on the Gulf or the Atlantic Ocean. He finds it convenient to travel by yacht."

"How nice for him," I said ironically. "If you don't know the name or location of the marina he uses, what is the phone number you call when you want to speak to him?"

"He does not answer the phone when I call. I am told to leave a message at the marina, and he will call back, presumably from a pay phone."

"So your conversations cannot be traced, I suppose?"

"Hmm, I hadn't thought of that. Perhaps you are right!"

"Glad I could give you an epiphany. Or is it a revelation?" I asked.

He did not react visibly to my feeble effort at sarcasm.

"You want the phone number?" he asked.

"If you don't mind. Or, even if you do."

He took a slip of paper out of a desk drawer, consulted a phone index and wrote down the number. He handed it over with a flourish.

"Okay. I hope you have been telling the truth, Mister Clarke," I said. "Because, if not, we will be right back. And, in a very bad mood."

He did not respond. Dan and I went to the door. Like Columbo, I paused and turned around with an afterthought. "By the way, I suggest you *do not* phone Elliot Jones in the next hour. If you do, it will prove to us that you are as guilty as he is of attempted murder and kidnapping."

15

Once we had left the church, with the distraught minister stewing in his own juice, I called our office number on my cell phone. Josie answered and reported that Special Agent Peter Fox of the FBI had left a number for me to call. I decided it was time to level with the Feebies. I called the number in Fort Myers.

A girl's voice: "Federal Bureau of Investigation."

"Special Agent Fox please."

The internal phone rang. "Fox here."

"Agent Fox, this is Maury Smith. I understand you received our Fax okay."

"Yes, we did. Sorry to hear about the abduction of your daughter. We are in a position to take over the investigation right away. But we need more facts. Where can we meet?"

"Sorry, er, Peter," I said. "Can't meet right away. My partner and I are following up a lead. Let me fill you in briefly. I believe my daughter is being held to prevent me from revealing a fraudulent scheme being operated by the Everglades Church of Redemption, here in Fort Myers. It is a combination Ponz/Pyramid operation being run by a swindler by the name of Elliot Jones from Georgia. My partner and I have just left the minister, Reverend Clarke. He is involved, too. But Jones is calling the shots. The loot from the fraudulent scheme was being counted in the basement of the church when we were there. I suggest you raid the place before everything is hidden."

"Wait a minute, Mister Smith."

"Call me Maury."

"Smith, Maury, whatever," Fox said, sounding very unhappy. "I can't proceed on your say so. I would need a search warrant. Furthermore, if there has been a kidnapping, it certainly takes priority. *Where can we meet?"*

"Peter, I agree with you about the abduction taking precedence. That's why we are following up a lead in an effort to find this guy Elliot Jones."

Fox interrupted, "It seems you and your partner are trying to take over this investigation. You PI's have no jurisdiction. Hell, you are not even law enforcement officers."

"Look Peter, I have no time to argue. Jones docks his yacht at a marina on the Caloosahatchee River. We are trying to trace its location from a phone number. The number is 743-6457. Write that down 743-6457. We'll meet there. But hurry!"

Before he could say anything more, I hung up.

I said to Dan, "Let's trace the marina.

"How?"

I told him by dialing 911.

Another female voice: "911, is this an emergency?"

"It certainly is. A matter of life or death. Operator this is an urgent FBI matter. I need the name and location of a marina on the Caloosahatchee River. The number is 743-6457. Hurry please."

She came back on within a minute. "Marinaville. North shore of the river. Just over the bridge on US 41. You could have looked in the Yellow Pages."

"No Yellow Pages on my cell phone. But thanks, Miss."

I told Dan to take Cleveland Avenue (US 41) across the bridge and turn right at the first intersection. We ran a couple of amber lights, beat a red by the skin of our back bumper, and approached Marinaville in record time. No sign of the FBI yet.

Marinaville was situated in a basin off the river, probably man-made by lots of earth-moving equipment. It was full of boats and yachts of all shapes and sizes. The biggest was a motor-sailer, anchored offshore. I fetched the binoculars from our big canvass bag. Luckily, the stern of the big yacht swung towards shore and I was able to read the name – *Halcyon III, Tampa Florida.*

The large, ketch-rigged craft seemed to be our best bet. But first we had to verify its ownership. From the promontory above the marina, where Dan had pulled up the car, we descended, and stopped in a spray of gravel, to the single building bearing a sign 'Office'.

Since my identity was known to Elliot Jones who might have been alerted by Rev Clarke despite his promise, we decided Dan should do the honors, in scouting out the motor-sailer. Dan got out of the car and strolled casually into the marina office at the entrance to a long dock. I watched from the car, as a flock of ravenous gulls circled around in search of sustenance.

Fluffy white cumulus clouds drifted overhead, creating shafts of light and dark on the river. But the sun was low in the sky, reminding me how short were the daylight hours at this time of the year. The orange globe would drop below the horizon by 4:45 and darkness would settle in soon after that.

According to my watch it was nearly 4:00 already.

Dan returned from the marina office, whistling and carrying two cans of Classic Coke. He handed me one and leaned on the car's window sill.

"That's our quarry, Elliot Jones, all right," he said quietly. "I made instant friends with Chuck, the dock-master by slipping him a twenty. He confirmed that a call had come in from Rev Clarke asking Elliot Jones to call him. It seems that Jones has a phone answering machine on board, on which Chuck left the message."

"So much for promises," I said. "We should have shot the son-of-a-bitch in the knee when we had the chance."

"I don't relish the thought of approaching the motor-sailer in broad daylight," Dan said. "But as soon as it gets dark, we might be able to board her. I spoke to Chuck about renting a small row-boat. He said that would be no problem."

"Let's keep watching the *Halcyon III*," I said. "Motor-sailers are a hybrid between a deep-keeled sailboat and a power craft. No doubt she has twin diesels and can move along faster than any pure sailing boat."

I raised the binoculars again and my stomach clenched. "I see activity on the bow. I think they are preparing to lift anchor and take off.".

"That means we can't wait any longer for the Feebies," Dan said. "And we are going to need something faster than a rowboat to catch the son-of-a-bitch."

I eased myself out of the car and followed Dan back into the marina office, with me limping and favoring my bruised left leg. The proprietor, Chuck was behind the counter. He appeared to be in his early sixties, with sun-weathered skin and a short, gray beard.

Chuck said, "You boys seem to be in a mite of a hurry."

Breathlessly, I replied, "Damn right. We need a fast boat. What have you got that'll keep up with that motor-sailer that's just leaving the harbor."

Chuck smiled, showing smoke-stained teeth. "Well now, let's see. I can let you have a Donzi with twin 250 Merc-Cruiser outdrives, sitting there in the slip. Some gas in her. She'll do seventy knots, wide open. That fast enough for you?"

"Hell yes. How much?"

"We'll settle up when you get back. Leave your credit card. How long will you need her?" Chuck asked.

"About two or three hours, I guess. Just long enough to have a showdown with Mister Elliot Jones. I think he has my daughter aboard, against her will."

He raised his gray eyebrows. "You think she's been snatched?"

"Yes, dammit. The FBI have been notified, and we have been waiting for them to show up. Can't wait much longer."

While Chuck and I were talking, Dan relieved me of the binoculars and stepped outside. He came back in and said urgently, "The motor-sailer is underway. There's no time to lose!"

"Okay, boys," Chuck said, grabbing some life-jackets, "follow me. Who's going to be handling the high-powered beast?"

Dan and I looked at each other. Simultaneously, we both said, "I am."

Chuck looked at my bruises and swollen and bandaged arm. "Might be better to let your pal do the driving. He appears to be in better shape."

"Yeah, all right," I agreed reluctantly. I handed Chuck my VISA card and climbed on board. First thing I did was reach over and press the button on the dash marked 'Blower' to force gas fumes out of the bilge.

"Glad to see you know what you're doin'. Don't want an explosion," Chuck said.

After two long minutes, Dan fired up the twin engines. Should have been four, but we were in a hurry. Chuck released the docking lines and spring lines and we started to back out of the slip.

"Hold it. FBI," a voice yelled from behind Chuck. A figure in a blue jacket ran past the elderly proprietor and down the dock. "Are you Short and Smith?"

"That's right," I yelled back over the idling motors. "Hop on board."

He jumped over the gunwale and landed on the seat beside me. "What the fuck are you two Private Eye clowns doing?" he demanded to know. "Why didn't you wait for me?"

"Cool it Mister FBI," I replied sarcastically. "We are not clowns, but we *are in a hurry.* The bastard who abducted my daughter is in a yacht that left the harbor a couple of minutes ago. We waited as long as we could without losing him."

I stuck my hand out. "I'm Maury Smith. The guy at the controls is my partner Dan Short."

We shook hands. "Sorry, I'm Peter Fox," he said. "I've had better days. Why did you hang up on me?"

Special Agent Peter Fox, was a handsome dude, dark-haired, clean-shaven, in his thirties, with steely gray eyes. His blue jacket had FBI in big block letters on the back. Tan Dockers, white Nike sneakers and a Florida State baseball cap completed his ensemble. I wondered if he dressed for the occasion.

"I hung up because there was no time for a long conversation, with my daughter missing and the need to follow a lead quickly," I replied. "If Elliot Jones gets away, it may be days before he is located again."

"Are you convinced she is on his yacht?"

"It's the most likely place he would be holding her," I said. "The only way to find out for sure is to board the yacht."

Dan had been exceeding the No Wake speed limit in the harbor. Once outside, in the river, he goosed the twin Mercs up to a loud roar, pushing us all back in the bench seat, three-abreast. The needle-nosed Donzi literally jumped out of the water, leaving a rooster-tail six feet high. Within five minutes, we were trailing the *Halcyon III* by about one hundred yards, or meters for those metric inclined. Dan eased the throttles and slowed down to match the speed of the big yacht. The motor-sailer was towing a small dinghy, used for getting ashore when the yacht was anchored in the harbor.

"What is your plan?" Fox asked over the sound of the throbbing engines. "We can't go onboard uninvited, without a search warrant. It would be illegal trespassing."

"I don't give a damn about legalities," I replied. "One way or another, I am going to board that fucking yacht and search for my daughter. If you don't want to participate, I suggest you look the other way."

Fox waved his hand impatiently. "I don't always go by the book." He leaned past me and shouted at Dan. "Pull up beside the yacht and I'll try to get us on board."

Dan did as requested, pushing the speed up until the Donzi was alongside the *Halcyon III.*

"Is there a loud hailer on this boat?" the FBI agent asked.

I looked around, but could not see a megaphone or anything resembling one. There was a marine radio and a CB set. The Citizen's Band had an amplifier that could act as a loud hailer. I turned the set on and spoke into the microphone. "Testing, One, two, three, testing." Then I turned the amplifier up a couple of notches and handed the mike to Agent Fox.

He grinned and pulled a .38 Smith & Wesson out of the holster he was wearing under his left arm. Holding the mike in his left hand and the gun in his right, he hailed the yacht, while we bounced around in its disturbed bow waves.

"Halcyon III, this is the FBI. Come to a full stop. If you continue, you will be fired upon."

We all waited for the result. There was none. The young helmsman on the yacht just ignored us and carried on. The twin diesels did not skip a beat.

Peter Fox repeated the warning, but nothing changed. The helmsman did not even look our way.

Dan allowed the Donzi to fall back in the wake of the motor-sailer, beside the towed dinghy.

"Decision time," I said. "Now what, Peter? It looks like she is headed for the Sanibel Island causeway bridge and it will soon be dark."

"That, of course, was a bluff. I will give the Coast Guard a call to see if they can help."

By this time we were opposite Pine Island and following the big yacht as she turned onto a Southerly heading towards the lift bridge. The sun was setting, a golden globe sinking below the tree-line of Sanibel. I looked up the call sign for the Florida State Marine Patrol on the chart attached to the steering post.

Peter made the call on the marine radio. We could all hear the response. They were unable to help the FBI at the moment, as there had been a boating collision off shore just North of Naples. They were rescuing survivors.

Next he called the Coast Guard. They said the only available vessel was chasing some suspected drug smugglers in the islands South of the Isle of Capri.

I was feeling frustrated. With no help in sight, I was desperate. It was getting dark, and we were nearing the lift bridge, which opens for boat traffic every half-hour. Looking at my watch, I feared *Halcyon III* would be able to get past the Sanibel causeway and would then head for the open waters of the Gulf of Mexico. No doubt her diesel tanks were kept full, so she would have tremendous range and could just keep ignoring idle threats and outdistance the Donzi, losing us in the darkness.

Trailing the yacht, we cleared the bridge. It was at that point I made my decision. "This is a futile chase," I announced. "So, I am going to get aboard that dinghy. Dan, pull up alongside, please, so I can jump."

16

Peter Fox looked at me like I was out of my mind, which was not too far from the truth. Frustration will screw up sanity every time.

"Don't be foolish," he said. And Dan threw in his two cents worth, too. But when I threatened to jump overboard and try to swim for the dinghy, he relented, figuring a jump for the dinghy would be the lesser of the two stupid alternatives.

At that point, one of the motors in the rear of the Donzi coughed a few times and quit. On one motor, he pulled up beside the dinghy. I grabbed a life preserver and jumped, landing on my sore arm in the sole of the little 14 foot boat. There were no gunshots or threats of retribution from the yacht, so I guessed the bad guys didn't think anyone would be crazy enough to attempt such a maneuver.

The Donzi veered off and headed in the direction of Sanibel, no doubt in search of a marina, where they could get a refill of fuel. Before many minutes *Halcyon III* was rounding the South point of Sanibel, where an old lighthouse was built to ward off unwary shipping.

Now we were out into the open waters of the Gulf. *God only knows where we are headed.* I stayed curled up in the bottom of the dinghy, with my head resting on the padded life preserver. The sea breeze was cool, and I wished I had borrowed the FBI jacket Peter Fox was wearing. In the event of a confrontation, that would give me the appearance of authority. Not that these bastards were paying any attention to the FBI or any law enforcement agency.

Peeking over the bow, I could see that the big yacht was running without any visible lights. Fortunately for me, the gentle offshore zephyr did not create any seaway. Except for the wake produced by the motor-sailer, waves were minimal.

The rumble of the twin diesels was soporific. It was not long before I drifted off, a sleeping, unwanted passenger, whose destination would be determined by Elliot Jones, a madman, and his crew.

I woke up with a start, not knowing how long my weary, battered body had been catching up on its sleep. I looked at the Timex on my wrist, a cheapo with a very useful night light feature named 'Indiglo' by some marketing genius. The small hand was at the ten and the big hand near twelve.

Nothing much had changed, except we were no longer within sight of land. I was shivering with cold. Probably the ambient temperature was in the sixties. But my beat-up body was not capable of comfort in anything less than the average daytime eighties.

I wondered if I were just a few dozen feet away from my captive daughter. Wherever she was being held, the poor kid must be scared out of her wits, not knowing she was being treated as a hostage to bribe me to keep my mouth shut.

Considering my options, I decided I had enough passivity. I donned the life jacket and started pulling on the long, nylon towline, to draw the dinghy closer to the mother ship. As I hauled it in, the distance to the transom shortened. But the closer the dinghy got to the stern of the big motor-sailer, the harder it was to make any further headway, and the more my sprained ankle complained, shooting waves of pain up my bruised leg. Finally, I realized I could not get close enough to the transom to get a grip on anything, and I had to release the painter back to its full length. Exhausted, I lay back on the sole of the dinghy while I regained my breath.

As an amateur astrologer, but non-believer in its mysticism, I remembered that the sign of the Zodiac for this period was Capricorn the Goat. I could feel a kinship to that worthy animal. Even the full moon was covered by clouds that formed offshore. Like Murphy's Law, it seemed that everything that could go wrong, had done so. An airplane passed overhead, beneath the clouds. No savior there. The crew and passengers were in their own little world, completely oblivious to the problems of one earth-bound, water-trapped private investigator.

While I dozed, another two hours passed. Looking over the gunwale, I could see the distant shoreline again, on the port side, presumably to the East. Over my left shoulder there was a glow reflected off the clouds, probably representing the street-lights of Naples.

A half hour later, *Halcyon III* made a major course change, turning almost ninety degrees towards shore. I figured Elliot Jones had enough of late night cruising and was planning to dock his big yacht in or near Marco Island.

As we passed, in tandem, through the buoys marking the entrance to the Marco River, I had feelings of *déjà vu,* having visited this area many times in my numerous fishing expeditions. The yacht slowed down to nine knots, as mandated by the signs at harbor entrance. Soon, the bright lights of Shea's Restaurant slipped by, a familiar landmark with its docking slips out front.

Even thinking about food was painful to me. The Big Mac I had grabbed at noon was no longer providing energy or sustenance. I tried to put Shea's, and its delicious choices of seafood, out of my mind.

To my surprise and relief, thinking of certain discovery if Elliot Jones had ordered a stop at the well-known eatery, I slumped down further on the sole and behind the bow of the little dinghy.

Nor did *Halcyon III* pull into the next point of refuge, the Marco Island Yacht Club. The big yacht proceeded slowly and inexorably down the main channel and under the causeway bridge marking the entrance to the Ten Thousand Islands.

The Islands are not land surrounded by water in the usual sense. Many are made up of discarded oyster shells, built up over generations by Osceola Indians who inhabited the Islands before white men arrived in Florida to create Indian Reserves and change the lifestyle of the natives forever.

I had explored the Ten Thousand Islands by boat in my youth. There were literally thousands of brackish water channels separating the tangled, impenetrable clusters of mangrove from each other. Some channels or waterways resembled small lakes, others were so narrow that even a small boat could not pass through. Of the whole area, thousands of acres are covered in mangrove and about three times that in fresh and brackish water. Navigating among the mangrove islands is like getting lost in a maze, as everything looked more or less the same.

Separating the Ten Thousand Islands from the mainland is a wider channel leading to the small fishing village of Goodland. And that was where *Halcyon III* was headed. I recalled that there are a couple of popular eateries in the village specializing in fresh seafood. Since they are located on the water they are accessible to both mainlanders by automobile and mariners by watercraft. Nevertheless, Goodland is situated on a, more or less, remote backwater bay, and no doubt that appealed to the despicable Mister Jones in his present need to evade the Law. *What he hoped to accomplish by his flight from Fort Myers, I could not fathom, unless he planned to dump my daughter's body somewhere in the remote water wilderness of the Islands. I shuddered at the thought.*

Of one thing I was certain, as we approached Goodland, I could not hide in the dinghy any longer. As soon as the twin diesels stopped turning the props of the yacht, and an anchor splashed into the water, I slid over the side of the dinghy and worked my way along the side of the yacht, away from the lights ashore. Before entering the dark water, I had made sure that my Beretta and cell phone were tucked in the top of the life jacket.

As I hid in the watery shadows, holding on to an inflated rubber fender on the starboard side of the teak hull, I could hear male voices. Two men boarded the dinghy and proceeded to row ashore. It appeared the owner and members of the crew were going ashore to one of the restaurants, two at a time. That left two aboard the yacht, plus Melanie, if my guess was right. I could not imagine Elliot Jones giving precedence to anyone, so he was probably one of the two men now going ashore.

When I figured the dinghy had reached the docking area, I worked my way along the line holding the rubber fenders. On reaching the transom, I was relieved to see a swimming platform attached to the stern and a small chrome steel ladder providing easy access to the stern cockpit. As quietly as possible, I climbed aboard.

A small overhead light shone on the piloting station, featuring the engine controls and helm. A man was sitting on the pilot's seat, facing forward.

Approaching silently from the rear, I stuck the Beretta in his ear.

"Freeze," I said, "or you're dead. He froze. "Where is the other member of the crew?"

"Below," he said in a quivering voice. Just a teenager, he could not have been more than nineteen. "We'll go below," I said. "What is your name, son?"

"Paul Kincaid, sir." Good-looking youngster, blond, about six feet.

"Ahead of me, Paul. Smart of you to defer to the man with the gun."

"Yes, sir."

The second member of the crew was coming up a companionway that led below decks. His head was down, so he did not see us at first. An older man, he was dressed, as Paul was, in a snappy blue uniform, with the name of the yacht stitched in white lettering over the breast pocket. When he looked up, his eyes bulged in surprise. Of middle age, he had a droopy moustache, swarthy, weathered skin and reptilian eyes. He obeyed slowly, when I ordered him to raise his hands carefully and slowly.

"Did Elliot Jones go ashore?" I asked. Iguana-eyes did not answer.

"Yes, with the Captain," Paul Kincaid volunteered.

"Good. Now listen carefully. This weapon is small, but lethal. The first wrong move from either of you, and it will send a bullet through your head. Understand?"

"Yes. Yeah," they echoed each other.

"Where is the girl," I asked.

Paul spoke up again. "Mister Jones' wayward daughter is locked in the forepeak cabin."

"Like hell she is his daughter," I fired back. "She is *my daughter* being held captive. And you two are aiding and abetting in a kidnapping."

Both men looked shocked.

I tapped Paul on the shoulder. "I want you to go to the rope locker and get the necessary cord or rope to tie both of you up. And find some duct tape. While you do that, your pal will be my hostage. If you are foolish enough to signal ashore, or if you are not back here in about one minute, bullets will start flying. Your friend will be dead and you will be next. Incidentally, they are mushroom shells and make a helluva mess of a person's face."

"Yes, sir," Paul said submissively.

"On your way, then."

When he came back with the rope and tape, I made Paul tie up the older man. I inspected the knots, and removed a knife from the scabbard. Then I stuck a length of gray, duct tape across the man's droopy mouth and moustache."

"I've changed my mind, Paul. I want you to lead me to the cabin where my daughter is being held captive."

"Yes, sir," he said obediently, "Follow me." Over his shoulder, he added, "We were told that the girl was Mister Jones' daughter, who had been misbehaving and was locked up as punishment."

"That's just about the way Elliot Jones would treat his family," I replied. "Your boss is a liar, swindler and kidnapper."

I followed him down the companionway to the lower deck. We passed along a long corridor, with doors leading to several rooms, including one bearing a sign 'Engine Room'. Finally, we arrived at a locked mahogany door, marked Sail Locker. Paul pulled out a ring of keys and unlocked the door.

The forepeak was dimly lit with a small night light. The small room held two bunks in vee-formation, one on each side of the hull. Where they joined, a smaller door appeared to give access to the actual sail locker. Paul stood back to allow me to enter.

On one of the bunks, a girl's figure, fully clothed, reclined in a fetal position. Although she was asleep, I had no trouble identifying Melanie. She was still wearing a T-shirt, jeans and sneakers, the clothes in which she was abducted.

I sat on the opposite bunk and said, in a loud voice. "Time to wake up, Melanie. You can sleep when we get home."

Bleary-eyed, she put a hand up to her face. "Is that you Dad? I thought I was dreaming. Cripes, what a nightmare!"

She got up and wrapped her arms around my neck, tears of relief coming instantly.

I responded by shedding a couple of tears of my own. "Thank God you are okay," I said. "But let's get out of here. We are not out of trouble yet."

She stood up and looked at Paul, and then back at me. "Don't hurt, Paul, will you, Dad? He is the only one who has been helping me get through this. He thinks I am Melanie Jones. That's what Mister Jones told him. I couldn't convince him otherwise. But he has been kind to me."

I thought instantly of the infamous Stockholm Syndrome, where the prisoner falls in love with the captor. But I guess that would be a stretch in such a short period of imprisonment.

I assured her Paul would not be harmed. But I was not about to trust anybody at this stage. Gun in hand, I followed the two youngsters back to the stern cockpit. Melanie was sobbing quietly.

Once on deck, I punched 911 into my cell phone and asked the operator for the Collier County Sheriff's Office. A duty deputy answered. When I identified myself, she said, "Oh, Mister Smith! Hold one please." After a short break, Dan Short came on the line.

"Jesus, Maury. Am I ever glad to hear your voice," he said. "The Sheriff's Marine Patrol has been scouring the Gulf waters for *Halcyon III*. Where the devil did you get to?"

"We ended up in Goodland harbor, Dan. I have Melanie with me, but we could still have problems. Please get a couple of Sheriff's deputies over here in a hurry. When last seen, Elliot Jones and the yacht's captain were heading for the Inn at Goodland, for dinner. Meanwhile, I am holding two members of the crew at gunpoint. It's a fluid situation. So, please get the cavalry on their horses pronto. Okay, Dan?"

"You bet, pal. The FBI has sent an APB to all law enforcement agencies, to pick up Elliot Jones. Just a second.... The dispatcher is sending a Sheriff's patrol based in Marco Island, with two deputies. Help is only ten to fifteen minutes away. Agent Fox and I will not be far behind."

While Melanie and I relaxed on a deck seat, discussing her experience, Paul Kincaid asked me to put in a good word for him with the Sheriff's officers. I said, in view of his cooperation, I would try. But that he happened to be in the wrong place at the wrong time, and he could expect to be arrested, along with Elliot Jones and the yacht's captain, as well as the other crew member.

Soon, we observed the welcome sight of flashing blue strobe lights on a police cruiser ashore, beside The Olde Inn. Very soon thereafter, the Collier County Marine Parole power-boat pulled into Goodland harbor and rafted beside the motor-sailer. I helped them tie up.

The two deputies wanted to know about the crew members, one of whom was still lying on the deck, tied up and gagged. I gave them a brief version of what had transpired, knowing that I would have to repeat the story in an official statement when we returned to Naples.

Paul Kincaid and the other crew member were informed of their rights and taken ashore. Melanie and I joined them on the patrol boat. As we left the dock in front of the inn, Elliot Jones and his captain, both handcuffed, were being close-marched to a squad car. The light was sufficient for Jones to recognize my daughter and me. He pulled back, looked at my wet and bedraggled condition, and asked me, "Where the hell did you come from, Smith?"

I was not about to reveal trade secrets. "Mister Jones, you conniving bastard, you should have taken your own advice."

"What advice?"

"You should have kept looking over your shoulder."

Before he could respond, he and his captain were shoved into the back seat of the cruiser.

Physically, I was near the end of my tether when Dan Short and Special Agent Peter Fox drove into the parking lot, beside the Inn. Fox assured me that Elliot Jones, was being charged with kidnapping and attempted murder, his captain and crew members as accomplices.

I informed the FBI guy that there was some serious doubt that the captain and crew of the yacht knew that Melanie was the victim of an abduction, that Elliot Jones had misled them with a fairy tale about Melanie being *his* misbehaving daughter. Also, I mentioned that Sarah Briscoe had attempted to repay any profit she had made from her participation in the church scam.

"Did you take any action about the Ponzi/Pyramid scheme being operated at the Everglades Church," I asked Peter Fox.

He nodded. "With probable cause, and a search warrant, I sent a raiding party to the basement of the church. Reverend Clarke tried to hide the evidence, but some of the staff members who were hired to open the white envelopes admitted skepticism about how the funds were being used. The investigation is continuing."

We decided to have a meeting to discuss the whole rotten mess, as soon as I recovered from my physical infirmities. Tentatively, late afternoon seemed soon enough. Having been operating purely on adrenaline during the past few hours, I was beginning to sag physically, and ready to hit the sack. Dan said he would drive Melanie and me home, to which I readily agreed.

And, so ended my first case as a 'private eye'. Except there was an unexpected addendum. When my weary head hit the pillow that night, I thought the Golding file could be closed. Little did I realize that there were more unforeseen adventures ahead, and a sad development in my love life.

17

I awoke the next day wondering what kind of truck had run over my poor, martyred body.

Melanie, on the other hand, seemed to have recovered completely from her traumatic experience – ah, the resilience of youth! She entered my bedroom wearing a bright smile and carrying a tray of steaming coffee, bacon, eggs and toast, with the morning paper tucked alongside. I thanked her and began attacking the food like a starving animal.

"It's a lovely day, Pops," She said. "And thanks again for rescuing me."

She landed a smacker on my bristly cheek, making martyrdom all seem worthwhile. "You have made the news again," she added, "as the knight in shining pants. And I am a media star, according to the radio reports. The newspaper, however, went to bed before the breaking story could be printed. That's the way the radio reported it. I think they were gloating."

"No doubt," I agreed. "Thanks for the update, Mel. But remember media stars are very transient creatures by nature. Like yesterday's paper, they are here today and gone tomorrow."

"Anyway, Dad, I have been telling all the media people who want to interview you to come back later. Some of them are still parked outside, waiting for you to surface."

"Damn," I said. "We've got to think of some way for me to get past them. I should be going to the office."

"Mister Short called earlier, asking how you were feeling. I told him you were sleeping. He said to not bother coming in to the office today. However, he did ask if you could phone Mrs. Golding. She has called a number of times about something urgent."

Rolling stiffly out of bed, I headed for the shower. Over my shoulder, I said, "Please call him for me, Mel, and tell him I'll phone her as soon as I have showered, shaved and dressed."

Melanie laughed. "Hey, it's only the phone, Dad. Not television. She won't care how you look."

"Quite true, my dear. But I would not want anybody to even *think* I could look this bad."

"Oh, I almost forgot," she said, tapping the side of her head, "Joanne Carter called."

I turned around at the bathroom door and went over to the phone. There was no answer.

Melanie was grinning like a Cheshire cat.

"She has Pooch, you know," I said lamely.

"Sure, Dad. Uh huh!" Melanie, the tease.

Mrs. Cynthia Golding's maid answered her phone on the first ring. And her ladyship was almost as prompt.

Breathlessly, she explained she had been reading about my 'accident' on the freeway. "Oh, Maury, you poor man. I read in Monday's paper about your accident on the Interstate. Are you all right now?"

There seemed to be no point in telling her I was operating at about fifty percent, thanks to her daughter's fling with higher finance. So I just said, "Just shaken up, really. But thanks for asking."

"I understand that congratulations are in order. The radio report said you helped the police capture those kidnappers and con men."

"Yes, my daughter got back safely. They were holding her as a hostage."

"I hope she is not any worse for the experience, Maury. Now, how does all this leave my daughter, Sarah?"

"Well, she co-operated in attempting restitution. So I am hopeful that will be taken into consideration, if she is charged. Anyway, the Feds may be satisfied to deal with the big fish and not charge the smaller fry, whom were taken in by their fraudulent scheme."

"I will be so glad when all this is behind us, Maury," she said. "And I do thank you so much for all you have done."

"All in the line of duty, Cynthia," I replied. "I will have our gal, Josie, send you a statement of our expenses and fees for service."

"Please do. But don't hang up, Maury. I really must see you. There is another matter pending. But I'd rather not discuss it on the phone."

"Is it urgent?" I asked. "I have a meeting this afternoon with the FBI, to make a statement, and hopefully get immunity for Sarah, from any potential charges that they might be considering."

"Certainly I don't want you to miss that meeting," she said, "but is there any possibility that we could meet briefly, before the meeting? I could come to your office immediately. It's a *very personal* matter, Maury. And, yes, it could turn out to be very urgent."

I looked at my trusty Timex…11:30. "Okay, Cynthia, I can meet you at my office, just off Airport Road, in a half hour."

"Thank you so much, Maury. That's very good of you, after all you've been through. I'll be there."

Almost as soon as I hung up, the phone rang. "Good morning, Maury. Dan here. How are you feeling, old cock?"

"Like a really old cock, partner," I said. "I don't feel ready to face the world yet. But I have to face Mrs. Golding in a half hour. I was just about to phone for a cab."

"Don't do that, Maury. "I'll be around to pick you up. I have a surprise for you."

"Not too big a surprise, I hope, in my weakened condition."

"Fear not. You can take this one sitting down."

A few minutes later, Dan walked in, smiling broadly. He handed me a set of car keys, attached to one of those little remote door opening devices.

"The surprise is an '04 Ford Taurus, my friend. Just like the police chiefs use. Only it's not as beat up as most police cars."

I was concerned at such a large expenditure. "Can we afford this, Dan?" I asked. "I need wheels. But these babies don't come cheap."

"Not to worry, Maury. Insurance money from the claim on the fucked-up Focus will cover most of it. And, this is a purchase with low, *low,* payments. I did the dealer a favor once and kept him out of jail. Now he's balancing the books."

"Thanks, Dan. Now for the tough part. Getting past the media people waiting out there."

He smiled. "Not any more. I told them there would be a news conference outside our office at two o'clock."

I decided not to remind him that I would be in a meeting with the Feebies at two o'clock. I'm sure he remembered.

When we arrived at the office, Cynthia Golding was seated in our modest waiting room. She was dressed in a beige suit, paisley silk scarf, pearl earrings and necklace, hair neatly coifed. Her usual cigarette in a long holder was ignoring our No Smoking sign.

After introducing her to Dan, I ushered Cynthia into my equally modest office. She appeared distraught and tense. Not her usual suave self.

"As I mentioned on the phone, Maury," she began, "I have another problem. This is another instance where I would prefer not to go to the police. I hate gossip, innuendo and the wrong kind of publicity that might come out of what I'm going to tell you."

"What's the nature of your problem, Cynthia," I asked, adopting my Father Confessor mode.

I noticed she was calling me Maury rather than Smitty. But I did not care one way or the other. As long as she didn't call me Maurice. I preferred the shortened version over my real name.

"A marital matter, Maury. It's about my husband, Gary."

"Is he being unfaithful?" I ventured.

"He is missing. Has been for about three weeks. But maybe unfaithful, too. I don't know what to think."

"I see. Start at the beginning please, Cynthia," I urged her.

She took a long drag from her cigarette. I wished I had an air cleaner in my small office. There is nobody fussier about second hand smoke than a reformed smoker.

"Okay, as I mentioned before, Gary and I have not been getting along very well. He is a compulsive gambler, which I only discovered after we were married. Gambling is an obsession with him. It seems to be his only interest since he retired from the investment banking business. Filling the empty space in his life, I suppose."

"Well there are worse things than gambling," I pointed out. "Even state lotteries are a form of gambling. It's a principal form of revenue for some states."

"But that is not the type of gambling Gary is interested in," she said. "He's what they call a high roller. Likes baccarat mainly, and sometimes poker. For really high stakes."

"Your marital difficulties are about his gambling?" I asked.

"That would not bother me, if he were not away from home so much," she replied, as she stubbed out her cigarette in her coffee cup. "He's often away three or four days, or up to a week at a time. But this time, it has been three weeks and I'm getting worried. Because of his reputation as a big money gambler, he is usually comped, given complimentary flights and accommodation at Las Vegas and Atlantic City. He likes to move around. But he has never been away so long without phoning me."

"What about closer casinos, like the Seminole Indian Casino at Immokalee, for instance?"

She snorted. "You must be kidding. Gary would not be caught dead in Immokalee, with all those migrant farm workers."

I tried to ignore the expression 'caught dead', which could be prescient.

"When was the last time he was at home?"

"Monday, December 5th. We had an argument about his gambling. He is kind of a headstrong man. And, when I complained about his being away before Christmas, he became angry. He booked a flight somewhere and left the house in a huff. I have not heard a word from him since then."

"I see," I said. "Does he usually say where he is going and keep in touch by phone?"

She nodded. "He always has phoned in the past, unless he is only going to be away a day or so."

"This time, he did not say where he was going, or when he would be back?"

"No. I'm afraid not," she replied. "He was so angry, he just got in his car and took off, presumably for the airport.

Thinking he would get over his anger given time, I did not worry too much at first. But now that he has been away almost three weeks, I am concerned that he might be the victim of foul play. As you know, gambling attracts some unsavory characters."

I picked up a pen and started to make some notes. "Would you please describe your husband for me, Cynthia. Physical description, please – height, weight, age color, race, hair and eyes color, any identifying marks."

She lit another cigarette and blew smoke. "Okay. Height about five-eleven, 185 pounds, age 65, ten years older than me. Short gray hair. Skin fair, I guess. Race, as the police say on TV – Caucasian. No identifying marks I can think of."

"How was he dressed when you last saw him?"

"Casual clothes, for travel. But he always carries a dark blue suit and change of clothes in a flight bag."

"Religion?"

"Gary is Jewish, but more of an atheist".

"Any teeth missing?"

"He wears dentures," she said smiling. "So I guess they are all missing."

I could not help but think how closely Gary Golding resembled the floater. But I did not want to jump to conclusions, or upset Cynthia at this point.

"And he drove to the airport?"

"Yes, he took his dark gray Lincoln Town Car, with a vanity plate, Gary100. He would not be happy with just Gary1, and Gary 1000 was too long for the plate, I guess. "

"How does he book his flights, Cynthia?" I asked. "Travel agency, or does he phone for tickets directly to the airline?"

"He is a computer nut, Maury. He gets on the Internet and looks at the flight schedules. Then he books his flight, using a credit card."

"May I see his computer, Cynthia?" There may be some record of his flight booking in the memory."

"Certainly, Maury. When?"

"I'll see. Perhaps tomorrow. Okay? I must get going to Fort Myers for my meeting with the FBI guys. Since I am going to be passing the International Airport, I can check in the parking area for his car. Don't worry. I should be able to trace your husband's whereabouts fairly quickly."

"Thanks again, Maury," she said, handing me another roll of one hundred dollar bills. "Put this on my account."

"Wait a minute, Cynthia,' I said. "Josie will give you a receipt."

She waved her hand as though a thousand bucks was inconsequential.

"Whatever, I trust you Maury."

As she was leaving, she gave me another peck on the cheek. I was doing well in that department today.

18

When Cynthia Golding left our office, I glanced at the calendar on my desk. Tuesday, December 20th. Where did the days go?

It suddenly dawned on me that there were only four more shopping days until Christmas Eve. I picked up the phone and tried Joanne's office number again. The receptionist at Mercury Realty put me right through.

"Hi Joanne. It's Maury. I called earlier, but you were out selling one of those million dollar condos in North Naples."

She laughed. "I wish! Oh, Maury, I have been so damned busy, I have had to neglect poor Pooch. How are you feeling? Do you feel well enough to pick him up at my villa? I am so glad to hear you were able to get Melanie back safely. And put those rotten kidnappers in jail."

"Whoa Babe." I said. "First, I'm okay, Joanne. And Melanie suffered no serious problems in her brief captivity. Finally, sure, I'll get my little guy on my way out to Fort Myers. I have to leave shortly, but I am sure I can find a shaded parking spot for him. I apologize for not mentioning this earlier, but Melanie and I are looking forward to having you with us for turkey dinner on Christmas Day. Mel has become quite a good cook, which is fortunate, as I am not."

"Maury, I am really sorry," she said. "I can't make it this time. I have been invited out to dinner on the 25th. When I didn't hear anything from you, I accepted an invitation, not wanting to spend Christmas day alone."

"Gee, Joanne, I am sorry, too. It's my fault for not mentioning something to you earlier. Anyway, I am glad you will have a nice dinner out. Anybody I know doing the entertaining?"

There was a pause, before she replied. "Er...I won't lie to you, Maury. It is somebody you know. But, let's not get into that now. You know our arrangement, which has been in effect as long as I can remember. No commitment, no pack drill; if one sees someone else, that's okay. Variety, being the spice of life. Or something like that."

I swallowed hard, trying to grasp this new and unexpected turn of events. "That's very true, Joanne. We did agree to that arrangement long ago. Neither of us wanted to make a permanent commitment after the disaster of our first marriages. But I love you. And I guess I am jealous. I hope this will not turn out to be a change in our relationship?"

"Gotta go, Maury. A client is waiting for me. Do pick up Pooch, and we'll talk later. You still have the key to my villa?"

"Sure. Okay, Joanne. Let's talk, as soon as possible. Bye, I love you."

Damn! How could I have been so stupid? Letting the only gal I really treasured get away. Somebody I know? Who the hell could that be?

I   left   the   office   with   a   heavy   heart. *Damn...damn...damn! Maury, you idiot.*

Even picking up my dog and getting a heart-warming greeting, did not change my self-condemnation. I made an advanced New Year's Resolution to be more attentive to Joanne from now on. I realized that I had started to take her for granted. I thought we would be friends and lovers forever.

I was not blaming her. It was all my own fault, for forgetting that other men – and she would have been more open, if it were a girl friend she was planning to go out with – would be as attracted to Joanne as I have always been. I had not yet selected a Christmas present for her. But it had better be a good one, to prove I love her!

These were the thoughts that ran through my mind, as Pooch and I sped towards Fort Myers along I-75 in the new Taurus. In other circumstances, I would have appreciated the beautiful new automobile more. But for now, all I could think of was Joanne and me. Me and Joanne. Our long history of making love together. To share her with another man was more than I could accept gracefully. I wondered how long she had been seeing the other guy. Probably not too long, or I would have sensed a change in her attitude towards me. She had never seemed so guarded before.

It was hard to concentrate on business. However, I could not just drift along, staying on I-75 indefinitely. Exit 21 would be coming up sooner than usual. Funny how depressing thoughts could make time pass more quickly. Is it equally true that happy thoughts would make the journey seem longer. Anyway, happy thoughts were well beyond reach at this time. What I needed was a good shrink to help straighten out my love life.

At Exit 21, instead of turning left down Daniels Road at the light, I turned right to the Fort Myers International Airport. In a matter of minutes I was walking through the Long Term Parking area, looking for Gary Golding's Lincoln Town Car.

The parking building was jammed. It seemed like everybody and his brother was trying to get somewhere for Christmas – back to family or friends. Or coming the other way to visit Floridians. Many travelers were going to be disappointed. A major storm had brought heavy snow, ice and freezing rain to Central and Eastern States. According to reports on the radio, many flights were cancelled. Meanwhile, Lee and Collier Counties were experiencing fine weather, with daytime highs in the low eighties.

After searching for a few minutes, I finally spotted a gray Lincoln Town Car bearing Gary Golding's vanity plate, Gary 100. It was tucked away in a corner of the parking building, covered with a fine film of dust, indicating that it was not a recent arrival. Although I was tempted to make enquiries of the various airlines in the airport, I realized more could be accomplished by phone, or by checking Gary's computer than by attempting to get information from harried airline employees during the Christmas travel crunch.

I located the building in which the Fort Myers office of the Federal Bureau of Investigation is located, and was fortunate in finding a street parking space under a tree that someone had recently vacated. Leaving windows partially open for air circulation, but not far enough open that some bad guy would try to reach in and open the door, I patted Pooch on his head and told him I would be back real soon. My guard dog responded with a whimper, making me feel guilty. I gave him a dog biscuit from the supply in my pocket, put lots of change in the parking meter, and went to meet with the Feebies.

The building directory board indicated that the FBI offices were on the seventh floor. I took the elevator and walked down the corridor to a door bearing the distinctive, round FBI logo. The cute receptionist with dimples and a short hairdo, said that I was expected. She pointed to a door labeled Special Agent Peter Fox. I knocked and was greeted by Fox himself, who introduced me to a trimly-dressed woman in a blue business suit with pants rather than a skirt, giving her a masculine look.

"Meet Agent Diane Wilson, Maury," Peter Fox said. "She is my good right arm and knows all about the Everglades Church case."

Agent Wilson gave me a warm smile. She appeared to be in her thirties, about the same age as her boss. About five-six, a slim brunette, with short hair barely covering her ears, she could pass as a school teacher of younger grades, if she dispensed with the holstered weapon bulging under her jacket.

"Nice to meet you, Mister Smith," she said. "I believe we spoke briefly on the phone, before your wild ride on the dinghy last night. Congratulations on helping to apprehend those villains."

"Thank you," I said, as Peter Fox motioned me into a seat across from his desk. "Please call me Maury." Wilson took the other chair.

"I guess we should get right down to business, Maury," Peter Fox said. "I hope you have recovered to some extent from your ordeal?"

I smiled. "Better than last night, anyway. I can sign my name, if necessary."

"Good, because we need a formal statement from you, to please the Bureau pen-pushers in Washington. We will be taping your verbal comments, and then we'll have a written statement transcribed for you to sign."

He reached over and started a tape recorder. Then he gave a short introduction, identifying those present, the date and time, for the benefit of anyone reading the transcript.

It took me the better part of a half-hour describing all the events leading up to the capture of Elliot Jones and his crew, and the release of Melanie, last night in Goodland.

During my dissertation, I mentioned how Elliot Jones had torn up the check that Sarah Briscoe had given me. I handed Peter a photocopy of the check as evidence of its existence. I also pointed out that Elliot Jones had probably misled the crew of *Halcyon III* into believing that it was his daughter who was locked in the forepeak cabin, because she had misbehaved.

As far as Reverend Clarke was concerned, I said the fact that he had sent a warning message to Elliot Jones of our attempt to intercept his yacht, made him as guilty of conspiracy to kidnap my daughter as Jones himself.

At the conclusion, Peter Fox turned the tape over to his receptionist to have it transcribed.

"Will that take long?" I asked, thinking of Pooch out in the car.

Peter smiled. "Ten years ago, it would have, Maury," he said. "But we have the latest in voice recognition equipment. It's a great time-saver."

"I was hired by Mrs. Cynthia Golding," I said, "to try to get her daughter, Sarah Briscoe out of the mess she had gotten herself into with the fraudulent church scheme. I hope her willingness to return so-called Heavenly Abundance profits and commissions will save her from being charged."

"I can only present the facts," Peter Fox said, "but I would think the federal prosecutor would go easy under the circumstances."

"That's fair enough," I said. "There are those who have benefited financially from their participation and have shown no remorse, or have not had an opportunity to do so. May I ask if you have uncovered a list of those who became converts, disciples, apostles, ambassadors, or whatever they were named?"

Fox looked across at his female sidekick. "It was Agent Wilson who organized the raid on the church basement and is leading the investigation. Diane?"

"Not exactly a list per se," she said. "But we have ordered the bank to turn over all their records of the transactions in the church's account. So, we can get at it that way. The church's split of the revenues with the Heavenly Ministries Trading Company was an even 50-50 deal, according to Reverend Mister Clarke. Our Atlanta office is looking into possible activities of the so-called trading company in connection with other churches."

I thanked them and took my leave. It was agreed that I would be kept informed of the outcome of the investigation, since it was Short & Smith who unearthed the con game.

19

On arriving back in Naples from my brief visit to Fort Myers, winter home of Thomas Edison, as their Chamber of Commerce likes to remind everyone, I took Pooch back to the condo, where be was given a big hug by Melanie. He demonstrated his happiness at being home by running through his repertoire of tricks, including tearing through the apartment like a dog possessed, until he exhausted himself and turned over on his back to have his tummy rubbed.

When he finally settled down, I told my daughter I was going out to do some shopping.

As I was leaving, I said, "You did a great job of decorating the tree, Mel. Is there anything I can do for you while I am out?"

"Sure, Dad," she said jokingly. "Give Santa a kiss and ask him if he got my list."

"There are some things you can do best yourself, Melanie," I said. "Also, if you have a list, it would be in more capable hands with me than with some old coot whom allegedly flies all over on Christmas Day giving children gifts they didn't ask for. Furthermore, Joanne will not be with us for Christmas dinner."

"Oh! You were not so cynical about Santa, when I was a little kid, Dad. And I detect a certain amount of dejection about Joanne's rejection. Has she got a new boy friend?"

"So it would seem. Apparently I am the last to know."

"While you are out, I will ask Pooch for the lowdown. He has been with her since you went joy-riding on the Gulf."

"Ungrateful wench," I said, tongue-in-cheek.

"Just kidding, Dad."

"I know, but I have temporarily lost my sense of humor."

"If I find it, I'll let you know. Don't bust the budget, Pops."

"Bye.".

Knowing that the gift Melanie would like most of all would be a home computer system, I took off for Circuit City.

With mail-in rebates, the bottom line did not look too bad. The young Asian salesman convinced me the package was a bargain when he threw in a three month subscription to America Online (AOL). Next, I visited a jewelry store in the same mall and nearly blew the budget and my credit rating on a beautiful ring for Joanne – a single natural pearl mounted on a gold band. Simple, but effective. Not exactly an engagement ring, but hopefully it would warm the cockles of her heart.

Fortunately, Christmas comes but once a year. I was pre-spending a dividend Dan had talked about from Short & Smith. It might keep me out of debtor's prison.

That evening, I wrapped Joanne's gift in a large box and phoned to see if she was home. The ring itself, in the center of a lot of wrapping paper, was housed in a nice blue velour setting box.

Joanne answered after a couple of rings (phone rings) and I asked if it would be alright if I dropped by. She assured me it would be, but said she was just going to have a shower, and to give her a half hour.

I watched television for a half hour. Then I jumped in the car and drove over to her villa.

Another car was in the driveway. As I walked past it I noticed a number 10 in the lower corner of the rear window. Just like a police car to identify 'unmarked' vehicles.

Joanne met me at the door, looking embarrassed. "I'm sorry, Maury," she said. "A friend dropped in unexpectedly. But he is leaving now. So come in."

Behind her, in the vestibule, was Detective Lieutenant John Weatherby. He was in civvies, of course.

Unbelievable! Standing at the door, I looked past Joanne, at Weatherby, trying to take in the situation.

"Good evening, Maury," Weatherby said with a self-satisfied smirk. "I'm just leaving."

Having finally gathered my wits, I asked. "What's going on, Joanne? Is this an official visit?"

"No, Maury," Joanne said. "Just what it seems. John is a friend, who just dropped by unexpectedly. I told him you were on your way over, so he said he would drop by later."

I saw red, and my quick temper took over. "Well, he does not have to leave, Joanne, because I am leaving. I don't think much of your taste in friends. If you wanted to end our relationship, you could have told me to shove off, which I am doing now. Here, take your Christmas present."

"But, Maury…".

"No buts. Goodbye." I turned on my heel, got in my car and roared back to *The Pallisades.*

When I got back to the apartment, Melanie could tell I was blowing smoke out my ears. "What's the matter, Dad," she asked. "You look like you are ready to burst a blood vessel."

I tried to calm down. It was not easy. "Joanne has my worst enemy as a friend. I have been cuckolded, I guess."

"Dad, you are not married," she reminded me. "To be cuckolded, your wife has to be unfaithful, not your girl friend."

"Don't quote technicalities at me, Mel. I am in no mood to quibble. I wouldn't be surprised if the S.O.B. singled her out because he knew we were *almost* married."

Before she could remind me further of my unreasonable attitude, the phone rang. Mel was closest and picked it up. She said hello and listened. Without a word, she handed the phone to me.

"Maury, this is Joanne. I am sorry for what happened. Please don't be mad at me. John is just a friend. I didn't know that he was the guy that had you fired from the Naples Police. He explained the situation to me, and I don't blame you for being upset."

I said nothing for a while, trying to sort out a reply, through my residual anger.

"Maury? Are you there?"

"Yes, I am here, Joanne," I answered coldly. "I'm still trying to figure out how you could become friendly with that arrogant, two-faced prick, my worst enemy on God's green earth. If you set out to hurt me, you could not have done better. And, he didn't fire me. I quit and told him to shove his freaking job. I've been listening, but I didn't hear you say you were through with him."

"Maury. Listen, please," she said, "I realize now that you two did not hit it off. But John is not a bad person. You said yourself that there were to be no strings attached to our relationship."

"Either you can't judge human nature," I said, "or you will find to your sorrow that John Weatherby is nothing but an arrogant, overbearing, unreliable asshole. He is only interested in himself, not you. He has an all-consuming ambition to deal the last blow – to get the last little bit of revenge, because I made him a laughing stock in the squad room when I told him to shove his job. To get back at me, he is stealing *my girl* – the only person I have ever loved. So, I wish you both much happiness, and I never want to talk to you again. Goodbye and good luck." I was still seething when I hung up.

Melanie heard the whole conversation, at least my end of it. She looked at me with raised eyebrows. "Da-a-ad. Do you think it was wise to hang up on her like that?"

"Wize, smize. Who gives a damn? If that's all I mean to her after all these years, it is better we should call it quits and get it over with."

"I know your feelings are hurt, Dad," she said. "but I doubt if Joanne knew how bitter your feud was with Mister Weatherby. In the long run, you may be sorry you were so rude to her."

"Spare your lecture, young lady. I know I will miss her," I admitted, "but I do have some pride, and I wouldn't share her with John Weatherby if she were the last woman on the planet."

"Okay, Dad. You are wiser than I am in these things…I hope!"

20

Still smarting from the ignominy of having lost the love of my life to the bastard Weatherby, I decided to immerse myself in work-related projects, rather than dwelling on my unhappiness. I phoned Cynthia Golding to ask permission to pay a visit and check out her husband's computer.

As expected, she said by all means come over. And as expected there was a damned password problem to be solved before I could get any information out of the stubborn techno beast.   It seems these days, in this computerized world, a person has to know a password or PIN number to access any-thing.

I sat alone in Gary Golding's study, a book-lined room on the second floor of his splendiferous mansion. For a frus-trating half hour, I tried inputing on his keyboard various possible passwords, none of which would admit me into the inner sanctum of his computer's hard drive.

As a computer nut - his wife's description- I figured Gary would use some password so sophisticated as to be be-yond guessing. Just when I was about to give up the whole idea as a lost cause, I tried the most obvious passwords. First I tried 'Cynthia'. But no go. Then I tried 'Briscoe'. Still no go. Finally, I tried a combination of his wife's maiden name, 'CynBris'. Eureka! Bingo! Halleluja! It worked!

Windows Home XP started up and the usual icons be-gan to appear on the 'desktop'. I was in like Flynn. With the mouse, I placed the blinking cursor on the icon for Outlook Express and hit the left mouse button twice. Up came the menu panel. I highlighted "Sent' – the box that would contain e-mail messages that Gary had sent recently. There was a very short message to a person whose Internet address was LesMil1940@aol.com.   The message simply said *Confirm arrival Naples date and time for airport pickup. Gary.* Obviously, Cynthia's husband was a man of few words.

Interesting, but not what I was looking for. So I looked for a folder labeled 'Gary' in his mailbox. And found one containing a goldmine of information. One dated 12-04-05 From Delta Airline confirmed a First Class ticket he had purchased departing Fort Myers International for Las Vegas. Another from Hideaway Club, Las Vegas, received on the same date, confirmed his reservation, arriving 12-05-05. I printed copies of both messages about his trip, as well as the one from LesMil, and placed them in my pocket.

After shutting down the computer, I went downstairs to find Cynthia.

"Did you have any luck, Maury?" she asked from her lounge chair on the rear patio.

"I think so, Cynthia," I said non-comittaly. "I'll know better when I have checked a few things out. Meanwhile, I am going home to spend Christmas Day with my daughter. I hope you don't mind if I pause briefly in this investigation until after Christmas. I can't achieve much anyway, with most everything shut down. But I'll be back on your husband's trail on Boxing Day. Is that okay?"

"Oh, certainly, Maury. Since it appears Gary will not be here for Christmas, Sarah has invited me to her place in Fort Myers for the holiday. It's better than being alone."

"That's nice, Cynthia," I said. "The investigation may lead me out of town. But, I'll keep you posted on any major developments. Meanwhile, I can assure you progress is being made."

"If you'll be traveling, will you be all right for funds?" she enquired.

I smiled and patted my jacket pocket. "Don't worry, I still have my credit cards, Cynthia. Please don't bring any more cash from the bank. I worry about you carrying so much cash around in your purse. It's an invitation to bad guys to mug you. Can't you just write checks?"

She looked at me with raised eyebrows, as though I had said something stupid. "Sure, I can write checks. But then Gary might find out I am paying a private detective and the bank employees will also. That's how unwanted rumors get started. I'll stick with cash, if you don't mind."

"Of course. I should have thought of that," I admitted. "Well, be very careful. You might consider buying traveler's checks. They can't be traced, except remotely at Amex head office. If lost or stolen, they can be replaced."

"Good idea, Maury," she said. "I'll do that next time. Have a good holiday."

"You, too, Cynthia. Take care."

There was no mistletoe over the entrance, but as I opened the door, I got a lingering peck on my cheek.

When I returned to the office, I asked Josie to book me a flight to Las Vegas on Boxing Bay, departing in the morning. Also, to reserve a room for me at any hotel except the Hide-away Club, whatever that was. Later, I had a word with Dan about my plans.

"Dan, I have to go to Vegas on Boxing Day. That's where Gary Golding is holed up, or deceased."

He was sympathetic. "Sorry you have to travel on a holiday, Maury," he said. "The Fort Myers International Air-port is stacked up with people whose flights have been can-celled by that big storm up North. Do you think you can get a flight?"

"Josie is working on it, Dan. Which reminds me, what are we doing for her regarding Christmas?"

"I have a Christmas bonus check for her," he replied, "and one for you. Yours is the same as mine – One Thousand Bucks. I would have discussed this with you before, but you have been busy lately. So I just went ahead. Josie's is for two-fifty."

I whistled. "I hope we can afford this, Dan?"

He smiled, and moved the ubiquitous toothpick to the other side of his mouth. "We can. It's been a good year, just like the tire company."

"Josie has been a treasure, Dan," I said. "Although she has been with us a short time, she deserves the bonus. I'm not sure about mine, though."

"You have earned yours, old buddy, and I agree with you totally about Josie. Here, you give it to her." He handed me two envelopes, one with my name on it. "Merry Christmas, partner," he said.

"You too, Santa. And thanks for the bonus."

When I handed Josie her envelope. She opened it and said, "Wow! Gee, thanks Mister Smith."

I said, "Don't thank me, Josie. Thank Santa in there. It was his idea."

"Well thank you both, and Merry Christmas. By the way, you are booked on United Flights 300 and 201, Fort Myers to Denver and Denver to Las Vegas. Don't lose your shirt in the gambling casinos," she quipped.

"Thanks, Josie. And, don't worry about my gambling. I know the house odds. Trying to beat them is for suckers. However, I might venture a buck or two on the slots, just for the hell of it."

She smiled. "That's right, Mister Smith. Live danger-ously. Incidentally, here is something for your trip."

She handed me what appeared to be a thick printout from the computer. The first page was a description, with full color pictures of the Monte Carlo Resort and Casino in Las Vegas. The caption read, 'located in the Street of Dreams, the Arcade and Midway offer state-of-the-art motion simulator, virtual reality, video, redemption, midway games and golf simulator. The Arcade and Midway are for the young-at-heart'. The remaining pages, twenty in all, were printed in single column style, headed, 'A Little Gaming History'. In-trigued, I sat down opposite Josie's reception desk and skimmed the contents: Gaming History, Modern Forms (of Gambling), Government Control, followed by a list of various gambling games: Baccarat, Blackjack, Dice Games, Keno (A sucker's game), Roulette, Poker (Draw and Stud), Bingo and Slot machines. Full descriptions were included of each game and how it's played.

I looked up from reading and asked Josie, "How the heck did you come up with all this stuff? It's incredible!"

"When I heard you were going to Vegas," she replied, "I just called up Yahoo, which, as you know, is a search engine for the Internet. I asked it to search for 'gambling', and up came a whole web page of gambling sites, including Las Vegas, Reno, Atlantic City and so on. There was a link to

'Hotel Reservations'. That's how I made your reservation at Monte Carlo Resort and Casino. Simple really."

"Simple, maybe," I observed, "but really impressive, Josie. I suppose you made my flight reservations on the Internet, too."

She smiled again, showing teeth white enough to qualify for an ad by Crest. "You guessed my secret," she said. "You can pick your tickets up at the airport."

21

The dry desert air in Las Vegas was much cooler than the balmy climate of Southwestern Florida. But the sun was just as bright and the sky equally blue. No complaints about the weather. I was prepared for cool weather at this time of year, and had brought along a topcoat. The weather really didn't matter anyway, since I had no intention of playing golf, fishing or sight-seeing on this occasion. Furthermore, after being squeezed in an aisle seat by a fat lady sitting next to me, and listening to a shrieking kid for a couple of hours, I was more than ready to leave the flight and stretch my legs.

I could have flown First Class, I suppose, and Cynthia Golding would not have raised an eyebrow at the expense. But ex-cops are not accustomed to such luxury, and we are creatures of habit...damn it!

Christmas Day had been very quiet. Melanie and I spent several hours getting the home computer system installed, and up and running. We had to use an old, folding card table which I retrieved from storage, as a temporary substitute for a dedicated computer desk and hutch. I decided, as a matter of priority, to blow some more of my year-end bonus on a corner computer desk which would fit nicely into Melanie's bedroom without taking up too much floor space.

After my Boxing Day landing in Vegas, I rented a Chevy Cavalier from Budget-rent-a-Car, again being economical in connection with Cynthia's expense account. I hoped she would appreciate my thrifty nature.

At 6:15 P.M. local time, the winter sun had just gone down behind purple mountains in the distance. In the dusk of early evening, I cruised Las Vegas Blvd North, which was starting to look like an extravaganza of neon and flashing lights spelling out the locations of the many hotels and casinos.

I should not have been surprised that the broad, palm-lined streets of the nation's gambling capital seemed to have a plethora of expensive automobiles and a shortage of modest economy cars like my rented Budget Cavalier.

My brief orientation run ended when I pulled in to 3770 Las Vegas Blvd South, the address of the three thousand room, glowing edifice, Monte Carlo, obviously named after the famous casino city in the Principality of Monaco.

At the entrance, I humbly turned the keys to the Cavalier over to a parking attendant while wondering if he had ever deigned to provide valet parking to such an insignificant vehicle. Knowing that he had me sized up as a small tipper, I reasoned it was all the more reason to justify his judgment.

My room was not modest. There are probably no rooms in Vegas answering to a description of modesty. I had heard that accommodation in this city of gambling iniquity is subsidized to lure more people in to the casinos. So, I was not about to ask the price of the room when I checked in.

After showering and dressing in a conservative-looking dark gray suit, white shirt and blue tie, I figured I had sufficiently disguised my Florida cracker background and was ready to face the city that never sleeps.

But first I had a couple of scotches to negate the effects of jet lag, followed by dinner at The Pub. Then I asked the concierge for directions to The Hideaway Club.

He quietly looked me up and down before replying, "If you don't have connections there, sir, I have to tell you that is one exclusive joint, only for the highest of the high rollers. If you are one of those, just take a right and follow the main drag right out to Riviera Drive. The location is past most of the hotels and casinos. Like its name, The Hideaway Club is hiding behind a high stone wall, with no sign or bright lights, kind of camouflaged by trees and bushes. I thanked him and tipped him generously with a fiver. The same for the undeserving parking attendant. Sorry Cynthia – when in Rome!

Presumably to prevent people like me from bothering the super high rollers while they patronize the gaming tables, a guard was stationed at the front entrance when I arrived. He resembled a Field Marshall of a third world country. Tall, heavily built, dressed in a purple uniform with gold epaulettes and gold cord stretched across his ample chest, ending in a tassel. Only a ceremonial sword was missing.

Again I was inspected closely. "Are you a member, sir?" he asked, making no move to let me pass.

"No, I cannot claim the honor of membership," I confessed. "However, I am here to meet with a member, Mister Gary Golding. It is a matter of utmost importance and urgency."

He seemed to be singularly unimpressed, no doubt having heard that or better stories from would-be punters any number of times. I reached in my wallet and handed him a twenty, hoping to at least prolong the conversation.

He put the bill in his pocket without comment. But he didn't offer to give it back, either.

"May I have your name, sir? I'll see if Mister Golding is in."

I handed him my business card. He looked at it, sniffed, and turned back to use a wall phone. Speaking very softly into the mouth-piece, he waited for about a minute. Then he came back and instructed me to wait outside the entrance door. I figured that was a step up from being sent to the tradesman's entrance. After waiting a couple more minutes, the massive oak entrance door swung open. A man who looked like Jeeves, wearing a tuxedo and accompanying finery, invited me to enter and take a seat in the spacious lobby. I wondered if formal dress was *de rigeur* for the hired help in this spiffy club.

As I waited on an armchair covered with brass-studded red leather, I thought to myself that the founders of The Hideaway Club had tried to make the décor as different as possible from the gauche commercial casinos and hostelries in Vegas. In the tradition of old England, the décor was reminiscent of Early Tudor, with stucco walls, thick ceiling beams and dividers of black walnut.

A full suit of knight's armor, lance in hand, stood in one corner, hopefully minus an occupant. The floor was tiled in lacquered and polished field stone. Over a Duncan Fyfe table hung an oil painting of horses and riders engaged in a steeplechase. The artist's viewpoint was at ground level; with the thundering herd advancing directly overhead. How dramatic!

But the artist must have died of injuries shortly after making his sketch, unless he was standing in a manhole at the time.

My reverie was interrupted by the massive inner door bursting open.

A scowling man, dressed in a dark blue suit, white shirt, striped tie, glared at me from the doorway. His gray hair was close-cropped. Physically he matched Cynthia's description of her husband, Gary. Horn-rimmed glasses hung by a black cord from around his neck.

Looking at my business card, which had been passed on to him, he asked, "What the hell do you want, Smith?"

I smiled, trying to match his discourtesy with clever incivility, "Mister Golding I presume. Just seeing you standing there, living and breathing, makes this visit all worthwhile."

That remark seemed to catch him off guard. He approached me. I noticed that his piercing eyes were brown behind his glasses.

"What is that stupid remark supposed to mean," he demanded to know.

I got up from the armchair, so that he would have to look up at me, instead of looking down, a maneuver that could be called one-up-man-ship.

"You have proven to me that you are not dead," I said. "although, until I report back to my client, you will still be listed as missing."

"Stop talking in riddles, Mister Smith," he demanded. "If you do not clearly explain your business, I'll have you thrown out of here."

"Sorry, I don't mean to be obtuse," I replied, "but I have flown all the way from Naples today for two reasons. Number one, your appearance matches, to some extent, a drowning victim that I came across in the Gulf of Mexico. Obviously, you are not him."

"No. I am certainly not the floater you found."

I blinked, when he mentioned 'the floater', when I said 'drowning victim'. "So you read about the floater in the newspaper?" I enquired – a Catch 22 question, because the unsolved mystery of the floater's identity was almost forgotten, being seldom mentioned any more in the Naples news media.

He just nodded, and I pressed on "And, two, I was hired by your wife to try to find you, as she has been very worried about having no word from you in the past three weeks. She explained that you and she had an argument just before you left the house. But, she thought you would get over your anger and phone her if you were going to be away more than a couple of days. Your wife thought something might have happened to you, so she hired me to allay her fears."

"Well, she has lots of money of her own," he said, "and if she wants to waste it on private dicks, that's her problem. I didn't call her because she deserved the cool treatment, and that is what she got. Now, that's enough of interfering in my personal affairs, Mister Smith. So you can just fuck off."

When I showed no sign of disappearing before his very eyes, he headed back to the door to his gambling den. But his curiosity got the better of his desire to have no further truck with a private dick.

"Oh, by the way," he asked over his shoulder, "how did you find me?"

I could not resist the temptation. "How did I find you?" I asked, repeating his question. "In a word – *obnoxious!*"

Before he could think of an adequate rejoinder, I turned on my heel and left him red-faced and gulping for air.

Arriving back at the Monte Carlo, I phoned Cynthia at her daughter's apartment in Fort Myers. I reported her husband was alive and well, or as well as his nasty disposition would allow.

She expressed relief and thanked me. But she did not ask when he would be returning home. Nor, had I asked her husband about his itinerary, assuming his reply would be another impolite expletive. However, I did want to meet with her when she returned home. So, we made an appointment for coffee on her terrace at 10 A.m. on December 28th.

Before leaving Las Vegas, I had to satisfy my curiosity. I blew ten dollars on a slot machine, confirming my suspicion that I would never ascend to the ranks of the high-rollers, nor even to the low-rollers of the gambling world.

22

Naples, Florida Tuesday, December 27, 2005

When I arrived back at our condo following my quick trip to Las Vegas, Melanie and Pooch met me at the door. In the Naples eighty degree weather I felt ridiculous carrying a topcoat over my arm.

"How did it go, Dad?" Melanie asked. "Did you bring back any souvenirs from Vegas?"

"Just a little decoration for your room, Mel," I said. "I am relieved to see that you are not missing this time."

I was thinking of Melanie while I was waiting for my flight at McCarran International Airport. Not wanting to return empty-handed, I visited a gift shop and picked up an Indian carving which I thought she would enjoy.

"Great, Pops," she said when I handed her the artifact. "Next time, take me with you, okay?" I was rewarded with a hug.

An easy promise to make. "Sure, Mel. If there is a next time."

Melanie waited until I had deposited my overnight bag and topcoat, before she said, casually, "Joanne called while you were away. She returned your Christmas gift."

"Well, that's okay, Dear. I rather thought she would," I said. "Did she bring it over herself?"

"Yes, Dad.   When she heard you were away, she stopped by and we had a nice visit."

"What did you two talk about? My bad temper?"

"No, she just wanted to say she was sorry the way things turned out," Melanie replied. "And, she left you a note. Here it is."

The note was in a sealed, heather-colored envelope, with her name and address embossed on the back flap. A faint aroma of lavender wafted to my nostrils when I opened it.

December 26, 2005

Dear Maury:

What a lovely gift! And, how sad I am, having to return it. I fully understand how you felt, when John Weatherby showed up unexpectedly. I had no idea that you and he disliked each other so much.

Under other circumstances I would love to keep the ring. But that would be totally unfair, until we resolve our relationship and have a better understanding of our mutual responsibilities. If you are so inclined, I think we should sit down and talk candidly about you and me and the future.

Please give me a call anytime,

Love, Joanne

I read the note over and over, trying to decipher what Joanne was saying between the lines. It appeared, from the tone of her words, that she was interested in some fence-mending, but not prepared to concede that she should tell John Weatherby to get lost.

How could I share Joanne with my worst enemy? Or, with anyone for that matter?

For years I had been faithful to our agreement – that we should lead separate lives – but remain committed to each other. At least, that was what I thought we had agreed upon, that fateful evening in 1995, when we shared our innermost feelings and convictions. At that time, neither of us wanted to take a chance on marriage again.

I did not think Joanne would react any more favorably than Loretta had to being a cop's wife. I could not read Joanne's mind, but I believed she wanted to pursue her career in real estate unfettered by more household responsibilities than she already had as a single person.

Anyway, it seemed over the years we did want to keep seeing each other on a regular basis, without any firm commitment. I thought that meant, by tacit consent neither of us sharing our love life with anyone else. Joanne seemed to be telling me she was free to do as she damned well pleased, with whomever she chose. I admit she made some such of a proviso away back when. But now that she seemed to be actually putting it into practice made me very unhappy.

In the past three months my circumstances had changed. I was no longer a cop, and I did not have to take orders from anyone. But, whether a private eye ranked higher than a cop on the social register was a moot point. Neither means of earning a living ranked right up there with the professionals, like doctors, lawyers and public accountants. Maybe more like the pros who walk the streets. As Roger Dangerfield said, we don't get no respect!

Anyway, the point of all this introspection was whether a firm and exclusive commitment between two people was necessary for their happiness. And, if they loved each other, whether co-habitation was necessary, or monogamy for that matter. Joanne seemed to be saying it wasn't. I was convinced it was.

Did I want to ask Joanne to be my wife? Sure as hell not as long as she was seeing John Weatherby! Even if she discovered the error of her ways – according to my way of thinking – would she look favorably on an offer of marriage? To a private dick with a hot temper, probably not.

Melanie pretended to busy herself with dusting the apartment, while I was still holding Joanne's note, deep in thought. I suspected she was watching me out of the corner of her vision.

I decided to show her Joanne's note, with a view to asking my twenty-year-old daughter's advice to the lovelorn.

"What do you think I should do, Mel?" I asked plaintively. "I don't know what she is trying to tell me. Is she just letting me down lightly. Or is there a message for me between the lines?"

Like Ann Landers, she asked sagely," Do you love her, Dad?"

"Yes, Melanie, I do," I confessed without hesitation. "That must be obvious. But, dammit, she is not offering to end her affair with John Weatherby."

"Are you sure it really is *an affair,* Dad?" she asked, "or do you think Joanne is speaking the truth when she suggests they are just friends?"

"I have no idea how far their relationship has progressed, Mel," I replied. But as long as he is hanging around, I don't want anything to do with her."

Looking at the note again, Melanie said, "She says she is prepared to discuss things with you, so why don't you take her at her word, and meet with her for a discussion? Swallow some of your pride and give her the benefit of the doubt."

"All very well for you to say, Melanie. But much harder for me to do," I said. "The stumbling block is that horse's ass Weatherby. Why can't she just get rid of him?"

She smiled enigmatically, like a junior Buddha, "Look at it this way, Pops. Maybe she is using him as her bargaining tool, to get you to make a commitment."

"Hell's bells! I've been committed to her for ten years. I thought she was likewise committed to me. Now she has changed the situation by seeing someone else. Maybe I could tolerate some competition, if it were anyone else but Weatherby. Then again, I don't really want to share her with *any* boy friend. I can be monogamous. Why can't she?"

"You had better ask her, Dad. Perhaps she no longer wants to be tied down. Or, maybe she *does* want to be. I can't read her mind, either. For heaven sake, just *ask* her. Hopefully, she'll tell you."

"Thanks, Mel," I said. "Probably good advice. But you are involved in this situation, too. Would you want Joanne as a step-mother?"

"Sure, Dad. I like Joanne. Anyway, I'm grown up enough that it would not make much difference, one way or the other. It would be more like a sister to sister relationship, than mother and daughter. Who knows? One of these days I might be asking you if you would like a son-in-law."

I should have thought of that. I had to stop thinking of Melanie as a youngster.

"Anybody in mind, Mel?" I asked.

She laughed, "Not at the moment, Dad. But as a semi-mature adult, I reserve the right to make my own decisions."

"Of course. Of course." I hastened to assure her. "In matters of the heart, you are probably more mature than I am. But don't spring any surprises on me, okay?"

"Relax, Pops. It won't happen till the fat lady sings."

"Let's change the subject, Mel," I sad. "I'd like to take you out to dinner, while you are still unwed."

"That would be nice, but do let me know what you decide to do about Joanne."

"As I've promised many times before, you'll be the first to know."

She chuckled. "I hope Joanne will be the first to know!"

"We'll see," I replied.

I was still on the horns of a dilemma. Or, somewhere between a rock and a hard place. Bitched, buggered and bewildered.

That night, as I tossed and turned, unable to sleep, my overactive mind in a turmoil about Joanne, for some inexplicable reason, my subconscious took over and changed the direction of my thoughts. I had an unsettled feeling about Gary Golding's hasty departure from Naples and his long stay in Las Vegas. He was acting almost like a fugitive. I had a hunch there was more to his actions than about paying his wife a lesson. I made a mental note to check out my hunch.

23

After a lot of soul-searching and very little sleep, I decided to write Joanne a note. I did not want to call her, in case that rotten sod Weatherby might be there, when he should be solving crimes on behalf of the good people of Naples.

December 28, 2005

Dear Joanne:
Thanks for your note. Sorry about the ring. It is safely stored in the refrigerator, right next to the eggs.
I would very much like to have a discussion.
When you have resolved your relationship with Mister Weatherby, please let me know, and I'll be on your doorstep with flying colors.
All my love,
Maury

After mailing the note to Joanne's home address, I Taurus-ed over to Port Royal for my 10 A.M. coffee meeting with Cynthia Golding.

She answered the door herself, explaining that she had given the Jamaican maid, the day off. This time, she said she had made espresso, and it sounded good to me.

Cynthia was back in a more relaxed mood, now that I had assured her she was not a widow again. Husband Gary still had not returned home. But that did not seem to worry her.

She wore a very revealing yellow sun dress, complementing her long, tanned legs and slim body. No bra. Her nipples were clearly defined. Once again, I felt the primal urge of incipient tumescence, which seemed to happen whenever I was in her presence. She made matters worse by taking my hand in hers, leading me to the back lanai, where she served espresso in little cups, while chattering away like a magpie.

When she had inserted a cigarette in her mother-of-pearl holder and blown a couple of smoke rings, she was ready for some serious talk.

"Now, tell me all about your trip to Las Vegas, Maury," she said.

"There is not a whole lot to tell, Cynthia," I explained. "After discovering your husband's car at the Fort Myers airport, I knew he had taken a flight somewhere, but I still did not know where. Then, courtesy of Gary's computer, I was able to trace his flight to Las Vegas and his accommodation booking."

"I see. And which hotel was it that Gary decided to patronize to get away from me for the past three weeks.

"It was not a hotel or casino in the usual sense, but rather a private club for high-rollers – gamblers who like to bet for really big stakes."

"That's Gary all right," she said with a note of disapproval. "So you found him. Then what?"

"It was very simple." I said. "I went to his club, appropriately named The Hideaway Club, and asked to see him. He came out, holding my business card and demanded to know what was going on."

She nodded.

"I said you had hired me to find him, so that you could stop worrying about his prolonged absence. He indicated that he didn't care if you wanted to waste your money on a private dick. Since his demeanor was, to put it bluntly, nasty, I could see no purpose in trying to prolong the discussion. I went back to the hotel, caught a morning flight and here I am."

She reached over and patted my hand. "Poor Maury! You had to be exposed to his lousy temper on my account. I'm sorry."

I laughed. "Don't give it a thought, Cynthia. I developed a thick skin a long time ago. In the police and private eye business one meets all kinds of characters. It gave me some satisfaction to tell him he was being obnoxious."

She laughed too. "Good for you. He needs more people to stand up to him when he starts acting over-bearing. Anyway, so much for my long, lost husband. He will probably return home in his own good time. Meanwhile, I am going to stop worrying about him."

It seemed like a good time to change the subject. "Cynthia, I have a request. Despite being flung about in a small dinghy for several hours the other night, I am still a boating enthusiast. Would it be possible for me to have a look inside your husband's lovely fifty foot Hatteras that's docked at the back of your property? I'll never be able to afford such a yacht, but I would love to see inside one."

"Why, certainly Maury," she replied. "I wish I had known of your interest before. I could have asked Henry Johnson to give you a tour. I know very little about the monster, and seldom go out in it. But Henry and his son are part time Captain and First Mate, respectively. They look after maintaining the yacht and running her. Gary leaves everything to them."

"Well, I don't want to trouble them, Cynthia, or you for that matter. If it's all right, I can see myself aboard for a quick look around, just to satisfy my curiosity."

"Sure. Not a problem, Maury, she assured me. "Wait just a minute, and I'll get the keys. You don't want to start the engines do you?"

"Heck, no. My knowledge of engines does not go beyond 150 horsepower outboards. I imagine this one has twin diesels, or some such power."

She chuckled lasciviously. "Gary is always talking about the twin screws. Rather impolite, don't you think?"

I wasn't going to touch that one. So, she got up and went to get the keys.

"Are you coming along, Cynthia?" I asked, when she returned.

"No thanks, Maury," she replied. "I've seen enough of the big beast. You go ahead, while I clean up in the kitchen."

"Okay, thanks Cynthia. I won't be long. What is she named?"

She smiled. "*Cynthia,* of course. At least, that's her current registered name."

As I was going out the back door in the wall surrounding the pool, I thought how many people would love to have even a short cruise in such a yacht. 'Monster' and 'beast' indeed!.

From the high dock, I was able to jump aboard and un-zip the stern curtain accessing the large rear cockpit. The actual helm and control station was at the forward end of the cockpit on a raised platform, reached by a short set of steps. There was also a high, flying bridge with dual controls accessible by ladder, but I did not bother climbing up. What I was looking for was no doubt in the lower bridge section. But first, I used a key to open the main stateroom and stick my nose inside. Paneling and hand rails were beautifully finished in polished mahogany. Red leather seats, surrounding the perimeter of the large cabin, were built in. I did not enter, but stepped back to examine the area next to the chrome wheel in the lower bridge. There was a hinged door next to the helm which was locked. I found a key that opened a roomy compartment.

It contained an assortment of charts and various navigational items, and what I was looking for – the yacht's Log Book!

Eagerly, I searched through the pages of the log, and came across an interesting entry in September. The Captain's handwriting was quite clear and concise.

Monday, September 5th, 2005

First mate Trevor Johnson topped up both fuel tanks at Naples Marina- 36 gallons. Returned to pick up Mister Golding and his friend at 10 P.M. for evening cruise in the Gulf. Arrived back at Port Royal dock at 12:16 A.M. Sept. 6th. Engine clock shows 2:16 hours for this cruise.

Henry Johnson, Capt.

I wondered who the mysterious 'friend' might have been, and why he or she had not been named.

When I returned to the pool area, through the back door, Cynthia was relaxing on a chaise lounge, after completing her household chores. She wore a slinky abbreviated one-piece, white bathing outfit, which contrasted with her tanned skin.

"Well, what did you think of the yacht *Cynthia*, Maury?" she asked as I handed her the keys.

"She's a beauty," I replied with enthusiasm.

"Did you see all you wanted to?" she said with a broad smile.

"Yes, thank you, all except the engine room," I replied. "Perhaps, sometime when Captain Johnson is here, he can show me the diesels."

"Of course, he'd be glad to, Maury. But right now, I'm going to take a dip in the pool. Care to join me?"

"I'd love to, Cynthia," I lied. "But I must get back to the office. Having been away for a couple of days, I can't spare the time. Some important things have been neglected."

She pouted. "Am I not important, Maury? Come on, be a sport. I let you see the yacht, so you owe me one. We have lots of swimming trunks. And there is a changing room right over there," she said, pointing to a small separate building beside the pool.

I could see she was determined, so I gave in gracefully.

"Okay, Cynthia," I said. "But it must be a quickie."

I wished I hadn't said that, because she burst out laughing again.

I found a pair of swimming trunks hanging up in the changing room and returned to the pool. I almost tripped over a skimpy, white swim suit that she had abandoned on the patio floor. Obviously, she had abandoned it to swim in the nude. I looked around nervously, but the high privacy wall guaranteed that any Peeping Tom would have to be very athletic or airborne.

Don't get me wrong. I like swimming in the buff. As kids, we used to take off our swim suits once we were far enough out in the Gulf that nobody could see us. There is nothing to compare to the smooth feeling of gliding through salty water on all of one's skin, unhindered by trunks. But I was not a kid anymore. I was afraid that my lower appendage would misbehave in an embarrassing way, in the close proximity of a nude, female swimmer.

Heck, even a dumb old ex-cop like me is smart enough to know that this particular female, swimming in her birthday suit, and devoid of the tender ministrations of her husband for at least three weeks, might very well be planning to seduce me. Perhaps it was more than a coincidence that she had given the maid the day off.

Such thoughts were racing through my mind, as I stepped out of my recently donned swimming trunks and tossed them down beside the skimpy outfit of my hostess. She was smiling and treading water at the deep end, when I plunged into the pool. As a native Floridian, I am an excellent swimmer, if I do say so myself. I did the Australian crawl for a few laps, being particularly careful to avoid contact with the other nude swimmer. Then I returned to the steps at the shallow end of the pool and sat down on one of the lower steps with my lower extremities still under water.

Smiling seductively, Cynthia slid up, like a mermaid, with her bare breasts resting on my chest, so that my little friend, now a big one, was receiving a free massage. I dare anyone to control their basic urge in those circumstances. Even though Cynthia was about fifteen years older than me, she was still a very attractive woman. It was time to come up with some reason why I should not give her what she obviously wanted. If Joanne Carter had not started two-timing me with my worst enemy, or if Gary Golding had been a nicer guy, I might not have screwed his wife. But I did. Not an earth-shaking event. It was a simple roll on a beach towel by two consenting adults.

Afterwards, however, I did explain that I thought such liaisons were not in the best interests of an uncomplicated detective-client relationship, and should not be repeated.

Like a small child whose favorite candy had been taken away from her, she whimpered at the loss, but reluctantly agreed.

As I was leaving, Cynthia handed me a sheaf of One Hundred Dollar Amex Traveler's Checks, all signed and counter-signed, but with the payee left blank.

"You can make them out to yourself, if you wish, Maury," she pointed out. "Some or all."

"Not on your life, my dear," I said. "would I cheat on my partner."

I took out a pen and entered 'Short & Smith' on all the checks.

"There," I said, "now I don't feel like a gigolo."

She smiled, "Come again real soon, Tiger."

Absolutely incorrigible! Some women are never satisfied.

24

On returning to the office after my coffee and 'extras' meeting with Cynthia, I kept wondering about Gary Golding's unnamed 'friend' as entered in the Ship's Log. It seemed the best way to get more information would be through Henry Johnson, or his son Trevor.

I knew Johnson was a common name, but I did not realize how common until I looked in the Naples Phone Directory. The listing showed something like 683 Johnson(s), of whom there were five Henrys. So, I looked for any Trevors and found there were none. There were a few T. Johnson(s) listed, so I simply called them all, asking for Trevor. Finally, a lady answered, without telling me I had the wrong number. She said Trevor was at work, and was expected home at 5:30 p.m. I left my home phone number and asked that he call Mister Smith.

When I got home, I told Melanie of my ongoing investigation of 'the floater' affair, and told her I was expecting a return call, in case she answered the phone. Naturally, I did not mention my morning fling with Cynthia. Why give my daughter an excuse to do likewise? I felt guilty about betraying Joanne, but also justified by her apparent refusal to give up Weatherby.

"Have you done anything yet about Joanne?" she asked. I wondered if she was psychic.

"Yes, I wrote her a note and mailed it to her home address," I replied.

"Did you agree to a discussion, as she suggested?"

My kid, giving me the third degree.

"Yes," I answered. "Conditionally."

"Conditionally? What does that mean, Dad? What was the condition?"

"On condition that she get rid of her new boy friend," I said.

"Hmm, that should make her jump for joy," she said sarcastically.

"Well, I'm not going to compromise on that issue, Mel, and now she knows it."

At that point, the phone rang. I pointed at myself, indicating I would answer it. "Mister Smith? This is Trevor Johnson. You called?"

"Yes, Mister Johnson; thanks for calling back. I was looking over the Golding yacht, the *Cynthia,* with Mrs. Golding's permission, of course, and I wanted some information on the engines. Could you help me, if I dropped around in a few minutes?"

He hesitated. "Have you talked to my father?" he enquired.

"No, I could not reach him," I said.

"Well, okay. I'm sort of the engineer for the yacht," he said. When would you like to come over?"

"You live on Golden Gate Parkway, right? I could come over immediately. Should be there within fifteen minutes."

"Fine," he said, "but don't be late, because my wife is preparing our evening meal."

As I hurried out, I told Melanie I would be back soon, short circuiting the grilling she was giving me about Joanne. It occurred to me that Mel would make a damned good lawyer.

On arrival at Trevor Johnson's address, I parked in front of his ranch style bungalow and dodged a small curly-headed boy hurtling down the sidewalk on his two-wheeler. The boy's father opened the front door and yelled at the boy: "Time to come in Johnny. It will soon be dark."

The youngster said, "Aw, gee." turned his bike on its side on the coarse, Bermuda-grassed front lawn and ran inside. I followed him to the front door. His father held the door open for me.

"Mister Smith, hi," he said. "I'm Trevor Johnson. Come on in," he said, as he led me in to the living room and indicated I should sit in a wicker chair. "Would you like a beer?"

"Thanks, but no thanks," I replied. "I'll make it a quick visit. You mentioned it's close to your dinner hour. Call me Maury, please."

Trevor Johnson was a working class type, stocky build, freckled arms and face, with curly red hair, about thirty years of age. He looked at my business card. "Yeah, Mrs.Golding said you were a private eye, an ex-police detective. I phoned her right after I spoke with you."

"Wise move," I said. "Anybody can cook up a story, to get in the front door."

"She said you visited the Hatteras this morning, but didn't go into the engine room."

"That's correct, Mister Johnson..er Trevor. Did she give you permission to speak with me about the *Cynthia*?"

"Yep. She said to give you any information you asked for about the yacht."

"Good. What I want to know, Trevor, if I may use your first name, is not about the engines," I confessed, "it's about an evening cruise which was taken on September 5th. Do you remember that particular cruise?"

He got red in the face and frowned. "Of course I re-member. But I am only cleared to answer questions about the diesels, not about any cruises. If you want that kind of infor-mation, you will have to ask Mister Golding."

"Who is not available. Would you rather talk to the police, Trevor?"

"What do you mean?" he asked nervously.

"Did you know that being an accessory to a crime makes you a criminal, too?"

By now, his face was flushed, matching his red hair. "I don't know what you are implying, Mister Smith. I have nothing to hide. If you are going to keep making threats, you can leave right now."

"Fine with me, Trevor," I said, getting up to leave. "Better get your dinner. There will be a Sheriff's squad car here to pick you up within a few minutes. I have reason to believe that something unlawful happened on that evening cruise. As a former officer of the law, I am obliged to take the matter to the police. If my suspicions turn out to be factual and you refuse to co-operate, you could be charged with obstruc-tion of justice, as well as an accessory to the crime."

His face drained of its former crimson blush, as he considered the implications of my warning. The possibility of a few years in prison is a powerful persuader.

I reached the door before he relented. "Okay, I'll tell you what happened," he blurted out. "But I want you to protect your source of the information."

I shook my head. "Sorry. Can't do that. You may be called upon to testify later on, if the case goes to court."

"Look, I haven't done a damn thing," he said. "And I don't want to lose a lucrative part-time job on the yacht."

"Is that what Gary Golding threatened you with, losing your job? Or was there monetary inducement as well?"

He did not look at me. His eyes were focused on the floor. "Some of both. But my dad would kill me if I said anything more."

I smiled, trying to be the friendly cop. Or, rather ex-cop. "Let's do it this way, Trevor to keep you off the hook. I'll describe what I think happened the night of the cruise. You can simply nod your head if I am right."

He nodded in agreement, his eyes not meeting mine.

"When the *Cynthia* was well offshore, Gary Golding and his guest had an argument about money owed and not paid," I suggested. "The argument became violent. Mister Golding pushed his guest, an elderly man in his sixties with shortish gray hair. The man lost his balance and toppled over the railing. It was a dark night, and by the time the yacht could be turned around, the guest could not be found. Golding ordered you and your father to remain silent about the unfortunate incident. Then the *Cynthia* returned to dock behind the Golding mansion in Port Royal."

He was nodding. "That's approximately right. They had both had a lot to drink in the early part of the cruise. I did not actually see what happened. I was in the main cabin when I heard Mister Golding yell 'Man Overboard'. Then we searched for a while, but could not find the man. We had been doing thirty knots, and that big cruiser does not stop on a dime. Mister Golding was, of course, very upset. When we returned to his dock, he asked us to wait. He went inside and came back with a check for each of us, my Dad and me, for One Thousand Dollars each. Do we have to give it back?"

I shook my head. "I don't think so, Trevor. But you and your father should have gone to the police. Do you know the guest's name – the man who fell overboard?"

"No, I don't. And I doubt if my Dad does. We are just part time employees, and are not usually involved too much with his guests. Also, it was dark when they came aboard, and they went right to the main salon, where the bar is located."

"All right, Trevor," I said. "You have been co-operating with me. So, here is what I want you to do. Go to the Collier County Sheriff's office and ask for Deputy Fred Baker of the Marine Patrol. Tell him what you just told me. He will then ask you to sign a written statement. He will want to interview your father, too. So you should phone your dad tonight, to prepare him for the arrival of the police. If Deputy Baker is not available, it might be because he is on shore patrol. Just ask the receptionist to make an appointment for you."

He was thoroughly subdued by now. "Okay, Maury. Anything else?"

"Don't say a word to Mr. or Mrs. Golding about this conversation with me. And, don't tell Deputy Baker you spoke to me first. The same with your dad. You can make a joint statement. I want the statement to be your voluntary confession, and not because I had warned you of the consequences if you didn't speak up. It may seem like you are breaking your word with Mister Golding, but he is already in trouble with the law, by attempting a cover-up. You don't want to take the fall with him do you?"

"No sir, I sure don't," he said.

"Good. Do it tomorrow. The longer you keep your silence, the deeper you and your dad will be in with the law," I said. "I will be talking casually with Deputy Baker to make sure you have gone to him about the matter. If you don't speak up, I will have to. Okay?"

"Sure, Maury. I understand. I will phone my father right away. And, thanks for helping us."

We made final eye contact. "Just remember. Not a word to the Goldings, *ever!*"

"You have my word," he promised.

Yeah, and Gary Golding had his word, too. I left him with no great feeling of assurance that he would do the right thing.

25

Having set the fox among the chickens in my meeting with Trevor Johnson last evening, I was anxious to know whether he and his father would actually contact Deputy Baker as Trevor had promised.

Finally I was fairly sure how 'the floater' had turned up near my boat, when Pooch had alerted me to the floating body. One person who could clear up the mystery of the man's identity was Gary Golding. But it was not up to me to question him, or accuse him of his foul deed and attempted cover-up.

If Trevor and his father, Henry, followed through with Trevor's promise to go to the Sheriff's office with their story, even at this late date, they would probably be cleared because of their co-operation with the law. Then the whole focus of the investigation would be on Gary Golding. A warrant would be issued for his arrest and he would be brought back to Naples under armed guard. From my perspective, it couldn't happen to a nicer guy!

Although I felt slightly guilty about my manipulative role in the affair, because it would probably impact on Cynthia's marriage, it appeared that she and her husband were close to a break-up anyway. *Que sera, sera.* What will be, will be.

Meanwhile, I brought Dan up top speed on the whole unseemly affair. He said 'tsk' tsk' when I told him my frolic by the pool with Cynthia. However, the sheaf of traveler's checks to be credited to her account seemed to take his mind of the scolding I had so obviously earned.

After all the weeks that had passed since the body of 'the floater' was discovered, surely he would be listed as a Missing Person. So it would be a simple matter to re-open the investigation by searching the Missing Persons database, readily available to any law enforcement agency. On the other hand, if he lived alone, he might not have been missed by anyone, except perhaps the paper delivery boy, who may have cut him off when the newspapers started to accumulate. Or the U.S. Post delivery service, who might, in any case, not be concerned if he lived in an apartment. He could have asked the superintendent to empty his post-box and keep his mail until he returned.

Because of all those possibilities, it occurred to me there is one sure way that a law enforcement agency such as the Collier County Sheriff's office could identify the body, if the ISP (Internet Service Provider), in this case, America Online (AOL), would co-operate. LesMil1940, the person to whom Gary Golding had sent an e-mail message on September 4th, stating that he would be met at the airport on the 5th, must be listed by his name and address with AOL's records.

Since I was the only person, other than Gary Golding, who knew of the e-mail message, I decided to advise Deputy Fred Baker of my strong suspicion that the owner of the e-mail address LesMil1940 was, in fact, the unidentified drowning victim.

However, I wanted to give Trevor and Henry Johnson every opportunity to contact the Sheriff's office voluntarily before I did. So, I waited until mid-afternoon, before I phoned Baker.

When I called his office, I was put right through.

"It's Maury Smith, Fred," I said, trying to sound casual.

"Hi Maury, what's new?"

"I was wondering if *you* had anything new, on the identity of that drowning victim whose body was picked up last September."

"No, Maury. It has been put on the back burner, considered as an unsolved case. If you have any information that would help, we would certainly like to have it."

"Yes, I have an idea that might help. But first, have you been in the office all day?"

"Actually, I have been catching up on some paperwork. But why do you ask?"

"I sent some people to contact you this morning. Would you check with your receptionist and enquire if there are any messages for you?"

"Okay. Hold on."

A couple of minutes passed. Baker came back on the phone.

"Nobody has been in to see me, and no outside phone calls, other than yours. What's going on, Maury?"

"I have some information that might help identify the drowning victim, Fred. But I would rather not explain how I obtained it. Just consider it comes from a private informant."

There was a short silence on the line. He was beginning to sound annoyed. "Okay, Maury. But let's not play games. If you have information, spit it out."

"Sorry, Fred. The whole situation is complicated by the fact that I have *no proof* of anything at this time. I have worked out a scenario that *might have* happened. I am still checking on my facts and need a little more time. Meanwhile, if my suspicions are correct, the man's identity might be traced through his e-mail address, provided his Internet Service Provider will co-operate with your office. In the past, I believe ISP's have been reluctant to divulge the names of their subscribers. But, perhaps if you obtained a warrant..."

Baker interrupted. "Let me get this straight, Maury," the deputy said. "Are you suggesting we obtain a warrant to obtain the name of a person from their internet service, based only on your *suspicion* of a certain scenario – an event, or something that *might* have happened, but of which you are not sure?"

"I know it sounds kind of weak," I said. "But if I can get some proof of my hunch, will you at least try to follow through with the man's ISP?"

"Sure. But we'll need more than a hunch. What is the name of the ISP?"

"America Online. AOL."

"That's a big, sophisticated outfit, Maury," he said. "Before we ask for their help in identifying one of their subscribers, we had better be sure of our facts. I suggest you take that extra time you say you need, and then get back to me. Going off half-cocked could get both of us in trouble. Right?"

"Right," I agreed. His logic was unassailable! "Leave it with me, Fred. I will get back to you as soon as I have my facts straight and confirmed."

So much for my effort to be a helpful citizen and private eye. Or, semi-helpful, anyway. If I had been completely honest, I would have continued the conversation. I would have told the deputy about my talk with Trevor Johnson and his broken promise to me that he and his father would contact him and explain their part in the September 5th evening cruise of the yacht *Cynthia.*

I wondered if Trevor had talked to his dad, and, if it were a joint decision to ignore my warning of the consequences. In any event, their window of opportunity to make a voluntary disclosure was now closed.

Trevor had, more or less, confirmed my version of what had occurred when the passenger on their evening cruise went overboard. Crime, or accident, there was a drowning, and the attempted cover-up should not be allowed to continue. I went next door, to Dan Short's office, to bring him up to date on my discussion with Deputy Baker and get his opinion on how I should proceed.

But Josie informed me that Dan had to leave for the day on a surveillance job for one of his clients.

I had decided to phone Fred Baker again and tell him the whole story, when a call came through from Cynthia. She seemed to be agitated about something.

"Maury, it's Cynthia," she said. "I really must see you right away. It's something about Gary. Can you come over? I don't want to discuss it on the phone."

"All right, Cynthia," I replied. "I should be there in ten or fifteen minutes."

I had no idea what might have come up involving Gary Golding. As far as I knew, he was still in Vegas being a high-roller. What now? I wondered if he had returned. If so, it would simplify having him arrested for the attempted cover-up. I told Josie I was leaving and would not be back until tomorrow. I would have to phone Deputy Baker in the morning.

Cynthia met me at the front door, as soon as I drove in. I noticed that the gray Lincoln Town Car was not parked in the driveway, although it could be in one of the three-car garages attached to the Golding mansion. It was unusual for Cynthia to answer the door herself. Perhaps she had given Marjie, the Jamaican maid, another day off.

"Come on in Maury," Cynthia said in rather a sullen, strained voice. "I have a surprise for you." She waved me ahead, as she followed and secured the bolt lock with a key. I entered the living room ahead of her.

The 'surprise' was Gary Golding standing in front of a large Picasso painting with a revolver aimed at my head.

"Sit down in the armchair, Smith," Golding ordered. It seems you have been sticking your nose into affairs that are none of your business."

I sat down, watching him closely.

"Maury, he made me phone you..." Cynthia started to say.

"Shut up, Cynthia," her husband snapped. "And, don't leave this room until I say you can."

She turned away, teary-eyed. A bruise on her cheek was turning from red to a darker hue. It looked like Gary had been using strong-arm tactics on his wife.

"Now, it seems I will have to close the eyes of the private eye permanently," Golding said. "I hear you are interested in the power plants of my yacht. So, you will have the opportunity to hear them working, until you can hear no more."

I made no attempt to reply to his threats. Long ago, I had learned one should not argue with a man holding a gun. I simply stared at him, while trying to figure out some way to thwart his plans to shorten my life-span.

I had already figured that Trevor Johnson and his father had decided to take their problem to Gary Golding, rather than to the Sheriff's office as I had advised.

I, too, had a gun – a small Beretta that I had been carrying in a right ankle holster ever since the Clarke/Jones affair. My problem was that by the time I reached for it, I could be dead. So, I sat very still and did not make a move.

Gary Golding had acquired a pair of police handcuffs. "Trevor," he said, "come in here."

Trevor Johnson entered the room and looked at me with a slightly embarrassed expression. He was wearing his nautical uniform with the name *Cynthia* embroidered on his blue jacket. Just like the crew on the Jones yacht. Not very original, but money does not always buy originality.

"Put these cuffs on him, Trevor," Golding ordered, tossing the cuffs to his First Mate.

Trevor, staying low, out of the line of fire, reached up and snapped the handcuffs on my wrists.

Breaking my self-imposed silence, I said to young Johnson, "You are making a big mistake, Trevor. By helping Golding, you are as much a murderer as he is."

"Be quiet, Smith," Golding said. "You are in no position to give advice. Thanks, Trevor. Now stand by outside until I call you."

"Aye, aye, sir," Trevor replied, in the best nautical tradition, earning at least a tot of rum.

While her husband was making preparations to carry out his threat to whack me, Cynthia was sitting in a corner of the room, quietly sobbing. Why do women always resort to tears when all else fails? Probably because it was their best weapon. Anyway, I was pleased to see that she was not part of her husband's scheme.

"Now, Cynthia," Gary said, "make your self useful. Get out to the kitchen and make up some sandwiches and a thermos of coffee. We may want a snack when we are out in the Gulf."

"Aye, aye, sir," she said sarcastically, as she headed for the kitchen.

From the kitchen, Cynthia's voice could be heard, "Trevor get the fuck out of my kitchen."

"Yes, ma'am," he replied, retreating out of her sight, towards the back of the house.

Gary Golding and I were left alone in the living room. It seemed my best chance.

"Are you sure that cannon is loaded?" I asked, taunting my would-be executioner.

For the smallest fraction of a second, he took his eye off me. I reached down and pulled out the Beretta in a two-handed motion, hindered to some extent by the handcuffs on my wrists. Gripping the handle in my right hand, I fired at Golding, strictly by instinct. There was no time to aim. The single shot put a neat hole in a very expensive Picasso painting on the wall behind him. On its short journey, the bullet grazed his left ear. Blood started gushing from the ear wound, distracting him enough that I got off another shot, this time more accurately. The 9 m.m. bullet hit his hand, and he dropped the revolver on the thick Persian rug.

Hearing the shots, Trevor rushed from the back of the house. He saw his meal-ticket holding his bleeding fingers, with blood gushing from his ear.

"Holy shit," Trevor exclaimed, kicking the small gun out of my grasp. Before I could get out of the armchair, he picked up the revolver Golding had been holding, and put the muzzle in my face.

Knowing when to quit, I just relaxed to await developments. Cynthia appeared at the door, behind Trevor. Taking in the situation, which was no longer in my favor, she closed the door quickly. I hoped she remembered the numbers 9-1-1.

"Get the engines started," Gary Golding ordered. "We'll use the first aid kit on board the yacht. No time to waste. Cynthia, are you coming with us?"

"What about the sandwiches and coffee?" she asked.

"There is not time for that now," her husband said, as he held some Kleenex tissues over his injured fingers and bleeding ear. "The neighbors might have heard those shots. Come on. Move it."

She obeyed. I followed. Trevor hid the revolver in his pocket, nudging me from behind, as we all filed out the gate at the back of the pool, to the yacht.

Captain Henry Johnson already had the powerful diesels warming up. His son removed the docking lines and the big Hatteras was underway in about one minute. Once the yacht started moving out of the canal behind the Golding mansion, Trevor brought out the first aid kit, and began administering to Golding's wounds. Although not life-threatening, ear wounds tend to bleed a lot. He managed to staunch the flow by applying a large field bandage that covered the whole left ear. The fingers were less of a problem, as they were only skinned. He applied small plastic bandages to the individual fingers, while his employer cursed me and all my ancestors.

Under goading from Golding, Henry Johnson illegally goosed the fifty-footer up to about twenty knots in the narrow waters of Gordon Pass. Giant waves from the wake crashed against the rock-lined walls of the breakwaters on both sides of the pass.

The big yacht ran through the line of red and green channel markers and was soon out in the open Gulf. I assumed my intended fate was to be that of the hapless floater. And that my corpse, in due course, would become bloated just like Golding's so-called friend, known only as LesMil1940.

In the main salon, seated side-by-side on the red leather bench seats, Cynthia and I were being held at gunpoint by Trevor Johnson, while a much bandaged Gary Golding scowled at the two of us.

"You won't win any marksmanship medals with that kind of shooting, Smith," he sneered. "And you won't have another chance before you visit Davey Jones' locker."

"Don't kid yourself," I replied. "If I had been less humane, I could have put that second shot right between your eyebrows. If you are such a gambling man, I would welcome a duel on the poop-deck, with the winner getting to live."

He laughed grimly at my challenge. "What a dreamer you are. I play the odds, when I gamble. But you don't have any odds. You are going to die by drowning. In your birthday suit. It will be weeks before anybody discovers your bloated corpse."

With that happy thought echoing in my ears, he left us and went out to talk to Captain Johnson.

I nudged Cynthia. "Any luck with the phone," I asked hopefully.

She whispered back, "Got 911, and left the phone off the hook."

Good girl, I thought. There was still a chance. It was very dark, with the moon hiding behind heavy clouds. The *Cynthia* was running at high speed, with her navigational lights off. The breeze was still offshore, causing two foot waves, hardly noticeable in the fifty-footer. I figured the cool salt water might be swimable, but not for ten miles or so, and not in handcuffs.

Listening to the roar of the twin diesels, I was trying to estimate the speed the yacht was making and the distance, by dead reckoning. I didn't like the 'dead' word, though. After about a half hour, the engines slowed down.

Golding came back into the salon. "Time for your dip, Smith," he announced. "I want you to strip down to naked skin. And, hurry it up, or Trevor will start shooting."

"Well, I don't want to start bleeding all over your lovely cabin, Golding," I said sarcastically. So, I guess I have no option. But with these handcuffs on, removal of clothing will be impossible."

"Good point, Smith," he admitted, handing the key to Trevor, "Uncuff him. But don't hesitate to shoot him, if he makes a false move."

Freed from the handcuffs, I began pulling off my clothes, while thinking how cold the Gulf water would feel after a few minutes. Probably my death would be by hypothermia, rather than just by drowning.

I was not worried about Cynthia seeing my bare body. Unknown to her husband, she had seen it before – and reveled in the pleasure it provided. The irony appealed to my warped sense of humor.

With the First Mate prodding my bare flesh, I was marched out on deck at gunpoint. I looked at the four foot railing surrounding the stern deck. There was not even a plank to be walked in the old pirate tradition. Just the cold, gray waters of the Gulf of Mexico beckoning me to a watery grave.

26

As I neared the gunwale, with Trevor right behind me, nudging my back with the muzzle of the revolver, I heard Cynthia scream. She ran at her husband, no doubt intending to pummel him into saving my life. He laughed and simply held her off with his good hand.

At the guard rail, I spoke to Trevor over my shoulder. "Stand back and give me a chance to jump over the rail, for chrissake!"

Obligingly, he removed the gun from my bare backbone. I took a step back at the same time, still facing the railing. Then I turned quickly, grabbed the wrist of his gun hand and twisted it with all the adrenaline my body could summon. The revolver clattered to the deck. Without releasing my grip, I pulled his right arm over my shoulder and bent forward, heaving him over the railing, into the Gulf.

Fortunately for Trevor, the yacht was no longer under way. Gary Golding was too stunned by the sudden turn of events to move. I ran to him and grabbed him by the scruff of the neck and seat of his pants, quick marching him to the rail and over into the dark water below, to join his First Mate. While the two of them floundered in the salty surf, I spotted a round life-preserver and threw it down beside them. Then, I picked up the revolver off the deck, and suddenly realized I had no place to put it. So, I held on to it. Meanwhile, Cynthia had grabbed another life-preserver and threw it over the side to her struggling husband. Still nude and shivering, I looked over the railing at the two men clinging to the round, white life-preservers. And waving for help.

During the turnaround on the stern deck, Captain Henry Johnson had not left his post at the bridge. He had stood, watching all the action without making any move to enter the fray. Rambo-like, I approached him, looking for a good fight. I was not just angry, I was seething.

"If you ever want to see your son and the mother-fuckin' owner of this yacht again, I suggest you get a move on and rescue them, because I am in no mood to save their lives."

"Aye, sir. Sorry about all this."

"No damned apologies," I said. "Now get moving, or it will be too late."

He stepped away from the helm smartly and saluted, "Yes, *sir.*"

Still angry and breathing heavily, I returned to the main cabin and started dressing. Cynthia came in and started to apologize. "God, I'm sorry, Maury," she said. He made me call you. He was hitting me and I was frightened."

"Sure you were, Cynthia, and you almost got me killed. Go and help the captain. I've had enough of the Goldings for one evening."

"Oh, Maury, don't be mad at me," she said, pleading for understanding. "I didn't know he was going to try to murder you."

"I'm sure you didn't have a clue," I said sarcastically. "Anyway, it's over. I hope the swimmers have been rescued by now."

A few minutes later, Henry Johnson herded in to the salon two dripping and bedraggled, fully-clothed, reluctant swimmers. They were thoroughly subdued and said nothing.

I told them all to sit on the bench seats. Too hell with ruining the red leather! "Now all of you listen up carefully," I said, holding the revolver at my side. "You are all under citizen's arrest. If anyone wants to challenge my authority, I am spoiling for a fight. Captain Johnson, you will take us back to port. Your son and Gary Golding will be locked in this cabin to dry out. Cynthia Golding, my ex-client, is free to wander around and look overwhelmed, as usual. I will be using your ship-to-shore radio to alert the police, who will be eagerly awaiting our return. So, let's get this expensive bucket of bolts moving, Captain."

Compared to the outward part of the cruise, the inward leg was uneventful. Cynthia sensed that I was still trying to get my temper under control, and she made no further attempt at pleading her innocence. In fairness, she had tried to dissuade her husband from making me food for fish. But, characteristically, her efforts were too feeble and too late. I thought she might have made a little more effort to warn me, before Gary got the drop on me in the living room. While I could not blame her for her husband's murderous instincts, I doubt if I could ever trust her again.

Once the yacht was underway again, I used the marine radio to invite a deputation from the Sheriff's office to meet us on our arrival. I explained I had made a citizen's arrest of three individuals, whom I was prepared to charge with attempted murder by drowning.

By the time the fifty-foot Hatteras had docked behind the Golding mansion, my adrenaline level was back to normal and my usual even temperament (?) had returned. At the front of the house, there seemed to be flashing lights galore, with the local police out in full force. Apparently my radio message had started a turf war between the County Sheriff's people and the Naples Police, both of whom responded to my call for assistance. Two officers from each department were waiting to greet us, while the yacht's captain himself tied the docking and spring lines to the cleats.

It made little difference to me which police force officially took custody of the culprits. The attempts at murder had taken place in both jurisdictions – the City and the County. The fact that my nemesis, Lieutenant Weatherby, was one of the officers from the City, naturally made me favor the County.

As luck would have it, when I set foot on dry ground, dockside, the Sheriff's Marine Patrol boat arrived in the canal. Deputy Fred Baker jumped out to add strength to the County side of the jurisdictional argument.

Golding and Trevor Johnson were still locked in the main cabin, and I was not about to release them until I told my story to the police, City or County.

I was not too worried about Captain Henry Johnson's guilt or innocence in the attempt on my life, as I figured Trevor had contacted Gary Golding of his own accord. Henry was not innocent of the attempted cover-up of 'the floater' event, but he had played no part in trying to feed me to the fish.

Ignoring Weatherby, who was all smiles of goodwill in congratulating me, I drew Deputy Fred Baker aside and quickly outlined the events of the evening. Weatherby and all the other police officers edged in to hear my story. Of course, Baker was more familiar with the earlier situation as it applied to 'The Unidentified Floater' case. He pointed this out to the other officers.

Weatherby was reluctant to withdraw his jurisdictional claim for Naples Police. He could envision the favorable publicity that would result from the solution to the multiple crimes attributable to such a prominent and wealthy citizen as Gary Golding.

When I had concluded my description of what happened earlier in the evening, as well as the ill-fated September 5th cruise of the *Cynthia,* Weatherby could not keep quiet.

"Maury is only three months retired from the Naples Police," he said proudly, to the assembled crowd of officers. "And it was his training in the Detectives Division that led to his solving these crimes. You County guys should let the Naples Police take over."

With that I burst out laughing, doubled over with exaggerated mirth. I went over to Weatherby and slapped him on the back, hard. He stumbled forward under the impact of the blow. "That's right, John," I said. "I learned everything from you. How to run roughshod over your subordinates. How to take credit for the work of other officers. How to kiss the Captain's ass. How to take advantage of your position of authority to get me to retire prematurely. So, congratulations asshole. It was all valuable training."

Weatherby started to splutter and was barely able to speak coherently.

"You can't speak to a police lieutenant like that. I'll have you charged with insulting an officer of the law, you insolent son-of-a-bitch. No wonder I wanted to get rid of you." He walked away, continuing to curse me. The Naples Police pulled out of the driveway, having lost the jurisdictional struggle.

I turned to Deputy Fred Baker, smiling. "See, Fred. The jurisdictional problem was easily solved."

He smiled back and the other deputies laughed loudly.

"Look Fred," I said. "It's almost eight o'clock and I have had a tough night. Do you mind if I give you my statement in the morning? Here is the key to the main cabin, where the bad guys are locked up, and here is Gary Golding's revolver. Will you take over from here?"

"No problem, Maury. You've done well. I'll take Golding and the two Johnsons into custody. Get a good night's rest and I'll see you in the morning."

I was about to leave, when Baker said, "One final thing, Maury. Did you find out the identity of 'the floater'?

"No, Fred. And I no longer care. You can get that information from Gary Golding, using thumbscrews if you wish."

27

Melanie had taken Pooch for his morning walk and checked the postbox on returning to the condo. I was still asleep when she gave my bedroom door a double tap.

Bleary-eyed but now awake, I said, "Come in."

"Wake up Dad," she said, as Pooch jumped up on the bed and started licking my face. He knew how to get me going in the morning. There is nothing like a dog's saliva to make a person want to head to the bathroom to wash one's face.

When I came out, Melanie handed me an envelope. "I found this in the mailbox," she said, "and I knew you would not want to waste any more time sleeping."

"The time wasn't wasted, Mel," I said. "After the events of last night, I needed to catch up on my zees.".

"Yes, but I think that's a message from you-know-who that you have been hoping for."

I recognized the writing and could hardly wait to break the seal. Inside was a small piece of paper. The message read as follows:

December 29, 2005

Dear Maury:

You were right
I was wrong
I turfed him out
And now he's gone!

Love, Joanne

With a big smile on my face, I showed the little ditty to Mel.

"I know where she got the idea for that little poem," I said.

"Where, Dad?"

"From a tombstone graveyard at Boot Hill, Tombstone, Arizona. It's kind of famous for its irony. I looked up an album. Here is a picture of it:"

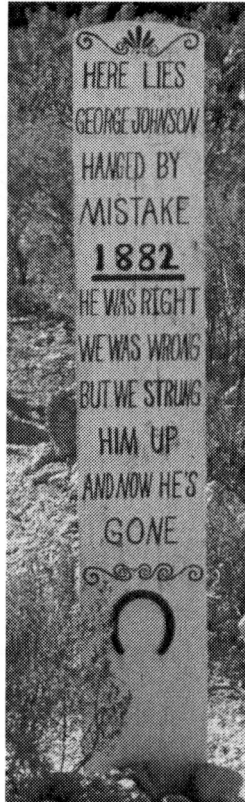

> *HERE LIES*
> *GEORGE JOHNSON*
> *HANGED BY*
> *MISTAKE*
>
> *1882*
>
> *HE WAS RIGHT*
> *WE WAS WRONG*
> *BUT WE STRUNG*
> *HIM UP*
> *AND NOW HE'S*
> ***GONE***

Melanie laughed. "Gee, Pops, how macabre! I hope she didn't string up Mister Weatherby."

"If she did, he deserved it, for using her to get back at me."

I picked up the phone and dialed Joanne's office number. She answered on the first ring. "It's Maury, Joanne. I got your note and loved your poem. When may I see you?"

"How about this evening, Maury? Are you available?" she asked.

"Sure. 7:30, 8:00, you name it?"

"Let's make it 8:00 o'clock, Maury," she replied. "I need some time to recover. Our receptionist quit, without notice. I have been filling in, answering all the calls and trying to put off some clients who are hot to trot. It's not even noon and I am ready to call it a day."

"Sorry about that, Joanne. Are you sure this evening is okay?"

"Yes, Maury. I don't want to put it off. You might change your mind."

"Not a chance, sweetie. I'll bring the Chinese and wine."

"Oh, good. In that case, make it 7:30!"

I phoned Deputy Fred Baker at the Sheriff's office. He said he was waiting for me to arrive to record my statement outlining the events of last evening, resulting in the arrest of Gary Golding and the two Johnsons, father and son.

When I had spent about a half hour explaining what happened from the time of my arrival at the Golding residence until the yacht *Cynthia* was docked again about two hours later, I was told the recording would be transcribed and a copy would be available for me to sign later in the day. Deputy Baker confirmed that Collier County did not have the same high-tech equipment of digital voice translation as the FBI. A typist would have to sit down and convert my voice statement to paper, the old-fashioned way.

I asked Fred Baker what happened after I left the scene of the arrests last evening.

"We brought the perps in for interrogation, Maury, and obtained sworn statements from all three. Gary Golding requested the opportunity to make a voluntary statement, and we gave it to him."

"Did he reveal the name of his guest, the one we have been calling 'the floater'?"

"Since you were responsible for solving the crime and capturing the bad guys, I guess I could let you read his statement. Here it is."

Gary Golding's voluntary statement, or confession, took up two sheets of legal-sized paper, double spaced. I sat down with a cup of potent coffee, supplied by the Sheriff's office and read:

I am Gary Golding, a resident of Naples, Florida, and this is my voluntary confession in connection with the events that occurred in the evening of September 5, 2005 and last night, December 29, 2005.

I first met Lester Mills at a gambling casino in Atlantic City. We had a mutual interest in high stakes games of chance, and became friends. That was in August, and I invited him to join me for a cruise on my Hatteras motor yacht, the Cynthia, for an evening cruise on September 5th. He flew in from New York City, where he lived, and we set out for an evening cruise in the Gulf. My crew consisted of Henry Johnson, an experienced Captain and his son, Trevor, as First Mate and Engineer of the yacht. There was nobody else on the cruise.

Lester Mills, a man in his sixties, a former CEO of a large pharmacutical company, was a pleasant companion, who shared my interest in high stakes gambling. We boarded the yacht at about 7 P.M. and were soon involved in a game of Showdown. It is a very simple card game, but one in which large amounts of money can change hands very quickly, depending on the pace set by the players. In my version of Showdown, each player has a deck of playing cards, which he shuffles and then exchanges decks with his opponent. By agreement, we used blue poker chips, each chip representing One Thousand Dollars. That was the ante for each hand.

First one player would draw a card from his deck and place it, face up, on the table. Then the other player would do the same from his deck. The player with the higher card would win two blue chips – worth two thousand dollars- his own ante and the opponent's one grand. From the outset, I was on a hot winning streak. The more I won, the faster Lester wanted to play, to try and regain his losses. It was not long before he was down $25,000. As we played, we both consumed a lot of booze. Gradually, Lester's pleasant personality turned nasty. I have been told by my wife that I become obnoxious, too, when I become inebriated.

It was not long before Lester accused me of cheating. And he said he would not be responsible for payment of my winnings. That started an argument. I was still sober enough to suggest that we go out on the deck and get some fresh air. I did not want the hired help, in this case Trevor Johnson, to overhear our argument. And, I hoped Lester would reconsider his decision to revoke payment of his legitimate losses.

Out on deck, however, he resumed his accusation that I had cheated in the card game. In the heat of the moment, he shoved me. And I shoved him back. Unfortunately, at the same moment, the yacht rolled in the trough of a large wave. Mills staggered backward, and toppled over the railing, into the Gulf. I immediately yelled 'man overboard' and threw a life preserver over the side, where he had fallen. Captain Johnson, who was at the helm, heard my call of alarm and threw the twin diesels into reverse, to try to stop the yacht's forward progress. But the Hatteras is a big, heavy vessel. We were traveling at about twenty knots, and it took some time to get stopped and turned around to try to rescue Mills.

First Mate Trevor Johnson may not have heard my distress call. But he heard the change in the sound of the engines when they were reversed. He came out on deck when the yacht turned around to retrace its path. We tried for over an hour to find Lester Mills. But it was an impossible task in the darkness and three-foot to four-foot wave action of the Gulf waters.

Finally, we had to give up. I instructed Captain Johnson to return to port. Meanwhile I considered my options. Since I had argued with Lester, and had shoved him, I figured the best chance of avoiding the consequences of my actions was to seek the co-operation of the yacht's crew in a cover-up. When we arrived back at the dock behind my house, I asked them to wait until I returned. When I did, it was with a check for One Thousand Dollars for each of the Johnsons, in exchange for their promises not to reveal what had taken place that night during the cruise. They readily agreed. But, when Mister Maurice Smith snooped around and discovered I had an unnamed guest on board that night, he suspected there was a connection with the unidentified drowning victim.

According to Trevor Johnson, Smith advised him and his father to go to the police. Instead, Trevor phoned me at my club in Las Vegas. I flew home immediately and persuaded my wife, Cynthia, to ask Smith to come over to the house. He did so, and that is when we had our confrontation. I believe he has told you what happened after that.

And that is the true story of what transpired. I will answer any questions, to the best of my ability and knowledge.

Deputy Fredrick Baker identified himself and asked the accused if he had been read his rights at the time of his arrest. The accused confirmed he had, but waived his right to have a lawyer attend the interrogation.

Baker: Mister Golding, you say you persuaded your wife to call Smith and invite him to your home. Did you use physical persuasion?

Golding: Yes. I hit her, when she would not co-operate. Then she agreed to do so.

Baker: When Smith arrived, did you threaten him with a gun?

Golding: Yes. I wanted to shut him up. He had threatened Trevor that he would go to the police if the Johnsons failed to do so.

Baker: Did you instruct Trevor Johnson to handcuff Mister Smith?

Golding: Yes, but he failed to search Smith to see if he had a weapon on his person.

Baker: And, still handcuffed, Smith shot you?"

Golding: Not once, but twice, once in the ear and once in the fingers of my right hand.

Baker: The fingers of the hand that held your gun, right?

Golding: That's correct.

Baker: That was quite an accomplishment, considering the handcuffs. Right?

Golding: I guess so. But I understand he was formerly a police officer. It would have been more impressive, if he had no prior training with weapons.

Baker: Let's stick to the facts. He was able to shoot you, even though you had a revolver trained on him.

Golding: That's right. The son-of-a-bitch distracted me. Then he shot me – twice.

Baker: Good. We now have that straight. Did you then take him, at gunpoint, to your yacht?

Golding: To be accurate, Trevor now had the revolver, and followed my instructions.

Baker: And you planned to silence Mister Smith by drowning him? To maintain your cover-up of the Lester Mills tragedy? Is that right? Yes or no.

Golding: Yes. I had nothing against Smith personally. He was impolite to me when he traced me to Las Vegas. But, I did not consider that sufficient grounds to, you know, do away with him.

Baker: By 'do away' you mean kill him, murder him by drowning? Right?

Golding: Right. I had to shut him up. Or end up in prison for my cover-up of the Lester Mills affair. However, Trevor Johnson was going to do the actual deed.

Baker: But Mister Smith turned the tables on Trevor at the last minute and threw him overboard?

Golding: Yes, and then he did the same with me. We both might have drowned.

Baker: Isn't that what they call 'poetic justice'?

Golding: If you say so. I call it attempted murder by drowning.

Baker: Anyway, the yacht was stationary, Smith threw you a life preserver and before long you and Trevor were rescued by his father, with the help of your wife. Correct?

Golding: Correct. What happens now?

Baker: You are permitted one phone call. I suggest it be to your lawyer and not your wife, in the circumstances. Then you will return to the holding cell.

Golding: Is Mister Smith being charged with two cases of attempted murder by drowning?

Baker: I think not. He was only trying to defend himself when he threw young Johnson overboard. With you, he may have been trying to make the punishment fit the crime, but more importantly he was preventing you from attacking him again. I doubt if any judge or jury would find him guilty. Self-preservation is not a crime. In my view he deserves a medal for helping solve a case that might otherwise have remained unsolved.

28

I arrived at Joanne's villa promptly at 7:30, bearing Chinese and a 1995 Bordeau blanc from the cellars of Baron de Rothschild.   She answered the door, wearing a pant-suit of shimmering beige silk and a welcoming smile. While my arms were full with the dinner fixings, she slid in close, maneuvered her arms under mine and kissed me lingeringly on the lips. It felt so good, I almost dropped the packages.

"Hi Hon," I said, "and thanks for the warm welcome. But let me take this stuff to the kitchen before I drop something."

She followed me to the roomy kitchen at the back of the villa and stood by while I deposited the packages on the counter.

She hummed to herself, while turning on the oven to keep the several boxes of Chinese food warm.   Then she looked at the label on the bottle of pre-chilled Bordeaux.

"Maury, you must have spent a fortune on the wine," she said. "1995 was the year we first met. How thoughtful of you, Darling!"

I smiled at the thought of that year and our first date, at King Arthur's Court, and of our pledge to each other to be friends, very good friends, but with no commitment.

"Let's pour the wine and take it out to the lanai, for our discussion," I suggested.

"Yes, let's do that. I have something I want to bounce off you," she said.

When we had settled ourselves together on the settee, she snuggled up and I inhaled the fragrance of her bath soap. It blended with the other nice aroma drifting in from the nearby white jasmine flowers.

"You first," I murmured, as I kissed her and nuzzled her blonde hair with my nose. "I'm waiting to have that 'something' bounced off me."

"Maury, I have to admit," she confessed "that I was using that creepy lieutenant to shake you out of your complacency about our relationship. Any other suitor would have done equally well. But he happened along, and served the purpose. Honestly, though, I didn't know that he was at the top of your most hated list."

"Last night, I got even by insulting him in front of other police officers," I said. "I think the Weatherby-Smith books are about balanced now."

"If you insulted him, I am sure he deserved it," Joanne replied. "When I sent him packing, he finally admitted his interest in me, was primarily because of the way you made a laughing stock of him in the squad room when you resigned. We were never lovers, you know."

"I assumed you were. I was jealous," I said.

"Not a chance," she said. "I think he likes boys better than girls."

"Oh. Well not this boy! I only wish you had chosen a less traumatic method of getting my attention. I was very depressed when I thought our long-lasting relationship was over. I love you Joanne. What do I have to do to prevent a recurrence of our temporary separation?"

She looked up and kissed me again. "There will be no recurrence, Maury. It was a dumb idea. I suffered, too. I love you, and want always to be with you. I think our non-commitment pledge of friendship has run its course."

"Are you saying we should get married? At last, make a commitment?"

She smiled. "That's not usually the way proposals go. But our arrangement has been pretty unusual, you must admit. Yes, that's what I am saying. I woke up one morning and realized I am thirty-five, nearing the end of my biological productive years. I decided, before it's too late, that I want your child."

I gulped. "You mean a baby. Our baby?"

"That's the way they start out, Maury, as you well know, having had one. And now she's a lovely young lady.

Melanie and I had a little chat the other evening. She is all in favor of the idea. But, what do you think?".

I reached in my pocket and pulled out the velour box, and slipped the Christmas ring on her finger. "I think it's a great idea, my love. I can hardly wait to get started."

She giggled. "Chinese first."

"To hell with that," I said. "Us first!".

BOOK TWO

Cat
&
Pearly

A Crime Novel

AUTHOR'S NOTE: Cat & Pearly is a Canadian Story – therefore Canadian spelling for certain words is used (e,g, check becomes cheque; center becomes centre, etc.) But as in U.S. English, non-essential vowels are dropped.

1

Until his fortieth year, Leo Kanaskis had been satisfied with his career as a petty thief, engaging in relatively minor felonies such as convenience store robberies, car theft, and the occasional break and enter.

That was before he was married.

It was his wife, Muriel who complained about his meager and irregular income. Because of her nagging, Leo mentally blamed her for his unsuccessful attempt to move up the ladder of crime, to the reputedly more lucrative world of bank robbery. Leo had started dating Muriel when she was working as a waitress in Ginty's Restaurant and Sports Bar on Yonge Street in downtown Toronto. An attractive blonde, with an hourglass figure, Muriel was ten years younger than Kanaskis.

A regular evening visitor to Ginty's, Leo Kanaskis was seduced by two 40 inch television screens, and a handy source of good draft beer. He liked to watch sports events, such as Maple Leafs hockey and the Toronto Blue Jays baseball or the basketball Raptors, in the congenial company of his little pal, Pete Pattino and other bar flies, some of whom had connections with the criminal underworld.

Leo Kanaskis, six-three, two-fifty, ebullient, handsome in a ruggedly casual way, liked to joke around with Muriel when she served their drinks. For her part, she was impressed by his masculine good looks and the generous tips he left for her when he paid the tab.

She was not aware of the frequent periods when Leo was flat broke and had to borrow from his drinking buddies for his next meal. Nor was she aware that his expansive nature obscured the fact that he was basically lazy, always looking for an easy way to 'earn' a living. In short, Leo *looked* to Muriel like the answer to a maiden's prayer. The *reality* only sunk in after their marriage. After a few dates, she was happy to say 'Yes' when he asked if she would like to get hitched. When she queried Leo about his occupation, he smiled and said he was in hydraulics engineering. "You know, liftin' things." Little did Muriel realize that what he was lifting was money, without permission of the rightful owners.

A few days before Leo posed the big question to Muriel, he had experienced a windfall, when he and Pete Pattino succeeded in ripping off an ATM machine at a bank drive-in. His share produced enough funds to pay the first and last months' installments of rent, and new furniture for a nice apartment in a high rise building on Steeles Avenue. Muriel was thrilled and suitably impressed with the nice apartment and all the lovely furniture, when Leo carried her across the threshold of their new home.

But Leo was unable to sustain his economic good luck, and soon the pseudo hydraulic engineer was revealed to his wife for what he was, a small time thief.

Several weeks after Leo's tainted funds had dried up, under direct questioning he admitted reluctantly that his only source of income was from petty crimes.

Muriel was furious that he had misled her. But she hoped she could make him reform. She started by haranguing him mercilessly.

"Leo, for crissake, get some gumption," Muriel chided, when she was confronted with the fact that she had married a crook. "Get a life. It's high time you got off your duff and applied for a regular job. I'm sick and tired of trying to make ends meet, with a few bucks here and a few bucks there. No steady income. Starvation diet until your next score. Then we have to scrape along until you and your idiot pals think up some way to steal a few more bucks. At least, when I was waitressing, I had a steady salary, plus lots of tips. Since I gave up that job to be your wife, we've used up all my savings and are still behind in the rent."

Leo hung his head contritely. "Geez, Muriel, I've tried to get regular employment, but every time it looks like I might be taken on, they check on my background and find out I've spent some time in jail. Then some lucky young jerk, not as qualified as me, gets the job."

"Excuses, excuses, Leo. You're just plain lazy. You're a reasonably intelligent man, so you could at least set your sights higher in life than an occasional 7/11 heist. Even when you score, you only bring back a few hundred dollars. Besides, one of these times you are going to get caught again. With your history and crime sheet, any judge in his or her right mind would throw the book at you."

Faced with the disagreeable prospect of having to resort to honest labor, Leo was deliberately vague. "I promise I'll do better Muriel. Don't give up on me. You know I love you."

He put his brawny arms out and pulled her to him.

She softened momentarily. "This isn't about love, Leo. We can't eat love. Get a job, you big lug. You hear?"

"Okay, okay. I get the message. I'll do my best. I promise. Meantime, I don't suppose you want to ask for your old job back?"

Muriel pulled back and shoved him away. "Oh no! No way am I going back to waitressing so that you can live off my labor like a retired jigolo. You start bringing in some legit money, or we're through, you hear?"

"Yes, dear. I hear."

That evening, at Ginty's, Leo discussed his problem with his partner in crime, Pete Pattino, a younger guy whom he had teamed up with in the successful ATM 'withdrawal'. Their partnership was a Mutt and Jeff combination, Leo being six-three and a robust two-fifty, compared to Pete's five-four and one-thirty-five.

"I've gotta get some big money, and quick, pal, or Muriel is going to leave me," Leo said. "You got any of that ATM loot left over, I could borrow?"

"Nope. Lost most of my share at Woodbine, Leo, bettin' on the nags."

Kanaskis looked dejected and ordered another beer to brighten his spirits. "So you need some quick dough, too. Got any ideas, little guy?"

Pete hated being called 'little guy', but chose to ignore it. "We could rip off another ATM."

"Naw, we got lucky once. But they got cameras on all them machines. Too risky."

Pete laughed. "You want a quick payoff, you gotta take some risk."

"How about a holdup. A bank holdup?" Leo suggested.

"Armed robbery ain't our specialty, Leo. Get caught, we'd get ten to twenty. Happen to shoot a teller and we'd get life."

"How about an *unarmed* robbery, Pete?".

"You mean walking in and handing a teller a note, pretendin' you're packin' heat?"

"No, that's risky, too. There might be a shootout, like at the OK Corral. I have another idea. But I need a driver for the get-away vehicle. Will you help me for a third share? As the driver, that's all you gotta do."

Pattino thought for a minute "Tell me your plan and I'll decide."

Leo told him very briefly what he had in mind. With some trepidation, because he had never been involved in a daylight bank job before, twenty-eight-year-old Pete Pattino agreed to be the wheelman.

2

Toronto, Monday, July 10, 2000

During his casing of a bank branch near the corner of Lawrence and Avenue Road, Leo Kanaskis had noticed that members of the staff began arriving for work at eight-thirty a.m., although banking hours did not officially begin until nine. They would press a buzzer on the door frame, and any nearby member of the staff who had arrived earlier would unlock the thick, glass door to permit entry.

But an older man had used a key and entered before any of the staff. Leo assumed this guy must be the manager. Around 8:45, when most of the staff had arrived, the man usually went next door to the Second Cup for coffee and a donut. Then he invariably reappeared just as the branch opened for business. Leo figured the fifteen minutes, while the manager was away, was his window of opportunity.

On a bright Monday morning at 8:45, an attractive dark-haired teller, whom Kanaskis recognized from his obser-vation the previous week, approached the front door of the bank, and when the door was unlocked, he walked right in behind her, carrying a black attaché case. He was dressed in a business suit, and was neatly shaven for a change.

When the girl turned around, with a questioning look, Kanaskis smiled at her and told her his name was Edgar Porter, the branch inspector who was assigned by the bank's head office to check on procedures at the branch.

"Is the manager here, Miss?" Kanaskis asked.

"He is next door, but will be right back, Mister Porter."

"Then I'll just wait for him. Ah, your name, Miss?"

"I'm Marion Stewart, one of the tellers."

Leo smiled again. "Nice to meet you, Marion." He handed her a business card, which one of his friends had made up on his computer. The card displayed the bank's logo in the upper left corner, the name Edgar Porter in the centre and Senior Branch Inspector in the lower left corner.

Once inside, like an important head office person, Leo Kanaskis walked through the door marked 'Manager' and sat on an armchair in front of the manager's desk. *So far, so good, he thought, with an inward smile.   The plan was actually working!* Meanwhile, Marion Stewart proceeded to the vault, where a senior female accountant was distributing cash drawers to the three tellers, so they would be ready to serve customers when the branch opened at 9 A.M.

When Marion Stewart took her usual position behind the counter, Leo walked up beside her and said quietly, "Before customers arrive, Marion, first thing I need to do, as part of our head office inspection, is check the amount of cash that's issued in each of the cash drawers. I'll start with you."

She looked confused and frowned. "Isn't that unusual, Mister..er..Porter?"

"Just a routine inspection, Marion. Don't worry. I'll return the drawer to you before the branch opens.".

Drawer in hand, he walked unhurriedly to the manager's office, leaving the door partially open, so that he could watch the main entrance door.

Quickly and quietly, he pulled the bills from the drawer and placed them in his empty attaché case. Then he waited inside until the front door was opened for the returning branch manager. With the black case in hand, when the door was opened, Leo walked out, nodding casually, as he passed the unsuspecting manager in the doorway.

Marion Stewart was discussing her weekend with the teller next to her and did not notice Leo's departure. The bank manager went straight to his office and was surprised to find a cash drawer, containing only coins, on his desk. He went to the senior teller at the vault to ask for an explanation.

While his partner was putting on his branch inspector act, Peter Pattino was parked near the exit of the bank's adjacent parking lot, in Leo's decrepit twelve-year-old Ford 150 pickup. On seeing Leo Kanaskis walk out from the bank, he turned the key in the ignition, while his partner walked casually across the lot and jumped in on the passenger side.

The starting motor turned over, but the engine did not start.

Desperately, Peter Pattino continued engaging the starter with the ignition key, while he pumped the accelerator pedal. A cloud of black smoke came out of the exhaust pipe, and finally there was a loud backfire.

"Hey stupid," Leo Kanaskis shouted, "take your foot off the gas. You've flooded the sucker.".

"Shut up, I'm trying everything. You shoulda taken this old heap to the dump and rented somethin' newer."

Three minutes later, the battery was gradually giving up the ghost. The starting motor produced a weaker and weaker sound, until finally the battery ran out of power.

Then came the strident sounds of high-pitched police sirens, slowly winding down to ominous silence, as two squad cars blocked both the exit and entrances to the parking lot.

Seated beside his partner, Leo was sweating and swearing. "What the hell you doin' for crissake? Why didn't you *leave* the motor runnin'? How stupid can you get, Pattino? Time's run out!"

"You didn't tell me to keep the motor runnin', so don't blame me.".

Before his red-faced partner could complain further, a police officer reached in the open window and put a handcuff on Pattino's wrist, attaching the other half of the cuff to the steering wheel. Another officer opened the passenger door, holding his revolver leveled at Leo Kanaskis.

"Hand me the case, you dumb creep, step out and hold your hands behind your back," he ordered.

"You mean me, officer?" Leo asked innocently.

"Of course, you, asshole. Move it, *now!*"

"Alright officer. No need to shout. As you see, we're not going anywheres."

Before he stepped out, Kanaskis gave his partner a little clip on the back of his head, as a final reminder that he should have kept the engine running. Then he turned over the attaché case to the officer, and obeyed the instruction to put his hands behind his back, so he could be handcuffed.

A crowd had gathered, with the bank manager standing in the forefront, watching with a satisfied smile, as both

Kanaskis and Pattino were led to the squad car parked at the exit. They were roughly pushed into the back seat. Like a couple of school kids, the two unsuccessful bank robbers continued to blame each other.

"Your fault," Peter murmured.

"Shoulda left the engine running, dumbo."

The younger man changed the subject. "One good thing, though.".

"What?" Kanaskis asked, still glowering.

"The fuckin' old truck will be impounded."

The senior partner saw the humorous side: "And they'll have to tow it.".

They both started to laugh.

But Kanaskis quickly sobered up. "What the hell are we laughing for? We're both going to jail. And my wife will never let me forget this bungled job."

3

Toronto, July, 2000

$\mathbf{A}$fter their arrest, while awaiting arraignment, Kanaskis and Pattino were locked in a temporary holding cell at the nearby police precinct. When they had been formally charged with attempted bank robbery and illegal possession of funds in excess of $5,000, the Provincial court assigned a different lawyer to each of them. Then they were transferred to the notorious, medieval Don Jail, while the creaking wheels of the Province's justice system slowly turned.

It was late afternoon three days later, when the two handcuffed men were escorted through the entrance of Toronto's jailhouse for so-called short-term detention.

Dating back to 1863, Toronto's Don Jail has been described by an Ontario judge as being so overcrowded that it has become 'an embarrassment to the Canadian criminal justice system.' Originally designed to house 275 prisoners, the ancient building often has a population of almost 700.

After being turned over to a surly guard, Kanaskis and Pattino, still manacled, were processed in the reception area, for incarceration. Then they were led by two uniformed guards, down a long corridor of occupied cells until they reached one that was to be their home until their case came up for trial. As they tagged along in single file, the first thing they noticed was an unpleasant odor that seemed to pervade the whole cellblock.

"This place stinks," Pittano mumbled.

"Quiet!" the surly guard ordered. The second guard pushed Pete forward.

A high steel door, barred from waste high, was opened with a key by the first guard. As Kanaskis and Pattino were shoved unceremoniously into the cell, one guard stayed outside, while the other guard removed their handcuffs.

A man appeared to be sleeping on the lower bunk. There was a vacant upper bunk, but no third bed of any description. Just the bare, and dirty concrete floor, with a drain hole in the centre, covered by a steel grille, and a toilet with no seat, in a back corner of the cell.

After their manacles were removed, the steel door was slammed shut and the two guards started back down the corridor. Leo protested loudly to the receding guards. "Hey, there's been a mistake here. There are three of us, and only two bunk beds."

One guard came back to the barred door. He rattled a key along the bars to emphasize his annoyance.

"This ain't the Ritz, as you'll soon find out. And it's no secret we got more prisoners than beds. One of you losers has gotta sleep on the floor. You can draw lots, or take turns at the two bunks, or give priority to the two guys with the biggest dicks. Use any other method you want to decide who gets the bunks and who sleeps on the floor. But if you are gonna fight over it, just beat each other up *quietly*. Now, shut up or you won't get no dinner."

The formerly somnolent prisoner, who had been reclining on the lower bunk, was now awake and sitting up. He turned out to be a large, black man with an attitude. He stretched and yawned as he stared with hostile malevalence at his new cellmates. Both Leo and Pete winced, as they watched, while the guy hocked up some phlegm and spit on the floor.

"Yo' all heard the guard," said the man with the ebony complexion, in a deep, gravelly voice, "One of us has to sleep on the floor. But it ain't gonna be Rastus, 'cause I was here first. You guys decide who gets the upper."

Little Pete looked at his partner, big Leo. "You gonna put up with that shit, Leo?" he asked. "We got some rights here. We should take turns, sleepin' on the bunks."

Leo Kanaskis looked at the black man, who stood up beside the disputed bunk bed, folding his brawny arms in a gesture of defiance. He was even taller than Kanaskis and must have weighed close to three hundred pounds.

"Um, maybe we should discuss this problem," Leo said, in a conciliatory voice. "We don't want no trouble. But as my partner says, it just don't seem fair that *he* should not have a turn at one a them bunks."

"Wait a minute! What the hell!" Pete protested. "I didn't say *that*. I said we should *all* share the bunks."

"Yeah. I guess you did say that, Pete," Leo conceded. "But when you are the smallest guy in the cell, you ain't got much bargaining power."

"Son of a bitch," Pattino cursed. "You got us inta this mess, Leo, and now you won't stand up for *our* rights."

"Just giving you a lesson for the future, Pete. You shoulda kept the engine runnin'. If you had, we'd still be free and wealthy. Your mistake, you didn't keep the engine runnin'."

The black man, who called himself Rastus, laughed deeply. "Well, that's decided. Now, Pete, if that's your name, I should tell you how it works in here. You get an extra blanket for sleepin' on the floor. That's the one you pull over your head, to keep the rats and cockroaches off'n yer face."

4

Toronto to Kingston, October, 2000

Kingston Penitentiary (KP) a maximum-security prison on the north shore of Lake Ontario, was opened in 1835, under the reign of King William IV. For the first 99 years of its history, women and men were incarcerated, although segregated, as well as children as young as 8 years old, within its high stone walls. Originally designed by an American from Auburn, New York, the complex encloses a number of buildings. Two Main cellblocks surround exercise yards. Other smaller buildings, are used for administration, training, educational and support purposes. With a rated capacity of 431 in the cellblocks, nowadays the prison is usually filled near to that figure.

On arrival at KP from Don Jail, Leo Kanaskis and Peter Pattino were not interested in the history of the institution, as much as the length of time they were going to have to spend, without freedom of choice in their daily activities. After the notoriously overcrowded and odoriferous Don Jail, they were pleasantly surprised to find that living conditions in KP were a considerable improvement over those in their recent experience.

When their case had come up in Provincial Court, in early September, their court-appointed lawyers advised them to plead guilty. Both men were reminded that they were caught red-handed at the scene of the crime, so there was no credible defense. By saving the province the expense of a costly trial, it was suggested that they would receive lighter sentences by agreeing to a guilty plea. Pete Pattino's lawyer had claimed his client should receive special consideration and a lighter sentence, because he was influenced by his older partner who was a chronic offender. Pattino being *only* the driver, the attorney claimed, was not personally involved in the actual theft of money.

In passing a sentence of five years to both men, the judge said he considered them equally guilty of the crime. The only good news was that the sentence could be reduced to three years, with good behavior.

On her first and last contact with her husband, in the visitor's room at KP, Muriel Kanaskis made her announcement on a hand phone, through the glass partition. She informed Leo that she was filing for divorce, on the grounds that she was deliberately misled about his criminal background at the time of their marriage.

Leo's usual calm demeanor was shattered when Muriel made her unexpected announcement.

"I was hopin' you would wait for me, Muriel. You know, askin' for a divorce, with your husband in prison is like kickin' a man when he's down."

"Don't give me that crap, Leo," Muriel replied icily. "I warned you that you had to start bringing in some legitimate money, or we would be through. You just weren't listening. If you think I'm going to wait five years for a shiftless loser like you, you are dreaming in spades."

"I might be out in only three years, with good behavior," Leo pleaded. "Time will pass quickly."

"Three years, four years, or five years, I'm not waiting, Leo. I told you to get a life. You ignored my warning and chose to risk our marriage on a stupid bank heist."

"Actually, not so stupid," Leo argued. "The plan worked. I walked out with a nice bankroll, but the old truck wouldn't start. My dumb partner didn't keep the engine runnin'."

"Well, Leo, that's enough excuses. This is goodbye. As a future reminder of your stupidity, I got your old pickup out of hock and put in storage. If you are planning any more bank heists when you get out, you'd better get the motor tuned up."

"Thanks for that, Mur. And for the cigarettes you left for me with Security. How are you going to get by, with nobody to support you?"

Muriel laughed derisively. "Support me? That's a sick joke. When did you ever support me? Anyway, I'm going to make some real money, in my new profession."

"New profession? And what might that be m'dear?"

"I've been hired as a masseuse in a massage parlor. And, in the evenings, I'll be a call girl."

Leo snorted with skepticism. "Call girl? You mean call *lady*, doncha? You'll just be a glorified prostitute. You have been lecturing me about going straight, and you are planning to sell your body. That's just as illegal as bank robbery."

She raised her nose haughtily. "I'll only be dealing with a select clientele. Besides, there's nothing illegal about turning an occasional trick. You may recall that Prime Minister Trudeau said the government has no business in the bedrooms of the nation. If wealthy johns want to pay me for a fling under the sheets, that's their business. It's not a crime, like that bank job you and that little squirt tried to pull off."

"Well, Mur, attractive as you are, don't forget you are not gettin' any younger. You'll never make it in competition with those young broads that keep comin' to the big city and end up becomin' street-walkers and call girls."

"Don't be so sure, Leo. I've got what those skinny young kids don't have. Experience. Most men prefer mature and experienced women. I know how to please men. I pleased you didn't I?"

"Sure. It was great while it lasted," Leo replied wistfully. "If you won't stick with me, maybe I'll be a client, when I get out of here."

"Don't get your hopes up, Leo. My evening rate is two hundred dollars an hour. And the rate will be going up with inflation."

"Well, maybe just for old times sake, eh Mur?"

She discouraged his plea. "Dream on, big fella, if it will make the time pass quicker," she said, as she was getting up to leave. "But watch out for those nasty homos. I hear prison is full of horny guys who don't take no for an answer."

Leo made a big fist. "They come near me, or my buddy, Pete, and I'll break their horny necks. See ya Mur. Don't forget, I love you."

There were no bunk beds at KP. Prisoners were assigned to individual cells. The reception officer could see no reason why Pattino and Kanaskis should be denied their request for adjoining cells, provided they behaved themselves. So, they were able to communicate with each other, by talking through the barred steel doors.

First day indoctrination, included an offer from Correctional Services of Canada of free Adult Basic Education. The brochure said: 'to equip offenders to deal more effectively with daily problems encountered in the community. Moreover, the sense of achievment and confidence that results from successfully completing such a program may encourage offenders to make further positive changes in their lives' Like two-thirds of the prisoners in the maximum security prison, Pete Pattino had not remained in school beyond Grade 8. Leo Kanaskis had moved on to High School, but had quit while still in Grade 10.

"You want to take some classes to upgrade your education, Pete?" Leo asked, when they were taking a breather from the mandatory exercise program.

His diminutive partner stared at Leo like he was losing his mind. "You mean *study*, read books, write *exams*; all that crap? No friggin' way. I had enough of that while I was in public school. But I might take somethin' practical, like Weldin' and Metalwork. That way, I can earn some extra pay. The daily allowance is only a buck a day, if I don't do nothin'. But. I unnerstand we can make as much as $6.50 by workin' and take some kind of training."

"I don't know that I would want to try to go all the way to Grade 12," Leo said. "But, I might take a course in English. It's not my first language, you know. My parents were immigrants. At home, we spoke mostly Russian."

"Do what you like. But it's prob'ly just a waste of time."

Leo laughed. "Time is something we got lots of, partner. Far as vocational trainin' is concerned, I might take the Auto Mechanics course. Then if some idiot can't get a pickup truck started *in a bank parkin' lot*, maybe I can solve the problem."

"Damn you, Leo. If you keep needlin' me about that fuckup, we ain't gonna be friends no more. So, leave off, okay?"

The big man patted his little partner on the shoulder. "Sure, I'll let it go, if you don't mention my divorce, which I can't do nothin' about."

"Heck, man, I ain't that cruel. I may be a mean little bastard, but I ain't no sadist. Besides, I need some protection around here. I figure, if I let it be known that I'm your buddy, them so-called horny ladies of the night will leave me be.

"Deal?"

"Deal," Leo said. They shook hands.

"One more thing," Pete said. "All the inmates I've talked to, seem to have nicknames – names like Tiger, Ace, Skip, Frostman, Boomer. It might help our repatations if we started callin' each other by nicknames."

"Uh, huh. What kind of name did you have in mind for yourself?"

"You can call me Pearl, or Pearly, on account of my past history as a jewel thief."

"Okay, Pearl. So you've been thinkin' about this. What about me? What moniker do you want to stick on ol' Leo?"

"That's an easy one. Leo the Lion, the king of the beasts. You're big like a lion. You have reddish hair like a lion. In kids' books, your real name, Leo, even goes with Lion."

"Let's not get carried away here, Pete, or Pearly. I start settin' myself up as a monarch of the KP jungle, and every tough guy will want to take a round outta me. I'll end up with a knife in my back, or up my cassoo!"

"Yeah, I guess you're right," Pattino agreed. "But let's stay in the cat family, because it's so appropiat. How about just Cat?"

Leo thought for a moment. "Okay, Cat it is. Can't do no harm. No more Leo and no more Pete. Just Pearly and Cat. Or, better still, Cat and Pearly."

A few days later, Cat and Pearly were getting comfortable with their new routines, and their new nicknames. They were having a smoke, after the group exercises. Finishing off the carton of Matinees Muriel had left for Cat as a farewell gift.

"I guess Muriel sent the smokes as a form of apology for divorcing me," Cat said. "How is the welding going, partner?"

"Okay, Cat. First they gonna teach us weldin' and cuttin' with a oxy-acetylene torch, and then after we learn that, we get to do electric arc weldin'," Pearly replied. "And they got me workin' half days in the metal shop stampin' out car plates. How about you?"

"Well, I have been workin' in the prison laundry for starters," Leo admitted, morosely. "Hell of a menial way to have to spend my time, just to make some extra income. But it's only half days. I'm taking Auto mechanics and Auto body repairing in the other half. And English Grammar three nights a week."

"No shit. English? You learnin' any new words?"

"Not so far. But the instructor told me I shouldn't drop my 'g's' at the end of participles. And I've got to stop runnin', or rather running my words together, like 'gotta'. Should be *got to.* Got that, Pearly?"

"Sure, I got that, Cat. But I've forgotten what a participle is. And I don't really want to know."

"Don't you want to improve yourself, Pearl?"

"You mean *torture* myself. No way! My lingo may not be good. But it's gotten me by, so far, and I *hate* the idea of studyin' just to be corrected by Correctional Services.

"Also, the instructor told me to stop using double negatives. It ain't proper English. Nor is ain't for that matter"

"What?" Pearly asked.

"Like in 'Don't ask me what no more'. It should be 'Don't ask me what *anymore.*' "

"I ain't gonna ask you nothin' no more. So stop showin' off. You and your high falutin' English. You're becomin' unsufferable, Cat."

5

Toronto, Saturday, November 15, 2003

Six weeks after their release from Kingston Penitentiary, in October, 2003 Leo 'Cat' Kanaskis and Pete, 'Pearly'
Pattino were back at Ginty's Restaurant and Sports Bar discussing the sad state of their finances. Pearly was wearing his
usual basic black outfit. Black, long-sleeved turtleneck shirt,
black cords and boots. Cat wore a long-sleeved, beige and blue
checkered work shirt and brown corduroy slacks with brown
suede shoes.

"How did the job interview go, Pearly?" Leo the Cat
asked.

"You mean the openin' advertised by J. Herman
Locksmith and Associates? In two words – it didn't."

"Any particular reason?"

"Sure. I tol' Mister Herman that I had a lot of experience as a locksmith. He wanted a reference. So, I had to
give him the name of my ol' employer, hopin' he wouldn't
check no further. But the son-of-a-bitch phoned and got a
earful, because I had swiped all the key blanks and machinery
when I got tired of workin' my ass off for the minimum wage.
So, I been blackballed in the only trade I know, except weldin
and sheet metal. Unfortunately there seems to be a surplus of
welders and metalworkers."

"Same with me, partner." Cat said. "There's lots of
auto mechanics around who are experienced on all the new cars
and trucks. And, giving KP as my former employer doesn't
create a very good impression."

"I hardly have enough cash left for beer, let alone
food." Pearly complained, keeping his priorities in the right
order. "I've just about used up my severance pay from Kingston. And, my landlady has given me notice. I'll be on the

194

street, if I don't cough up some dough in the next couple of days."

"I'd lend you some money, Pearl," Cat said. "but I'm getting down to last of my twonies and loonies, too."

Pearly signaled the waitress by holding up two fingers and pointing at their empty glasses. "So, what are we gonna do, Cat? Go on the pogee?"

"You mean Welfare? Nah, that's sinking too low,"Cat said. "At least when we were in KP we had free lodgings and three square meals a day."

"Wanna go back?" Pearly asked, half-serious.

"No," Cat admitted. But it would be easy enough. Just stop reporting to our parole officers, and the fuzz would be out looking for us."

"What, then?"

"I have been thinking about making a big score and then getting out of the country."

Pearly looked at the big man skeptically. "Seems to me, we were tryin' to make a big score when we got caught and sent down."

"No, Pearl, that was a *little* score. I'm talking millions, not hundreds or thousands. It was Muriel who told me I had always set my sights too low, although she wanted me to earn *legitimate* money the hard way, not stealing to get it."

"You seen her since you got out?"

"Yeah. She looks great," Cat said morosely. "I visited her at the Paradise Massage Parlor. Got a massage, and that's all. Cost me fifty bucks, which I could ill-afford. Anyway, she is rolling in dough. She loves to lord it over me now. Says she owns a Jaguar, and lives in a high-rise costing over two thousand bucks a month."

"Did you hit her up for a loan," Pearly asked.

"Yeah. I was getting desperate. She told me to get a job, even if it meant digging ditches, or dumping garbage cans. I thanked her for the advice and walked out."

"A couple of weeks ago, I borrowed a few bucks from my new girlfriend, Sam," Pearly said. "She said she is supporting her mother in a nursin' home, so I can't go back for more."

"Sam? What kind of name is that for a girl?"

"Sam is short for Samantha. But she hates her full name and only goes by Sam."

"I didn't know you had a girl friend, Pearl. What does she do?" Cat asked.

"She's a smart cookie. Works in the computer department for a big insurance company on University Ave."

"Hmmm, an insurance company, eh?" Cat mused, rubbing his day-old beard. "She might fit into my idea for a big score," Cat said.

"She won't do nothin' to break the law, Cat. So, forget it."

"It would not be really breaking the law, Pearl, what I had in mind. It would just be doing a bit of overtime to help us out. And she could be offered a nice reward."

Pearly pulled out a packet of cigarettes and prepared to light up. Cat reached over and took the cigarette. "While we were in the jug, Pearl, they changed the law. If you want to smoke you have to go outside."

"What the hell! Fuckin' politicians. I'm gonna smoke right here."

"Thousand dollar fine. Or a month in jail. Probably in the stinking old Don Jail, Pearl," Cat warned.

"Jesus." Pearly took the cigarette from Cat and put it back in the pack. "I'll never forget how you made me sleep on the floor in that dump."

Cat grinned. "Not my fault, Pearl. Blame that big old black rascal, Rastus."

"No use blamin' him. I hear he's a lifer at KP. Was sent down for rape and murder; slittin' a girl's throat."

"That's why you slept on the floor, Pearl. I didn't want any part of messing with that nigger. Or I guess I should say Afro-Canadian. But I think he was actually from Jamaica."

"Who cares! Next time, I get the top bunk, okay?"

"Sure. Because there won't be a next time." Cat replied confidently.

"You mean we'll skip Don Jail and go straight to Kingston?"

"Don't be so skeptical, Pearl. Now order us another beer and I'll explain the plan."

6

Toronto, Friday, November 28, 2003

In Cat's old pickup truck, he and Pearly spent several days cruising around Toronto's wealthier neighborhoods. After being promised a large payoff following their forthcoming 'project', Pearly's girl friend, Sam, had done a little night work on the computer database of the insurance company and printed out a list of policyholders with life insurance policies in excess of One Million dollars. They finally settled on the home of an investment broker named George Monroe. The joint beneficiaries of his policy were his wife, Marsha Monroe, and his daughter, Carol. The address of their home was on The Bridle Path, an exclusive enclave in a green area, north of Lawrence Ave. East..

They drove by the Tudor mansion several times, noting the wide landscaped lot and long setback of the house from the quiet street. Privacy was provided by high cedar hedges on both sides of the property. It seemed like an ideal candidate for break and enter, to fit in with Cat's more ambitious plan, which was to abduct the daughter and hold her for ransom.

Parked a few doors down the street, the pair of would-be kidnappers were arguing about their next move, whether they should stay awhile, or look at some other possible victims, when a silver Mercedes sedan pulled out of the Monroe driveway and drove past them. A young girl was at the wheel, with an elderly man seated beside her in the passenger seat, and a white-haired woman in the back.

"I'm going to follow them," Cat said, as he started the motor, "see where they're going." The Mercedes was moving slowly, as the street was slick with snow from a light snowfall overnight. When it had turned the corner, Cat backed into a driveway and followed the Mercedes behind several other cars in the busy traffic on Bayview, heading North. When the Mercedes turned onto the ramp for 401 West, Cat continued to follow at a distance.

"I wonder where they is goin', Cat?" Pearly asked. "Maybe to a shoppin' mall?"

"I don't think so, Pearl. They wouldn't all go together, just for shopping. They could be heading to the airport."

"I hope not. If they are flyin' someplace, our plan is scuppered, for a while anyways. We need to get our hands on the girl."

"Let's just follow and see where they go. The girl may be just driving her parents to the airport."

When the Mercedes passed the ramp to 427, Cat thought his guess about their destination would turn out to be accurate. Sure enough, the Mercedes exited 401 and took Dixon Road towards Pearson International, finally ending in front of International Departures at Terminal 2.

Cat and Pearly stopped at curbside a short distance from the Monroe vehicle, watching as a red cap porter removed two suitcases from the trunk of the Mercedes, and loaded the luggage on to a cart. Then he returned with a wheelchair for the woman, who was helped out of the back seat. The girl got out to help and hugged her parents goodbye.

When the couple disappeared into the terminal entrance, the silver German car took off, with the girl still driving. Cat pulled out from the curb and followed.

Off the Express lane going East, onto the Collector lane, they followed her down Avenue Road and eventually to a parking lot for the University of Toronto. The girl, wearing a ski jacket, and carrying a book satchel over one shoulder, locked the car and headed for one of the limestone buildings.

From where they had parked on the street, Cat said: "Looks like she is going to class. Let's wait for her at the house."

7

For Pearly, picking the side door lock at The Bridle Path mansion had been quick and easy. And, the two ex-cons were lucky in another respect. The Monroes had always depended on a sophisticated Chubb security system to protect their home while they were away. But, on this occasion, George Monroe had assumed that his daughter, Carol, had set the system in operational mode when they all departed for Pearson Airport. Carol, on the other hand, thought her father had punched in the numbers on the security keypad.

So the keypad went unpunched, and the house went unprotected. If the security system had been operational when Cat and Pearly broke in, they would have quickly departed the scene. As it turned out, they enjoyed beginner's luck in their new field of criminal endeavor.

Once inside, Cat said to Pearly, "Let's wait in the basement, Pearl. Then we can surprise her when she returns."

After they descended the short flight of stairs to the basement, they were pleasantly surprised. They entered an opulently furnished lounge area, and walked through to a games room, equipped with a pool table and dart board. To the left was a furnace room, with a workbench and wall-mounted tools.

On returning to the lounge, Cat checked out the tall two-door refrigerator behind the mahogany bar counter. Pulling out a couple of cans of imported Heineken beer, he snapped the caps. Then he reached up to the shelf and took down a couple of pewter steins before pouring in the golden brew. He handed one of the steins to his partner, who was busily checking out the contents of a cigar humidor, which he found on the bar counter. While Pearly was lighting a long Cuban cigar, Cat walked over to a Lazy-Boy recliner and spread out his six-three frame on the leather upholstery, as he planked his size fourteen shoes on the raised pedestal.

"So this is how the other half lives," Cat said as he leaned back and closed his eyes. "Thank you, Mister Monroe."

Pearly had taken a seat on a Windsor armchair nearby, at a glass-topped table. He blew a smoke ring at the ceiling.

"I doubts it's a *half* that can live like this," Pearly argued. "Maybe one in a hunnert. They just ain't enough money to buy this kind of luxury for more than a privileged few."

"There you go again, Pearl," Cat complained. "I say something and you try to take it literally. I was only quoting a well-kown saying."

"Anyways," Pearly said, undeterred by his partner's annoyance. "I seen in the paper that the distribution of wealth in this country is like a puramid, see, with the haves at the top and the have-nots at the bottom."

"Pyramid, Pearly, not puramid," Cat corrected.

"Yeah, pyramid. Across the base of the pyramid you got your poor people – the welfare cases, transients, dead beats, ex-cons without regular jobs, and your homeless who the politicians keep trying to hide, to get them outa sight."

"Well, don't include ex-cons in the same breath as dead beats, Pearl. As you know, it's tough to get a regular job with a prison record."

"Yeah, you're so right," Pearly agreed.

"So, we ex-cons have to be creative. By cooking up this plan, we are being entrepreneurs." Cat shifted his big body to reach the stein on the side table next to the Lazy-Boy. "Have-nots, though, that's us. But that's going to change real soon."

Pearly nodded in agreement. "Then, in the next upward layer, you got your blue collar workers, your farmers and office types with steady incomes. They're called middle class. All the time the numbers are getting' smaller and the pyramid is getting' narrower."

Cat took a swig of beer and wiped his moustache with the back of his hand. "It doesn't seem fair, Pearl. I've been trying to get into the middle class all my life, and haven't made it yet. No wonder we have to resort to kid snatching to make a decent living."

"More'n decent, man," Pearly pointed out. "When we pull this job off, we'll be like this here George Monroe, whose daughter we're going ta abdicate."

"Abduct, Pearl. Abduct."

"Okay, abduct, snatch, or kidnap, whatever. Anyways, next layer up in your pyramid is your comfortable wealthy – business owners, educators, plumbers and professionals, like doctors and dentists. Finally, at the very peak, are your *really* wealthy – like CEO's, jet-setters who inherited big dough, professional sport jocks, movie stars and them people who make their fortunes cheatin' other poor suckers in the stock market. And we'll join them at the top, if we can pull this snatch off. We'll be rich as that ol' gink, Croesus."

Cat was getting tired of the pyramid analogy. "Who?"

"Croesus. You know, the rich ol' guy in Greek myth-lology. Or was he a Roman senator?"

Cat snickered. "How about an Ottawa Senator – on the hockey team? Anyway, you probably are referring to Midas."

"Smartass. Everybody knows Midas is a muffler chain."

Cat rolled his eyes and let out a sigh of exasperation. He was not about to explain about the great King Midas, the monarch with the golden touch, to an ignoramus like his partner.

"Forget it, pal. You don't know the difference between Midas and Midol."

Pearly ignored Cat's sarcasm. He was looking around the room at the opulence of the furnishings in the lounge – the imported silk woven wall coverings, the soundproof cork ceiling, the inset cove lights and the track lighting over the wet bar. On one wall was a gas fireplace of cut stone. He got up and fiddled around with the controls until a flame burst around the simulated logs. Oriental scatter rugs partially covered the gleaming parquet floor.

His gaze wandered to another wall on which a six foot long sailfish was mounted, its prehensile snout pointing along the room to a mounted moose-head.

"Hey, Cat," Pearly said, "look at them stuffed animals. This Monroe guy is elderly now, but he musta been some outdoorsman in his youth." With his eyes, Cat followed his partner's gaze. But, he was not impressed. "You can *buy* trophies, if you've got the money. Besides they are not both animals. One is a fish."

"Yeah, but a *big* fish, just like we're going to be, when we get our ransom money."

It was five-thirty in the afternoon, and late November dusk was falling, when twenty-year-old Carol Monroe returned from her class at the University of Toronto. Using the remote control to open the garage door, she parked the family Mercedes in the three-car garage, next to her beige VW Jetta. She walked back to the side entrance and used a key to open the side door. Carrying her books in a shoulder bag, she ran up the small flight of six stairs and reached for the light switch in the kitchen.

Cat's large, hairy hand grabbed her slim wrist and his other hand covered her mouth, smothering her attempted scream.

Pearly reached past the struggling girl and turned on the light switch. Carol's eyes were bulging, as Pearly slapped a thick strip of duct tape over her mouth and wound another piece around her wrists, while Cat held her from the back.

"Okay, Carol," Cat said. "You can stop struggling. We won't hurt you, unless you cause us problems. Carol, that's your name, right?".

Tears were welling up in her blue eyes, as she nodded.

"We know your old man has gone away with your mother." Cat said. "For how long?"

She shook her head sideways and kicked out, catching Pearly solidly in the groin. He let out an oath, as he gasped and doubled over in acute pain.

Cat reacted by putting one of his massive arms around her throat, lifting her slender body off the floor. Her feet kept bicycling in the air.

"Now listen, Carol, that ain't co-operating," he said. "So settle down. You hear?"

While his partner remained in a bent-over position, Cat hauled Carol up the winding stairs to the second floor. Choosing one of the six large bedrooms, he pushed her down on an armchair.

While Carol sat, with tears running down her cheeks, Cat went over to the leaded casement window and peered out into the semi-darkness. A section of the sidewalk was barely visible from that position, lighted weakly by an overhead street lamp. After pulling the heavy drape across the window, he gazed around the room at the attractive décor. It appeared he had chosen Carol's own bedroom for her temporary detainment.

The three-quarter-sized bed had an overhead canopy, with a flounced chintz border imprinted with blue daffodils. He opened the closet door and noted a wardrobe of girl's clothing, ranging from formal dresses to jeans, pullovers and seven pairs of shoes.

A scowling Pearly Pattino appeared at the bedroom door, having recovered enough from the attack on his genitals to again assume an upright stance. He walked over to Carol, who was still seated in the armchair, looking both distraught and defiant.

He slapped her across the face.

"That's for kicking me in the fuckin' gonads, sister," Pearly said. He had brought up more duct tape, which he began to wind around her ankles. "And there's more where that came from."

Cat intervened. "Let her be, Pearl. We want some information from her."

He bent over the frightened girl. "Listen, Carol. I'm going to take the tape off your mouth, if you promise not to scream. Okay? Nod if you promise."

She nodded her blonde head up and down. Slowly and carefully, Cat removed the wide tape from across her mouth. Still it hurt and she gasped with pain.

"Now you can talk, Carol. How long are your parents going to be away?" he asked.

She paused, before answering. Finally, she put her head down and murmured. "Three days."

"Where did they go?"

"Bermuda," she replied, in a small voice.

"Bermuda...for three days?" Cat asked. "You wouldn't be lying to us, would you?"

"No. They often go for a long weekend. Dad has a cottage in Southampton. He plays golf. They visit friends and go out to dinner in Hamilton. You know – stuff like that. But, they don't take long holidays. My mom has a health problem."

Cat turned to Pearly. "What do you think, Pearl?"

Feeling important at having his opinion asked, Pattino raised himself to his full five feet, four inches. "Possible, I suppose. But I don't see what the fuck difference it makes. We gotta get her outa here, before some nosey parker wonders what's going on and calls the fuzz."

Cat turned back to the frightened girl. "You look like a smart kid, Carol. So, I guess you have this figured out, eh?" You are going to be bait for some ransom money from your old man. In other words, you have been snatched. You are the kidnappee and we are the kidnappers. If you want to stay alive, don't make any trouble for us. We are going downstairs, to prepare the ransom demand, see? Now, hold still, while I put the tape back on your mouth."

Pearly nudged his partner. "They ain't no lock on the door. Stay with her till I get a hammer and nails. There's a workbench and tools in the furnace room."

"Okay, Pearl. Make it snappy. We got some planning to do."

8

In the basement lounge, with paper, a magazine, scissors and a container of Elmer's White Glue, the kidnappers were discussing how they could get paid off, without having to revisit KP for a much longer term.

"Okay, here's what we do," Cat explained, since it was his plan, as senior partner. "We demand two mil in used Canadian bank notes. Unmarked bills. Nothing over a C note. Packed in a big suitcase. To be left in a locker at Pearson Airport, which we lock beforehand. You make an extra key for us, Pearly. We leave our ransom note stuck on the door of the refrigerator in the kitchen, upstairs. *We say* in the note that if the cops are called, the girl gets whacked. How's that sound?"

"Let's whack the girl anyway," Pearly suggested. "Less trouble that way. 'Cause we don't have to look after her."

"No way, Pearl. Leo said emphatically. "Adding Murder One to Kidnapping? I say we keep her alive. I may be a snatcher, but I'm sure as hell not a murderer."

"Who gives a shit, Cat? We get life anyway, if we're caught. Dumb little broad, kickin' me in the nuts. Christ, that hurt!"

His partner laughed. "Yeah. She sure got your attention. But we don't figure on getting caught this time. Last time was that old pickup, we had to use for get away. This time, we have that nice new-looking Mercedes to drive.".

"Them Fritzies sure do know how to make cars." Pearly said.

"Right. We'll need lots of trunk space, and the Mercedes should have enough. Anything else you can think of?"

"What do we do about the old pickup?" Pearly asked.

"When we get where we're going, we take the plates off, switch them to the Mercedes, and dump the old heap somewhere. Anything else?"

"Damn right. Major flaw. Have you ever seen even a million dollars in C notes? There's no locker would hold that many bills."

Cat stroked the stubble on his chin. "Hmm, hadn't thought of that. Okay, we ask for a cashable bond for two mil."

"A bond? Don't be nuts. We try to cash it and any bank would send out the alarm."

"Alright. Make it two cashier's cheques. Made out to Bearer, and cashable by anyone, like us. Plus ten thousand dollars in unmarked C notes, for emergency cash."

Pearly looked perplexed. "What do we do with the cheques?

"Fly them to the Cayman Islands by way of a US airport, like Miami, and open bank accounts in that Caribbean paradise, my friend. Their banks don't report to any government. And they don't give a hoot in hell where the money comes from."

"The Mercedes will be hot as blazes," Pearly pointed out, "once our clients get back from Bermuda."

"Clients, yeah! I like that," Cat said, grinning and displaying the gap in his two front teeth. "I like the sound of that. Classy sounding, just like frigging lawyers. Anyway, long before they show up, their expensive car will be in pieces. We can turn it over to Joe Carboni's chop shop out in Weston. Get him to give us another car in exchange."

Pearly took a pull of a Cuban cigar he had lifted from the humidor at the bar.

"Fuckin' A, man," the junior partner said excitedly. "I hope they sell luxury cars in the Caymans. With a mil to spend, I could afford *two* Caddies, one for me and one for my girl friend, Sam. I promised her a nice gift for helpin' us with this here project."

While the two kidnappers were trying to put the final touches to their sketchy plan, the 'kidnappee', upstairs was busily trying to remove the duct tape from her mouth. Her hands were taped together, as were her feet, and as an extra precaution, she was taped to the only armchair in her bedroom.

Despite her initial sensation of terror, Carol Monroe was beginning to sense a lack of professionalism on the part of her captors. In fact, their actions smacked of amateurism. They had left her alone for at least a half hour, with her hands taped *in front* of her, so that she could work away at the tape binding her to the armchair and the tape on her mouth, which was not nearly as sticky, having once been removed and reapplied, wet with perspiration.

In a few minutes, she had removed the tape on the arms of the chair and her mouth. Next, she tore off the tape around her ankles. She was then able to make her way over to the drawer of her dressing table, where she knew there were a small pair of scissors. Though her hands were taped with the palms facing each other, there was some wriggle room. It took her a few minutes, but finally, after many attempts, she succeeded in getting her hands free. She went to the door and tried to open it, but the large nail, hammered through the door and into the frame held against all her desperate efforts.

Carol went to the window and opened it. Darkness had descended, with only the weak glimmer of a street lamp relieving the blackness of the November night. The outside air was chilly. When she breathed out, she could see the mist created by her breath.

In the dark shadows of the street light, about a hundred feet away, Carol thought she saw a person passing by. She started screaming.

Down in the basement the two ex-cons were trying to piece together the ransom message from words they had cut out of several magazines.

"I haven't had anything to eat since this morning," Pearly complained. "Them beers just made me more hungry."

"Let's not worry about our stomachs now," Cat said testily. "We have to finish this note."

"Maybe we should send out for pizza," Pearly suggested, with a mischievous smile.

Cat glared at him.

Pearly put his hands up defensively. "Just kiddin'. Just introducing a little levaty inta tha situation.".

"Geez, Pearl. How can you think about food, when we're asking for a couple of mil in ransom money?"

"We didn't have to wait till we captured the girl to make up tha note," Pearly pointed out.

"So we got the cart before the horse. Or the snatch before the note," Cat argued. "Who gives a shit, pal."

"I can't find words to cut out that say two million dollars," Pearly mentioned.

"Print it then. Use your ingenuity."

Suddenly, Cat stopped and slapped himself on the forehead. "Son of a bitch, Pearly, I just realized we are wasting our time. We must be stupid."

Pearly gave his partner a vacant look. "How come?"

"Because our goddam fingerprints are all over the house. We shoulda worn gloves. You know, like in the hospitals."

Pearly objected. "Naw. My hands perspire like mad in them plastic gloves.".

"*Any kind* of gloves would do, for crissake. Anyway, it's too late now. Our fingerprints are on file. And the cops will be sure to run the impressions they lift from here, through the computer," Cat lamented. "And there goes our perfect snatch."

Pearly's face fell. "Not only have we lost the advantage a bein' anominous. But they'll know who we are."

"So, we might as well just write the note longhand, and sign our names to it," Cat concluded, ignoring his partner's double speak.

At that point, their discussion was interrupted by a series of loud screams from above. The two men looked at each other, and simultaneously bolted out of their chairs.

They stumbled up the steps, getting in each other's way, as they scrambled to the second floor.

9

By the end of training camp and the beginning of the regular National Hockey League season, most professional hockey players are in top physical condition. The strenuous demands of the long NHL schedule leaves little room for any player suffering from a debilitating leg injury to be given ice time.

When healthy, Murray Hammond was the answer to a coach's dream. Rock solid at the blue line, he was also a rushing defenceman, with a prolific goal scoring record, who often led his team, the Toronto Maple Leafs, in assists as well. Not since the early retirement of legendary Bobby Orr had a defenceman's knee injury received so much concern, as the one Hammond had received, when he crashed into the boards in the last game of the previous season. As he was assisted off the ice, to the cheers of appreciation and encouragement from home town fans, it was with the certain knowledge that his now famous left knee would again require the attention of a prominent Toronto orthopedic surgeon.

Twice before, in his long and illustrious career, Murray Hammond had injured his left knee, so badly that operations were required to repair ligaments and cartilage damage. So, sports columnists were gloomy in their predictions that the Leafs were about to lose permanently the services of their thirty-eight-year-old superstar player.

But after an arthroscopic operation in July 2003, a determined Murray Hammond had other ideas. By mid-August, he had embarked on a rigorous program of exercise to rebuild strength in his damaged knee and restore his general physical condition.

Murray preferred to do his fitness workout indoors and the necessary roadwork in the evening outdoors, when there was less pedestrian and automobile traffic than in daytime. He found running and jogging in the upscale area of The Bridle Path, exhilarating and addictive. There was a welcome solitude, while passing the huge homes of the wealthy on the dimly lit street, a peaceful interlude that did not exist in the daytime. He allowed his mind to wander. But this night his thoughts were brought sharply back into focus as he passed the spacious grounds of a large Tudor mansion.

He had been doing wind sprints, alternating with jogging. But the pain in his knee had built up to the point where he slowed down to a walk, when a series of loud screams interrupted his thoughts.

He stopped abruptly. Retracing his steps, he peered up the long driveway that circled in front of the entrance and branched off to a garage at the back.

A young, blonde girl was leaning out an open second floor window, waving with both arms and screaming shrilly.

Forgetting the throbbing pain in his left knee, Murray paused momentarily and then sprinted up the interlocking gray brick driveway. As he arrived at the steps leading up to the front door, he looked up, just as a hand covered the girl's mouth and she was pulled back into the room. The leaded casement window was slammed shut, and the drapes were pulled.

In darkness, Murray approached the massive, solid oak door, which was attached to its frame with large black, cast iron strap hinges. He grasped the horseshoe-shaped knocker and rapped loudly several times.

There was no response from within, for at least two minutes.

When nobody answered the door promptly, he was in a quandary as to what to do next. But at last a pair of coach lights, positioned on both sides of the entrance, was switched on. The door swung open, and a large man with unkempt auburn hair and a full moustache, appeared on the threshold. He was wearing brown, corduroy slacks and a beige roll-neck shirt.

"Good evening. What can I do for you?" the big man asked in a friendly voice.

Murray was taken aback by the casual manner of the question. And he realized that he must be a strange sight at that hour. His warmup track suit was saturated with perspiration. A baseball cap was perched backwards on his head. But then, he had not planned on making house calls.

"Excuse me for intruding," Murray began politely, "but I heard a lot of screaming from a girl, up on your second floor."

"Sure you did," the man replied smoothly. "And, I'm very sorry if she disturbed the whole neighborhood. That was my daughter, who just had another epileptic seizure. The poor girl becomes hysterical and screams a lot after one of her convulsive fits. Sorry if it got your attention, while you were passing by. We should not have left her alone in her bedroom. But you never know when she'll have another attack of epilepsy."

"But she screamed something about being abducted and she was asking for help."

"Yeah. That's too bad, she often does that. You see she becomes mentally disoriented and thinks somebody is out to harm her. She yells all kinds of crazy stuff. The seizures are really frightening to her."

"Uh, huh." Murray said dubiously.

"Sorry to keep you waiting at the door. You see, we were just calling the doctor. When he arrives, he'll give her some sedation. That will calm her down, so that she can get a good night's sleep."

To Murray, the man's explanation seemed plausible. More or less satisfied, he started to turn away, when the man said: "Wait a minute. Are you Murray Hammond, the hockey player?"

"Yes," Murray admitted.

"Hey. I'm a big fan of yours. Always cheer for The Leafs. How is the knee coming along?"

Murray was surprised at being recognized. "Er. Oh. Yeah. I'm working on it. It's gradually improving. Thanks for asking. Sorry to have bothered you, Mister...?"

The man stuck out his large hand. "My name is George Monroe. I'd invite you in, but I must get back up to my daughter."

Murray shook his hand, with the uncomfortable feeling that he might be talking to a con artist. But, he did not believe he could press his enquiry further, in the circumstances.

"Okay. I understand. Nice to meet you, Mr. Monroe. Hope she will be alright."

"Thanks, gotta go now. 'Bye."

Cat Kanaskis closed the door with a sense of relief, and turned out the coach lights.

Murray retraced his steps down the driveway, deep in thought. He was unable to identify the reason for his continued unease about the screaming girl.

After giving his explanation, Cat congratulated himself on his quick thinking. He hurried up to the second floor. On entering the bedroom, he noted that Carol was seated quietly in the armchair, with her wrists, ankles and mouth retaped. Pearly was standing in front of her, in a threatening posture, holding the claw hammer he had used to remove the nail in the door.

Cat said: "Take it easy, pal. I got rid of him. It was a goddam hockey player, name of Hammond, out jogging. Heard her screaming. But he bought my story, that she was having an epileptic seizure."

"I tol' you, we shoulda whacked her," Pearly grumbled.

"Just shut up and grab her legs," Cat ordered. "We gotta get her out of here."

"What about the ransom note, Cat?"

"No time now. If that guy has second thoughts, the fuzz could be here any minute. We can mail the note later."

As they were carrying their hostage down the stairs, Pearly asked, "Hockey player? How did you know who he was?"

"Saw him interviewed on television. Don't ask so many questions and don't let her bump on the stairs for crissake!"

Depositing the girl's body on the kitchen floor, they quickly ran to the basement and pulled on their jackets.

"Now listen, Pearl." Cat said. "I found the keys to the Mercedes in her book-bag. We'll have to stuff her in the trunk. Then, I'll drop you off down the street, at the pickup. We'll drive both vehicles to Joe Carboni's. You know where that is?"

"Sure. Out on Weston Road. South of 401. Been by it lotsa times.".

"Okay. When you turn the ignition key in the pickup, don't use the accelerator, or you'll flood the goddam engine again."

"You promised you'd never mention *that* again. You're the fuckin' auto mechanic, why don't you drive the pickup?"

"Don't argue, Pearl. Just do it."

"Alright, Cat. But we shoulda whacked her. Then we could *both* ride in the Mercedes."

"Forget it. This is an abduction, not a murder."

10

Kathy Blake was sitting cross-legged on the scatter rug in front of the fireplace, reading a book, when Murray Hammond entered his penthouse suite on the top floor of the Welkin Arms Apartments on Lawrence Avenue East.

He walked across the room to where she was seated, bent down and gave her an affectionate kiss on the cheek. A drop of perspiration fell on her open book.

"Stop, you animal," she said, as she patted his cheek with one hand, and then pushed him away with the other. "You'll ruin this book and my make-up."

He laughed. "It looks like a library book, and half-ruined anyway. As for your make-up, why do you care? It's almost ten o'clock and I won't be able to see your make-up in bed."

His logic was unassailable. She changed the subject. "How many miles did you do? And how was the knee?"

"About five, and okay, in that order," he replied, as he walked over to pick up the phone. For a brief moment, he stood deep in thought.

"Whom are you phoning at this hour, Murray?" she asked.

"The police," he replied. Her curiosity, he thought, knew no bounds. "It's a long story."

"Oh, good. I like long stories."

"I'm not sure you'll like this one. It's about a scream-ing woman."

"What screaming woman? Don't tease me. Tell me."

"Listen my dear and you shall hear…"

"About the midnight run of Paul Revere?"

"No. Murray Hammond. And, it's only ten o'clock."

"Well, it is midnight somewhere," she said.

He punched in 911, grinning at her quick comeback.

"Operator. I'd like to speak to the police." He paused, trying to decide whether it was urgent. "Yes it's urgent. It's about a possible kidnapping. I'll give them the details. My name is Murray Hammond."

There was a buzzing sound on the line. In a few seconds a central police operator came on the line. Meanwhile, he looked at Kathy, who wore an alarmed expression under her smudged make-up.

"Yes, operator, I wish to report a suspicious incident. My name is Murray Hammond," he repeated.

The operator said, "Just a moment, please. Don't hang up."

A male voice came on the line. "May I help you? Constable Dixon here." The officer's voice was husky. Perhaps he had treated his larynx to too many cigarettes and cups of coffee.

Murray went on to report what he had seen and heard, giving the address on The Bridle Path. Then he described the conversation he had with the man who answered the door.

"Sounds suspicious. We'll check on it, Mister Hammond," the policeman said. "Should be able to get a squad car there within the next ten minutes. Would you give me your full name, address and phone number."

When the information was given, the officer's voice brightened up and became less official. "Say aren't you Murray Hammond, the hockey player?"

Murray admitted that he was.

"Well how's that knee coming along? I'm in a hockey pool here at the precinct. And, I win big if the Leafs win the Stanley Cup."

Murray laughed. Funny how complete strangers became so interested in another person's ailing limb, in the name of sport. "The knee's coming along fine, officer. But I thought gambling was supposed to be illegal."

Constable Dixon also laughed. "You're pulling my leg, eh? You hockey players love to kid around. Anyway, let's just forget what I said, okay?"

"Okay by me," Murray said. "I hope you know how to wipe the incriminating remarks from the recording of this call. Anyway, will you let me know if my suspicion is confirmed?"

The constable's voice became official again. "Of course, Mister Hammond. As soon as a report comes back from the investigating officers, we'll get back to you. Thanks for reporting the incident. And have a good evening, sir."

When Murray replaced the phone, Kathy was standing in front of him, wide-eyed. "Do you really think there was a crime committed, Murray?" Her voice contained a trace of mischievous skepticism. "Do you think you have fingered a perpetrator?"

He blushed slightly, wondering if he had made a fool of himself in reporting the incident. Kathy's questions were not making him feel any better.

He shrugged. "We'll see."

Realizing his sensitivity, she apologized. "Sorry, hon. You did the right thing by reporting it. Most people would have just ignored the girl's plight and would have gone right on by. I'm proud of you, however it turns out."

"Yeah. Yeah. Well, I was just trying to cover all the bases. Anyhow, I'm for the shower. And, young lady, it's past your bed time. You'd better be between the sheets when I come out."

She giggled. "Yes, master. If I didn't know you better I would think you were trying to order me around. Perhaps I made a mistake in taking you to see The Taming of the Shrew."

"Seems to me the Shrew was also a spirited lass, and *also* named Kate. But she was tamed in the end. Shakespeare had the right idea."

He pulled her shapely body to him and against his wet, smelly track suit. After they kissed deeply, she gasped: "That track suit has got to go. Mur. To the washing machine. Forthwith."

He grinned, revealing his expensive bridgework, replacing his two front teeth, almost a trademark of pro hockey players. "Not until I'm out of it, m'dear."

"Well, don't just stand there. Hurry. It's not fair to get a girl all excited and then keep her waiting."

He smiled and started towards the bathroom.

"Oh, I forgot to tell you," she said. "I've got the tickets."

Murray had become accustomed to his roommate's habit of starting a conversation with a seemingly irrelevant or disconnected statement. Or, sometimes of answering a question a couple of days after it was asked, just as though nothing had occurred in between.

He loved her and considered these scatter-brained statements among her more endearing traits. Life was never boring with such an unpredictable personality.

"Tickets for what?" he asked as he removed the top of his semi-wet track suit, while wincing at the thought of a possible ballet, or symphony.

"Tickets for our trip to Rome over the Christmas holidays."

"Damn it Kate. I could be back with the team by then. You should know the only holidays I can take are during the summer."

She looked sheepish. "I got them just in case you were not able to play."

He refused to be drawn into a discussion about his future with the team. He fell back on his usual philosophical statement. "We'll see."

Heading for the bathroom again, he decided he would not pursue the question of tickets to Rome, or anywhere else. He knew Kathy could return tickets, as easily as she had purchased them, because she worked in a travel agency in Yorkville.

Murray did not relish the idea of breaking into his training program, even for a week. He hoped to get back on the ice by Christmas. He was being paid millions of dollars for his services, and Murray believed in quid pro quo.

11

Toronto, Friday night, November 28, 2003

"**H**ey Joe, It's me, Cat.   How're you doing, buddy?"   Kanaskis was calling from a cell phone he had discovered in George Monroe's car.   He had punched in the emergency number displayed on the back lane gate of Carboni Import Export off Weston Road.

"Cat?   Who the fuck is a cat?"   Joe Carboni sounded annoyed with a phone call late in the evening, from some looney calling himself with a stupid nickname.

"Cat *Kanaskis*.   Don't you remember me Joe?   We used to be friends for crissake.   You know.   Down at the end of Lake Ontario.   Place called KP."

"Oh, yeah, yeah, yeah.   Da big boardin' house, with da lumpy beds," Joe was beginning to sound less hostile.   "Leo the Cat' Kanaskis.   It all comes a back to me now.   Been a long time.   So, how is da world treatin' you, Cat?"

"Not bad, Joe.   I wouldn't call you this time of night. But, I got some very urgent and important business for you."

"Oh.   Urgent, eh?   What is it, and where are you at, Cat?"

"I'm parked outside your gate that says Carboni Import Export, in the back lane, in a 2003 Mercedes."

"Hmmm.   Must be your lucky day, Cat. New Mercedes are very much ina demand.   Stay put.   Be right over."

Housed in a formerly abandoned warehouse, Joe's Body & Paint Shop and Carboni Import Export were each part of a dual operation.   The front two-thirds of the building housed a thriving business dedicated to the repair of vehicles. Some damaged in traffic accidents, almost always involving insurance claims.   In addition, there was the source of repair work Joe liked to call 'the salt business', repairing and repainting damage from corrosion caused by sodium chloride. Salt, mixed with sand, when spread on city streets during the winter, was a godsend to motorists in preventing accidents. At the same time, it was a godsend to repair shops such as Joe's, as a regular source of business. Then too, there was the other end of the same equation, the 'oil business', an oil-spraying service, which some motorists bought to *prevent*, or at least slow down the erosion caused by the 'salt business'.

However, the big money for the Carboni enterprises was not in the front two-thirds of the big warehouse building, nor in the steadily declining 'salt and oil' business, because car makers were using better materials to combat rust and corrosion, but in the back third, which housed Joe's 'chop shop'. Although the space devoted to the back end was less than front end, the revenue generated by this illegal activity was many times larger.

For secrecy reasons, Joe had only two auto mechanics working in the so-called Import Export business. They were Vittorio and Gino Carboni, younger brothers of the owner. As family members, they were well paid for their expertise in disassembling or disguising stolen automobiles. For their own security, the Carboni siblings and their respective families were expert at keeping their mouths shut. Joe's brothers did not associate with the staff of the legitimate body and paint shop. As far as any connection was concerned, the entire back third of the building might as well have been located in another county.

The chop shop required a continuing source of automobiles, to fill orders from customers, who did not worry about the fact that the vehicles might have been stolen. Depending on the current demand, sometimes only a repaint job, new plates, plus filing and changing the registration number was necessary to disguise the vehicle. In other cases, the whole vehicle was disassembled and sold for parts. Sometimes, whole vehicles, or just parts were shipped overseas in large containers. That accounted for the 'Export' part of the name. There was little or no reason for the word 'Import' in the title, except that it sounded more customary, and therefore more legitimate.

Rather than taking a chance on amateur car thieves, Joe Carboni relied entirely, for his product, on freelance professionals, who specialized in the latest techniques in making automobiles disappear from the streets of Canada's largest city. He did not care how they were taken, only that they were delivered at certain hours of darkness, down the back lane, when the front shop was closed. He always paid cash, usually a fraction of the actual value of the vehicle.

Car thievery was a big problem for law enforcement, right across Canada. An average of five hundred cars was stolen each day. With insurance companies, manufacturers and the police on one side and car thieves on the other, it was a constant battle. Increasingly, late model cars were being equipped with ignition-interrupters and alarms. There were ways of disarming the alarms and bypassing interrupters, but the risk of being discovered in the process of working inside the vehicle was hardly worth the effort. Even 'The Club' the much-advertised device that could be locked on a vehicle's steering wheel could be removed by simply cutting the wheel rim with heavy wire cutters. There was no foolproof protection against car theft. Thieves, both pro and amateur, were always on the lookout for careless drivers who did not bother, or sometimes forgot, to remove their keys from the ignition.

A few minutes after Cat's call, Joe Carboni drove along the back lane to his chop shop entrance, in a sleek, white Cadillac De Ville. A middle-aged, balding Sicilian, with light coffee skin and a corpulent belly, Carboni was addicted to solid black shirts, white ties, venetian silk suits and hand-made Italian shoes.

With his two brothers, Joe Carboni had arrived in Canada at the age of nineteen, in the company of his immigrant parents. In due course, he found employment as an apprentice auto mechanic in an east end auto body shop. Over the years, by hard work and by fencing a few stolen cars on the side, he was able to raise enough money to open his own chop shop business in Montreal. There was no shortage of customers for his cars. The prices were about half the actual retail value. Unfortunately for Joe, one of the eager buyers turned out to be an undercover cop.

Near the end of his prison sentence, Joe met Cat Kanaskis and Pearly Pattino, who were still doing time at KP for their unsuccessful bank robbery a couple of years after Joe Carboni was released.

Needing a fresh start, Joe Carboni moved his business to Toronto, where he opened a legitimate body and paint shop, as a front to his secret chop shop.

The back section of the Carboni compound on Weston Road was fenced in with a ten foot high wooden wall, to thwart prying eyes. The younger Carboni brothers and their families followed, shortly after Joe set up his dual operation.

Joe walked over and opened the lock on the high gate with a key. He waved the Mercedes in, and followed in with the Cadillac. Before Joe could close the gate, Pearly drove in with Cat's ancient pickup.

Joe Carboni looked at the pickup with a frown. He beckoned Cat over with a curled finger. Although Joe had lived in Canada for many years, he had never studied English, and dialect was still influenced by his Sicilian roots.

"What da fuck isa *dat*?" Joe asked, indicating the old vehicle. "He with you?"

Cat came over to Joe, followed by Pearly.

"Joe, remember my partner, Pearly Pattino?" Cat asked.

"Yeah. I do now. But his wheels looka awful sad."

"That's my old pickup Pearly's driving," Cat said. "We want to offer you a two-for-one deal."

Carboni looked skeptical. "Dat's a godawful lookin' piece a junk you got Pearly, I hope you ain't gonna leave it here. You should be ashamed, Cat, admittin' dat's yours."

"Still runs good, Joe. Ford don't make 'em like that any more."

"Well, thanka god for dat, my friend. It'll cost ya twenty-five bucks, if you want me to get rid of it. Now, what about da Mercedes?"

"It's a little warm. So, we'd like to trade it for another set of wheels."

Joe laughed: "You mean, it's *hot* and will need some immediate attention. Right?"

"Yeah, Joe. That's why we're here. What can you do for us?"

Carboni walked over to the Mercedes and gave it a quick inspection. "I see it's a current model and low mileage. Come inta my office and we'll talk."

The two wannabe kidnappers followed the chop shop operator, as he unlocked the outer door and led them in to a small office, featuring a steel desk littered with papers. Carboni indicated they should sit, while he pulled out a yellow pad from his desk and a ball point pen from his inside pocket. "Leta me see. Ona da market, repaint, with a new serial number, and new plates, I can probably get about fifty grand for the Mercedes. But the car isa hot. So I can only allow thirty thou' for it, as I'ma takin' all da risk. I won't charge for disposin' ofa da old heap. How's at sound, you guys?"

"Sounds like highway robbery," Cat moaned. "But we don't have a choice. Anyway, we need wheels. Something we can take right away. And not a small car, because we need trunk space."

Joe smiled. "Again, your lucky day, biga fella. I got a three-year-old Lincoln, justa been repaint. Ready ta roll."

"How about plates, and registration?" Cat asked.

"We'll switch da plates off yer old Ford pickup, already registered ina your name."

"But the registration slip says Ford," Cat pointed out.

Carboni looked pained. "Who da fuck you think makes Lincolns?"

"Never mind. If we have to show the slip, we're in trouble anyway," Cat decided. "But we want to switch something from the Mercedes trunk."

Carboni got up and walked over to hit a switch, opening the large garage door.

"Okay. Drive a da Mercedes in here. Da keys are in da Lincoln ignition. I don't even want to know whatsa in da trunk. You do da trunk business, while I get a wrench for da plates."

After moving Carol Monroe's body from trunk to trunk, Cat drove the Lincoln Town Car back onto Weston Road and headed north, towards the ramp to 401.

In the passenger seat, Pearly buckled his seat belt. "Better do yours up, Cat. We don't want to get caught on no technacality. Besides the fine is a hunnert bucks."

"Good thinking, partner. We gotta get out of the city pronto. Let's head up towards Barrie on 400 to find ourselves an empty cottage. We can write that ransom note and mail it when we go to Pearson airport to rent a locker."

"There's the ramp, Cat. Turn right"

"I can see fine, Pearl. No back seat driving."

"I ain't in the back seat. Besides, I think the locker is a bad idea for collectin' the ransom.

"Why bad. You got a better idea, spit it out." Cat sounded miffed.

"Bad because the girl's old man will call the cops. When we tell him to put the ransom money in the locker, the police will be watching like goddam hawks," Pearly pointed out.

"Sure they'll be watching the locker. But all that's needed is a diversion, something to get their attention elsewhere. Maybe a small bomb nearby. It isn't all that complicated."

"You're so fuckin' smart, how come you didn't think about them fingerprints until we spread them all over the house?"

"Well, they were *your* fingerprints, as well as mine. How come *you* didn't think of them?"

Pearly decided to change the subject. "You think the little bitch is okay?"

"I don't know. And, she's a girl, not a bitch. I just hope she's getting enough air."

"She seemed kinda limp, when we loaded her into the trunk."

Cat frowned. "I don't want a dead hostage on our hands. But we can't stop now.".

"Get in the right lane, Cat. There's the sign for 400 North."

"Try closing your eyes, and your mouth, partner. I'll let you know when we get there."

"Just so you don't bust your brain, makin' all the wrong decisions, big guy," Pearly said sarcastically. "You know what they say about grass that don't grow on no busy street. And you with all that hair on yer head. I wunner how I got along all those years on my own. Stealin' jewels takes brains, ya know."

"Awright, awright," Cat said with exasperation. "So you're a fucking genius. Let's drop it, Pearl. We've got to find a cottage that's empty, private and winterized, so we don't freeze. And we're going to need a tape-recorder."

"Tape recorder? What for?"

"So we can get the girl to say something to her parents, to prove we've got her."

"Good idea. A real tear jerker for the parents."

Cat looked across at his partner, and shook his head in disgust.. "You're all heart, Pearly.".

"And you're a damned softnik and a control freak."

During the next few miles of the trip North, the two partners maintained a sullen silence. After passing the low flatland of Holland Marsh, Cat was the first to speak again. "Pearl, for crissake say something. You're getting on my nerves, just sitting there with your bare face hanging out."

"Somethin'", Pearl said.

"What?"

"You said to say somethin', and I said it."

"Well, let's call a truce. We have to finish this job and get our two mil."

"Okay," Pearl said. "Long as I get to have some say in what we do. Yer not gonna call all the shots in this here operation."

Reluctantly, Cat agreed. "You got it. But if you screw up…"

Pearly cut him off. "My first decision is right now. We don't go to Barrie, see. The OPP will be watchin' all the major highways outa Toronto, as soon as the hostige is reported missin'. So the sooner we get off 400 the safer we'll be."

"Makes sense," Cat admitted reluctantly. "Where do you want us to go, glorious new leader?"

Pearly referred to a road map of Ontario that he found in the glove compartment. He turned on the overhead light and advanced the dial of the car heater further into the red zone.

"We can turn East on Innisfil Beach Road. That's prob'ly on Lake Simcoe. "

When they saw the highway sign, Cat turned the big Lincoln onto the off-ramp and they proceeded down Innisfil Beach Road. Fortunately for the two cottage-seekers, in the increasingly cool night there was a brilliant full moon. They cruised along the shore, with the waters of Lake Simcoe unusually calm, giving the appearance of a large silver platter.

Many of the cottages were too close to the road for privacy, and a few appeared to be occupied, with cars or pickup trucks parked in the yards. Some that appeared to be unoccupied were obviously basic seasonal residences. Cat finally stopped in front of a property that featured a dense cedar hedge across the front of a wide lot, also bordered on both sides with tightly grouped trees. From the main road, they could see the outline of a substantial two-storey building with a steeply pitched roof and a stone chimney. The rural mailbox out front bore the name 'Murphy'. The place appeared to be unoccupied, with no lights visible and all the windows covered with wooden shutters.

"Let's drive up the lane, Cat," Pearly suggested. "If anybody's home, we can make some excuse about askin' for directions."

"Okay," Cat agreed, as he wheeled into the long driveway. "Looks like a first class hideout. Nice and private."

The cottage, built on a slight elevation, turned out to be a large, modern building with brown stained exterior. At the back, there was a one-car garage and a small utility building, presumably for garden equipment. At least a cord of firewood was stacked along the side of the garage. A light green propane tank was partially visible behind the building.

Cat pulled the Lincoln right up to the back of the house, so that it could not be seen from the road. While Pearly walked over to check the garage, Cat opened the trunk by pushing a button inside the glove compartment. The little trunk bulb lit up the inert body of the hostage, with duct tape on her mouth, wrists and ankles still intact. He checked her pulse, which was faint, and he anxiously put a hand on her forehead. There was some evidence of a mild fever. He was glad to find that she had at least *survived* the trip huddled in the trunk.

But her comatose condition was certainly cause for alarm.

12

Toronto, Saturday, November 29, 2003

The fact that Murray Hammond's room-mate was a pretty young female, and his lover, was not a universally popular situation. He knew his widowed mother, who lived with his sister in St. Catharines, prayed every night for her only son's lost soul.

Kathy and Murray had met at a party put on by one of her girl friends two years earlier. When they were introduced, their mutual attraction was instantaneous. But he was so shy at the outset that she had to practically force herself on him. To Kathy, Murray was a puzzling contradiction – a Jekyll and Hyde personality. Seeming to take special delight in the mayhem of professional hockey, Hammond earned his reputation of being an aggressive player – one to avoid. So, he received great respect for his deadly body checks and rough treatment in the corners. Murray's alter ego, off the ice, was entirely different. Outside the game, he reverted to his natural disposition, as a quiet introvert, modest and retiring. Despite his tendency to be self-effacing, Kathy could detect an inner strength in her boy friend, which she found very masculine and attractive.

Kathy Blake's parents were both academics. Her mother, also named Katherine, but nicknamed 'Katie', taught journalism at Ryerson. Her father, Gordon Blake, was a history professor at York University.

The Blakes were not critical of their daughter's decision to co-habit with a hockey player eight years older than her thirty years. They understood that the young couple did not want to make a permanent commitment while he was playing in a professional sport which kept him away from home a good deal of the time, traveling from city to city in North America, with an occasional trip to Europe for exhibition games.

Aside from the welcoming approval of her parents, who immediately took a liking to Murray, Kathy was not in the least concerned about the opinions of others. She loved Murray and could not care less about anyone with raised eyebrows, critical of their arrangement. Let their tongues wag until they fall off. Besides, she had read somewhere, co-habitation in the early stages of a relationship was far better than a hasty marriage and then a possible divorce after the first bloom of passion had withered, like the last rose of summer with a bug on it.

When Murray came out of the shower, whistling tunelessly, and wearing a bath towel around his waist, Kathy was already propped up on two pillows on their king size bed. She was wearing a very transparent nightie and reading the same book which he had inadvertently defaced slightly by letting a drop of sweat fall on one of the pages. He climbed on the bed beside her and read the title on the cover.

He announced the title aloud, and burst out laughing. "The Joy of Sex. Are you learning anything you don't already know, Hon?"

She tossed the book on the night table and turned out the light. "Just so much theory. There's nothing like practical experience. I'd rather you taught me, lover."

Pulling him to her, she pressed her mouth on his smiling lips. Then she kissed each of his eyelids, and blew her hot breath in his left ear.

"Hey! That ear trick is new," he commented. "What else did you learn in that book?"

"What do you expect? I'm only up to Chapter Three," she said in a low, sexy voice.

She undid the knot on his damp bath towel and ran her fingers gently and slowly over the contours of his torso, ending at his male erection. Soon, her gentle stroking began to get him too excited, too soon. "Whoa babe," he gasped. "Easy does it. Or we'll have the denouement before the prologue. Let's go back to Chapter One."

By Saturday afternoon, having heard nothing from Constable Dixon, Murray phoned him and asked about the outcome of the police investigation.

"It's kind of strange, Mr. Hammond," the officer said. "When the cruiser got to the address you gave us, there was no answer at the door, and no lights on, or any other indication that anyone was home. The registered owner of the property is George Monroe, an investment broker."

"More than strange," Murray observed. "How long before they got there?"

"Ten minutes after you called. But, of course, you had to return home from the house on The Bridle Path. So, in total, I suppose that would make it a half hour after you spoke with the gentleman at the Monroe house."

"Still doesn't add up, as far as I'm concerned," Murray said. "They were supposed to be calling their doctor. Why would they leave the house so quickly?"

"Don't know. Anyway, the same officers followed up this morning. They found the house still unoccupied, so they talked with some neighbors. They were told the Monroes were a quiet couple and did not mix much. A young daughter, living at home, attends the University of Toronto."

"Did any of the neighbors hear the screaming?" Murray asked.

"Nobody reported any screaming. The foggy night, the size of the lots in that neighborhood, plus the mature trees and high hedges would kill any sound to some extent. Unless a person was outside, as you were, it is understandable that there were no other reports of unusual sounds, particularly of a woman screaming."

"So, what is the next step in the investigation?" Murray asked.

"We have sort of put this one on the back burner, for now," he admitted. "It is possible that Mister Monroe took his daughter to the hospital, or some other medical facility. That might explain why there was no answer this morning when the officers followed up. Anyway, the owner's explanation seems reasonable enough."

"Or plausible enough," Murray suggested. "How about getting a search warrant to have a look around, inside?"

"Not a chance. There must be some real evidence that the law is being broken," Dixon replied. "There has to be reasonable cause for the police to enter the premises. There is no such evidence. Just your story, or rather, your report. These days, we have family disputes coming out our ears, and we're drastically understaffed. A record of your call has been recorded in our computer data bank. If anything further turns up, we'll get back to you. Sorry, I've got to take another call."

Hearing the dial tone, Murray replaced the phone.

13

Innisfilin Beach Road, Early Saturday, November 29, 2003

Cat gently closed the trunk lid of the Lincoln, without latching it. Pearly had come from the garage, which he said contained some gardening equipment and a lawn tractor.

"The girl is unconscious, Pearl. So we've got to stop wasting time and get her inside. This is your moment to demonstrate your expertise, partner," Cat said. "Show me how you can open the back door. I'll hold the flashlight."

Pearly examined the lock. "A piece of cake," he declared. "Common type of cheap lock you get at hardware stores. Nothing too complicated for ol' Pearly." He pulled a set of lock picks out of his jacket pocket and went to work. In two minutes they were inside.

Proud of his demonstration of quick break and enter, Pearly led the way up a short flight of stairs to the kitchen. He pushed a light switch and an overhead light came on. "Hey, Cat. There's power and even some heat on, judgin' by the temperature.

"Not too surprising, Pearl. Looks like they keep low heat on during the cold weather, so that the concrete blocks in the basement won't crack."

"I seen a propane tank out back," Pearly said. "Mebbe they got a propane furnace down there."

They went down to the basement.

"Fantastic!" Cat enthused, as he looked at a high efficiency propane furnace. "Just what the doctor ordered. Central heat. All we have to do is turn up the thermostat." He walked over to a laundry sink and turned on a tap. No water. "They drained the plumbing system for the winter."

"The fuse panel is right over here," Pearly said. "I'll turn on the water pump."

Almost immediately, Cat could hear the gushing of water upstairs, in the kitchen and bathroom, as well as the sanitary tub in the basement.

"Quick! Turn that pump off, dammit," Cat yelled. "When they drained the system, they left all the taps *open*. All the valves have to be closed *before* the water is turned on. Hurry up, or we'll flood the whole place."

"Okay. Okay. *You* run up and turn all the valves off," Pearly said resentfully, "while I stay here and wait for your *permission* to turn the water pump on."

"How did I ever find such a frigging genius for a partner," Cat grumbled as he headed upstairs.

When all the necessary 'turning off and on' functions had been completed, they went out to the yard and carried the inert body of Carol Monroe in, and laid her on the four-seater sofa in the living room. Cat pulled off the tapes that had been applied to keep their hostage silent. She still had her school clothes on; white turtleneck shirt under a light blue, wool sweater, designer jeans, wet in the seat, and Eddie Bauer rubber-soled runners.

"She's wet her pants," Pearly observed.

"Are you surprised? Cat asked, "she's been confined in that trunk since five-thirty this afternoon and it's away past midnight now."

He placed a finger on her throat and then a hand on her forehead. "Weak pulse. Bit of a fever. Her skin feels like she's half frozen. And I guess she didn't get enough oxygen. Lucky she hasn't cashed in her chips."

"Well, as I said earlier," Pearly reminded his partner. "We don't *need* her alive to cash in *our* chips. Alls we gotta do is let the parents *think* she's alive."

"Don't be stupid for crissake. We want to send a recording with the ransom note, to *prove* she's alive. Her dad is not going to pay two mil for a dead daughter."

"Awright. Have it your way," Pearly said. "But, far as I'm concerned, she's just excess baggage. Anyways, I thought we agreed that I was runnin' the show now."

"Only until you screwed up," Cat reminded him. "And you just did that when you kept suggesting we murder the girl or just let her die. That's what I call screwed up thinking."

"Well aren't you the gutless wonder," Pearly said sarcastically. "Mama's boy wants a big payoff, but is afraid to get his hands dirty."

"That'll be enough, Pearl, unless you want a taste of this." Cat said, scowling and clenching his huge fist. "I think she needs some medical attention, or she'll croak."

"What? We go to all the trouble of grabbing a hostage and now you want to get rid of her? You do that and I'm outa here."

The big man laughed. "How you going to do that, Pearl? "I've got the keys to the Lincoln."

"Don't give me that shit, Cat. I can hotwire that fuckin' Lincoln before you can blink. I can pull out anytime I want to."

"Listen chump. We're in this together," Cat said, waving his fist ominously. "If you don't agree with my decision about the girl, I can beat you to a pulp and throw your mean little carcass in the lake."

Pearly thought for a minute before he replied. He decided it was time to let his partner think he was going along with his decision.

"Okay, Mister Universe. Or rather, Miss Manners. What do you want me to do?"

"I want you to help me wrap this girl in warm blankets, so I can take her to a hospital."

Pearly said nothing more. While Cat went looking for blankets, he stayed with the comatose hostage. But his mind was working on a plan.

When Cat returned, with several blankets in his arms, they rolled Carol into them and carried her back out to the car. This time, they loaded her wrapped body stretched out, into the spacious back seat.

"I'm heading up to Barrie, Pearl," Cat said as he got behind the wheel. "Are you coming along?"

Pearly got in on the front passenger seat. "You ain't leavin' me much choice."

He reached down to his pant-leg and pulled out a small, silver Beretta, 9 m.m. revolver, which he leveled at Cat.

Looking down the barrel of the small weapon, Cat was surprised, but reacted calmly. "Where did you get that, Pearl? You didn't tell me you were packing."

"Never mind where I got it, big guy. I've had it all along. Being little can be a disa'vantage. But this here is a great equalizer. Makes me as big as you. No. Bigger'n you. . Now you'll have to do as I say. For starters, we ain't goin' to no hospital. If she kicks the bucket, that's too bad. Nothin's changed, except I'm the boss from here in."

Cat turned on the ignition and started the motor. "Well, Pearly, my boy, you got a lot of learning to do about your partner. If you want to shoot me, go ahead,"

He backed the Lincoln around and coolly turned on to the driveway. "We are on our way to the hospital. If you want out of this deal, I'll let you stay in the car until we get to Barrie. Then, if you want wheels to go somewhere, you can find another car and hot-wire it."

Pearly realized his bluff was being called. He stared at Cat with disbelief. Then slowly he lowered the Beretta and shoved it back into his ankle holster. "Fuck you, Cat," Pearly snarled. "You think you're so goddam cool. Well, we'll see about that. Push me hard enough and you'll die of lead poisonin'."

Cat continued to ignore Pearly's empty threats, as he drove the Lincoln at 120 km, about the speed of the rest of the light traffic at that early hour. He secretly wished they could stop at the McDonald's at the service centre at the intersection of 400 and 89. They had hardly any food or drink since breakfast, except for the beer and light snacks from the Monroe refrigerator. He was hungry and thirsty, but too worried about the girl who was stretched out on the back seat, to stop. Passing the second McDonald's, as they entered the outskirts of Barrie required even more determination about saving the girl's life.

He glanced at the clock on the dashboard, as four-lane Hwy. 400 took them through downtown Barrie. Unbelievably, the clock showed 4:30. Where had the time gone? Pearly's eyes were closed, his head leaning against the window. Cat wondered if his devious, ferret-like partner was putting on an act, feigning sleep.

Cat turned off 400, onto the service road and drove up to the entrance of imposing new Royal Victoria Hospital. He followed the signs to Emergency, slammed on the brakes, jammed the gearshift into Park and rushed around to the back door, leaving the motor idling.

Pearly woke up with a start. "What's goin' on?" he asked.

Cat pulled the inert body out of the back seat and said: "Back in a minute. Park somewhere out of the way of ambulances."

He carried Carol through the automatic doors and looked around for help. Spotting a receptionist who looked half-asleep, he approached her.

"I have an emergency patient here, who needs *immediate* attention."

The receptionist looked at him and then at the body he was carrying. "Certainly, sir, sit over there, and I'll ...."

"No sitting," Cat bellowed. "I want some action. My daughter is dying of exposure. Get a doctor *right now!*" He saw an empty gurney a few feet away. So he carried Carol to it and stretched out her slim body, still wrapped in blankets. So that she would not roll out, he pulled up the sides of the mobile bed. Her face was almost blue, and she was breathing raggedly.

An arm, clad in a white coat, tapped him on the shoulder. Cat turned and faced a beautiful dark-haired woman. He tried to read her lapel sign, as he was gently shoved aside.

"Are you a doctor?" he asked.

"Yes," she said curtly. She was frowning as she pulled the blankets away from Carol to exam her chest with a stethoscope. The receptionist, a middle-aged woman, was standing behind the female medico, with a defensive look on her face, apparently expecting another outburst from the big man.

"How did she get this way, Mister....?"

"Simpson, Harry Simpson," Cat supplied. "We're new in the area. She went for a walk and got lost in the woods. I traced her footsteps in the snow and found her half-frozen, hardly breathing. Her name is Carol."

"Alright Mister Simpson," the doctor said. "We'll take care of her. Just give the information to triage."

"What's triage, or whatever you call it?"

The receptionist pointed to herself and smiled. "I'm triage. Come with me."

He followed her back to the cubicle marked Triage. Looking over his shoulder, he saw an orderly pushing the gurney through some double doors.

The middle-aged receptionist had pulled out a form. "Do you have your daughter's Ontario health card, Mister Simpson?"

"Umm, not with me. I didn't want to delay, looking for it."

"We are not supposed to treat patients without a health card. Otherwise, some guarantee of payment is necessary."

"I'll guarantee payment," Cat promised. "But I'll have to get to my bank before I can pay for her treatment."

"That's alright, do you live in Barrie?"

"Innisfilin. We just moved there. Bought an all-season home from a fellow by the name of Murphy. He lives in Toronto."

"Uh, huh. What is you daughter's full name?"

"Carol Eaton Simpson."

The receptionist stared at him in disbelief.

He grinned. "Her mother liked department stores," he lied. "Bless her soul. She died in childbirth. "I've had to raise Carol as a single parent."

"I see. It must be difficult for you. "Your new address, please."

"R.R.1, Innisfilin, Ontario. I'm not sure of the postal code."

"Phone number?"

"Er...phone not installed yet. I'm using a cell phone. The phone and number is out in my Lincoln." He mentioned the upscale model of automobile to impress the receptionist with his ability to pay for Carol's treatment.

"Your occupation Mister Simpson?"

"Ah, hydraulics engineer. You know, for lifting things."

"Company?"

"Harry Simpson Hydraulics Engineering Inc. That Inc. at the end, is for incorporated. I'm the president.".

She was writing all his answers down. "What is the nature of your daughter's illness?"

"Suffering from over-exposure. I'm not qualified at diagnosis, except in things to do with hydraulics."

She sniffed. "Of course not. Does she have any allergies, particularly to drugs, like penicillin?"

He paused before answering. "Um, no allergies." He hoped he was right.

"Please sign this form and take a seat now, while the doctor examines your daughter?" She still looked sort of tentative, considering his initial rampage.

He signed and thanked her. "I'll be right back. I think I left the motor running in my car, in my anxiety to get Carol medical treatment."

He walked out the automatic double doors, with no intention of returning.

The Lincoln was nowhere to be seen. After searching the almost empty parking lot, he concluded that Pearly had taken off with his wheels. He was not surprised, considering their argument about the hostage.

After checking out the parked cars, he could not find any that were unlocked. It would not have mattered if he had found one, he decided, because he had no screwdriver or any other tool to hot-wire an ignition.

Rather than face the receptionist at Emergency, who would ask again for his cell phone number, he walked around to the front entrance and called a taxi, using a pay phone. When the cab showed up ten minutes later, he asked to be delivered to the nearest fast food restaurant that was open.

"There are none open this early, sor." The foreign cab driver said. "Not that I know of. McDonald's and Wendy's on Bayfield Street open at 7 a.m." Leo thought the dark-skinned driver was either a Paki or an Iranian, judging by his accent. Probably white-skinned drivers had more sense than to be working all night.

"What about the McDonald's at the service centre, the other side of town?" Cat asked. "It was all lit up last time I passed it at night."

"Yeah, that one stays open all night. But, it's on the wrong side of the highway. So, I'd have to go to Molson Park to get turned around."

"Tough beans, buddy. Don't tell me your problems, I'm hungry as a bear. So just *go!*"

"Yes, *sor!*

When he was dropped off at McDonald's on the southern outskirts of Barrie, Cat paid off the driver and sent him on his way. He just had enough money left to satisfy his hunger and thirst with two Big Macs with fries and a large chocolate milk shake. He positioned himself at the glass doors facing the parking lot. As a single driver was leaving the restaurant, Cat asked for a lift to the Royal Victoria Hospital, where he said his daughter was in serious condition, intensive care. Cat explained that his car had broken down and had been towed to a garage on Essa Road.

The young driver, who said he was heading north to Orillia, appeared sympathetic and told Cat he would drop him at the ramp leading to the service road leading to the hospital. They chatted amiably on the 400 route through Barrie and Cat thanked the man for the lift. His feet were cold by the time he had trudged the two blocks through the snow to the hospital parking lot. He thought he could have relieved the young man of his wheels, but he was not impressed with the rusty five-year-old Mazda Protégé, having been spoiled by the Lincoln with which his partner had absconded.

His Mickey Mouse watch said 6:30 as he ducked inside the Emergency sliding doors to get warm. After a few minutes, he noticed a black BMW sedan approaching the portion of the lot reserved for medical personnel. He beat the car to the lift gate and stood behind it, as the sole occupant of the black bimmer placed a card in the slot and waited for the single barrier to rise.

Noting the MD plate on the car, Cat tapped on the window and the unsuspecting driver obligingly pushed the button to lower the power window.

"Good Morning, Doc," Cat said. "We are offering V.I.P. parking this morning," as he reached in and pulled the keys from the ignition.

The doctor's jaw dropped in surprise and indignation. "What in blazes is going on? I've been called in for emergency surgery. But I usually park my own car, thanks."

Cat grabbed the doctor by his coat collar and easily lifted him out from behind the wheel. The little medico weighed perhaps 140 lbs in his expensive cashmere overcoat. The big car hijacker had the advantage of at least one hundred pounds in weight over his victim, and three years' of arduous muscle-building in the gymnasium at KP. Operating the remote control on the key chain, he quickly shoved the struggling surgeon into the spacious trunk.

In his newly-acquired 'ultimate driving machine', Cat turned on the stereo radio to drown out any noise emanating from behind the back seat. He drove south on the service road until he could get back onto 400 South. Past Molson Park, he left the superhighway and took a concession road until he reached a remote area, where he stopped and opened the trunk.

The doctor was swearing loudly as he emerged from the trunk of his own car.

"Might as well save your breath, Doc," Cat said, with a smile. "There's nobody around here who can hear you. And my late, sainted mother would not want me to listen to all those four letter words."

"But, how am I going to get back to the hospital? It's urgent."

"I checked out the glove compartment of your BMW, Doc. Your I.D. is Doctor Clarence Good. Nice to meet you, Clarence, old boy. I saw the hospital number on your phone list. And, I can use your cell phone to tell them of your pre-dicament. If they need you, they will send transportation. Have a nice day."

On the way back to 400, Kanaskis phoned the hospital to tell the Surgical Ward where they could find Dr. Good.

When Cat pulled the BMW in behind the Murphy all-season cottage on Innisfilin Beach Road, he was not surprised to see the Lincoln parked behind the back door. Pearly opened the door, wearing a large grin, and holding a steaming cup of coffee out for his partner.

"Hi, Cat. What took you so long?"

"Some son-of-a-bitch took my wheels. That's why." He took a sip of the coffee.

"Are you pissed?"

"Sure. But not surprised. And I've had time to get over it."

"Will ya be holdin' a grudge?"

"Nah. I am aware that you think we should have whacked the girl. You lost the argument, so I was not surprised you took off with the Lincoln."

"I see you picked up a decent replacement."

"Yeah," Cat replied. "BMWs are okay. And hijackers can't be choosers."

"Should be able to raise a few bucks on the bimmer from Joe Carboni."

"Let's go," Cat said. "I'll take the Lincoln. You can drive the BMW."

14

Highway 400, Saturday afternoon, November 29, 2003

Cat in the Lincoln, and Pearly in the BMW drove down 400 in light traffic and almost zero visibility, due to a low ground mist, moisture sprayed from passing trucks and a heavy overcast sky.

Pearly had started out ahead, but had to stop at the Esso service centre for gas, when he noticed the fuel gauge showing a red warning light. He figured Cat was aware that the BMW was low on gas, and that the switch of cars was his partner's way of getting even for last night.

Meanwhile, Cat smiled to himself as he saw that Pearly had to pull in for gas. He continued on at 120 Km per hour.

Just as he reached the top of the hill at the south end of Holland Marsh, he heard a siren. Looking in the rear view mirror, he had a sinking feeling. An O.P.P. cruiser was right on his tail, with a 'Police' light flashing and a roof-mounted blue strobe light rotating. Slowly, Cat pulled over on the shoulder and stopped.

The O.P.P. vehicle drew up behind the stationary Lincoln and the uniformed officer got out. As a precaution, the officer undid the dome fastener on his service revolver and approached the driver's side of the Town Car. Cat used the button to roll down the window.

"Good afternoon, officer. Was I going too fast?" Cat asked innocently.

"Yes, sir. May I see your driver's license and the vehicle registration please?"

Cat stalled for time, pretending to reach in the glove compartment. Over his shoulder, he said: "I didn't realize you were behind me, officer. What speed was I going?"

"I clocked you at 120," the officer replied. "As you know, the speed limit is 100. Your driver's license and ownership please."

Cat frowned and turned back to the officer. "Hey, I thought you guys only issued tickets for speeding *over* 120. That's not really speeding. Heck, all the other cars are going at least that fast."

The young officer was trying to contain his temper. "Sir, I'm not going to debate the issue with you. You were speeding. Now, I'll give you fifteen seconds to produce your driver's license and ownership."

There was a squeal of brakes from behind and a black BMW came alongside, pinning the officer against the side of the Lincoln.

Pearly lowered the passenger window and apologized. "Geez, I'm sorry, officer. The steering system on this expensive car needs replacing."

Like a pair of well-trained performers, Cat and Pearly acted instinctively. Leo Kanaskis opened the driver's door of the Lincoln and relieved the struggling officer of his service revolver. Meanwhile, Pearly Pattino got a tire iron out of the trunk of the BMW and went back to the cruiser. He smashed the two-way radio and drew the keys out of the ignition. He tossed them in the adjacent field.

"Time to roll, partner," Pearly said to Cat, as he got back in the BMW. The two vehicles were on there way, leaving a dazed O.P.P. officer standing helplessly at the side of the fog-bound highway.

Using the doctor's cell phone, which he had switched to the Lincoln, Cat phoned Joe Carboni at Carboni Import Export, as the ramp to 401 loomed ahead.

When Carboni answered, Cat said: "Hey, Joe. It's Cat again. With more business for you. Can we meet you at the shop?"

"Okay. But not until after dark. That'll be about five a clock. Gimme an hour. Will ya?"

"We'll need some cash, Joe."

"Not a problem. But don'ta show up until five."

"Gotcha."

Cat and Pearly cooled their heels in a coffee shop on Weston Road, while waiting for the magic hour of five. Later, when darkness had fallen, they drove the two cars down the back lane to the tall wooden gate, which swung open as they arrived.

"You guys have a been busy, I see." Joe Carboni feasted his eyes on the black BMW. "Nice a wheels."

"How much for the bimmer, Joe?" Cat asked.

"Hmm, for cash. Twelve grand. But I only gotta ten ina da safe."

Cat was not about to argue. They needed cash to continue to survive and make their big haul. "We'll take it Joe. And we'd like to trade the Lincoln back to you for different wheels."

"You mean, it's a *hot*, too? Shame on yous. Okay, you can a have da Mercedes. It's been a repaint dis morning and da serial changed."

"Gee. That's fast work. Show us."

Joe opened the big doors and pointed to the Mercedes formerly the property of George Monroe. It had been expertly repainted a lovely sandy gold color.

"New plates, too," Joe pointed out. "Come inta da office and we'll do new o'nership and driver's license. What was a dat name I gave ya. Simpson?"

"Can't use it anymore, Joe," Cat said. "The name's hot, too."

"Jesus, man. Can't yous stay outa trouble?"

"No. Seems like trouble follows us around. Anyway, let's try the name Parson, William Parson for a change. Maybe the dicks will think I'm a preacher."

15

Toronto, Saturday, November 29, 2003

Murray Hammond preferred to do his jogging and wind sprints in the evening hours. But, giving in to his curiosity, he jogged slowly past The Bridle Path mansion Saturday afternoon. There was no indication that anyone was home. After hesitating briefly, he finally decided to turn back and walk casually up the cedar-lined driveway. When he reached the front entrance, he went up to the door and used the big knocker to announce his presence.

There was no answer, no sound from within.

When he returned to his apartment on Lawrence East, he was glad that Kathy was out. She had said earlier that she wanted to spend a couple of hours with her parents, who lived near High Park. Realizing that she was skeptical about his amateur sleuthing, he felt he did not want any more heckling from the cheap seats. He picked up the phone and punched in the number for the police precinct.

A female voice answered. "Police department. Constable Watters here. May I help you?"

"I'd like to speak with Constable Dixon please."

"Sorry. He's off duty. Would you like to leave a message?"

"No message," Murray said. "I was speaking with him about a suspicious incident I encountered last night. Just wanted to check again to see if anything new had transpired."

"When did this suspicious incident occur, sir?" The police woman had a nice clear voice, but very brisk, clipped, and to the point.

Murray decided to match her no-nonsense approach. "Friday night at 7:15. On The Bridle Path. Woman screaming," he replied tersely.

There was a pause, presumably while Watters pulled up a report on the computer. "Yes, I have it here. You are Mister Hammond?"

"Yes. Murray Hammond. I live on Lawrence Ave."

"After the follow-up investigation this morning, there is nothing new to report. Unless you have some additional information, no further police action seems to be required, since there is no firm evidence of wrong-doing. Have you thought of anything that would justify re-opening the investigation?"

"Well, I was jogging past the house this afternoon and there is still no indication that anyone is home. The girl who was screaming claimed she was being abducted. Surely that is a very real possibility, despite what that guy said, who claimed he was her father. Now that I think of it, he was kind of a rough looking character, at odds with the nice home and upscale neighborhood. Did the investigating officers get a description of the owner?"

"Just a minute." There was a pause, while the constable read the report. "Here it is. The owner, Mister George Monroe, is an elderly gentleman, gray hair, Caucasian, five-eleven, brown eyes. His age is sixty, according to his registered driver's license. Does that match the description of the man you spoke to last evening?"

"Not even close, officer! The guy I spoke to was at least six-three, red-haired, and his eyes were blue. But he *said* he was the girl's father. So, everything he told me was a lie. I still believe she was being abducted."

"From your description of the man representing himself as Mister Monroe, I would certainly agree with you. I am glad you have persisted with this enquiry, Mister Hammond. I will see that a detective is placed in charge of the investigation right away. Will you be home for a few minutes, in case we want to get in touch with you?"

"I'll be in the shower for about ten minutes. After that, I can answer the phone."

"Right. You may expect a call from a detective very shortly."

Murray Hammond was just finishing dressing after his shower, when the phone rang.

"Hello."

"Murray Hammond?"

"Yes, this is Murray Hammond."

"Detective Sergeant Ian Scott here, I understand you have serious misgivings about the Monroe matter, and believe that there has actually been an abduction. Constable Watters has filled me in on your conversation of a few minutes ago. How long has it been since you were by the house on The Bridle Path?"

"I guess it's been about three-quarters of an hour. I could see no sign of occupancy. Even when I knocked on the door, there was no answer."

"Hmm. We have had one of our patrol cars follow up after your call. And the officers confirmed that the house seems to be unoccupied at present. Under the circumstances, it sounds like there is enough probable cause to suspect a crime has been committed, allowing us to obtain a search warrant."

"Will you let me know the outcome of your search, Sergeant? The girl was screaming from the front window on the second floor, above the bay window on the first floor."

"I have a better idea, Mister Hammond. Would you be willing to come with me and show me exactly where she was before someone pulled her back and closed the window?"

"Certainly. Anything I can do to help. Will you pick me up?"

"Yes, in an unmarked green Ford at the front entrance. I'll phone as soon as I am leaving the precinct, and we'll pick you up within ten minutes of my phone call. Okay?" Scott asked.

"Okay. I'll be waiting at the entrance, after you phone."

A half hour later, Hammond was waiting just inside the front door of the low-rise apartment building when the green Ford sedan pulled up in front. Wearing his Maple Leafs jacket, and a blue touque, he hurried down to the street. A man stepped out from the passenger side and introduced himself as Detective Sergeant Ian Scott. They shook hands.

"I appreciate your taking the time to come with us, Mister Hammond," the detective said, as he opened the back door for Hammond to take a seat.

"This is my boss, Inspector Ben Christopher. He obtained the Search Warrant and decided to visit the crime scene with us," Ian Scott explained.

"Hi Inspector," Murray said, as he climbed in the back seat of the non-descript vehicle. "Please call me Murray. Mister Hammond is my father."

The man in the front seat grinned and laughed at the little joke. He waved his gloved hand at Murray. The Inspector wore a light weight top coat unbuttoned, over a dark blue business suit, with light blue dress shirt and maroon tie. The Sergeant was less formally dressed, in a black leather bomber jacket and gray Dockers slacks.

On the way to the to the Monroe house, Ian Scott explained that they were meeting a team of criminal investigation specialists, whom would be dusting the house for fingerprints and collecting any available evidence.

"Then you agree there has probably been an abduction?" Hammond asked, feeling his persistent efforts to get some action were finally vindicated.

Detective Ian Scott replied: "It's certainly beginning to look that way. Your report of the man who answered the door, representing himself as the girl's father, does not agree with the physical description we received from the neighbors, nor does it agree with the details on Mr. Monroe's driver's license. He has gray hair and brown eyes and his height is listed as five-eleven. Apparently, not at all like the guy with whom you talked last evening."

When the green sedan pulled in to the driveway on The Bridle Path, there were two vehicles already parked there. One was a blue and white squad car and the other a white van with Crime Lab markings. A uniformed officer was stationed at the front door.

Murray Hammond accompanied the two detectives up the flagstone steps, where they paused in front of the gothic arch over the entrance, so that he could point out the window from which the girl had been screaming. The uniformed officer spoke to the inspector.

"Sir, a piece of duct tape has been found in the bed-room, and a hole in the door where a nail has been driven. In the basement, there are beer steins, a cigar butt and evidence that the perps were trying to make up a ransom note, when they were interrupted. The girl's Jetta is in the garage, but her father's Mercedes is missing."

Sergeant Scott looked at his wristwatch and made a note in his black pad. He drew Murray aside. "Thanks for confirming the location of the room where the girl was being held. Have you thought of any other descriptive marks or features that might help us trace the man you spoke with here at the door last evening?

Murray thought for a moment. "Yes, come to think of it, he had a small lump of some kind on his forehead, just above his right eye. Other than the wild red hair, blue eyes, moustache and linebacker size, six-three or four and perhaps two-fifty, that's about all I remember about him. Did I mention that he was wearing brown corduroy slacks and a beige turtle-neck pullover?"

The detective continued to make notes in his book. "No, but that's a very complete description. Do you think you could identify him in a line-up?"

"I believe so. But, of course, you have to find him first. Seems like he, or they, if more than one, got a good head start."

"That's true, but if this is a straight forward kidnap-ping, and not sexually motivated, there is a good chance the perps will try to contact Mister Monroe to demand a ransom."

"Speaking of Mister Monroe, have you traced the girl's parents?"

"Not yet. It seems unlikely, if there is going to be a ransom demand, that the whole family has been taken hostage. It is more likely that just the girl was abducted. Taking three people hostage is a lot for anyone to handle. The parents may be away for the weekend."

Inspector Christopher waived to Scott, indicating that he was going inside.

"Got to go," Sergeant Scott said. "Do you mind wait-ing in the car, Mister err…or rather, Murray? I can drop you off at the apartment in a few minutes."

"Not necessary, Sergeant. I'll just jog home. It's not that far. Will you let me know how this turns out?"

"Sure. But, it'll be all over the news media, now that we know it's definitely a kidnapping. Thanks again for all your help."

16

Innisfilin Beach Road, Saturday evening, November 29, 2003

When the two wannabe kidnappers drove north on Weston Road, after leaving the Carboni chop shop, they both felt much better about their financial situation. They had acquired a newly repainted 2003 Mercedes sedan and $10,000 to show for their efforts of the past two days. And Cat had the satisfaction of knowing that the hostage was in good medical care in Barrie. Hoping that she had been delivered to the hospital in time to save her life, he had used Doctor Good's cell phone to get a report on her condition. The report was still vaguely disconcerting. Carol Simpson was comatose and being treated for pneumonia, caused by hypothermia.

"It's getting late, Pearl," Cat said, "and unless you have a better suggestion, I think we should return to Mister Murphy's emporium on Innisfilin Beach Road."

Pearly simply nodded agreement. He was greedily counting the large pile of cash paid by Joe Carboni, and splitting it in two equal amounts.

As they drove up 400 again, Cat looked across at his partner. "Now that we are sitting pretty financially, for the first time in years, I wonder if we should just forget about going after the big haul. Five grand each would take care of our expenses until we could find a way to make an honest living. Or, should I say, a living honestly?"

Pearly stopped counting, and looked at his partner in disbelief. "You getting' cold feet again, Cat? There's a helluva difference between five grand and over a million bucks each."

"Of course there is," Cat agreed. "But, there is also a huge difference in the risk factor, between accepting what we have, as opposed to trying to complete the plan. *My* plan, incidentally."

"Well it may be your friggin' plan, Cat. But the important part is the ransom, enough to live on comfortably the rest of our lives. I didn't realize I had hooked up with a quitter."

Leo Kanaskis was quick to point out that he was only thinking out loud. "Don't go jumping to conclusions, pal. I was just weighing the odds. Taking the hostage was easy compared to collecting the ransom. The last part of my plan *might* work, or it *might not*. Besides, I still have hopes of getting Muriel back. And the only way I can do that is to get an honest job."

Pearly looked disgusted. "Make up your mind, Cat. Because, I'll do it alone, if you quit. I'll collect my share of the ransom, and you can go back to yer wife, the hooker, with yer hat in yer hand. I promised my girl friend, Sam, a nice reward, and I am not gonna back out now."

Cat did not put up any further objection. "Okay, okay. We'll carry on with the B part of the plan. But I hope we won't regret bumping against the law in a big way. Tomorrow, we have to get hold of Boomer Boudrealt to make us a small bomb. We need a bomb that can be detonated by remote control. Do you know how we can contact Boomer?"

"Let me use that cell phone," Pearly said. "I know his sister's number in T.O. and she will know where he is."

"Okay, next thing on the agenda is to rent a locker at Pearson airport so that you can make a duplicate of the key. Our ransom note will include a key, with instructions to leave the ransom in a large envelope. We'll demand two certified cheques of One Million Dollars each payable to Bearer, plus Ten Thousand dollars for expenses, in used, unmarked bills, nothing larger than a fifty, to be delivered in a suitcase and placed in the locker."

"Just a reminder, Cat – tomorrow is Sunday."

"Doesn't matter. The airport operates 7/24. And we'll give Monroe a day to come up with the dough. Provided Boomer Boudrealt can supply the bomb in time, we can pick up the ransom money Monday night."

"The fuzz will be watching the locker."

"Yes. But they won't recognize us. Tomorrow morning we have to visit Malabar's, the costume people." Cat said.

"How are we going to get the ransom note to Mister Monroe?"

"Did you say your girl friend, Sam, has a younger brother?"

"Yes. His name is Tommy. He's fifteen." Pearly replied.

"Give him fifty bucks to drop off the note at the house Sunday, after we visit the airport. The police can't charge a juvenile."

"What if Carol comes out of her deep slumber and fingers us?"

"Then Monroe will realize that his daughter is no longer a hostage and he won't pay a cent. That's a risk we have to take."

"Geez, I tol' you we shoulda whacked her."

17

Toronto, Sunday evening, November 30, 2003

$\mathbf{A}$ir Canada Flight 147 from Bermuda's International Airport to Toronto's Pearson, Terminal 2 arrived on time, at 6:30 Sunday evening. George Monroe had told his daughter Carol not to bother trying to meet the flight, that he and her mother, Marsha, would take a limousine home, on their arrival.

When her legs would not function properly, Marsha Monroe had been diagnosed with multiple sclerosis (MS) in December, 2000. The neurologist at St. Michael's Hospital explained that the disease was incurable, in the present knowledge of medical science, but could be mitigated to some extent with drug treatment. Although the advance of the disease was relatively slow, it was inexorable and she had become confined to a wheel chair most days. When George was playing golf with friends at the exclusive Mid-Ocean Country Club in Bermuda, Marsha enjoyed accompanying the foursome, as a passenger in her husband's golf cart.

In his sixtieth year, George Monroe was still in robust good health. The only downside to his character was a quick temper, which he tried to keep in check when in the presence of his wife. The wheelchair Marsha was sitting in at the curb outside Terminal 2 belonged to Air Canada.   So, George thought nothing of 'doing the honors' in carrying his wife and placing her carefully in the back seat of the limousine. The weather in Toronto was still damp and foggy, as the long, black airport limousine arrived at the Monroe house on The Bridle Path.

When the driver attempted to pull up to the house, a uniformed police officer stood in front of the headlights with his hand raised. There was yellow crime scene tape across the driveway, marked POLICE – Do not Pass

"Looks like we can't go any farther, Mister Monroe," the driver said.

George Monroe stepped out of the rear door and approached the constable. "What in blazes is going on here, officer?"

"Are you Mister Monroe, sir?"

"I certainly am. And I have my invalid wife waiting in the limousine to get into our house."

"Just a moment, sir, I'll let the Inspector know you are here." He spoke into a walkie-talkie. In about thirty seconds the large, oak front door opened. The two plain clothes detectives, Christopher and Scott hurried down the steps and the uniformed policeman returned to take up his usual post at the front entrance.

"Mister Monroe, I am Inspector Ben Christopher and this is my associate, Sergeant Ian Scott. We have been trying to locate you since Friday night. I am sorry to have to inform you that your daughter, Carol, has been abducted and is being held for ransom."

George Monroe was visibly shocked. "Good God, man, this is unbelievable. My wife and I have been away for a little holiday in Bermuda for the weekend – and we come home to learn our daughter is missing and our home overrun by police. When did all this happen and what are you doing about it?"

"Our nearest estimate of the time, sir, is Friday evening about five-thirty or six o'clock. A passer-by heard a cry for help about that time."

"In that case, why were the police not able to stop the kidnapping?"

"Rather than getting into a detailed discussion out here in the cold, why don't we all go inside. We understand your wife is disabled, so I can have a couple of our men help get her inside."

"That won't be necessary, Inspector. She weighs very little, and I am used to carrying her."

When the Monroes had removed their outer garments, George Monroe tried to get his wife to retire up to her room, using the small escalator adjoining the spiral staircase. But she would have no part of being kept out of the conversation. Although teary-eyed, as a result of the news about Carol, she was determined that she would not be kept in the dark about the situation.

The two detectives and Carol's parents all gathered in the huge living room, seated in beautiful antique furniture. The gas fireplace had been lit and one of the uniformed policemen volunteered to make tea in the kitchen.

Inspector Christopher started the discussion by asking if the Monroes had anyone, other than their immediate family living in the house.

George Monroe was annoyed. "You can answer my question first. Why did the police not take action when a passerby reported hearing Carol call for help?"

Christopher explained how one of the abductors had answered the door and pretended to be Carol's father. He went on to outline the chain of events leading up to the decision to obtain a search warrant to carry out the investigation.

"I see," George Monroe said testily. "So the kidnappers of our daughter were smart enough to mislead the passerby and, in turn, the police, enabling the criminals to make their getaway."

"Yes, Mister Monroe, there is no doubt in retrospect, we should have investigated further at the time of the first report. But Leo Kanaskis told a convincing story, which deflected suspicion for a while."

"Who, may I ask, is Leo Kanaskis?"

"One of the kidnappers, sir. His partner in this crime is Peter Pattino."

"So you *know* who the kidnappers are?"

"Yes, sir. They left lots of fingerprints. Both have prison records. But this is not their usual *modus operandi*. They are small time crooks, whom we believe are completely out of their depth. In the past, they have always been robbers, not kidnappers. We expect to catch them when they claim the ransom."

"Then they have sent a ransom note?"

"Yes. A young boy delivered the note this afternoon, by handing it to an unsuspecting uniformed officer on traffic duty. He passed it along to our precinct without delay."

"Did the officer collar the boy?"

"No. As I said, he was not expecting anything, and he knew nothing of the abduction until he read the note. Meanwhile the boy ran away and got lost in a crowd. But that is not important, as he was no doubt just a paid messenger."

"Bah! Faulty police work," Monroe blustered. The kid might have led us to where they are holding Carol. I should report your incompetence to the Chief of Police."

Marsha Monroe finally spoke up. "George, cool down and be reasonable. These detectives are making progress. They have, at least, identified the kidnappers. And, they know about the ransom demand. When the kidnappers try to collect the ransom, surely they will be caught."

"The ransom demand," her husband repeated sarcastically. "And what good news do you detectives have about that, if it is not too much to enquire."

"The demand is quite substantial. Two certified cheques, payable to bearer, each for one million dollars..."

George Monroe looked as though he was about to have a fit. "Good heavens! They must think I own a Swiss bank. There is no way I can raise that amount."

"I hadn't quite finished, Mister Monroe," the Inspector said. "They also demand ten thousand dollars in unmarked bills, none over a fifty dollar denomination."

"What's that for?"

"Presumably for incidental expenses. In other words, they are broke and need some quick cash, even before they try to cash the hypothetical cheques. The cash is to be left in a locker at Pearson airport in a big suitcase. They have supplied the locker number and a key."

"That's bloody ridiculous. They can *demand* until the cows come home. I won't pay a cent."

"George, before you get on your high horse, *think* about our daughter," Marsha pleaded. "Carol must be suffering terribly, certainly mentally and perhaps physically, in the hands of those two criminals."

He calmed down and went over to stand beside his wife. "Okay, dear. You are probably right. Let's hear what the police say. Inspector?"

"As I said earlier, sir, we fully expect to catch these two small-time crooks when they attempt to collect the ransom. It is only to be hoped that your daughter has not been harmed in the meantime. May I make a suggestion?"

"Go ahead. We are listening."

"It seems to me that you have two choices. Either put up ten thousand dollars, explaining that you cannot raise two million. If we collar the one or both of the kidnappers, when they attempt to open the locker, your money will be returned to you anyway. Or simply leave a suitcase full of blank paper in the locker. Hopefully, when one or the other of the kidnappers is caught, he will reveal where Carol is being held. We can be very persuasive during interrogation. But, the Toronto police may not use Gestapo tactics to get information. So there is always a chance that he or they, will refuse to reveal the location of their hostage."

Monroe pondered the alternatives for a moment. "Inspector, my wife and I would like to discuss our options privately. When do you need to know our decision?"

"Actually, we *don't* need to know what you are going to put in the suitcase. But the note says the ransom must be paid by 6 p.m. tomorrow. Or else."

"Or else, what?"

"They don't say. Just 'or else'."

18

Toronto, Sunday, November 30, 2003

After speaking with Jacques 'Boomer' Boudrealt's sister on the phone, Pearly reported to Cat that their luck was holding. Her brother happened to be on the VIA Rail train en route from Montreal to Toronto, due to arrive at 4 P.M.

"Excellent," Cat said. "Let's form a welcoming committee of two to intercept old Boomer before he disappears into the bosom of his sister's family, or gets on a motorcycle to North Bay with one of his Hell's Angels buddies."

"You heard his sister, Alicia, married a member of the bike gang?" Pearly asked.

"Yeah. She got hitched to another 'angel from hell', Pierre Dubois, likewise a Frenchie. Supposed to be the kingpin in the recently formed Ontario branch of the drug-dealing hardasses. Boomer got his nickname from blowing up the clubhouse of the rival Centurions. Nice people we have to work with."

"Well we can't be choosey, Cat. We need Boomer's expertise. If we made a bomb ourselves, we might blow up Terminal 2."

"Unintentionally, of course," Cat agreed.

"Of course, partner."

When the passengers arriving from the Montreal train streamed out on the concourse of the Union Station, Cat and Pearly spotted Jacques 'Boomer' Boudrealt, carrying a well-worn black travel case. The explosive expert was wearing a black leather jacket, blue jeans and brown, tooled, high-heeled cowboy boots. His long black hair was caught in a ponytail, partially hidden by a red toque bearing the logo of Les Canadiens hockey team.

"Hey, Boomer," Pearly said, holding out his hand, "how ya doin'?"

The brown-eyed, six foot tall French-Canadian stared malevolently down at Pearly like he was inspecting a piece of bad meat. "Who wants to know?" he asked.

From behind his partner, Cat intervened, trying to save Pearly from further embarrassment. "We do. Pearly and Cat. You know, from Kingston."

Boudrealt frowned, as though he were trying to remember some long forgotten catechism. "KP? Oh yeah. So what's with the big deal? You two just happen to meet my train?"

"No, Boomer," Cat said. "We need to talk to you about a project. Let's go across the street. There's a bar downstairs at the Fairmount Royal York."

"I dunno," Boomer said. "My sister is expectin' me for dinner."

"This won't take long," Pearly said persuasively. "And there's big dough in it."

"Okay. I'll give yez a half hour max. Then I gotta catch a cab."

"We'll do better than that," Cat said. "We'll drive you to your sister's place in our new Mercedes."

"You punks got a Mercedes? Next t'ing ya know pigs will fly."

In a secluded corner of the bar, over several beers, Cat outlined his plan to collect the ransom, and the need for a diversion so that they could open the locker at Pearson Terminal 2.

"So yez are wantin' a small pop device that is remote controlled and won't kill nobody, right?" Boomer said. "How much is da ransom?".

"Ten thousand cash," Pearly said quickly.

"Is dat all?" Boomer asked. "I thought yous said it was big dough. Dat's peanuts. Hardly worth da risk. Aside from makin' the explosive device, you expectin' me ta get involved for a measly five large?"

"We hadn't actually discussed a figure," Cat admitted. "But we thought you might drive the car to pick us up at the airport."

"Forget it, yous guys. No way will I stick my neck out for only five."

"Come on, Boomer. We need you," Cat said. "Make it ten grand."

Boudrealt became steely-eyed. "You fruitcakes fuckin' with me? How can ya pay me ten grand, if the ransom is on'y ten? Yous must t'ink I'm an idiot."

"No, no, Boomer," Cat said soothingly. "Pearly said we're asking ten grand *cash,* and he was telling the truth. The rest of the ransom is not cash, and the amount is our business. But we'll pay you ten grand up front. Won't we, Pearl?"

Pearly nodded. "But it'll clean us out. And we need some cash for other expenses."

"Okay. Tell yous what. I'll take da ten grand right now. And I'll *lend* yous a grand until you get your payoff. If sometin' goes wrong, yous'll still owe me a grand, even if we all end up back at KP."

"Gottcha." Cat agreed. "Pearly, fork over your five and I'll give Boomer my five, less a thou'."

"No, Cat. I'll give him forty-five hunnert and you can do the same. Geez, what a con man I got for a partner!"

Cat smiled. "Whatever, pal. Takes one to know one."

19

Toronto, Monday, December 1, 2003

After concluding their deal with Jacques 'Boomer' Boudrealt, Cat and Pearly drove him to his sister's home. Alicia Dubois lived with her husband, Pierre, in a split level on Islington Avenue in the west end of the city. It was agreed that they would pick Boomer up at 6:30 Monday evening, so that they could be out at Pearson International Airport around 7:00. The bomb expert said there would be no problem assembling a remote-controlled, small explosive device ready for use at the old Terminal 2.

According to the airport authority, the original Air Canada Terminal 2 building, will be eventually leveled to make way for a new and more efficient building. Meanwhile, it was rendered almost miniscule by the huge and impressive new Terminal 1, to be opened in April, 2004.

Rather than drive all the way back to Innisfilin, to spend Sunday night, Cat and Pearly booked into a room at the Quality Hotel & Suites at 2180 Islington Ave. The busy desk clerk did not notice the absence of luggage. Many travelers check in first and get their luggage later.

Cat was kept awake for several hours, listening to his partner snore fitfully, and wondering whether Carol Monroe was going to recover from her long ordeal confined in the icy cold trunk of her father's Mercedes. Once again, he was having second and third thoughts about his kidnapping plan, which had put an innocent girl's life at risk.

Before his mother died, when Leo was a teen-ager, she had learned of his frequent scrapes with the Law. On her death bed, as she was reaching the final stages of cancer, which had wasted her body to a mere shadow of her former self, she held his hand and whispered to her son in a croaking voice:

'*There is nothing wrong, Leo, with being poor. Your father and I have been living below the poverty line almost all our lives, but we have survived happily for many years and never harmed a living soul.* (Cough) *We have always offered a willing hand to any of our neighbors who needed help. One of the worst sins is selfishness – always grasping for more. There is enough sadness in life, without any member of the Kanaskis family creating more unhappiness by stealing what rightly belongs to others.* (Pause for breath) *The scriptures talk about sinners going to hell, but even before you leave this life on earth, you will experience hell, if you fail to heed your own conscience.*'

"*Amen, mother,*" Leo thought to himself. "*But I hope you cannot see what is going to happen in the next twenty-four hours. It's too late now to cancel the plan.*"

At 7:00 A.M. Pearly woke up and immediately accused Cat of keeping him awake by snoring loudly. Since Cat could not hear himself when he snored, he could not refute the charge. He just tuned Pearly out, and went into the bathroom to have a shower.

Pearly was reading the Toronto Star, a complimentary copy of the Monday edition, which he had found outside their door. The kidnapping had made the front page:

University Student Kidnapped
Daughter of prominent Toronto investment dealer being held for ransom

Toronto police have identified two suspects in the abduction Friday evening of Carol Monroe, from her parents' home on The. Bridle Path, in the upscale North York area of the city.

Based on fingerprint evidence, the Star has. learned that Leo 'Cat' Kanaskis and Peter 'Pearly' Pattino carried out the kidnapping. and are holding for ransom the 20-year-old. daughter of George and Marsha Monroe.

A province-wide search is underway for the. two ex-convicts, who were released recently. from Kingston Penitentiary.

(*See 'Kidnapped' on Page A6*)

Pearly turned to Page A6. "Hey, Cat, they've printed the pictures they took at KP."

Cat looked over his partner's shoulder. "Why do they show our prison numbers in the pictures? Makes us look like a couple of hoods. Anyway, I don't think anyone would recognize us now. Those photos were taken over three years ago. And I hardly recognize myself. Come on, Pearl. Let's get some breakfast."

"I've already called Room Service, while you was in the shower, Cat. I figured there would be less chance of one person recognizin' us, than if we went to the restaurant."

Cat patted him on the shoulder. "You know, every once in a while you make sense. Keep up the good work."

20

Sergeant Ian Scott did not argue with his boss when Inspector Ben Christopher said the locker at Pearson International had to be kept under constant surveillance, starting at 5 P.M. Monday evening.

"Do we have a problem with jurisdiction if we stake out the ransom pick-up at the airport, Sir?"

"No. I spoke with the Superintendent of the Airport Division of Peel Regional Police. Because of our familiarity with the case, and the fact that the abduction took place in 31 Division, he is happy to leave the stake-out to us. He has, however, offered assistance from his men. And the airport security officers have been informed of our stake-out plans."

"So you are putting me in charge of the take down, when the perps show up?"

"Yes. You're in charge of the operation, Ian. So how many do you want, knowing that the precinct is stretched for bodies with two murder investigations under way, in addition to the Monroe kidnapping?"

"When you put it that way, I guess I can grab the two amateur kidnappers, when and if they show up, if I have one other plainclothes dick to back me up, and another one to watch the entrance. Three detectives in plain clothes should be able to handle the arrest. We don't want to have a lot of uniforms around, as a show of force might scare the kidnappers away, and they might not have enough nerve to try to open the locker."

"Well, they don't seem to be lacking in nerve. For example, there is interesting news from up north," the inspector commented, "news that could have a bearing on the kidnapping case. First, a short term abduction of a doctor from the parking lot of a hospital in Barrie. Description of the perp matches that of big Leo Kanaskis. The doctor's car, a late model BMW, was stolen, and the doctor was dropped off on a remote concession road."

"Any idea what Kanaskis was doing in Barrie?"

"His presence there might tie in with a second report. The cottage of a Fred Murphy of Toronto was broken into over the weekend. It is located on Innisfilin Beach Road, south of Barrie. A next door neighbor found the back door unlocked. The heat was turned up and some food was found in the refrigerator. The O.P.P. is checking for fingerprints in the cottage."

"It does sound like there is a connection," Sergeant Scott agreed.

"Report number three, and this one has the Provincials hopping mad. One of their officers on Highway 400 patrol stopped a Lincoln Town Car for speeding. When the officer was about to write a ticket, a BMW came along, pinning him against the Lincoln. The drivers of the two cars took his service revolver, threw away the ignition key, smashed his two-way radio, and drove away, leaving him fuming and helpless."

"I presume the description of the drivers matched that of the two ex-cons?"

"Exactly."

"When we catch those two car-thieving, kidnapping, cop-baiting desperados, the O.P.P. will owe us one."

"Yeah," the Inspector agreed. "But the Provs have short memories. So don't expect your names to be added to their Christmas list."

"So Ben, what are the O.P.P. doing about the all these obviously related events?"

The inspector leaned back in his chair and clasped his hands behind his head.

"A massive search along 400, right up to Barrie, is under way, although the ex-cons were headed south, towards Toronto. The Barrie police force is co-operating."

"Sure. Leo and Pete have to collect the ransom, and they can't do that from up north."

"On the other hand, they did not have the girl with them, unless she was in the trunk of one of the cars. So, she could still be in the Barrie area."

21

Pearson International Airport, Monday, December 1, 2003

At 5:45 P.M., a British racing green Jaguar coupe stopped at the International departures entrance to Terminal 2. The blonde driver, Kathy Blake, leaned over and kissed Murray Hammond goodbye.

He pushed a button to pop open the boot, (English parlance for the trunk) and took out the large canvas bag containing all his personal hockey equipment. He also took out a small carry-on case. He waved to Kathy and entered the Terminal building.

After lining up at the Air Canada check-in counter, he returned with a boarding pass. That was when he spotted Detective Sergeant Ian Scott, sitting on a plastic contoured chair, part of a long bench, near the bank of lockers. Another plain-clothed detective was seated beside him. Scott had recognized the hockey player when he entered the terminal. He had hoped Hammond would not see him, thus calling attention to his stake-out. But his hope was in vain.

Murray Hammond walked over and smiled.

"Hi there sergeant. Are you traveling Air Canada?" Murray asked.

"Um. No. Just waiting to meet someone. How about you, Murray? I noticed you were carrying your hockey stuff. Is the knee all better so soon?"

"Not completely. But I can skate a little, and I am joining the team to help with the coaching for the game tomorrow night in Detroit."

"Well, good luck then."

"Thanks. I'm glad I brought a paperback. The Detroit flight does not depart until seven o'clock.

The detective had hoped that the hockey player would not stay. But, to his dismay, Hammond sat down near him and his companion and started to read *The Murder Room,* a mystery by famous British author and peeress, Lady P.D. James.

Meanwhile, a large elderly lady was getting out of a gold colored Mercedes sedan, which had pulled up to the terminal entrance. The lady's face was heavily made up, and she was dressed in a long fur coat with a red fox skin collar. Perched on her head was a ridiculous wide-brimmed hat sprouting a pink ostrich feather.

The driver deposited her large suitcase and a smaller train case on the sidewalk, while she looked around for a porter. A small, dark man approached, wearing a navy blue pea jacket and the red cap of a porter. She pointed to the luggage as the Mercedes moved away. A few quiet words were spoken by the little porter. "I seen a plain clothes dick at the entrance, and two more seated inside," the porter whispered.

"All right, my good man," she replied in a loud falsetto voice. Just take my bags inside, and keep an eye on them, while I make a phone call."

"Cert'ny ma'am," the porter replied and touched his cap.

He piled the luggage on the hand cart and towed the cart inside, with the lady following.

Although the two detectives who were seated observed the elderly lady, they paid her and her porter scant attention, as they intently watching the bank of lockers. Murray Hammond, seated nearby, had his nose buried in the murder mystery.

The lady walked away in the direction of some telephones, while the porter stopped his cart close by the detectives. He pretended to go back to the glass entrance doors some distance away, ostensibly to watch the driveway for further arrivals. When he saw the lady reach in her purse for a small black remote control, he quickly got behind a large pillar.

B-O-O-M!

The blast from Boomer's home made device, located in the lady's luggage, sent shock waves in all directions. The two detectives, and the nearby hockey player, as well as the bank of plastic seats on which they were seated, were simply blown over. They were bruised, temporarily stunned and deafened. Several people who were walking along the long concourse were knocked off their feet.

Following the blast, there was instant confusion, as the crowd milled about afraid there might be further explosions. Panic prevailed. Some terrified people ran out of the terminal, fearing another terrorist attack like 9/11 in New York.

The detective who was at the entrance, was about to run to the aid of his companions, when he noticed the large lady putting a key in the locker holding the ransom suitcase. He rushed up to the lady and tried to hold her. She turned, and gave him a sharp uppercut to the jaw. He fell to the floor, unconscious.

In all the confusion, the large lady carrying the ransom suitcase, joined the porter outside on the sidewalk, and was whisked away in the gold-colored Mercedes.

When a female flight attendant, who had witnessed the scene from a safe distance, was later questioned by the police, she said the sight of the elderly lady knocking the man unconscious with one well-aimed punch was one of the funniest things she had ever seen in her life. The investigating officer did not share her sense of humor.

Eventually, an ambulance arrived. The three plain-clothed detectives and the hockey player, who were closest to the explosion, were rushed to the Emergency Department at an Etobicoke hospital.

Following Leo's plan, Jacques 'Boomer' Dubois, drove the gold Mercedes, with the two airport thespians as passengers, around to Terminal 3. The red cap porter got out, followed by the large lady, carrying the piece of luggage containing the ransom.

Dubois then drove the Mercedes to the Long Term parking facility, where he abandoned the vehicle that could be easily identified because of its unusual color and license plates. He was picked up by his brother-in-law on a modified, high powered Harley-Davidson motorbike. The two Hell's Angels zoomed out of the airport, with Boomer Dubois riding tandem.

Once inside cavernous Terminal 3, Pearly found a Men's washroom, entered a stall and removed all traces of his former disguise. Cat entered the Ladies washroom, removed the ridiculous hat and overcoat, which he had rented from

Malabar's, and stuffed them in a waste bin. He was wearing his usual clothes underneath. All he had to do to become his former self in appearance - except for his shaved off moustache - was roll down his trouser legs and wash his face. As he reached the door, a young woman in the light blue uniform of an airline hostess, almost bumped into him. She raised her eyebrows, about to say something. But Cat beat her to it.

"Sorry, lady, I was caught short and the Men's was full."

"That's no excuse," she said indignantly. "The nerve of some men!"

Pearly was waiting outside. He had a mischievous smile on his face.

As they hurried to the main concourse, Cat asked him what was so funny.

"Guy in the next stall lost his wallet, when he let his pants fall to the floor. And I found it. Money and credit cards inside. Ain't that a coincidink!"

"Congratulations, Pearl. Very timely," Cat said. "Just use the credit card and driver's license to buy us a couple of tickets for the next flight to Miami."

"We can't leave the country yet," Pearly protested. "I promised my girl friend, Sam, I'd take her along."

"Don't worry, Pearl. It's just another diversion, to throw the fuzz off our trail. Next stop is a car rental counter."

"Oh yeah, I forgot. We goin' north again?"

"Right. You can drive this time because the car will be charged to your new credit card, and I'll annoy *you* by pointing out where to turn, like you did to me."

"Let's rent a Caddie. I always wanted ta drive one."

"You got it partner. I hope this guy's credit card isn't maxed out. Now let's get the tickets and then to hell out of here. What is his name?"

"Who?"

"The guy you ripped off."

"Oh." Pearly looked at the card. "Joshua Cross."

"Kind of biblical, ain't it? Or rather isn't it?

"Yeah. Joshua. Ain't he the guy that fit the battle of Jericho?"

Cat laughed. "Right. And his pants came tumbling down!"

22

When the three detectives and Murray Hammond were wheeled into the Emergency Room at the Etobicoke hospital, the E.R. doctor on duty was Farley Carmichael, M.D., known throughout the medical centre as a humorist. With a dark moustache, he not only looked like the late Groucho Marx, but he talked like him.

He was sharing the heavy workload with a younger hospital intern, Dr. Omar Kahdif.

The ambulance driver explained to the two doctors what had happened at Pearson airport.

Two of the battered and bruised policemen were examined by the young intern, while Dr. Carmichael checked out Sergeant Ian Scott and the hockey player, Murray Hammond. Both casualty cases had regained consciousness but were groggy and suffering from hearing loss and severe headaches.

The doctor put his stethoscope on Scott's chest. He listened for about thirty seconds and then looked into the detective's eyes and shone a penlight over the pupils.

Finally, Dr. Carmichael said to the patient, "I have determined that you are breathing and still have a chest and two eyes. And I suspect you also have a concussion and some hearing loss." He lowered his voice and adopted a confidential tone. "For example, you may think I'm speaking in a quiet voice. But the deaf patient down the hall has been complaining about my shouting."

Detective Ian Scott frowned. "No kidding, Doc?"

The doctor smiled. "Yes, kidding. Can you hear that?"

"Certainly. Plain as day."

"Then you are cured." He winked at the attending nurse.

"Good, I can leave?" Scott asked.

The doctor stroked his black moustache and took two long strides across the room. He brought back a blood pressure outfit, a wide band with bulb and round meter attached. The nurse rolled up the patient's sleeve, and Carmichael applied the band with Velcro closure. He pumped the bulb and observed the dial.

"When I am not using this on patients," the doctor explained, "I find it useful for pumping up the tires on my bicycle. Your blood pressure is up and your good judgment is down. You must stay overnight, under observation. And I will have to order some tests. Urine test, electro-cardiagram, blood test. Even a test of the tests. Certainly a CT scan, if you are not feeling better by tomorrow morning."

The detective sat up. "Geez, Doc, I want to get out and after those bandits."

"Forget it, my friend. You are so dizzy, you don't realize how dizzy you are. You may think I have been chewing garlic buds, but actually you are just nauseous from having your brain rattled around by the explosion."

Dr. Carmichael pulled back the white curtain separating the detective's bed from a prostrate Murray Hammond, who was curled up on a gurney and holding his left leg. He was obviously in considerable pain.

"And, here we have bomb victim number two. Or is it number seven? No. Number seven was Tim Horton's number. What's yours Defenceman Murray Hammond?"

Murray released his leg and tried to smile at the flippant medico. "Scotch and soda, please."

The doctor examined the hockey player's leg. Murray said, "Ouch."

"You will have to be more explicit. Regular scotch or single malt? Club soda or baking soda. How are you feeling, aside from the damaged leg?"

"Nauseous, Doc. And I can hardly hear you."

"That's called acute hearing loss and may be temporary, but not very cute. No doubt you have had concussions before?"

"Yes."

"I thought so. Then you have another. And, I think your leg is broken. I will be sending you up for X-rays. Do you have any last wishes?"

"Do you think it's *that* serious?"

"Only if you want to play hockey again. On two legs that is. I believe the left one was badly broken last season. Right?"

"No. Left. Yes. Damn it, the knee was just getting better. I was supposed to start skating..."

The doctor wiggled his bushy black eyebrows in Groucho Marx fashion. "I was supposed to start skating, too. But my wife hid my tiny bob-skates. Next time you sit next to Sergeant Scott, I suggest you wear a leg brace and your hockey helmet."

"I heard that, Doc," Ian Scott said.

"Good. Your hearing is improving. Now I understand we have more casualties awaiting my tender care. Nurse, see if you can find rooms, beds and bedclothes for these two, in this overfilled and underfinanced institution. I'll check on them in the morning."

"Certainly doctor," the nurse said, with a broad smile. "Up we go to the Sanity ward, from the Insanity Ward."

23

When Pearly drove the rented black Cadillac sedan away from Terminal 3, Cat was in the back seat with the precious cargo he had lifted from the locker in Terminal 2.

"How's it feel to be chauffeured in a Caddie, partner?" Pearly asked.

"It'll feel a lot better when we are miles from the city," Cat replied, nervously looking out the back window. "You drive and I'll navigate."

A Metro Police cruiser passed in the opposite direction, siren going and lights flashing.

They were approaching the intersection of four-lane highways 409 and 427.

"Take 427 North, Pearl, and turn right on Rexdale, then take the ramp to Highway 27 North," Cat ordered.

"You're confusing me with all them turns," Pearly protested.

"Just take it one step at a time. I'll direct you,"

"Why 27, Cat? 407 to 400 and north from there is a lot faster."

"Because, we have to get off the major highways," Cat replied. "The O.P.P will be setting up road blocks, or traffic stoppers, as soon as the Metros contact the Provs. They will send out an all points bulletin. Commonly known as an APB, my friend, which will say we are armed and dangerous. Suddenly we are right at the top of their Most Wanted list."

"That's okay," Pearly said. "I don't know about you, but *I am* armed and dangerous. If we get stopped, them cops are in big trouble."

"Well, I'm not armed. And don't intend to be," Cat said. "If we get stopped and can't talk our way out of it, that's just the way the ball bounces. I'd rather be back in KP than dead. I don't want any part of a shootout."

"You're a cat all right, Cat. Just a scaredy cat," Pearly said with a sneer. "Anyways, here we are on Highway 27 North. What now?"

Cat ignored the insult. "Just keep driving. We want to stay on back roads, as much as possible. When we get to the intersection with Highway 89 at Cookstown, you can turn left a few miles to a concession road, which will take us through back country to the village of Angus."

"You seem to know this part of the country. How come?"

"I'm looking at a road map, dumbo, the one you got from the rental agency. Besides, I was brought up near there."

"When are you going to open the suitcase, Cat? Let's make sure Monroe kept his end of the deal."

"Up till now, I've been more interested in escaping. But, you keep your eyes on the road and watch for cops. I'll open the case now," Cat said. "Okay. Here's the envelope, containing the cheques for two mil. But there is no cash. Just a lot of blank paper. Looks like used computer paper, the kind with sprocket holes along the edges."

"Who cares about the ten grand? As long as we got the two mil," Pearly said.

"I'm opening the envelope. Son-of-a-bitch! No certified cheques. In fact, no cheques of any kind. Just a note."

"What? Jesus. Read the friggin note. You mean to say we grabbed the girl, and practicly blew up the airport, but don't get no payoff? Over his shoulder, Pearly looked daggers at Cat. The car swerved, narrowly missing the headlights of an oncoming pickup truck.

"Watch out Pearl! Dammit, keep your eyes on the road, or we'll both be killed," Cat said. "The note says: *'To the kidnappers of my daughter, Carol. I am unable to raise any sum close to the Two Million dollars that you demand. I am in a position to pay you the Ten Thousand dollars cash, in unmarked bills of Fifty dollars or less, but only if you supply proof that Carol is alive and unharmed. Send me a tape recording of her voice, and I will see that you receive the money.*

If you have harmed or killed my daughter, I hope you rot in hell. Signed, George Monroe.'

"Geez! What a rip-off. Ya can't trust nobody no more," Pearly said. "I tol' ya we shoulda whacked her. But you insisted on takin' her to the hospital. We should snatch the girl from the hospital, punch her ticket, and send him a Polaroid of the dead body."

"Forget it, Pearl. Revenge is out of the question," Cat replied calmly. "By now, she is either already dead, or conscious enough to tell the cops what happened to her. The Toronto detectives have our fingerprints, and they know who we are. It is just a question of time before they pick us up. If we had two brains, instead of just one, we'd cut our losses and turn ourselves in."

"You can turn yourself in, if you want, Cat. But not me. I ain't goin' back to no prison. I'd rather be dead myself."

"When we get to Highway 89, there is a McDonald's at the service centre. Let's get a couple of coffees from the Drive-in and take some time to think about what to do next."

24

Toronto, Monday, December 1, 2003

After driving Murray Hammond to Pearson airport, Kathy Blake returned to their Wilket Arms apartment. In the luxurious penthouse condominium, she would feel lonely with Murray away. But it would only be for a couple of days before he returned. And Detroit did not seem all that far away, compared to some of the cities he usually had to visit during the long NHL season, such as L.A., Sacramento and San Jose. She could never figure how people in those warm weather cities could get excited about a game that is played on ice, natural or artificial. In her mind, hockey required a winter landscape to be properly appreciated. Ice in California and Florida should be reserved for beverages.

As she usually did when Murray was away, she turned on the 40 inch Sony TV to watch the evening news on CBC. However, tonight she was almost too late. The program, with Toronto regional news in the last thirty minute segment, was just winding up. Instead of the usual ending, a crawler came on the huge screen: 'Special News Report'. A male announcer's voice-over, in sonorous tones made the report:

"CBC Television has just received late-breaking news of an explosion at Pearson International Airport, Terminal 2. A CBC News crew is on its way to the scene, and is expected to arrive momentarily. Meanwhile, details are sketchy. It is known, however, that there have been some casualties. During the evening, regular programming will be interrupted to bring viewers first-hand reports on the latest developments. Stay tuned. More complete news of the suspected terrorist attack on the busy airport will be covered on CBC National with Pierre Hommeport at 10 P.M."

Throughout the brief report, Kathy's heart was beating like a sledgehammer. She was worried about Murray, knowing that Terminal 2 was still the main location for Air Canada arrivals and departures. Without waiting for further news, she pulled on her winter jacket and rushed down to the under-ground parking garage. The black Jaguar coupe was still warm from her earlier trip to the airport to drop Murray at International Departures. She burned rubber up to the Macdonald-Cartier Freeway, more commonly known as Highway 401, cursing the slow rush-hour traffic, as she tried to make time to the Dixon Road exit. Driving like a woman possessed, she ran a couple of amber lights and arrived on the congested road to Terminal 2.

The scene in front of the International Departures en-trance was one of utter pandemonium. Darkness had added another disquieting dimension to the near panic of people relating the unexplained explosion to the tragic events of twin towers in New York and the suicide bombings in the Mid-east. Rotating blue strobe lights and flashing orange lights mounted on ambulances, as well as red lights on an Etobicoke Fire Truck marked the International Departures entrance to Termi-nal 2.

The street had been cordoned off by the Peel Regional Police Department. Police officers, wearing fluorescent yellow jackets and carrying neon lights prevented vehicular traffic from approaching. News media crews who tried to get access to the scene were turned away, while rescue workers and ambulances were filtered through.

Frustrated at being unable to get near the entrance where she had dropped her fiancé off about an hour earlier, Kathy Blake parked the Jag illegally at curbside about fifty metres away from the temporary police barrier. She observed some enterprising reporters and photographers racing on foot to the nearby Arrivals entrance, doing a sort of end-run around the official obstacles on the street.

Doing a pedestrian version of a U-turn, she followed them. Once inside the terminal building she hurried behind the pack, up the wide carpeted corridor until they reached another barrier, this time a yellow tape bearing the crime scene mes-sage 'Police- Do Not Pass'. A burly uniformed officer stood behind the tape ready to enforce the order. He had already turned back a couple of reporters who had tried to sneak around the end of the tape, where it was tied to a post. He warned them not to try again unless they wanted to spend the night in jail.

The resilient crews began setting up their cameras and recording equipment just outside the tape. Kathy was mistaken for a member of the fifth estate, and they made room for her when she edged up to the forbidding tape and looked past the policeman to the actual scene of the explosion. A distinctive smell of burned fabric pervaded the concourse, marked by an area of the carpet blackened by the explosion. Off to the side, in a waiting area, a row of plastic seats had been overturned by the blast. It was there that Kathy's worst fears were confirmed.

Behind the row of overturned seats, she recognized a large blue and white canvas bag that Murray used to carry his skates, jock strap, socks and other personal hockey equipment. He had not yet checked it through. But Murray himself was nowhere to be seen among the crowd of rescue workers and airport security personnel who were working inside the cordoned off expanse.

Throwing caution aside, she ducked under the police tape and confronted the uniformed officer. "I know. I know. I shouldn't be here, officer. But I am desperate to find my fiancé. He may be injured, or worse. Where are they taking the casualties?"

"You go back behind the tape, young lady, and I'll find out for you. But you must stay back there."

While she obeyed, the cop glowered at the media people to hold them in place. Then he walked over to an ambulance driver, had a brief conversation and returned. "The nearest hospital," he said, "is Etobicoke Memorial. "The ambulance driver said he took the hockey player and three Toronto police personnel to the hospital on his first run. If you have a car, I suggest you follow the ambulance. But don't get in the way of medical workers."

"Thanks, officer." Kathy ran back to her car and pulled the Jag in behind an ambulance that was just departing from the group of vehicles parked at the entrance. She followed the ambulance, which had its siren going and lights flashing, all the way to the hospital. When the ambulance pulled in to the Emergency entrance, she parked the car under a street sign that said No Parking, beside a fire hydrant. She figured her emergency had a higher priority than any fire department that might need to put out a potential and theoretical conflagration. She hurried in the front entrance and followed the arrows to Triage.

A middle-aged woman, seated behind the counter, looked at her computer and answered Kathy's breathless question. "Murray Hammond? Yes. Room 427. He has been taken up to acute care. Take the elevator to the fourth floor. Follow the purple stripe to the Nurses' Station for the Active Treatment Pavilion."

With a mixed sense of relief that she had found Murray, and dread that he might be seriously injured, Kathy took the crowded elevator to the fourth floor. She followed the broad purple line painted on the walls to the Nurses' Station.

Kathy tried to get the attention of a dark-haired young lady wearing a white cotton smock. She had her head hiding behind a computer monitor. A tall man, with steely gray hair and dressed in surgical scrubs was peering over her shoulder. After clearing her throat several times, Kathy said: "Excuse me. I wish to see one of your patients, please. His name is Murray Hammond. And I am his fiancée."

"Oh. Mister Hammond has just been brought up from Emergency," the nurse said, with finality. "He is not receiving visitors this evening. And, he is scheduled for X-rays in the morning. But, you could come back tomorrow afternoon."

Kathy could feel her temperature rising. She did not like the girl's attitude.

"I guess you didn't hear me, Miss. I am Kathy Blake, Mister Hammond's *fiancée.* I know he has been injured and I don't intend to be put off. He does not need you or anyone else to protect him from his family or his future wife. If necessary, I'll raise some proper hell with the Medical Director, the Hospital Administrator, or even the freakin' Minister of Health. But it will save us both a lot of time and trouble if you just forget what you said and make a note that I checked in at the Nurses' Station as required. I am going to Room 427 now and don't try to stop me." She started down the hall.

The nurse blushed. She was used to giving orders without any argument. Her mouth was open and she was speechless. Suddenly mute.

The doctor, who had witnessed the confrontation, was grinning. He followed a few paces after Kathy . "Miss Blake. I am Dr. Morland, an orthopedic surgeon. Perhaps I could have a word with you before you see your fiancé. I have just finished examining the young man. I am afraid his hockey days are over."

"Is he seriously injured, doctor?" Kathy asked plaintively.

"Nothing life threateningly, Miss Blake. But his injured leg appears to have had an additional double fracture. We will know the extent of the damage after the X-rays are taken. Aside from that, he has a few abrasions and bruises. Nothing more than he might get in a professional hockey game. He will suffer some temporary loss of hearing, and he has a concussion from the blast. But his hearing should return to normal in a day or two. The concussion might take a little longer. Our staff neurologist will take a look at him tomorrow."

"Gee, thanks doctor. I have been so worried about him."

"Of course, Miss. Don't worry too much. He'll be glad to see you. Room 427 is three doors on your right."

Kathy pushed the door open gently, not knowing what to expect. The first thing she saw was a leg suspended in the air over a folding hospital bed. The leg belonged to Murray, who was resting in a half raised position with his eyes closed.

She walked over and kissed him on the cheek., across from a large bandage covering the other side of his face. "Hi Hon. I see they've got you strung up so you can't chase the nurses."

He opened his eyes and smiled. "It did not take you long to get here, Kathy. Thanks for showing up in my hour of need."

"I've been to the airport. Saw where the explosion occurred. Noticed your canvas hockey bag sitting all by its lonesome on the floor, and deduced that you were in the wrong place at the wrong time. Elementary my dear Murray."

"Any news yet? Have they caught the culprits?"

"Not that I know of, Mur. People are jumping to conclusions. Some think it was a terrorist attack. What do you think?"

"I think my hockey career is over, Hon" he said disconsolately.

"Oh, don't look so sad, Murray. Now we can get married and have our honeymoon in Rome."

He laughed. "I knew you'd find a way to use those tickets."

25

While Kathy Blake was visiting her fiancé in Room 427 at Etobicoke Memorial, Inspector Ben Christopher put his head in the door of Room 429, to check on his injured sergeant.

Feeling guilty and embarrassed that he had been out-smarted by the two kidnappers, Detective Ian Scott was not overjoyed to see his superior officer. When Christopher entered the room, Scott took one look at him and pulled the bed cover over his head.

Grinning at the sergeant's little joke, the inspector pulled up a chair. "Hi Ian. I understand the medicos would like to keep you under observation for a day or so. How are you feeling?"

"Very embarrassed, Inspector. I know I screwed up, letting those two low-lifes put one over on me."

"Never mind that, Ian. What about *you?*" You must be feeling pretty awful, if you had a concussion from the explosion."

Scott had a swollen black eye, dressings on his face and arms. Any remaining wounds were covered by the bed sheet.

"Yeah. I feel as though my head is going to burst," Scott admitted ruefully. "I can hardly hear what you say, Sir. Which isn't all bad, by the way. And I have thrown up my dinner. The medicos say I'll feel better after a good night's sleep. There should be no permanent injury, except to my pride. I should have asked for more backup."

"Nobody could have predicted that kind of diversion, Ian," the inspector said. "And I must admit the disguises those guys used proved they were not so stupid, or as out of their depth as we thought. However, they didn't get any ransom. George Monroe made his own decision, and they got only a suitcase full of shredded paper. He says he wrote them a note demanding proof that his daughter is alive and unharmed."

"That's risky!" Scott said. "I hope those two ex-cons won't take that as a signal they should off the girl in revenge."

"Probably they won't. They need the girl, because her father offered ten grand cash if they want to meet his demands. It is not anywhere near the ridiculous demand of two million. But it's not peanuts either."

"Assuming they agree, how can they collect the ten grand without getting nabbed?"

"We'll just have to see if they have anymore surprises up their sleeves. In the meantime, they must be feeling the heat of the O.P.P. on their tail, and of their mug shots in the paper. That's assuming they are still in the province somewhere, hiding out with their hostage."

"Think they might have skipped the country, Sir?"

"Not likely. They tried to fake us out by laying down a false lead, buying airline tickets for Miami. But, as far as we can determine, they never got on the aircraft. The tickets were charged on a credit card lost by a guy named Joshua Cross. He claims to be the victim of a pick-pocket who stole his wallet while he was in the can at Terminal 3. Luckily, he reported the loss right away to airport security, and they passed the info on to Peel Regional Police. Now we know how they escaped."

"Has a tracer been put on the get-away car?"

"Not necessary, Ian," Christopher said. The missing Monroe Mercedes has been located in Long Term Parking, Terminal 3, already repainted. I personally checked with the car rental agencies. A 2003 black Cadillac was rented by a little squirt answering to the description of Peter Pattino, using the Cross credit card and driver's license."

"I'd like to get out of here and help with the investiga-tion, Sir," the sergeant said plaintively.

"Don't worry about it, Ian. Just take it easy until the doctor says you are going to be okay. I know you want to make amends for the balls-up at the airport. But I doubt if the two ex-cons stayed in the city. So, they are probably out of our jurisdiction and into the wonderful and spacious world of the O.P.P. It's a big province, but the Provs are anxious to pick them up after the fiasco on 400. There are not a huge number of black Caddies on the roads at this hour."

Ian Scott shifted his weight and sipped from a glass of water on the side-table.

"Any report on the other two guys who were with me – Constable Miles and the hockey player?"

"John Miles was not hurt badly. Vern Goldman has a sore jaw, and would like a rematch with Leo Kanaskis under Marquis of Queensbury rules. Both of our men will likely be released in the morning. Perhaps you will be, too. As for the hockey player, his left leg – the one that got busted last year – got buggered up again in the blast. I doubt if he will be playing hockey again anytime this season."

"Too bad. The Leafs could use his talent on their porous blue line."

"Yeah. But I have a hard time feeling sorry for guys like Hammond, earning millions, while police officers are underpaid and overworked."

"Nobody said life was fair, Sir. How would you like to be Prime Minister and earn less than the lowliest rookie in the NHL?"

"If I were PM, I'd pass a law preventing it!"

26

Driving north on Highway 27, with Pearly at the wheel, Cat was in a despondent mood. His master plan to raise two million dollars in ransom money had fallen through, and they no longer had the hostage for bargaining power. Without Carol, they could not even meet George Monroe's demands in order to get the ten grand he was offering for proof that his daughter was alive and unharmed.

Pearly was glum, too. He still blamed his partner for being soft-hearted in delivering the girl to the hospital in Barrie. But he knew better than to raise the issue again with Cat. It was too late. All they could do now was try to avoid the police and hole up somewhere until the fuzz got tired of looking for them.

When they were on the outskirts of Cookstown, Cat finally broke his silence. "Pearl, I need some coffee and food. Turn right at the stop light and that'll take us to the McDonald's at Highway 89 and 400."

"That's taking a big chance." Pearly pointed out. "The fuzz love them fast food places. And, by now, they may have traced this Caddie through the rental agency."

"Yeah., yeah. I know that," Cat replied. "But I think they'll be watching the traffic on 400, rather than the Drive-in. They won't think we are stupid enough to show up in a brightly lit parking lot. So, using reverse psychology we can probably get away with it."

"And if we don't?"

"Then it's your fault for being stupid enough to hook up with a loser like me."

"Gee, Cat. I never thought you would admit being a loser."

"Well, don't expect any more admissions of failure. I'm pissed enough at the way things turned out, without being reminded that we got in over our heads."

They pulled up at the order microphone of the Drive-in. There were no other cars ahead of them at that late hour. And no sign of the O.P.P. Their luck was holding, such as it was.

Pearly was closest to the microphone kiosk and had to do the ordering.

"You order, please," the disembodied voice said.

Pearly looked at his partner. "What dya want, Cat?"

"Large coffee, black. Two Big Macs. With cheese. Fries, with ketchup, salt and vinegar. And a chocolate sundae for dessert."

"Jesus. How'm I supposed to remember all that., Pearly protested. "You are a human garbage can."

"Pull ahead and let me out. I'll order," Cat said.

When they finally got their orders through to the attendant, Cat got back in the car and handed Pearly a five dollar bill.

"What's this?" Pearly asked. "Five bucks won't even pay for the Big Macs, let alone all that other crap."

Cat grinned and said, "That's the smallest bill I have. All the rest are twenties and fifties."

"Well, for crissake, McDonald's will change bills. Give me a twenty, you cheapskate."

Reluctantly, Cat handed over a twenty and asked for the five back. "I'm not really a cheapskate, Pearl. I just like teasing you."

Parked in an obscure corner of the parking lot, Cat burped, partly with satisfaction, and partly to annoy Pearly.

"I have an idea," Cat announced.

"Oh no! Not another plan," Pearly said.

"Just for tonight. A place to sleep, without getting all cramped up in the car."

"Okay, what?" Pearly asked skeptically.

"My dad lives a few miles down the road, in Alliston. I haven't seen him in five years. Maybe he can put us up overnight."

27

Dimitri Olarivich Kanaskis was enjoying a quiet evening at home. On the screen of his 19 inch TV was a scene from the famous Russian opera 'Boris Gudenov'.

He was surprised when a knock came on the front door of his modest three-bedroom bungalow. The hour was late. He was not expecting company.

He looked at the time shown on his ancient VCR. It was 11:15. Who would want to be calling that late on a Sunday evening? He hoped there was not trouble at the plant. Most nights, he would be on duty at the auto assembly factory, where he was employed as a security guard for the local Japanese enterprise. But guards were allowed one night off every week on a rotating basis. Next week he would be off Monday night, the next on Tuesday, and so on. A former sergeant in the Alliston Police, Dimitri had been retired on his sixty-fifth birthday. He lived alone, his wife Gerta having passed away after a five year, losing battle with cancer.

A heavy set man of five-eleven and two hundred pounds, with close-cropped gray hair and beard, Dimitri struggled to his feet to answer the door, cursing the interruption in his favorite opera. Before opening the door, he took the precaution of turning on the veranda light and pulling back the cotton mesh curtain covering the small window beside the door. He saw two men stamping their feet to rid their shoes of snow, one of whom he recognized.

"Come in, Leo," Dimitri said as he unlocked and opened the door. "But sit on the bench and take off your shoes. I just finished cleaning the floors."

"Hi, Dad," Leo said as he gave his father a hug. "This is my pal, Pearly. His real name is Pete Pattino."

Without much enthusiasm, Dimitri submitted to the hug from his son and shook hands with his companion. He indicated the hall tree for their outer jackets. They followed him into the small living room. He did not invite them to sit down, but got right to the point.

"You two here to turn yourselves in?" he asked.

The blunt question took Leo by surprise. "What do you mean, Dad?"

"Your mug shots were in the paper. You kidnapped some innocent university student and are askin' for ransom. There's a province-wide search out for you two. Where is she? Where is the girl?" Dimitri's English was heavily accented with Russian, the principal language of his native Kazakhstan.

"Gee Dad," Leo replied, "we don't have any girl. The whole thing is some kind of mistake. They got us mixed up with two other guys. Just because we were in prison, the dicks in Toronto figured we took the girl. And, if we let them pick us up, we'll be right back in the slammer again."

"Uh, huh. So you came here, so that your father could be charged with bein' an accessory to the crime, for not turnin' you in."

"But, Dad…" His father cut him off.

"No buts, son. As an ex-police officer, you know I can't have any part in this. It is my sworn duty to uphold the law."

"Come on, Dad. You are not going to turn in your own son."

"Or his best friend," Pete Pattino chimed in.

"That's exactly what I will have to do, if you don't leave immediately. I'll just have to forget you were here. But my memory loss is only temporary."

He walked to the vestibule and handed them their jackets. "Where's your car?"

"Around at the back," Leo replied. It's snowing so hard nobody could see us drive in anyway. Covered with snow, all cars look the same."

"Well, I'm sorry son. I don't believe your story about the kidnapping. The Toronto Police would not put your mug shots in the paper if they did not have hard evidence of your guilt. It may be snowin' outside, but I'm not fallin' for the snow job inside."

The two fugitives from the police said nothing as they put on their jackets and shoes and started for the door.

"Not that way. Use the back entrance," Dimitri ordered. "I don't want the neighbors to see you, or I'll end up in prison with you two kidnappers."

Pete Pattino managed a smile. "Nice ta have metcha Mister Kanaskis."

"The pleasure is all yours," he replied icily.

Leo kept his head down dejectedly, as he opened the back door. "Bye, Dad."

"Bye, son. Do the right thing and turn yourselves in."

"We'll talk about it."

Pearly did not say anything until the snow-covered Caddie was on the outskirts of Alliston, heading east on Highway 89.

"Your dad said he was a cop," he said to Cat accusingly.

"That's right. A retired cop. I guess that was not such a good idea, putting him on the spot," Cat admitted. "Turn left at the next intersection, Pearl. We'll head north, for Angus."

"Ain't that where the Army camp is at?"

"Sure. But I'm not worried about the Army. The cops are enough to worry about. Anyway, before we get to Angus, we can find a farmer's field in which to park."

"Sheesh. If we are gonna keep runnin' away, we shoulda kept our disguises."

"Your disguise was easy – a freaking red cap. Mine was more complicated, Pearl."

Pearly giggled. "You sure looked funny, Cat. Particularly when you went to the Ladies' washroom."

Cat changed the subject. "How is the gas supply. Pearl?"

Pearly looked at the lighted instrument panel. "Looks like about half full."

"I sure hope it is enough to get us through the night. We don't have any blankets, and it'll be cold as a whore's heart.

28

Near the Village of Angus, Tuesday Morning, December 2, 2003

Incongruously, the black Cadillac, featuring the latest in high-technology bells and whistles, was parked beside an old manure wagon, under the bare branches of a gnarled and overgrown apple tree, part of an abandoned orchard on farmland, just south of Angus.

Far away, a rooster's strident call beckoned the morning. His lusty, high-pitched crowing sound warned the hens that he expected his libido to be satisfied before a new day dawned.

A ghostly apparition of white contours, the Cadillac had been covered with six inches of snow overnight. Little Pearly had slept better than his big partner. Lying on his back in the front, he was able to drape his legs over the console between the two bucket seats.

Cat had more difficulty. He kept trying to stretch out his six-three, beefy body, but the arm-rests attached to the back doors shortened the width and the folding arm-rest in the middle of the back bench seat, created an uncomfortable hump. He tossed and turned most of the cold night and was in a foul mood when smoke from Pearly's first cigarette of the day assailed his nostrils.

To conserve enough precious fuel to reach a gas station in the morning, they could not keep the motor running all night to supply warmth to the heater. The windows inside the car were covered with frost. Shuddering with cold, Cat could see plumes of mist leave his mouth when he let his breath out.

Struggling upright, Cat said, "Let's get the hell out of here, Pearl. We can get some heat from the engine and make the last several miles into Angus at the same time."

"Ten four, partner," Pearly said cheerfully, as he turned the key in the ignition. "See how quick a good car starts. Not like that old truck a yours."

"Shut up, Pearl. I am in no mood for an argument." Cat replied. He got out to wipe snow off the windows so they could back out of the field.

The dashboard clock read 7:45 when they reached Angus.

From the back seat, Cat instructed the driver to turn right onto the main street, Highway 90. Down the block was a Restaurant sign. And farther on was a service station.

"Tell you what, Pearl," Cat said, "it would be better if we were not seen together while you gassed up the Caddie. You had better drop me at the restaurant before you head for the service station. I'll bring you out a Western sandwich and coffee. You can come back and pick me up."

"Okay. But give me fifty bucks from your stash. These here big buggies use lots a gas and have big tanks to fill up"

Cat did not argue. He handed Pearly a fifty note from his wallet and got out in front of the restaurant. There were several vehicles parked out front. When Pearly drove away to the service station, Cat started to walk into the restaurant. Before reaching the door, he noticed an O.P.P. cruiser half hidden by a cargo van bearing a sign on the side panel for Holly's Flowers. He paused at the door and peered inside.

He could see a uniformed police officer seated at a table. The cop was chatting with the proprietor, who was wearing a white apron. At the eating counter there were a couple of other patrons who looked like farmers, or their hired help, sitting on stools. Cat knew a stranger in this small town would stand out like a sore thumb. He changed his mind about entering. He started to walk toward the service station.

Pearly was sitting in the driver's seat of the Cadillac while a young teen-ager filled the tank. Ignoring the gas jockey, Cat came up beside the car and tapped on the window. When the window was lowered, Cat whispered, "There is a Prov officer at the restaurant. Couldn't take the chance of being recognized. Give me the fifty and I'll pay for the gas and get some coffee and snacks inside."

Pearly handed the fifty note back to Cat.

While hi-test gas was being pumped into the tank of the voracious eight-cylinder Cadillac, Cat went into the service station and greeted the middle-aged man behind the counter.

"Morning squire. How's the world treating you?" Cat asked jovially.

The obsequious little guy had a wrinkled, weather-beaten face with a stubbly beard. He was wearing greasy overalls with a Blue Jays baseball cap mounted over straggly, shoulder-length dark hair.

"If it was treatin' me any better, I couldn't stand it, Mister. Coffee's freshly brewed."

A Goodyear Tire display consisted of three different size tires on a metal stand, covered with dust. An old Coca-Cola clock hung on the wall over a large 2001 calendar featuring Miss December, a topless, breasty blonde wearing a big smile.

Glad that the food items were protected by packaging, Cat began picking up pretzels, peanut and cheese crackers and several chocolate bars which he stuffed in his jacket pockets. "Two cups of coffee to go, please, both with cream and sugar."

While the little man began pouring the coffee, he said, over his shoulder, "That'll come to nine bucks, Mister."

Cat thought the proprietor was a mathematical genius, to be able to keep track of all the food items and come up with a nine dollar total. But he was not going to argue.

"Your boy out there is pumping forty dollars worth of gas. Here's a fifty. Keep the change."

"Thanks, Mister. You just passin' through?"

"Yup."

"Well, you have a real nice day. And come again."

Back in the car, Cat handed Pearly a coffee in a paper cup. "Watch the cup, Pearl, it's hot. We're headed towards Barrie on Highway 90. It changes to Dunlop Street in town.."

Looking in the rear-view mirror, Pearly noticed the O.P.P. cruiser pulling out of the restaurant parking lot. "Fuzz coming up behind us, Cat."

"Shit! Don't panic, Pearl," He watched in his side-view mirror, as the cruiser pulled into the gas station. The officer got out and walked casually into the building. "Okay, let's get out of here, Partner."

Pearly turned the Cadillac away from the pumps, toward the highway. "Do you want me to speed up, slow down, or what?"

Cat turned and watched through the back window. "I see he's coming back out. Let's see if he follows us. Don't go beyond the speed limit. It's sixty K until we clear the outskirts of Angus. Then it'll be 80."

"Do you think he's made us, Cat?" Pearly asked anxiously, as he kept looking in the rear-view mirror.

As the O.P.P. cruiser was pulling out of the station, an olive-green Army truck prevented the cruiser from tailgating the Cadillac.

"I don't know, Pearl," Cat replied. "But there's no point in speeding up and getting a ticket. Let's wait and see if the squad car passes the Army truck. There's a concession road at the top of the hill. Take a right there and we'll know whether that service station guy tattled on us."

When the speed limit sign for 80 Km appeared on the two-lane highway, Pearly revved the motor a little and set the cruise control at exactly 80 Km, until they reached the top of the hill. He turned onto the concession road and watched out of the side window as the Army truck continued on toward Barrie.

The O.P.P. car, a late model Ford Crown Victoria, turned on to the concession road and speeded up, with headlights flashing in sequence, a blue strobe light started to rotate and the lights on the top light bar began flashing sequentially. The high pitched siren began to wail, as the white cruiser closed on the rear of the black Cadillac. On the front fender of the police car, a red light showed the word POLICE. A light on the other fender flashed the signal STOP.

Pearly responded by tramping the accelerator pedal to the floor and the big Cadillac took off in a spray of snow, gravel and mud. "Fuck him," Pearly screamed. "I ain't gonna stop. He can't pass us on this narrow road without goin' in the ditch."

"Don't be nuts, Pearl," Cat screamed back, as he was pressed against his retaining seat belt, while the big car fishtailed at 115 Km, almost out of control. "You'll get us killed for crissake!"

The two vehicles continued on for a few kilometers, with the cruiser following dangerously close to the Cadillac. The police officer eased back the speed, to aim his revolver with his arm out the window of the cruiser. There were two popping sounds, and the Cadillac started to swerve towards the shoulder. Pearly swore as he hit the brakes, slowed down and swung the wheel back and forth to regain control. Finally, they stopped, with the police cruiser right behind.

"Son-of-a-bitch shot a rear tire," Pearly explained, as he opened the driver's door. In one motion, he reached down and withdrew his small Beretta from his ankle holster.

"No, no," Cat yelled helplessly, as he observed his partner's intention.

Meanwhile, the officer had stepped out of the cruiser, and was approaching the driver's side of the Cadillac, revolver in hand.

Pearly pushed the door wide open, leaned out and still-seated fired three shots at the officer at point blank range. The officer fired back a single shot and Pearly, shot in the head, fell out of the Cadillac, onto the road. The officer was down and writhing on the road when Cat got out of the passenger side.

He looked at Pearly and knew he was dead. Half of his face was missing, the remainder a mass of red flesh. Blood and brain matter were all over the inside of the driver's door.. A non-practising Catholic, Cat crossed himself over the corpse of his partner. "Well, Pearl, you finally got your wish," he mur-mured to himself. "No more prison for you."

He walked back to the officer, who was still breathing, but unconscious. Two of the 9 m.m. bullets had hit his chest and were embedded in the officer's Kevlar bullet-proof vest. The third had caught him in the throat, where bright red blood was oozing from the wound.

The officer's O.P.P hat had rolled onto the road, as he had been trying to put it on as he was approaching the Cadillac. Cat picked up the hat and dusted it off. He found it fit his head. It gave him an idea. He stripped the striped trousers off the inert body and exchanged them for his own. Then he dragged the body into the back seat of the cruiser. From a first aid kit he found in the glove compartment, he took out a large field dressing and applied it to the wound on the officer's neck to stop the bleeding.

Then he jumped into the front seat of the cruiser, which still had all the lights flashing and siren going. He speeded to the first intersection, turned the cruiser around and drove like a fiend to Barrie, passing all vehicles at high speed that did not move over for the siren. Turning north on Highway 400, in a matter of minutes he pulled into the Emergency entrance to the Royal Victoria Hospital.

Cat, wearing the officer's O.P.P. jacket, striped trousers and hat, was greeted by a male attendant, who had heard the siren, still wailing away.

"Wounded officer," Cat explained tersely to the attendant, "get a gurney, quick."

Within thirty seconds the attendant returned with a mobile stretcher and white-coated male nurse to help remove the inert body of the officer from the back seat.

"Take good care of him. Gotta return to the scene of the crime," Cat yelled as he jumped back in the cruiser and headed back to the highway.

Why did he try to save the officer's life? Probably, he thought, he was not cut out for a life of crime, even though he had been on the wrong side of law enforcement agencies most of his life. Paradoxically, because he was big and strong, he could easily inflict pain. But that was not his nature. When he saw somebody suffering, his sympathetic side took over, and he always tried to make amends. A good psychiatrist might be able to explain the contradiction. Cat just obeyed his instincts.

He decided to head north on Highway 11, rather than stay on 400 where it veers off toward Parry Sound and Sudbury. Another plan was formulating in his hyper-active mind. He wished Pearly were beside him, so he could explain it to him. He missed his little partner already. Now he had nobody to argue with, except himself.

If his idea worked, he would have a few more hours of freedom. He had no illusions about the final outcome. He knew he could not remain on the run indefinitely.

Kidnapping was a capital offence, punishable by a minimum of twenty-five years in a high security prison, without the possibility of parole.

Maybe Pearly had the right idea after all. Cat still had the wounded officer's .38 revolver strapped to his waist. Eating the barrel and pulling the trigger would be a quick way out. But, meanwhile, he was enjoying the excitement of out-witting the police.

29

Royal Victoria Hospital, Barrie Tuesday, December 2, 2003

Carol Monroe regained consciousness at 5 A.M. with registered nurse Miriam Langey at her side. While Carol was comatose, in critical condition, it was decided by the head of the Pulmonary Section that a close watch should be kept on the patient, around the clock. So, the R.N. had stayed with the young girl throughout the night, while Carol, although unconscious, instinctively fought for breath.

Diagnosed with early stages of double pneumonia, there had been a discussion about whether Carol Simpson – the name under which she had been admitted – should be hooked up to a heart-lung machine. But the equipment was already in use assisting another patient to breathe. Carol was put on an intervenous drip and antibiotics, with full time oxygen. She was also attached, by electrodes, to a heart monitor.

The first sound Carol made, when she woke up, was a long moan like a wind passing through a hollow pipe. Nurse Langley was immediately alert. The patient's eyelashes quivered for a few seconds before her eyes opened. Her chest heaved and she began coughing. When she recovered from the spasm, she looked up at the nurse with a vacant expression.

"Where....where am I?" Carol asked in a low whisper.

"Carol, you are in a hospital," the kindly nurse replied, placing her hand on Carol's forehead to feel for fever. "Your father brought you here Saturday morning. You have been unconscious. I am so glad to hear your voice."

"My father? Is he back from Bermuda? What day is it?"

After speaking, she had another coughing fit.

"It's Tuesday, Dear. Early Tuesday morning." Nurse Langley assumed Carol was confused about her father being in

Bermuda. "How do you feel? Would you like a sip of water? She held up a glass with a bent straw."

"No thanks. Not now."

"I need to take your temperature, Carol. Would you hold this thermometer in your mouth for a minute?"

"K" Her voice was thick and nasal.

After a minute, the nurse withdrew the thermometer and held it to the light. "Hmmm, that's better. Your temperature is down a little. It was dangerously high for a couple of days."

Turning her head, Carol looked around the room. "What hospital am I in?"

"The Royal Victoria, Dear."

Carol frowned. "Never heard of it. Where is it? Not in the city is it?"

"On the outskirts of Barrie, Carol. The City of Barrie."

Carol tried to sit up, but did not have the strength to do so. She lay back, wheezing and coughing from the futile effort.

"Barrie? Why Barrie? Wait a minute. I remember being put in the trunk of a car."

"The trunk? Why would your father put you in the trunk of his car? I think you have had a bad dream. Please keep your head on the pillow, while I see if the doctor can have another look at you, now that you are awake."

The nurse returned in a few minutes, with Doctor Laurie Paquette, the young intern on night duty in the Pulmonary Ward.

The doctor, a recent graduate of McGill's medical school, was doing her mandatory residency. She took Carol's limp left wrist and put a little pressure on the vein to feel her pulse. Then she put her hand on the young woman's forehead, just as the nurse had done earlier. It was wet with perspiration and very warm. Finally, she listened with her stethoscope to Carol's chest.

The doctor smiled with satisfaction. "You are on the mend, Carol. A few more days, and you'll be as right as rain."

"Uh huh. Do my parents know I'm here?"

"Oh yes. Your father brought you here, Carol."

"But the kidnappers put me in the trunk of their car."

Puzzled, the young intern looked at Nurse Langley. "Kidnappers? What does she mean, Nurse?"

"She seems to have had a nightmare," the nurse replied.

Carol overheard the conversation. "Not a dream. I was taken from my home by two kidnappers, and put in the trunk of their car. One man was big and the other small. The little guy was nasty to me."

"Nasty? How do you mean?" the doctor asked.

"He slapped me very hard on the face. And they tied me up with duct tape."

The young intern patted Carol on the arm. "Just rest, Carol. The nurse will be back in a couple of minutes." She gestured to Nurse Langley and they retreated into the hallway.

"What do you think, Miriam? Is she hallucinating?"

The nurse paused in thought. "She seems to be very definite about being kidnapped by two men. Perhaps we should call the Barrie Police to see if there has been an abduction recently."

"Good idea. Better to be on the safe side. Leave it with me," the intern suggested. "After being up all night you need a break. The day staff should be able to keep a close eye on the patient to monitor her condition."

Doctor Paquette went back to the Nurses Station and got an outside line. To save time she punched in 911 and got through to police headquarters. She identified herself to the police operator and asked if there was a recent kidnapping, explaining the claim made by the patient registered as Carol Simpson.

"Hold one minute, please, while I transfer your call." A man's voice came on the line. "Constable Bannister here. To whom am I speaking?"

"This is Doctor Paquette at the Royal Victoria Hospital, Constable. We have a patient who claims to have been abducted by two men. She was brought in Saturday morning by her father, and registered under the name Carol Simpson. We don't know if she was just having a bad dream, or if she might have actually been kidnapped."

After a pause, the constable said, "There have been no recent incidents of that kind reported in Barrie. But one was reported by the Toronto Police. You say her name is Carol Simpson?"

"Yes, but we have heard nothing from the father since he brought her in, suffering from hypothermia."

"The father's name, Doctor?"

"Harry Simpson, who said he recently moved to Innisfil.

"Wait a minute. Here it is. An all points bulletin. A Carol Monroe was abducted from her home by two ex-cons on Friday. That may be your patient. Did you ask her name?"

"No. How dumb of us. Hold the line a moment till I go to her room."

The doctor came back on the line. "She says her name is *not* Simpson. It is Monroe. Carol Patricia Monroe."

"Holy smoke! She has been right under our noses, so to speak," the constable said. "I'll get onto the Toronto Police right away. That's fantastic, Doctor. Her parents will want to kiss you on both cheeks."

She giggled. "Not today, officer. I've been on duty all night. Now I'm going to get some sleep."

"Okay. You deserve a rest. A detective will be over to the hospital within ten minutes. Can you stay awake till he arrives?"

"Just barely."

30

Orillia, Tuesday Afternoon, December 2, 2003

Still wearing his Ontario Provincial Police disguise, Cat drove the police cruiser in to the front parking lot of a new car dealership in Orillia.

When he walked in to the showroom, he gazed around at the new vehicles on display until he was approached by a smiling salesman.

"Good day, Sergeant. May I help you look at one of our new models?" The salesman appeared a trifle nervous, wondering if he had been observed speeding, while demonstrating a car to potential buyers recently. He tried to relax and appear confident.

Cat sensed the young man's anxiety and did not smile back. He was enjoying the feeling of power projected by the uniform of the O.P.P.

Finally, he said. "Yeah. I have been looking around, and have decided on a Pontiac Grand Prix. But the dealer in Barrie didn't have the color my wife likes. The dealer offered to check for the model with other dealers. But I had to come to Orillia on business anyway."

"The Grand Prix is for your personal use, of course?"

"Of course. Me and the little woman. But I am in the squad car most of the time and she is complaining about being stuck at home, without wheels."

"I see. And what color would she prefer?"

"A powder blue. Sort of a robin's egg color. Do you have anything like that in stock?"

"I think so, officer. Just a minute, while I check the inventory sheet."

While the salesman went back to his tiny office, Cat looked over a black Buick LeSabre in the showroom. If the

300

inventory did not include a baby blue Grand Prix, he figured he might settle for the Buick. Stealers can't be too choosey.

The young salesman returned, sheet in hand. "We have three Grand Prix in stock. One has just had the prep work completed and is cleaned up ready for the road. It is a dark blue, with light blue leather interior. Loaded with all the bells and whistles. A dream to drive."

Cat stroked his chin, pretending to think what his mythical wife might think of a dark blue exterior. "Tell you what. If I can talk my wife into the darker color, I'll take it. Maybe the light blue interior will do the trick. How much will it cost? The bottom line, including tax, please."

"Do you have a car to trade, sir?"

"No. The old heap she was driving finally packed it in. It is now crushed metal."

The salesman's eyes lit up. A clean cash deal, with no trade to have to sell or get rid of to an auctioneer was every salesman's dream. He did some figuring on a pad, and named a figure just below the MSRP (Manufacturer's Suggested Retail Price). Cat said that would be okay. He could handle it, and would bring in a certified cheque if his wife approved of the car.

"I'd have to show it to the wife, of course," Cat said. "Meanwhile, I can leave the cruiser as security. Hah, hah."

The salesman laughed at the joke. "Oh, no problem, officer. All I need is some I.D. and you may take the car. Keep it overnight, if you wish."

Cat fished out the wounded officer's wallet and showed the salesman the driver's license, with photo I.D. It was a lousy picture, as usual, and the salesman hardly glanced at it. The real Sergeant was vaguely similar in appearance to Cat anyway – six-one, two hundred pounds, blue eyes, fair hair, forty years of age. The salesman just went over to a copy machine and banged off a copy.

"Take the keys to the cruiser," Cat said. "You might want to put it inside overnight."

"Thanks," the happy salesman said. "I hope your wife likes the car. If not, we'll find one to suit her taste. Let me get a dealer plate and you'll be on your way."

Ten minutes later, Cat was back on Highway 11, driving the new Grand Prix northward, in the direction of the rugged lake and rock country of Muskoka. The highway was wet and heavily salted. He knew the shiny new car would soon be covered with a layer of white grime, eliminating its new car shine. He had removed his O.P.P. hat and jacket., and had slipped back in to his own jacket, which he had transferred from the cruiser. Once more he was a civilian. The striped trousers could pass as part of a jaunty ski outfit. He turned on the radio and played with the Scan button until he found a noon newscast. It was a Toronto station and he had to listen to a couple of stories about shootings in the east end of the city, until finally the announcer came to the item for which he had been waiting.

"It was happy news for the Monroe family this morn-ing, when the Barrie Police assisted the Toronto force in locating university student twenty-year-old Carol Monroe, who had been abducted last Friday from her home on The Bridle Path by two ex-convicts, identified as Peter Pattino and Leo Kanaskis. It appears that the young lady was taken by Kanaskis to the Royal Victoria Hospital in Barrie for treatment under an assumed name. She was suffering from a severe case of hypo-thermia, which turned into pneumonia. She is now happily reconciled with her parents, who rushed to her side when they learned that the kidnappers had given up their hostage to save her life.

In a related incident, the pair of convicts set off a bomb at Pearson airport Monday evening, as a diversion to obtain ransom money from the girl's parents.

This morning, in a shootout on a concession road near Angus, O.P.P.Sergeant Ivor Burbridge was wounded and fugitive Peter Pattino was shot dead His partner, Leo Kanaskis drove the wounded sergeant to the Royal Victoria Hospital for emergency treatment before escaping in the sergeant's police cruiser. Some people, are calling Kanaskis 'The Good Samaritan', for delivering Carol Monroe and Sergeant Burbridge to the hospital in an effort to save their lives. But law enforcement people prefer the name 'Bad Sa-maritan', as the slippery Kanaskis is still on the loose and wanted on several serious charges, including kidnapping. Despite the flattering description of his life-saving deeds, the public is warned Kanaskis is armed and dangerous. "

Cat switched off the radio, wondering if anyone at the Orillia dealership had heard the newscast. One thing was certain. He had to get rid of the orange dealer plate. He was feeling the pangs of hunger. The McDonald's at Gravenhurst beckoned, and was reachable in ten minutes. He remembered there was a hardware store in the same plaza, where he could buy a small wrench and screw driver, with which to relieve some parked car of its license plates.

He passed a sign advertising Royal Mail Ship 'Segwun' the only authentic steam powered ship operating in North America. Like the Phoenix, The Segwun had risen from its abandoned hulk and become a major tourist attraction for Gravenhurst, the town that proclaimed itself the Gateway to Muskoka.

Before pulling in to the McDonald's Drive-in, he paused out front to make sure there were no police cars in sight. Then he drove through the Drive-in and ordered two Big Macs, fries and coffee.

With the inner man satisfied, next on his agenda was the license plate problem. He drove to the Home Hardware, and bought the necessary tools, hoping he would not be recognized from the newspaper mug shot. The girl at the check-out desk did not even make eye contact. He walked out, just like a regular Samaritan, good or bad.

There were plenty of cars bearing Ontario license plates in the plaza parking lot. But he figured alarm bells and sirens would go off if he tried to remove a set of plates from a vehicle in broad daylight. Too many people were driving in and out, patronizing the various stores. The nosey parkers would report him to the local gendarmes or the Provs., if he tried to liberate some plates.

He got back in the Grand Prix and drove out to Bethune Drive. The fact that the Province of Ontario required vehicles to have two plates – one each, front and back – was a pain in the ass. Why not just a rear plate, like most states in the U.S. of A.? Unfairly, Ontario made the acquisition of plates by theft, doubly time-consuming. He decided to wait a few hours until darkness set in, before attempting to replace the orange dealer plate that was hanging out of the trunk of the Grand Prix. Next stop, Bracebridge, where he intended to spend the night. Only a matter of ten miles (16 km), but it would seem farther, driving with his fingers crossed.

31

As Cat drove past the Muskoka Airport, on Highway 11, just outside of Bracebridge, he looked longingly at the rows of private and commercial aircraft lined up on the field. If only he could pilot a plane and fly away into the wild blue yonder, leaving all his problems behind!

Cat was enough of a realist to know that the problems were all of his own making. He had chosen a life of crime and would soon be paying the penalty of spending the rest of his life in prison. Or not, if he chose the alternative. He could drive on to Huntsville, or North Bay, or even farther north. But he had no desire to string out his freedom by heading for the back country and living like a hermit, until he was finally apprehended. Whatever he did, wherever he went, the final outcome would be the same. So, he figured Bracebridge would be his last stop.

When the off-ramp for Cedar Lane appeared, he saw a small sign indicating an O.P.P. Detachment was on his route into town. He almost decided to drive in and give himself up. But he resisted the impulse and drove on by, down Taylor Road and into the main drag, which for some strange reason was named after another province – Manitoba Street!

He recalled that Bracebridge did, in fact, have a bridge spanning one of the falls of the Muskoka River. Since the early days of logging, the burgeoning town had become a thriving community. Nostalgically, he remembered that it was only a few more miles to the lovely summer resort of Windermere House, where he and Muriel had spent their honeymoon. If only he had taken her advice, they would still be happily married and he would not be a fugitive from the law.

He drove around for a while, getting his bearings and looking around for overnight accommodation. Near the intersection of Wellington Street and Highway 118 West, he checked in at a motel under a fictitious name, Fred Adams. He filled out a form giving an equally fictitious address in Toronto. By paying cash, he was not required to prove his identity. Backing the Grand Prix into the parking space in front of his room, with the dealer plate hidden in a three-foot snowbank, he decided it was unnecessary to steal a set of license plates. By tomorrow, he would not need the car.

The motel was within easy walking distance of a plaza with a Beer Store and LCBO. He walked in to the liquor outlet and looked over the well-stocked displays of domestic and imported alcoholic beverages. At the Scotch display, he selected a bottle of single malt Glenfiddich, which was packaged in a round cardboard container with a screw-on metal top. When he looked at the price his eyes bulged and he considered settling for something less expensive. However, it suddenly dawned on him that he did not have to worry about the cost, and could afford ten bottles, or a hundred, if he were so inclined. He also remembered that he had only a few hours of freedom left in which to spend his share of the funds from the chop shop, if he were to carry out his latest plan.

Cat paid for the 12-year-old scotch with a hundred dollar bill and walked across to Zeller's, where he made a couple of purchases.

When he returned to his motel room, he phoned for a taxi. He assumed that taxi drivers were among the most knowledgeable people in any community when one wants information. In about ten minutes, an ancient Chrysler New Yorker, with a Taxi sign on the roof pulled in to the motel parking lot. The driver was a gnarled-looking man in his sixties, with closely-cropped gray hair and beard. He defied convention by wearing a leather bomber jacket over a heavy wool shirt, and a sea-captain's hat with gold braid on the visor.

The elderly cabbie stepped out and opened the rear door when Cat approached from his room.

"Are you Mister Adams?" the driver asked.

"Yes."

"Where would you like to go?"

"Nowhere. But you can start the meter running, while we talk. I need some information and I'll pay for it," Cat said.

The taxi driver stared at Cat for a few seconds, and shrugged. "Okay. My minimum charge is ten dollars. What would you like to know."

"Here is the ten. And, I'll make it fifty, if you can help me. I just came in from out of town. I would like some female company for the evening. Do you know of anyone who would like to earn a hundred bucks an hour to spend, say three hours with me this evening."

The driver scratched his ear in thought. "I think so. But I'll need a few minutes to check it out."

Cat handed him a fifty dollar bill. "Take the fifty. If you can help me, keep it. If not, return half and we'll be all square."

"Fair enough, my friend. Where and when is the gal to report to you?"

"I am going out to eat, and will be back by six," Cat said. "She does not need to use the front entrance. The corridors are inside, but she can just knock on my room's sliding doors around seven. The room number is 105. Or you can, if you strike out and want to return twenty-five dollars."

By 7:30 Cat had almost decided he could kiss his fifty bucks goodbye. No female of any description had shown up. And no taxi driver. On the plus side, the bottle of single malt scotch was depleted by one-third, and was tasting better with each drink. Being basically a beer drinker, Cat had never before felt affluent enough to try the exotic premium libation of Scotland's world-renowned Glenfiddich distillery. He decided the smooth liquid mood-adjuster was to die for – almost as good as sex. But he would prefer to have both.

He had closed the curtains on the sliding doors, figuring he was going to spend the evening alone, when a light tap came on the exterior door. He pulled back one of the drapes. A female face, wearing a tentative smile, was peering in, with one hand raised to block the light from the table lamp. Cat jumped up from the armchair and slid the glass door open.

"Good evening, my dear," he said. "Do come in."

She entered the room, shyly looking around. "Mister Adams?" she asked breathlessly.

"That's me. Miss. But you can call me Fred. And what is your name?"

He drew the opaque drapes closed, and turned to look at her. She was much younger than he expected as a companion for the evening. Refined looking – nice smile. Dark hair, shoulder length. Oval face, creamy complexion. Rosy cheeks from the night air, or perhaps from mild embarrassment, being in the same room with a strange man. Very little make-up. About five-eight, with long, slender legs. Probably in her early twenties. She was wearing a hip-length suede jacket with a fur collar. This was no prostitute. More like Betty 'Princess' Anderson in the old TV show 'Father Knows Best.'

"My name is Penelope," she said. "People call me Pen, or Penny for short."

"Well, Penny, it's a pleasure to meet you," Cat said politely. "May I take your jacket and hang it up?"

"Sure," She shrugged out of the jacket, with Cat's assistance. He hung it up in the closet.

Beneath the jacket, she was wearing a red lambs-wool, V-neck sweater over a white, ruffled blouse, with a gray skirt of medium length and dark nylon stockings. She removed a pair of galoshes revealing a pair of black pumps with sensible heels.

"All I have to offer you is scotch, which I have been drinking on the rocks. Would that suit you?" Cat asked.

"Perfect. Add a little water, please. May I sit down?"

"Of course. Of course," He said apologetically, as he drew up another armchair. "Forgive my manners. I am not used to female company. Excuse me for a minute while I go down the hall and refill the ice-cube container."

He headed for the door, wondering how to deal with this seemingly innocent young thing.

When he returned, bearing a full plastic container of ice cubes, Penelope was in the washroom. Perhaps, Cat thought, she was having a nervous pee. The toilet flushed and she came out, with her lipstick renewed. She was trying valiantly to appear non-chalant.

Kanaskis poured two drinks, added water to hers and handed her the glass.

"Mind if I smoke, Mister Adams?" Assuming consent she produced a silver cigarette holder from her handbag.

"Not at all, Penny. You go right ahead. It's a non-smoking room, but I doubt if they will throw us out in the snow. I quit smoking three years ago, so that I would not die of lung cancer. As it turns out, I might just as well have smoked three packs a day."

She lit the cigarette. Looking past the flame of the lighter, she raised her eyebrows in a questioning mode.

"Did that get your attention? Yes, my dear. This is my last evening of freedom on Planet Earth. So, I appreciate your keeping me company for a while."

She inhaled lightly and blew out a stream of smoke, while wondering if Fred Adams was a nut case. "I don't know what you are talking about, Mister Adams. But at one hundred dollars an hour, you can say anything you please, and I'll listen."

"At that rate, I can buy three hours of your time, and to show good faith, I will pay you up front." He opened his wallet and handed her three hundred dollars.

She slipped the notes into her purse. "Thank you very much. Now what?"

"Now we can relax and swap stories. I'll tell you my story and you can tell me yours, Okay?"

She smiled. "I guess so. After we swap stories, are you going to ask me for sex?"

He laughed at her direct question. "That was my intention, because I have not slept with a woman in over three years. But when I saw how young you are, I decided to skip the imposition and just enjoy your company. Penny, you are very pleasant to look at, but you are young enough to be my daughter. Just talking to you is much better than being alone with my thoughts. I don't believe in taking advantage of young girls."

"Fair enough, I am happy to keep you company, as long as I don't have to reveal my real name."

"If Penelope is your real first name, it stands for faithfulness. Did you know that?"

"No. Tell me about it."

"If you took Ancient History in high school," Cat said, "you may remember that Odysseus wandered for twenty years on his way back from the Battle of Troy. His wife, Penelope, swore to everyone around her that she was tired of waiting for her husband to return. She declared she would divorce him because he had abandoned her, as soon as she completed her knitting project. But the project was never completed, because

she tore out the stitches each night, and started over again the next day."

She smiled. "She was either very faithful, or very dumb, or both."

"Now for my story. My name is not Fred Adams. My real name is Leo Kanaskis. Does that mean anything to you?"

She looked at him closely and slowly nodded. "*Jeepers!* I thought you looked familiar! Your picture has been in the paper. Something about kidnapping a university student in Toronto and taking her to the hospital in Barrie. It has been a front page story. The police are blaming you and your partner for an explosion at Pearson Airport, and a shootout near Angus."

"Knowing all that, aren't you frightened?"

"Sure, I'm frightened. I'm nervous as hell, even though you look and act like a nice man. But I *need* the three hundred dollars. And, don't worry, I won't phone the police."

He laughed sardonically. "It wouldn't matter if you did, Penny. I'll be phoning them myself in the morning. You see, I've decided to give myself up."

"I didn't mean to pre-empt your story. Is it all true? And, if so, why did you do it?"

"Yes, it's true," he admitted bitterly. "I've been asking myself why we did those things. My partner and I were greedy. We were after the big payoff, like in a lottery. But, of course, it was all illegal. My partner paid the price earlier today. He's is dead. And now it's my turn."

"Did you deliver your hostage, the Monroe girl, and the wounded policeman to the hospital, to save their lives, like it said on the radio?"

"That's right. She had developed pneumonia, through our carelessness. And he was wounded in the shootout. He had a bad wound, but I think he'll survive."

She shook her head in disbelief. "I can't understand this. You do all those bad things, and then turn around and try to save a couple of lives. It doesn't make sense."

He gave a self-deprecating laugh. "I know it doesn't I guess I was not cut out to be a full-fledged criminal. But I got started as a small time thief and never tried to hurt anybody. One thing led to another and I ended up in prison, for a relatively harmless, but unauthorized bank withdrawal. Not a robbery. Just a kind of scam. It was kind of fun outwitting the bankers. But, of course they took it seriously, and so did the police."

She was shaking her head with a bewildered look.

"Then, after we got out of prison," Cat continued, "my partner and I cooked up the kidnapping scheme, because we could not get regular jobs. Employers are not interested in hiring ex-convicts, when there are lots of other candidates around with clean records."

She stubbed out a second cigarette in an empty can Cat provided, from some Planter's Peanuts he had bought at Zellers.

"Wow! What a story," she said. "Too bad I'm not a reporter. I could write it up, emphasizing the good things you did. Then maybe the justice system would take it easy on you."

"Not likely, Penny. But thanks for the thought. I've decided to take my medicine like a man, and not beg for mercy. Now, we have talked enough about me. What about your story. Do you often accept evening assignments such as this with strange men?"

She blushed. "No. I'm not a prostitute, if that's what you are wondering. I'm just a single mother who needs to put bread on the table. Three hundred bucks will buy a lot of food for me and my daughter. She needs some new clothes and we both like to eat."

"How old is your daughter, Penny?"

"She just turned three, Mister Adams, or Mister Kanas, um Kanaskis."

"You can call me Cat. That's my nickname. Leo the Cat, as in Leo the Lion. Like in childrens' books."

"Okay, Cat. You don't look, or act like a bank robber, or kidnapper. I would even trust you with my little girl."

"Where is she, Penny? Not home alone, I hope."

Reflexively, she looked at her watch, which read 8:35. "She's in bed, I hope. I left her with a sitter, a young kid in the next apartment. She sits for me when I work at night. During the day, I have to stay with my daughter, Emily, because the cost of day care would use up most of my earnings."

They talked and talked, becoming more comfortable with each other as time passed. Penny found herself liking the big, ruggedly handsome desperado who had exhibited an empathetic nature. When she looked again at her watch, and realized that the three hours had passed, she felt a little bit disappointed.

Cat noticed her looking at her watch. "Look, Penny, I know the three hours is up. And I really appreciate the time you have given me. Knowing what I have to do in the morning does not make me happy. But all things, good and bad, including my criminal career, must come to an end. The hour is getting late, and your daughter needs her mother."

Penny got up, leaned over, and kissed Cat on the lips. "Before I go," she whispered, "I'd like you to remember me as more than a conversationalist. Please take off your clothes and make love to me."

"Are you sure…"

She smiled. "I'm sure. You see, like you, I've not had sex in about three years. I have my needs, just as you have yours. Call it a bonus, at no extra cost. I would enjoy an extra half hour with you as my lover. Then, perhaps you can face the morning with a smile on your face."

Cat was pleasantly surprised. "Well dear, I would hate to disappoint you. I'll just have to pretend you are not as young as you look!"

32

Cat woke up with a small shaft of sunlight coming through the slit between the drapes caressing his face. The L.E.D. readout on the bedside clock read 8:05. He flung an arm across the bed where Penny had been. She had left him, quietly slipping out the double doors, while he slept like a babe. Probably it was the wonderful lovemaking, combined with the therapeutic effect of half a bottle of single malt scotch that had sent him into dreamland. He was sorry he had not said goodbye and thanks for a memorable evening.

Now he had to face the inevitable. While he showered, shaved and dressed, he remembered wistfully, the feeling of her warm, delicious body and her ephemeral farewell gift of love.

He wondered if he should go to a restaurant for breakfast, but then decided against it. He did not want to ponder on his decision, or lose his resolve. Picking up the phone, he dialed 911.

A female voice answered. "This is 911. How may I help you?"

"Please put me through to the Ontario Provincial Police."

"Is this an emergency call, a problem of some kind, sir?"

"It will be a problem, if you don't put me through to the O.P.P."

"Do you wish to speak to the Provincial Police headquarters, or the Bracebridge Detachment, sir?"

"The Bracebridge Detachment, for heaven sake. And no more questions."

"Certainly, sir. I'm just following procedure."

There was a click on the line. "Bracebridge O.P.P. May I help you?" A girl's voice.

"Listen carefully, sweetie. Because I am only going to say this once. My name is Leo Kanaskis. I am supposed to be armed and dangerous, according to all the stories in the newspapers and broadcast media. The O.P.P. has killed my partner, and I have decided to give myself up."

The receptionist, Margaret Breen, remained calm. "Where are you now, Mister Kanaskis?"

He gave her the name of the motel. "I will be waiting in the parking lot. How soon can you send officers to pick me up?"

"A squad car will arrive within ten minutes, sir. When the officers show up, please put your hands in the air, so that they can identify you and make sure you are unarmed."

In the O.P.P. building on Cedar Lane, Sergeant Jim Ainsley and his partner Constable Shirley Newby had just arrived to start the day shift, when Reception called them on the P.A. system.

"Officers Ainsley and Newby, please report to reception urgently. Code Red."

Sergeant Ainsley burst into the foyer, followed by his partner, who was strapping on her service revolver.

Margaret Breen tried to contain her excitement. "You guys came in at the right time. Leo Kanaskis just called. He wants to give himself up. So get going and good luck."

"Where is he, Margaret?"

She gave him the name of the motel. "He says he will be waiting for you in the parking lot in front of the motel. "I told him to hold up his hands when you arrive, so that you can identify him and see that he is unarmed."

Sergeant Ainsley nodded. "We are on our way."

The morning traffic on Taylor Road was lined up at a red light. Not wanting to wait while the light changed, Ainsley hit the siren and flashing lights on the Ford cruiser and pulled out into the left lane to by-pass the cars lined up. Fortunately, the light changed to green just as the fast-moving police car hit the intersection. Past the traffic light, he veered the squad car back into the right lane and accelerated down curving Taylor

Road. Past the railway crossing, he turned up Hyman Street and slowed down at the stop sign on Ann Street. But then accelerated across the street and turned left, slowed at the next stop sign and speeded up again, until the red light at Manitoba Street again slowed down progress. With siren screaming and lights flashing, the police car entered the intersection and squeezed past drivers intimidated and slowed down by the high-pitched noise and flashing lights.

Constable Shirley Newby was silently praying. She had faith in her partner's driving skills, but despite that, there was always the unexpected that sometimes happens. A driver who wants to go through on the amber light. Or another saying, to hell with the police having the right-of-way, I'm in a hurry. Or a mother and small child trying to get across, caught in the middle of the 4-way intersection with a pram.

Finally, she let go. "Jim, take it easy. The guy won't walk away while we are trying to break speed records to pick him up. It's not worth risking our necks just to set a new world's speed record."

"Okay. Okay. You are starting to sound like my wife, with her back seat driver's advice."

"But I am not your wife, and I am in the death seat here. Slow fucking down! Or I'll put you on report for danger-ous driving."

"Well, we are almost there, so save your breath, part-ner. I can see him standing at the far end of the parking lot. He's raising his hands in the air."

The cruiser slowed down and stopped in front of the motel. Both officers got out and drew their service revolvers, with safeties off. This was a dangerous criminal. They were taking no chances.

"Leo Kanaskis?" Sergeant Ainsley shouted.

"That's me," Cat replied, his hands still in the air. "I'm turning myself in. So, come and get me."

The two officers, with guns drawn approached slowly and cautiously. It was like a scene from the movie 'High Noon'. Tension in the air was palpable. The two officers kept remembering that he was armed and dangerous.

Suddenly, when they were twenty paces away, Cat dropped his hands and pulled a weapon out of his waistband, waving wildly in the air in their general direction. Both officers fired at the same time. Cat sagged and then fell backwards into the snow-covered tarmac.

They closed in warily. Blood was gushing from a hole in his forehead, and one in his chest.

Standing over the inert body, Ainsley said to his female partner, "Nice shooting, Shirl."

She bent down and felt Cat's carotid left artery. "He's dead, Jim," she said solemnly.

Sergeant Ainsley pried the weapon from Kanaskis' right hand. "Holy shit, Shirl, it's a plastic Luger. A damned toy pistol."

With the two officers standing over the corpse, reality was setting in. His parting gesture at outwitting cops was to trick them into helping him commit suicide.

Constable Shirley Newby gripped her partner's arm. "Look, Jim! The son-of-a-gun is smiling."